WHITE FLAME

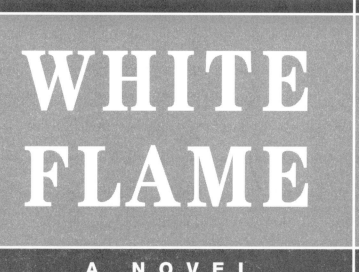

WHITE FLAME

A NOVEL

JAMES GRADY

DOVE
BOOKS

Printed in the United States of America

ISBN: 0-7871-0903-7

Dove Books
301 North Cañon Drive
Beverly Hills, CA 90210

Distributed by Penguin USA

Text design and layout by Folio Graphics Co., Inc.
Jacket design and layout by Rick Penn-Kraus

10 9 8 7 6 5 4 3 2 1

The author owes grateful acknowledgment to Rita Aero, Rich Bechtel, Nathan Blumberg, Taylor Branch, Lou C., Ulysses Doss, Danny Glover, Bonnie Goldstein, Harry Gossett, Melinda Hatton, John Holloway, David Levinson, Lou Mizell, the Pulaski crew (Alan, John, James), Ruth Ravenel, Michael Viner, Les Whitten, Bill Wood, and countless others. Any worthwhile insights in this work of pure fiction measure my debts to such good souls.

for Jane Grady

LAST EPIGRAMS FOUND IN THE
INTERNET JOURNAL OF FARON SEARS:

This is the doctrine of the Karma. Learn!
Only when all the dross of sin is quit,
Only when life dies like a white flame spent
Death dies along with it.
                    from *The Light of Asia: The*
                    Life and Teachings of Gautama,
                    by Sir Edwin Arnold, 1884

Instant karma's gonna get you.
                    John Lennon

Everything is burning.
                    Buddha

Chicago police lied about the crowd that filled a North Side street at noon that January 15, the anniversary of Martin Luther King's birth. The police told the press the crowd numbered 200 people; 450 was closer to the truth. The crowd surged toward the porch of a mansion where a man in a topcoat clutched a microphone.

"Why do so many people hate me?"

The man's amplified voice rolled over the shivering crowd. They wore Brooks Brothers topcoats, old Army parkas and labor union jackets. A woman in cashmere stood next to a youth in gang colors. The faces were Southside Black and Saigon café au lait, flushed with genes from Belfast and Krakow, from Milan and Athens. For a dozen tan faces clustered together, a woman translated the speech into the lilt of Veracruz.

"White people." The speaker shook his head, ran his hand over his cropped, kinky hair that was as black as his leather gloves. "Do white people hate me because they see a black man—another black man—with money and power and an attitude?"

Laughter rippled through the crowd.

"A black man with a mouth full of words like 'the terror of suffering.' Do white people hate me because of that?

"Black people," said this man of polished ebony. "Do they hate me because my success means I've 'become white' and 'betrayed' them? Do my black folks hate me because I refuse to let them or anyone define me by the mere color of our skin?"

On the porch behind the speaker were a dozen people who worked in the mansion: women, men, white and black, Hispanic and Asian.

"Do Jews hate me because I challenge them to give up their tribal taboos against assimilation and follow their codes of tolerance into a new era? Do Muslims hate me when I tell them their common roots with Jews make them brothers, not enemies?"

His magnified voice made the windows of the mansion tremble.

"Do politicians hate me because I refuse to twist myself into this party or that, into empty labels like liberal or conservative, candidate or not? From the intellectual graveyards of universities to the rent-a-vote halls of Congress, does the power elite hate me because I won't fight them for yesterday's political turf?"

A lone figure detached itself from companions at the edge of the crowd. Bundled in winter clothing, the figure could have been anybody. Two policemen in white riot helmets paid no attention. One cop sipped from a steaming plastic cup.

"Do the police hate me? Hate me because they had me in their prisons once and now can never cage me again?"

Hard-eyed men wearing open overcoats stood side by side below the porch steps. One spotted the lone figure coming closer, closer. The guard stepped aside to let the person move quietly up the steps. That inconsequential traffic drew no one else's attention.

"No, I am not hated by skin colors or religions or politicians or police. I am hated by people. People like you. People like me. And you know what's at the center of their hatred? Fear."

Discreetly, the figure entered the mansion behind the speaker.

"Fear that whispers to their hearts."

No one was inside the mansion to witness the lone figure hurrying to the mansion's second floor.

"Fear that they might be wrong."

From the front window of a deserted communications center, the lone figure stared down at the speaker and his crowd.

From there, you could see the great orator's beginning-to-go-bald spot.

"Fear that I might be right."

From inside his bulky coat, the figure drew out a book-sized computer, detached a phone cord from the desk nearest the window and plugged it into the hand-held machine. Typing a message on the keyboard took less than two minutes.

"And if you think they're afraid now . . ."

Message completed, the person hidden behind the glare of the mansion's window entered a command into the computer.

". . . wait until our headquarters opens in Washington, D.C.! Then you'll see true fear."

The computer's screen flashed with each ring of a distant phone. One ring. Two.

"That big 'they' out there keeps asking, 'If you say you're not a politician, why are you going to Washington, D.C.?' And I answer, 'Because it is the next step in the journey.' "

The liquid-crystal display flashed: "CONNECTION."

"They say, 'If you are not a politician, then who are you?' "

A message sped from the palm computer in Chicago through the phone line as the orator proclaimed:

"So to those who demand to know who I am, I say: I am alive!"

Wind whistled through pine trees along a remote two-lane Idaho highway. The pavement was snow-patched. Ten miles up the road, snow drifts had closed the pass through the mountains. Here, a glass phone booth stood like a sentry beside a rest stop the state locked after Thanksgiving. A red Toyota idled by the booth.

The man shivering beside that chugging car wore a black fake-leather coat and jeans. His name was Chris Harvie, and he rubber-banded his stringy blond hair into a pony tail. Chris yelled to the man in the phone booth: "This wilderness gig is for the birds!"

The man in the booth stood absolutely still. He wore a red parka over a black down jacket, ski pants, and arctic boots. Black ski gloves fit him like skin. His face was smooth as an egg, his dark hair was short. He cradled a hand-held computer he'd wired into the phone after snipping off the receiver. He used equipment from Radio Shack and followed a manual stolen from a trade-school library.

"Did you get it?" Chris blew into his cupped, bare hands.

The man in the booth stared at the message e-mailed into his machine. The liquid-crystal words burned into his memory. He exited the communications link without saving the message: Proof of its existence died instantaneously. He smiled: "Get what?"

"Don't keep fucking with me!" Chris stomped to the phone booth. "I'm freezing my ass off! If it weren't for me—"

"I wouldn't be here." The man unfastened his computer from the mangled pay phone cord, stashed the machine inside his jacket.

Chris shook his head. "Why the hell did we have to slip and slide a zillion miles out here to Nowheresville? Rig up a damn pay phone? We could have done this the easy way at the motel or—"

"Art is not supposed to be 'easy.' Art is . . . *an event.*"

" 'Event' my ass," said Chris: "You know how cold it is?"

"Not as cold as it gets."

"Oh, yeah?" snapped Chris. "How the hell cold does it get?"

His companion pivoted to the left, hands turning palm to palm, then whipping apart with a flash of sunlight. Crimson spray colored the day as the knife from his wrist sheath slashed Chris's throat.

Chris staggered forward, blood pumping from his slashed neck. He crashed into the phone booth, his dying hands grasping for help on the glass wall.

"It gets about that cold." The killer cleaned his blade on the dead man's jeans.

Dragging the body into the trees took twenty minutes. The radio predicted a blizzard by midnight. Before then, no one would come here; by spring, whatever hadn't melted would be a profound event for whoever found it. Aftershock as art. Ripple art.

He took the dead man's wallet, motel key, and pistol, washed the blood off his own face with snow, tossed his gore-splattered parka into the Toyota, climbed in and drove away.

*   *   *

Eleven miles down the road, the red Toyota reached the intersection of two state highways. Junk littered the crossroads. A pickup sat on blocks, a six-inch hat of snow on its cab. Civilization was a gas station and eleven dilapidated motel cabins.

Two cars huddled in front of Cabin 9. The killer parked in front of Cabin 4, the number that matched the dead man's key.

Those two cars weren't here this morning, thought the killer. His watch told him it was lunch hour in Idaho. Two cars, this county's tags, lunch hour: Somebody's Husband, Somebody's Wife. They posed no security problem: Their secret closed their eyes.

Inside Cabin 4, the man watching "Oprah" was huge. Buttons strained on his Hawaiian shirt. Electric ghosts from the TV danced on his tattooed arms. As the cabin door swung open, he jumped out of his chair and grabbed a .357 Magnum revolver off the table.

"Honey, I'm home!" said the killer. He shut the door.

"What the hell took so long?" grumbled the tattooed man.

"I didn't want to cut it short."

The room smelled of panel heat and whiskey. Cross-country skis and a backpack leaned against the wall. The killer ran his gloves over the skis. His peripheral vision watched the tattooed man put the Magnum back on the table.

The tattooed man turned his eyes to the door: "Where's Chris?"

"Waiting for you." The killer shot him in the chest with Chris's gun, a .22 Chris packed to feel like a Detroit pro.

The low-caliber bullet tapped the tattooed man back in his biker boots. His massive arms ripped his shirt open. He stared down: a little bitty hole, like a red . . .

The killer sent a slug through the tattooed man's forehead. He crashed to the floor, and the killer fired a to-be-sure round through the man's skull. The killer pocketed the corpse's wallet, got the skis and backpack, left the room locked.

Outside, he filled the Toyota's gas tank and two plastic five-gallon jugs from the motel's pump. He wore smoked ski goggles to hide his face, but the proprietor saw only the color of money.

Three miles from the motel, the Toyota left the highway

for a heavily drifted gravel road. Five times, the killer had to shovel snow from his path. The road topped a ridge overlooking the gray sheen of a frozen lake. The Toyota plowed a cloud of white powder as the killer gunned it down the hill. Inertia skidded the machine 50 feet onto the lake. The ice groaned, but held.

He shut off the engine, carried his skis and backpack to the shore. With binoculars, he made a 360-degree sweep. He saw walls of Christmas trees, white powder drifting in their branches, but no skiers, no snowmobilers. A hawk soared above swaying evergreens.

The killer soaked the Toyota with gasoline from the plastic jugs. He poured gas from the car's open fuel tank to the shore. His survival match flared with the first strike. He let the flame settle, then dropped it on the rainbow trail of gas.

A line of fire raced across the frozen lake. A fireball engulfed the car. Black smoke billowed to the sky—the big risk, the major *what-if*: If the smoke were seen, what would happen?

The Toyota's gas tank exploded. The car spun around on the ice. Steam rose to mingle with the black smoke. Fissures in the ice cracked out from under the burning wreck. Chunks of frozen water popped free. The ice opened up, swallowed the burning car, flames hissing as everything sank beneath the surface.

The water rippled, then was still.

By the time he'd strapped on his backpack and skis, a skim of ice had formed over that hole. He pointed his skis toward the town where Somebody's Husband and Somebody's Wife lived secret lives. Before sunset, he would rejoin the cross-country skiing charter group that had bussed him there. He paid by cash, acted shy, used a false name. No one knew him.

He corrected himself: None of them knew him *yet*.

Eight days later, a Tuesday morning, three men sat in a booth at a Washington, D.C., restaurant. Through the window beside them, they could see the complex called Watergate.

In the booth, Willy Smith told the men he faced: "You two ain't fooling me out. There's what you say, and then there's real truth."

"What is the 'real truth'?" asked the man in the booth with silver-flecked black hair, scars on his right cheek, and dark eyes. The leather case in his suit jacket identified him as Dalton Cole, Special Agent, Federal Bureau of Investigation.

From inside his denim jacket, Willy drew a pack of cigarettes and a lighter. He said: "*You* get real. I know what you're doing."

" 'Real' is it's illegal to light up in here," said D.C. Homicide Detective Nick Sherman. He had dusky hair, blue eyes, and a chipped-tooth grin.

Willy blew smoke at the two lawmen. "So arrest me."

"So what do you think we're doing?" said Nick Sherman.

"I know what you *say* you're doing." Willy wore a perfectly legal folding knife in a leather case on his belt. "Same thing the blue boys who rolled me up two years ago said they was doing."

"You mean," said Sherman, hoping that the tape recorder in his pocket was working, "the first policemen you talked to let you know you're a suspect in a series of felony crimes?"

"Oh, yeah," said Willy. "They said all the law-book words."

"We advised you of your rights, too," said Sherman. "Remember? First day we met you at your place."

"My two new buddies from the Cold Case Squad. You put it out: Innocent Willy Smith—somehow, he's a suspect in a carjacking."

"Carjacking, kidnapping, rape, and murder," said Cole.

"Let me tell you something." Willy leaned across the table. "You can't rape a woman lessin' if she wants it. All that stuff is bullshit the bitches use to keep real men down."

"You've been down, Willy," said Cole, a new edge in his voice. "You pulled two stretches for armed robbery."

"That was then, this is now."

"And two years ago," said Cole, "somebody grabbed Jenny Davis in the hospital lot. Stuffed her in her car's trunk. Afterwards he had her car, cash, credit cards. He'd . . . done what he wanted with his dick. He taped her eyes; she probably couldn't have ID'ed him. She was a good nurse who had a son and a husband. Why do you suppose he had to kill her?"

"Bitches always find a way to set a guy off. But since I walked prison, I've committed no crimes whatsoever." Willy stubbed out his cigarette. "See? But six weeks ago, you show up, run me through bullshit. Then every day or so, you happen by. Hell, I like the company. You guys take me out, buy me coffee, burgers—"

"Good thing you had time on your hands," said Cole.

"Hey, I'm off parole! So I can't find work: I'm a victim of these hard-ass post-Cold War times."

Cole said: "What kind of work do you do?"

"Oh, man!" Willy bathed the lawmen with his breath. "Not that shit again! I know what the hell you two are really doing!"

"What's that, Willy?" asked Cole.

"A scam! You figure, keep workin' one going-nowhere case, it'll keep your asses out of the bullet streets! But you can't trick that to your bosses—*unless* you got a suspect you're working!

"And that's me," said Willy as he lit a new cigarette. "Hell, you guys hanging on me, asking dumb questions—I'm keeping you alive by being here!"

"Willy," asked Nick, "did you figure that out by yourself?"

Willy shrugged.

"Clearly, you're destined to get a job as an astrophysicist," said Cole. "But have you ever worked in a car wash?"

"What's with my resumé shit? You two writing my life story?" Willy faced the exit. Dumb cops: Why'd they let him have the chair where you could keep an eye on who came in?

Detective Sherman sat on the outside of the booth, between Willy and the only way out. Reflected in the glass, he saw the waitress pick up the coffee pot, start their way. Sherman kept his hand below the table—out of Willy's sight—and waved her back.

"What's wrong?" asked Cole. "If you're telling the truth, what difference does a question like where you've worked make?"

Willy blew smoke at the hotshot FBI man.

Cole said: "So, you ever work in a car wash—*Mister* Smith?"

"Fuck you and no fucking way."

"Well," said Nick, "then we've got a real problem."

Willy saw iron snap in the murder cop's eyes. "What problem?"

"You just became our *Number One* suspect! Now you can 'splain to us how we're full of shit, or say nothing! You can get a lawyer, even if you're broke! We'll leave here, go take care of business."

They gave Willy a minute to worry. Then Nick said: "So you want to get all the way formal and go down to Headquarters?"

Willy knew that Headquarters meant starting down the justice line. His nonanswer legally spoke to both his knowledge and intent.

"We're talking about murder, carjacking, kidnapping, armed robbery, and rape," said Cole.

"Two years ago," said Detective Sherman, "D.C. police found the car where you dumped it with Jenny Davis stuffed in the trunk, naked and beat all to hell. Tore up and sexual lubricant in her."

"You must have worn condoms," said Dalton. "Kept your shorts up so as not to drop any hairs."

"So we got no DNA," said Nick. "No luck backtracking the credit cards you probably sold on the street. Forget her cash."

Smoke rose from Willy's cigarette to the ceiling in this bright, family-style restaurant.

"No witnesses," said Nick. "But we do got something."

Cole told Willy: "Your thumbprints. On the trunk of her car."

The lawmen watched Willy as his smoke disappeared. In the window glass, Nick Sherman saw the waitress start toward them, the check in her hand. Below the table, he again waved her away. She stormed back to the cash register.

"My prints on her car don't prove a thing!"

"Damn, Willy!" said Nick. "That's just what the prosecutors said! They said a defense attorney could come up with 'reasonable doubt' explanations of how your prints got on that car."

"My guess is you wanted to feel your hands on her," said Cole.

"So when the regulars couldn't turn up any more, they were stuck. Which is how you dropped into the Cold Case Squad."

"Into our hands," said Cole.

"Where you blew it."

"See," said the Fed, "even though you knew you were a suspect, in our chats, you eliminated every explanation your lawyer could throw at the jury about how your prints tie you to Jenny Davis."

"You told us you never met her," said Nick. "Never saw her or her car, never sold cars, never shopped at the grocery stores where she did. Never been in her neighborhood or to the hospital where she worked—not within a mile, I believe your words were."

"You told us you've never worked as a car mechanic," said Cole. "Never worked in a gas station, a parking lot. A car wash."

"So," said Nick, "Mr. Number One Murder Suspect, the only thing you haven't told us is how your thumbprints got on that car."

Cole said: "Any way you cut it, Willy, you're—"

From nowhere came the waitress: "Look, *Gentlemen,* you've been here for—"

Willy flicked his lit cigarette at the city cop's face.

Nick batted it away and lunged out of the booth. Willy pushed the waitress into Nick. They tumbled to the floor in a heap. Willy ripped the table free of the wall and heaved it on Cole.

"Don't fucking move!" yelled Nick from the floor.

The waitress froze, her body rigid on top of Nick.

Dalton pushed Willy. Silverware crashed to floor. Cups and water glasses shattered. Willy threw a chair through a window.

A thousand shards of glass exploded to the sidewalk. The chair bounced through a crowd of tourists gawking at the Watergate across the street. A security guard who'd deserted her post at the Watergate to buy smokes passed through the crowd as the glass exploded. She saw a man leap through the jagged hole in the window.

"Hey, mister!" yelled the security guard: "You OK? What's—"

A fist broke her nose. She felt the .38 revolver she was forbidden to take off-post jerked from its holster.

Cole leaped through the window a second before a chunk of glass dropped like a guillotine across the gaping hole. He saw Willy, saw his arm coming up, *black thing* pointed—

"Gun!" yelled Cole.

The .38 roared as Cole dove between two parked cars.

Tourists screamed. Ran like mice.

Cole popped above a car's trunk, his 9mm Beretta locked in both hands, scanning through the pistol's V rear sight.

"Get down!" he yelled. "FBI! Get down!"

Gun in hand, Nick Sherman jumped through the glass hole.

A girl, maybe seven, panicked and ran. Willy jumped out from between a parked tour bus and a car, revolver hunting the lawmen. Cole and Nick realized: *Citizen in the line of fire.* The city cop tackled the girl. Cole shifted his aim, shot out a restaurant window. The roar of Cole's gun and the crash of glass made Willy flinch. Nick dragged the girl between two parked cars.

Willy blasted two rounds into the car sheltering Cole, then ducked behind the tour bus. Tourists hugged the frozen sidewalk. Cole heard the girl sob.

"Nick!" whispered Cole.

"OK!" came the voice one car behind him. "Knee's hurt!"

Twelve years before, a drunk driver hit a police cruiser where Nick was riding shotgun, banged up the cop's back and leg.

Cole heard the cop radioing Code 13, *officers in trouble.* Somewhere a police car hit the siren. Cole crept down the sidewalk, alongside the bus, pistol zeroed toward where Willy had been.

Easy, Cole told himself, watching his reflection grow in the bus's side mirror. *Walk it easy.* When he reached the bus's front wheel, Cole flung himself between the bus and the car, his gun zeroed on that gap where Willy—

Wasn't.

A gun roared and a bullet crashed as Willy's shot drilled a hole in the bus. Cole saw Willy run toward the gas station at the edge of the parkway, dive behind the gas station's dumpster.

Cole's Beretta punched a line of holes in the dumpster's green steel. The terror of lead slamming into his cover scared Willy enough. He bolted toward the parkway.

Two bullets left in Willy's gun.

Willy jumped a winter-dormant flower patch, whirled, innocent cars cruising the street behind him, his gun . . .

Cole blasted three rounds into the earth at Willy's feet. Dust and dirt granules erupted in front of Willy. His eyes teared as he jerked the .38's trigger. The slug ripped past Cole.

He's got one left, thought Cole.

Willy ran onto Rock Creek Parkway, a crosstown racetrack for Washington's hyperactive denizens in their doomed challenge of the clock. Horns blared. Tires screeched. Taillights flashed. But no car obeyed Willy's frantic waves to stop.

"Drop your gun!" yelled Cole. "Give it up, Willy!"

Willy fired at the cop chasing him just as a panel truck from a chic bread bakery roared between Cole and him. The bullet slammed through steel to bury itself in loaves of honey-baked bread.

Empty gun, thought Cole as he raced after Willy.

Thompson Boatyard sits across Rock Creek Parkway from the Watergate. Willy ran past the boatyard's parking lot, crossed a footbridge. A tourist couple loomed in front of Willy. He hit the man with the empty gun, grabbed his wife, and pulled her toward the river, one hand yoked around her neck as he drew his knife from its belt pouch.

Behind Willy ran the rippling gray Potomac. He scanned the footpath for his pursuer. Willy whirled toward the boat-house: padlocks over steel doors. In the corner of Willy's eye, a blur streaked from the footpath to a Buick-sized tangle of driftwood. He jerked the tourist bitch around, covered his body with hers.

"I know you're behind there!" Willy yelled at the driftwood. "You do me, I do her! I'll die twitching my knife through her eye! Get out where I can see you! Get up!"

Twenty seconds passed before Dalton Cole walked from behind the driftwood, his Beretta pointed down by his side.

"Give it up, Willy."

Willy dragged the woman toward the dock. "Hey, fuck you, man, I got a hostage!"

"That's *your* problem." Cole marched closer.

"What?"

"You don't have a plan, do you, Willy? Life's roaring around you. You don't have a plan and you don't have a prayer."

"I got—"

"You got shit, Willy. Give it up, you'll go to prison, you'll live. Stop this bullshit, or you die."

When the FBI agent was twelve steps away, Willy felt the wood of the dock under his shoes. "You fuck with me, I'll kill her!"

The tourist rolled her eyes. Steel pressed against her cheek-bone drew a crimson tear.

"Go ahead," said Cole. "Makes it easier for me."

The FBI agent raised the Beretta. Willy saw Cole's dark eye centered by the pistol's sight, saw the bore of the gun and its black hole to forever. Cole thumbed back the Beretta's hammer.

"Are you crazy?" yelled Willy.

"Yeah."

Dalton squeezed the trigger. The hammer fell on a bullet-empty chamber with a dry metallic *click*!

"Shit!" said Cole, his eyes wide, his face stunned.

Willy threw the woman at Cole, ran toward the moored boat.

Cole swept the woman aside with his left arm, an arc that ended with his hand on top of the Beretta. He racked the slide and rechambered the pistol he had cleared behind the wood pile, the pistol he had cleared so the hammer would fall on an empty chamber, the pistol he had then loaded with a bullet-heavy magazine.

"Willy!" he yelled to the man at the edge of the dock.

Willy saw the gun pointing at him: It had clicked empty. Willy lunged with his knife toward the crazy FBI guy.

Cole fired three times. Willy fell backwards into the river.

Thompson's Boatyard was lousy with lawmen. Park Service cops. Washington FBI Field Office. D.C. Homicide Squad. Cold Case Squad. Lawmen in uniforms, lawmen in suits. Lawmen on motor scooters, in cruisers and unmarked cars, even two lawmen astride horses.

Special Agent Dalton Cole leaned against a Bureau sedan.

Across the boatyard parking lot, Cole saw the cruiser where Nick Sherman sat in the backseat, a cold pack on his knee from the ambulance that had taken the tourists to the hospital.

The Bureau and D.C. police shooting teams were keeping Agent Cole and Detective Sherman apart so the law could get a straight story without the involved lawmen getting their story straight.

Two morgue technicians wheeled a gurney supporting a lumpy black rubber body bag toward their waiting van.

Killed a man, thought Dalton Cole. Just like I had planned.

"You mean you *wanted* to shoot the suspect?" the FBI agent investigating the shooting had asked Cole after hearing that truth.

"No," Cole had explained, "but before I joined the Bureau, I settled with myself that if I had to kill a bad guy, I would."

"Just like that?" said the investigator.

"How else?" replied Cole.

The investigator made sure nobody stood close to them and said: "Look, stick to the jargon. And don't ever share that *philosophy* with anybody else."

A sedan bristling with antennae rolled into the boatyard. Four men got out: the driver, a Special Agent of the FBI; the Special Agent In Charge of the FBI's Washington Field Office, the SAC; the Assistant Director of the FBI's Criminal Investigative Division, the AD/CID; a Deputy Assistant Attorney General from the Justice department of the United States of America, the DAAG. The four men from the sedan walked toward Cole. As they did, the SAC beckoned the multi-agency shooting team to join them.

"Special Agent Dalton Cole?" asked the FBI's AD/CID.

"Yes, sir."

The AD/CID was one of the twenty-two most powerful men in the FBI, the most powerful law-enforcement agency in the United States. He asked the men who worked for him: "Clean shoot or no?"

"Sir?" replied the chief FBI shooting investigator.

"Is Agent Cole clean on this shooting or not?"

"Sir, the field investigation is not complete."

"Hear me. Is he clean or not—and tell me *now*!"

The lead FBI investigator licked his lips. "He's clear."

The Bureau executive turned to the city detectives. "Is that square by you and your people?"

"Hey," said the city homicide sergeant. "This is federal turf, plus our man never squeezed a round. If you square it with the Park Police, for us it's in the box."

The AD/CID turned to the local FBI SAC, Cole's nominal commander: "*You* square it with the Park Police; *you* make sure this agent is cleared for duty by start of business tomorrow. Any problems, you call me directly. I want zero calls. Questions?"

"None, sir," said the SAC.

"Agent Cole," said AD/CID: "Come with us."

As Cole took his first step, he asked: "Where?"

The Department of Justice sits halfway between the Capitol and the White House, a gray stone lady dwarfed by her tan sandstone child across the street, the J. Edgar Hoover Building, headquarters for the Federal Bureau of Investigation.

The fifth floor of Justice is a plane of power simultaneously held in awe and derided by the 95,000 employees of the department—including 24,000 of them who work for the FBI. The fifth floor holds the main office of the Attorney General of the United States, chief law enforcement official for the federal government. Down the dark, wood-paneled corridor from the A.G.'s suite is a conference room where portraits of Attorney Generals stare at a polished table and a dozen hardback chairs.

Dalton Cole sat at one end of that table, his heart pounding. No one had said anything to him during the ride here. All he could think was: *How have I screwed up this big?*

At the other end sat the Assistant Attorney General, the AAG. He told Cole: "You must be absolutely certain if you say you're fit for duty."

Fit for duty? Cole mumbled: "What happened, happened."

Then he realized: All this isn't about any mistake I've made! And whatever is happening here . . . I can't walk away from something that's *finally* this big.

"My conscience is clean. I may have nightmares, but I'll wake up. I can do my job."

The AD/CID sat to the left of the AAG, the Justice department's Number Two man. The DAAG sat to his boss's right.

Only one FBI executive, thought Cole. This is Justice's turf and these Justice people are stratospheric. *This is Justice's show.*

The AAG said: "Agent Cole, you are to consider even the existence of this meeting as classified. Do you understand?"

"Yes, sir."

The AAG said: "You are aware of Faron Sears?"

"Sure," said Cole.

The DAAG, who had been a Senate committee counsel prior to his political party winning the last presidential election, said: "Ross Perot, Jesse Jackson, Colin Powell, Minister Farrakhan: they were trouble enough. Now we got a billionaire Malcolm X or Martin Luther King or Bill Gates on a political-messiah acid trip—we got Faron Sears."

"I wasn't aware that Sears claimed to be following in anyone's footsteps," said Cole before he could censor himself.

"Hell," argued the DAAG, "he's bought and bamboozled himself two hundred thirty thousand followers, according to White House polls! What he wants—"

"Did you see that half hour of network TV he bought? Ran on his cable channel, too! Him voiced-over one scene after another: kids, old people, garbage dumps, rats, gang busts, amber waves of grain, war shots, bears in the woods, ballet dancers—Elvis Presley and Muddy Waters, for chrissakes! The Kennedys and King and Malcolm X and John Lennon and Arlington! Walt Whitman! An empty Detroit assembly line! Some white guy doing T'ai Chi! I sat through all that *'this is this'* stuff he was saying, and *I don't get it!*"

Cole said: "But you watched it."

The DAAG snapped: "So what does it *mean* come November?"

"Our job," interrupted the AAG, who like his assistant had been appointed by the victorious president, "is not elections."

He rubbed his brow. Locked his gaze on Cole: "In Chicago, two agents of the Bureau of Alcohol, Tobacco and Firearms got a tip that bodyguards for Faron Sears wanted to buy fully automatic weapons. The two agents . . . without authorization, they set up interceptions of Faron Sears's communications systems."

"They bugged him," said Cole. "Illegally."

"Call them over-zealous."

"Call them stupid," said Cole. "Nothing they get that way is admissible. It's a waste of time, and if you get caught . . ."

"These were old-time ATF guys trying to do their job under politically correct rules," said Cole's FBI supervisor. "They knew their boss wouldn't target a politician because of a snitch."

Cole said: "So they figured to get something out of the bugs that they could wash into court-clean information, or an 'inspiration' of where to look so they could make a legit bust."

"Sitting in this chair," said the DAAG, "I now appreciate J. Edgar Hoover. Miss the power he had to do stuff that needed doing."

The AAG pushed a sheet of paper down to Cole: "Those illegal taps intercepted this e-mail message from Faron Sears's Chicago headquarters to a phone booth in rural Idaho."

> *R.—*
>
> *He's scheduled for a White House meeting, but no matter what, we're moving F's H.Q. to D.C. Let him have a last Valentine's Day. Remember, Faron's assassination must be close-contact work. Your second mission will be cast after F. Clean up loose ends. Rise.*
> *U.*

"Shit," said Cole.

"On the day this was sent, the White House meeting was known only to Faron's headquarters and the White House," said the AAG.

"So it's genuine," said his DAAG.

"But is it *real?*" asked Cole. "Reads like an amateur's note to a weird wanna-be. The question is: *Is all that real?*"

"The answer is: We must assume it's valid," said the FBI AD/CID. "Suspect A sent the e-mail, Suspect B received it."

"*U.* and *R.*," said Cole. "Call them by their names."

"If we could do that," said AAG, "you wouldn't be here."

"We're trapped," said the Justice department czar. "Our government has illegally bugged a major political figure—who happens to be black. This on the heels of Ruby Ridge, Waco, and our bust of Malcolm X's daughter in an assassination plot to kill Minister Farrakhan. If this illegal bugging comes out, it will rip this administration apart and propel Faron Sears into the role of heroic martyr, making him more powerful than ever."

"And if Faron Sears is *assassinated*," said the FBI executive, "there'll be riots bigger than after the Rodney King verdict, possibly approaching the 1968 King assassination riots. Deaths, billions in damage, massive political repercussions."

"And if it comes out that the Feds knew he was at risk *beforehand*," said the AAG. "*If-if-if*—all the 'ifs' shaft us."

"Except one," said Cole.

"Yes," said the AAG. "If we stop the assassin before he strikes, most of the damage can be contained."

"To say nothing of preventing several crimes," added Cole.

"Twenty-four hours after they intercepted this," said Dalton's FBI superior, "the ATF agents had the belated good sense to blow their way into the office of the Secretary of Treasury."

The Alcohol, Tobacco, and Firearms Bureau is under the Treasury department, not the Justice department.

"The Secretary of the Treasury marched them over to the Attorney General," said the AAG. "Then the two cabinet members took it in to the president."

"I wouldn't have wanted to deliver that news," said Cole.

"That White House meeting was supposed to be between Faron Sears and just the chief of staff," said the AAG. "Nobody wanted to convey presidential status on Sears by having him in the Oval Office. When Sears sat down at sixteen hundred, we ambushed him with the Attorney General. The AG told Sears that intelligence reports gave us reason to suspect that a spy in his organization and an outside individual or group were plotting to murder him."

"You didn't tell him he'd been bugged," said Cole.

"Are you crazy?" said the DAAG.

"To effect the necessary warning, there was no need to disclose the sources and methods," said the AAG.

"Uh-huh," said Cole.

"He didn't care," said AAG, "or so I'm told. At least, he seemed . . . unconcerned about the news of a murderer on his trail."

"Hell," said DAAG, "he probably expected it. With his background, with a goon squad, with things he's doing that we don't know about: every mob boss expects a hit."

"What got his attention was the news that he had a traitor close to him," said the AAG. *That* kept him in the meeting. We proposed he declare himself a candidate for president . . ."

"Which would have stopped all his kid gloves, touchy-feely press, too," said DAAG.

"Which would have," said his boss, "allowed the president to assign him Secret Service protection. Allowed us to finesse an investigation of this along formal, open lines."

Cole knew: "Faron said no."

The DAAG said: "He's playing politics with his life."

"Doesn't everybody?" asked Cole.

"But his politics have put your life on the line, too," said the AAG, "because you're the only alternative he accepted."

"Guess he figures you can be trusted," said the DAAG. "After all, you got him out of prison. Let him walk on terrorist charges."

For a minute silence ruled the secret meeting.

Finally the AAG said: "This is the deal Faron gave us."

"Since when does the Bureau allow victims or targets of investigations to dictate deals?" Cole asked his Bureau boss.

Their Justice department superior said: "We make deals all the time. And this is the only choice we can swallow.

"Faron vetoed any routine investigation, said he'd fight us if we came at his staff like we'd have to. We'd lose that fight, probably while exposing our rogue Feds. We'd end up being the bad guys. Faron also refused our protection . . . with his people out shopping for machine guns, maybe he's way ahead of us.

"The deal is this: FBI Agent Dalton Cole can go into his organization, undercover. Investigate and protect. You, period. And he agreed to keeping that operation secret—from his people, from the press."

"No," said Cole.

"Excuse me?" said the AAG.

"No," said Cole. "The FBI is not a bodyguard agency. And no agent works alone. No one to watch your . . ."

Then Cole fell silent. *Imagined* it. The second hand swept

the clock twice before he said: "If I go in, I have one inside partner, one outside man."

"He won't go for a pair of agents," said the AAG.

"He's got gangbanger smarts. He knows I'll need a back-up. And obviously, he trusts me enough."

"Enough to what?" asked the AAG.

"We'll see."

"You know your job," said Cole's AD/CID. "Based on the clock ticking in that e-mail message, you've only got twenty-one days."

Cole said: "I'm a federal law enforcement official charged to investigate specific crimes. The only evidence of a crime here is a violation of Faron Sears's rights to not be bugged."

"We work cases all the time without prosecuting the first dirty sin," said the AAG. "Faron Sears's privacy rights aren't as big as his right not to be murdered."

"We'll find federal hooks for this," said the FBI exec. "We'll designate you an Inspector."

"You get what you want, when you want it, top priority," said the AAG. "Keep this son of a bitch from getting killed."

"The only caveat," said the DAAG, "is do this all quietly. No leaks."

"So," said the AAG. "Do you accept?"

"*Inspector* Dalton Cole. Yes, I do."

"What do you want?"

"First, the D.C. homicide cop who's been my partner on the Cold Case Squad, Nick Sherman. I want him as my out-side man."

"He's not Bureau," said the AD/CID, "not Federal, not—"

"He's got a D.C. badge, and here's where the hit might happen, based on that intercept. He knows killers. Knows how I work.

"Plus," said Cole, "he's a better shot than me."

The three executives looked at each other. Shrugged.

They're letting me do it! Confidence surged through Cole—confidence welded to certain knowledge that he'd be these men's fall guy for all failures.

Let them push, he thought. I won't fall down easy.

"Do you have anything else in mind?" asked the AD/CID.

"Oh yeah," answered Cole.

An hour later, anger radiated off a pregnant woman as she marched into Washington, D.C.'s Du Bois Housing Complex. Her swollen abdomen jutted beyond her tattered Navy peacoat. She wore loose black pants, had a clean jaw, an elegant African mouth. Her skin was flawless American chocolate.

DHC is scarred earth surrounded by rusted chain-link fence. A dozen fifty-unit cinder-block apartment buildings fan out like spokes from a traffic circle. Cars cruise the traffic circle. Even on a bitterly cold day like this one, the crews are there, waiting for customers, more alert for lethal rivals than for cops. Music blasts from cars and through apartment windows.

The woman frowned. Her swollen belly and flashing eyes faced one graffiti-smeared building that seemed no different from the others. A group of men lounged by the entrance, watched everyone who came their direction. The woman stopped on the sidewalk well outside their reach but well within their glare. She put a fist on each hip, hollered: "Jerome! Jerome Jones! You haul your ass out here and see wach you done!"

Echoes of her words skimmed through the icy air to the traffic circle. The crews glanced her way.

"I'm talking 'bout you, J.J.! You know who you are! Call yourself a man? Come down here an' face me an' see what's what!"

She saw the men by the tenement's doors cock their hips and show what-the-hell cool.

"J.J.!" yelled the woman. "Je-rome! Get your snaky ass out here! I ain't leaving till you do!"

One of the men guarding the doors drifted toward her. "Yo, bitch! Whassup this yellin' shit?"

"I ain't no bitch and I ain't yellin' for you," she said.

"Well, hell, mama," he said, now close enough to get a good look at her remarkable face, now dropping his voice so only she could hear, "fine as you are, you should be hollerin' for me!"

"I ain't no fool, and I ain't lookin' for one, neither. You go tell J.J. to get his mangy black ass out here."

"*You* take *your* hollering black ass out of here," he said, " 'fore somethin' happens to it."

"Something already happened to it, an' you know what an' you know by who. 'Bout the only thing you don't know is how mad J.J. gonna be if'n you run me off."

"What I don't know is you. You a lot of trouble for a bitch."

"And I'm damn sure worth it," she said. "Now you go fetch your homie J.J. and tell him to get out here and collect his dues."

"You ain't going nowhere," he said, like that was his idea. He went inside the building. For seven more minutes she paraded on the sidewalk, her challenges echoing through DHC. Then the doors to the building flew open.

Jerome Jones stepped outside to rule his world. He was six foot two, had a crooked nose and wore a tan cashmere topcoat over his bare chest, blue sweat pants and sneakers. His hands were thrust into his coat pockets. His voice was deep and jagged as he yelled to the pregnant woman: "Who the hell are you, bitch?"

"I told you, don't you call me bitch!"

"I calls you what I want."

"That's not what you said after you knocked back the bottle."

"What the hell you talking about!"

Hands in the pockets, she spread the peacoat wide. Showed him and his Bro's her body. Her voice lost its shrill edge.

"Why don't you come on here an' see what we're talkin' 'bout?"

A dozen heartbeats passed. J.J. took a step. Three of his crew started with him, but he pulled his right hand out of his

pocket, held it up, and held them back. He patted that pocket, stuck his hand back in it. Walked toward the woman. The man who had fetched him fell in three paces behind his boss.

"Look," said J.J. when he was fifteen feet away from her. "Maybe you got me mixed up with some other dude."

"How could I do that?" Her anger was still there, but he saw her fight back a smile. "I knows how you could forget, all them other bitches you been messing with, but me, how could I forget?"

"Yeah," he said, stopped just out of her reach. "Well . . . I'd've remembered you."

"I can do what'll make you never forget," she whispered.

"Maybe you can," he said. Shuffled a step closer.

"You done good, J.J." Her hand came out of the peacoat, reached across in front of her. "Here, baby. Let me show you."

She guided his fingers toward that stomach, his eyes on her breasts. J.J.'s fingertips brushed her blouse, felt the cold, spongy . . . steel bit J.J.'s wrist—*snap-click!* A second *snap-click!* sounded as the woman yelled: "Bulldog! Bulldog!"

Sirens screamed into the complex. The doors of the building across the street exploded. A dozen figures in blue nylon jackets emblazoned with giant gold letters charged out.

Handcuffs! realized J.J. as he jerked back. *The bitch cuffed my right hand to her left!*

"FBI!" she yelled. "You're—"

J.J. hooked his left fist smack into her face.

Lawmen charged across the complex. J.J.'s crew hesitated, uncertain what to do as a dozen cops charged them: "Police! Freeze! Don't move! Hands up!"

The bodyguard grabbed the woman's free arm: She was strung between the two men like they were a chain of paper dolls. J.J. pulled and she followed his force, set her balance, then side-kicked the bodyguard. His grip broke; he staggered back. She pivoted, slammed a roundhouse kick into J.J.'s stomach.

The bodyguard drew a pistol—spun around, hit the ground before the *crack* of the SWAT sniper rifle reached them.

J.J. sucked in fresh air as he groped for the gun in his pocket. The revolver the woman had drawn from under her coat slammed into J.J.'s forehead.

"Go for it!" she hissed. "Killing you is worth the paperwork."

Twenty minutes later, she sat in a Bureau car. Spinning lights on police cruisers bathed her face in beats of red and blue. The foam belly lay on the back seat beside the transmitter she'd worn to trigger the raid. She kept her hands pressed flat on the upholstery, refused to let them shake. Outside the car were agents wearing blue nylon jackets emblazoned with giant gold "FBI" letters. A helicopter chopped the air. The agent who commanded the fugitive squad opened the BuCar door: "Hell of a job, Pickett."

"Thank you, sir."

Over her supervisor's shoulders, she saw her partner, Harry, hurrying toward them.

"Excuse me, sir." Harry was a big man, and he edged their boss out of the open car door. "Sallie, you're not going to believe the call we just got on the cell phone!"

"Why me?" FBI Special Agent Sallie Pickett asked the man sitting across from her at the conference table. They were alone in this office on Justice's fabled fifth floor. Night had fallen.

"Because I said so," was his reply.

Inspector Dalton Cole, she thought: Somebody's made the man a star. Rising or falling? She said, "We don't know each other."

"No."

"Why do you think I'm the agent best qualified for this assignment?" she asked.

"In the Bureau, every agent is qualified for all assignments."

"You ordered me to be candid. And that book line about 'everybody's qualified' is absurd. I'm a brick agent."

"Me, too."

"Then don't . . . Did you pick me for this because I'm black?"

"Absolutely," he said. "And because you're a woman."

"That could be construed as racism and sexism."

"I would not pick you to infiltrate a Mafia family or the Ku Klux Klan." Cole frowned. "You've never filed a complaint about racism or sexual discrimination in the Bureau. Should you have?"

"How far does a black, split-tail agent's complaint about harassment get her these days?"

"Further than it did yesterday," he said.

"So far I've handled what I've been handed."

I'll bet, thought Cole. She sat in her chair as if she'd spent a lifetime preparing to be there instead of having been rushed here straight from a street bust.

"Now I'm handing you this," Cole told her. "If you agree."

"There are other black, female agents. More experienced."

"Your B.A. in psychology, grad classes in poli sci, give you background for our cover. You have no immediate family members who'll be negatively impacted by the twenty-four-hour intensity of this operation. You've worked half a dozen undercovers—"

"Never long term," she said. "Day, maybe two, then a bust."

"Plus," he said, "you pistol-shot in the top ten percent of your class, and you have martial arts expertise."

"I'm a first-degree black belt, Tae Kwon Do."

"Looks like you missed a block today," he said.

She touched her swollen cheek where J.J. had hit her. "Sometimes you take a punch to do the job."

Cole grinned. "That's the attitude I want."

Sallie couldn't stop her answering smile. "Then I guess you get the whole package."

At 9:07 that Thursday morning, a BMW sedan rolled east along Massachusetts Avenue toward Stanton Park. Dalton Cole drove the car; beside him rode Sallie Pickett. The car, the man's topcoat, and the woman's chic coat on the back seat had come from the Bureau's warehouse of goods used for undercover operations.

"Nervous?" he asked as they waited for a red light.

"Absolutely," she said, but matched his smile.

They found a parking place near a gothic red brick castle surrounded by a fence of six-foot steel poles.

"Lots of rooftops and windows," whispered Sallie as they walked toward the remodeled former church.

"The intercept said, 'close contact.' And that intercept means the threat is already inside."

The night before, Cole had told Sallie and Nick Sherman: "We're running two tracks: One, find and stop the assassin. Two, identify the conspiracy and their inside man. Our best chance is to concentrate on the assassin while we ease our way inside."

That morning, Cole pushed a button on the mansion's speaker box. An electronic buzz opened the steel gate.

"I feel naked without my gun," she whispered to Cole.

A six-foot-eight man of granite with a bowling-ball bald head opened the front door. He wore both his tailor-made suit and his rage well. "Who you?"

"We're expected," answered Cole. "I'm—"

"I knows your *names*. I asked who you *are*."

Sallie met the glare of the giant whose skin was black to her brown. "Mr. Sears is expecting us."

"So I hear." He swept them inside with a massive paw.

"You make quite a first impression," said Cole.

"That's my job, Cous'. Now head on upstairs." The giant padded behind them as they walked through a cacophony of phones, cheerful voices, chattering TV news, and radio talk shows. Three banners stretched along the wide foyer's walls:

DATA IS NOT TRUTH
INFORMATION IS NOT KNOWLEDGE
NOW IS WHEN

"Is there a place where we can hang our coats?" said Cole as he climbed the main staircase.

"You 'spectin' to stick around?" said the giant behind them.

Offices were off to each side of their trek down the second-floor hall. The scent of coffee came from one room.

"How long ago did you leave New Orleans?" said Sallie.

"You got good ears, girl. Nice walk, too."

"It gets me where I want to go." Her tone was firm.

"Well you's here now." The big man rolled open a set of double doors to a conference room where two men sat at a table.

Match their faces to photos in the intel file, thought Cole.

The first face was a white male, early forties, no tie, no jacket, blue jeans, and a dress shirt: *Jeff Wood.*

Newspaper clips about Faron Sears's "Movement" poked fun at Wood's indifference to fashion. After Sears's popularity swelled past the dismissive peg of "freak," the press began to note that Wood was a Vietnam veteran—a fact reported with implication but no explanation. A pundit christened Wood the Movement's *warlord.* As Cole and Sallie entered, Wood picked up a phone receiver.

Sallie recalled Wood's NCIC computer print-out: *Arrested and convicted, 1971, Chicago, disorderly conduct.* A demonstration against the Vietnam War by the anti-war Vietnam Veterans group. Wood had evolved from soldier to peacemonger. *Arrested, 1976, California, possession of a controlled substance (marijuana).* Misdemeanor, probation, $100 fine. The crusader was no Puritan.

Into the phone, Wood said: "They're here."

As Wood hung up, the other man stood with a smile and an open hand stretched toward Cole and Sallie: "Glad to meet you!"

Jon Leibowitz, thought Cole as he shook the hand of the man with a curly fringe around a balding dome. He was an ex-congressman swept into office with Jimmy Carter, swept out by Ronald Reagan. A powerhouse law firm hired Leibowitz the day after he lost his election. Through the Reagan-Bush years, Leibowitz walked the halls of Congress for anyone who could afford his shoes. Leibowitz had the prescience to be an early fund-raiser for the election bus driven by Bill Clinton, but Leibowitz's "legal services" for his other clients tainted him too much for a presidential appointment. Six months after Clinton's inauguration, Leibowitz jumped off Clinton's wobbling bus to become Faron Sears's full-time attorney.

No arrests, thought Sallie as she shook the man's hand. One client interviewed by agents investigating arms deals in the Iran-Contra scandal; another client investigated for labor racketeering.

Leibowitz nodded to the behemoth blocking the closed double doors: "My guess is Monk—Arthur—didn't introduce himself."

"Monk Badreaux." Cole smiled as if his knowledge were innocent trivia. "Linebacker for the Pittsburgh Steelers, LSU. You've been out of the pros about ten years. What have you been doing?"

"Minding my own business."

Leibowitz gestured toward the table. "Monk is Faron's right hand. He quarterbacks our logistics."

Plus, thought Cole, he runs a crew of heavies that the ATF informer fingered as customers in search of rapid-fire artillery.

"What we're wondering," said Jeff Wood in a smooth, even voice. "Is who you are, what do you do, and why are you here?"

"Where's Mr. Sears?" said Cole.

"Faron's around," said Wood.

Leibowitz said, "When we were informed about you by him—"

The double doors rumbled open. For a moment, all Cole saw in the doorway was Monk's bulk, then a woman stepped around the ex-jock, moved to the table, and said: "So, you're Faron's hired guns."

Lauren Kavenagh, thought Dalton. Her chestnut hair curled at her shoulders, soft lines bordered her wide brown eyes. She had ivory skin that needed more sun. Nylons crackled as she sat.

Too much blush, thought Sallie.

Leibowitz spoke the appropriate introductions. Cole smiled at Lauren. Corporate records gave her a dozen vice president and chief executive titles in Sears's computer corporations. One columnist called her the woman behind the guru. Several articles claimed she and Faron were or had been lovers. The Bureau backgrounder on her found no marriage, no kids.

"In our group of equals," said Leibowitz, "Lauren is closer to Faron than anyone."

"I know," said Cole.

"Really," said Lauren. Cole didn't know what he heard in her tone: a question, a statement, an explanation.

"But," said Leibowitz, "Lauren knew nothing about you."

"Until yesterday," she said, "when Faron announced that you worked for us."

Wood said: "Doing what is what we want to know."

Cole said: "How did Mr. Sears—"

"Faron," corrected Leibowitz. "He avoids 'mister.' "

"We're consulting political analysts," said Cole.

"Yes," said Leibowitz, "Faron told us you were associated with the James Group. That you'll be doing research and monitoring here—although you're not listed in our contractors' data base."

"The James Group handles our fee," said Sallie. "How they bill—as long as we get paid—you'll have to ask them."

"I did," said Leibowitz.

Cole and Sallie held their breath.

"The chairman—whom I know from the White House campaign—confirmed your . . . affiliation. Commended your work."

The head of the public relations firm James Group had

agreed to vouch for the Bureau's operatives without being told details.

"We owe him a big thanks," said Cole.

"This is Washington, I'm sure he'll collect," said Lauren.

"But he was vague on precisely what you did for him and what you might do for us," added the lawyer.

"We're here on an exploratory contract," said Cole. "We aren't sure that we can help."

Sallie said: "Faron felt that since you've discussed polls—"

"He's consistently rejected polls," said Lauren.

"Said you can't yes/no or this/that what he's building," added Wood. "And that poll questions create perceptions that roll into reality instead of telling you what's out there."

"What he wants us to do," said Cole, "is explore that assumption. And other ideas."

"Day to day," said Lauren, "what are you going to *do* here?"

"Monitor everything," said Cole. "By observing you and everyone who works with you, going to your meetings and rallies, watching people relate to Faron, we get a sense of areas that we can quantify and then target for—"

Wood said: "That sounds like horseshit."

Sunlight streamed through the silent room.

"But," Leibowitz said, "American politics runs on horseshit."

Lauren said: "Bottom line, Faron says you're here."

"We're here to help you," said Sallie.

"Of course you are." Lauren's smile sliced through the younger woman. "Now, Faron wants to see you. Monk will take you."

She stood: Her eyes weighed Sallie, brushed Cole. Leibowitz and Wood followed her from the room.

Monk led Cole and Sallie upstairs. Office chatter faded. Sunlight filtered through stained glass windows. Maroon carpet muffled their footsteps, ran like a red tongue to a closed door.

The man in a wooden chair outside that door wore a black suit with a black turtleneck sweater, black shoes. He uncoiled from the chair to his feet with a liquid grace familiar to Sallie.

"New people, Nguyen," said Monk.

The man in the black stood still, hands at his sides.

"Let's get straight," Monk told the new people: "My job is to make sure nothing happens to him. Don't put yourselves in my way."

"What we do depends on your boss," said Cole.

"He ain't 'my boss.' You're the hired hands, not me. I belong here. Two paper-dollar nobodies like you line up against me, Faron won't wave good-bye if I knock your asses into the street."

"We're here to help," said Sallie, "not bring you trouble."

"You won't be no trouble to me," said Monk. "Believe that."

A massive paw steered Cole toward the door.

"Faron left orders: he'll see you alone," said Monk. He knocked softly on the dark wood, then opened the door.

Dust floated in the sunlight flowing through the windows of the steeple tower. The big room was empty—except for a man sitting cross-legged on a mat. He wore dark cotton pants and a loose blue shirt open at the collar, black Chinese slippers.

The door closed behind Cole. He thought: *He doesn't see me. His face is turned this way, but he's not looking.* "Mr. Sears?"

"Those were the first words you spoke to me when we met," said the man on the mat. "You called me *'Mister Sears.'* Not 'nigger,' not 'Hey, you,' not 'prisoner' or 'boy': you called me *Mister*."

"Seemed appropriate," said Cole.

"But not usual. You walked into the interrogation room in your Bureau suit. I wore prison blues and a chain to the floor."

Like a butterfly, Faron Sears unfolded from the mat.

This time his eyes aren't shooting hate at me, thought Cole. Faron's handshake was dry, firm.

Cole said: "You've done well for yourself."

"And how have you done?"

Cole shrugged. "Sorry if I kept you waiting this morning."

"I wasn't waiting," answered Faron. "I was sitting."

"Is that what you call it?"

"I call it being here." Faron Sears smiled. "I'm glad to see you. By the time I admitted to myself that I owed you my thanks, you were no longer around. So now—for then: thank you."

"Just doing my job," said Cole.

"No, you were doing your *duty*. That must have made you popular on your *job*."

"My dance card stayed full."

Then—because the truth belonged in part to this smiling black man—Cole told him what he'd never dared articulate:

"Hell, for years I got one bottom-of-the-barrel transfer after another. Then I stumbled on a Mob crew and my efforts got recognized by a SAC who didn't give a damn about political correctness. He pulled me onto a strike force, we made a great case, and he rabbied me back onto the ladder."

"And no one blamed you anymore for freeing a radical Black Panther terrorist?"

"No one punished me for it anymore," said Cole.

"Nobody ever punished the fourteen Chicago cops who burst into my party leader's pad, killed him while he was asleep in bed."

"At least they didn't kill you," said Cole.

"Fools never knew that thirty-to-life would give me the world. They jobbed me out to the state data-processing center like a plantation field hand chained to an old mainframe computer. But in six months, I could program that dinosaur better than anyone."

Faron smiled. "I thought filing a civil rights complaint with the Bureau was a waste of time. Then *you* came along."

"Didn't take a genius to wonder why *seven* members of the Chicago police department's Gang Intelligence Unit pulled you over for a 'routine' traffic stop. *Regular* cops—"

"*Honest* cops," said Faron.

"They'd have pro forma traced that pistol they said they saw tucked in your belt. Found its owner—who'd reported it stolen. The burglar who got popped for that job had been arrested by one of the cops who busted you."

"I told you: they planted—"

"They didn't plant the shotgun. You bought it in Indiana."

"Legally," said Faron Sears. "And when I put it in the trunk of that car, its barrel was longer than the sawed-off steel that showed up in court. Even the snitch inside the Panthers knew that."

"Case closed. Now we're here and your people don't trust us."

"They're smart."

"What did you tell them?"

"That you're here to help," said Faron. "They're used to my unorthodox ideas, so they'll buy your cover if I say so. They don't imagine that I would betray them."

"Who wants to kill you?"

"No more than two or three hundred thousand people."

"That's helpful. Try something easier: who in your organization could be a spy or a traitor."

"The last time Judas sold me out, he was working for the FBI."

"Now I'm the FBI. I'll keep you alive. That's my job."

"Finding out who would betray us is the only reason I agreed to let you in here. And that agreement was for you and only you to do this. I've been told you're not alone."

"I have to sleep. Chase around the country after the bad guys and guard you. Simple physics—can't be in two places at the same time. So you've got two protectors." Cole's face hid the secrets of Nick Sherman, the weight of the Bureau. "Agent Sallie Pickett and me. Sometimes one of us will be around, sometimes the other. Trust her like you trust me."

Faron smiled.

"Good," said Cole. "We'll need unlimited access to—"

"No," said Faron.

"What?"

"Our deal does not include letting the FBI and the White

House pry open all my affairs and steal whatever information they want, to use however they want."

"You know that's not why I'm here."

"That may not be Agent Cole's mission. I trust him. But the men in the White House? Their mission is to stay in power. If you vacuum my life and my work into your investigation, they'll sift through everything you get and use what they can against me."

"Nobody will run their own agenda against you under my flag."

"You can't control your bosses."

"You have a traitor inside here with us. A killer out there. How can I find them if you make me wear blinders?"

Faron shrugged. "I don't have time now to meet your partner, but I must accept that you have one. Or get rid of you. But don't mistake my accepting your partner for license to range beyond our agreement. From now on, ask for what you want. Maybe I'll say yes."

"That might not be enough to keep you alive."

"I'm not worried." Faron smiled at the man from his past.

Leave it for now, thought Cole. He looked around the empty room. "What is it you think about when you're sitting?"

"Nothing."

"Then why do it?"

"If you can be still, the infinite can be perceived."

"But you make a great target," said Cole. "Now my job is to go and take care of that."

Cole realized his shirt was soaked with sweat. As his fingers touched the cold metal doorknob, he heard Faron say:

"Back then, when we first met . . . how much did you know?"

"I knew enough to do my job."

"Did you know I was guilty?"

The room shook as though with thunder.

"The police were right: I was planning to kill as many of the GIU cops who'd assassinated my leader as I could.

"They stopped me from that evil," said this man who commanded a movement that stirred throughout America. "For the wrong reasons and with the wrong methods.

"But you," he added, Cole falling into his eyes, "you rescued me from the consequences of my sins."

A black magpie soared above pine trees as two cars followed a dark ribbon highway into Idaho's snow-covered mountains. The first car bore the emergency lights and insignia of the Idaho Highway Patrol, two officers in front, Dalton Cole and Nick Sherman in back. The second car was a Bureau sedan carrying FBI agents from the Boise field office.

Cole suppressed a yawn. His case was barely begun, but he was already tired. Jet-lagged. Out of his element. Cole had originally planned on making the trip to Idaho alone.

"Bad idea," Nick had said. "A table-top Kansas City boy like you will get lost out there in the small towns and mountains."

So when Cole finished his introductory foray into Faron Sears's headquarters, he and Nick caught an afternoon flight to Boise.

"What are we telling the locals?" Nick had asked as their plane leveled off above the clouds.

Cole shrugged. "We're investigating wire fraud."

"Wire fraud! Nobody goes down for—"

"We're from Washington," said Cole. "They don't expect common sense from us."

"What about your people?" asked the city cop.

"Headquarters will tell our agents what they need to know." Cole shook his head: "I used to hate assholes who'd fly in and hotshot some hush-hush case on my turf, then fly out and leave working shoes like me to clean up after them."

"Then don't make a mess," said Nick.

The plane engines droned. The clouds turned purple and pink.

"We're almost over your country, cowboy," Cole told Nick.

The stewardess pushed the cart with its tinkling minibottles of Scotch past the two men she knew were badges carrying guns and thus not allowed to drink. Nick listened to the tinkling glass.

"No land down there that I ever owned." Nick remembered his mother, her straight black hair, her face smiling on the good days.

"So D.C.'s your forever home?" asked Cole.

"They gave me the badge. And my wife—she loved the place. She might have changed her mind if we'd had kids. Now that she's gone, the badge is what keeps me there."

"Guess you don't have any place else to go."

"Hey, partner," Nick said, giving Cole the big smile to lead him to laughter. "We're both on the same damn plane."

The next day, in the state car, the patrolman riding shotgun pointed down the road to a gray cinder-block, aluminum-roofed blockhouse. "Good thing we've had some thaws or we might had trouble getting here. There's the rest stop."

The driver parked twenty feet from the phone booth. Car doors opened and slammed shut. The FBI field agents joined their inspector and the patrolmen. Another magpie cackled, skimmed over the men's heads and disappeared in the pine trees.

"Now what?" asked the patrolman.

One of the agents handed Cole a pair of overshoes. The agent's face betrayed no disrespect for the hotshot from Back East who hadn't been sensible enough to wear mountain gear. Cole pulled on the overshoes, walked toward the phone booth. Cowboy-booted Nick limped beside him, winter tightening his battered knee.

The phone booth looked like a crime victim. Its broken door gaped half open. The severed metal cord dangled above ice on the floor that was clouded dark brown—brown like the smear down one glass wall.

"Nick," said Cole.

"Maybe. Maybe."

Cole waved for the others to join them. A bird call cut the morning air. Cole saw two black, feathered, V-tailed blurs disappear into the pines. To the senior agent, he said: "How long to get a crime scene search team out here?"

"Be dark in six, seven hours," said the highway patrolman. "If we could wait until tomorrow . . ."

"Call your SAC," Cole told the senior agent. "Have him get a warrant for this phone booth, have him call the phone company. Get a tow truck, a van: cut the whole booth out of its base and—"

"What the hell?" said the patrolman.

"Get it padded in the van—keep it cold; I don't want the ice on the floor to melt. Extreme caution in handling it: there might be prints inside and outside."

"Where do we take it?" asked the agent.

"Arrange for immediate refrigerated air transport to D.C."

"We're in the middle of nowhere," interjected the state officer. "We got no evidence of anything that justifies—"

"Patrolman," said Cole, "the Bureau appreciates your help."

"You know," said the officer, "last big deal the Bureau had out here, we all ended up splattered with ugly blood."

A magpie swooping over the parked cars caught Nick Sherman's eye. He watched it fly into the pines.

"We're not talking about a siege of a right-winger's cabin," said Cole, remembering how once upon a time, the Bureau had but to ask in order to receive. "We're talking about legally removing one phone booth for laboratory investigation. And we're not going to do anything that will get anybody hauled up before Congress."

I hope, he told himself.

Nick saw yet another magpie swoop into the pines. Same place. In a straight line between the rest stop and where the magpies disappeared into the pines, Nick saw a broken sapling.

"I'll call it in," said the trooper.

"Thanks," said Cole. As the troopers and the senior FBI agent walked toward their cars, Cole told the other agent: "You make sure nobody contaminates that phone booth."

"Yes, sir."

Nick circled the rest stop, eyed the padlocks on the bathroom doors. He stood ankle deep in snow between the cinderblock building and the tree line. His feet in his cowboy boots were cold.

"Dalton," he called, and watched the FBI agent who'd worn city clothes to assert his authority ruin his suit walking through snow.

"You ever do any hunting?" said Nick.

"Not for anything that couldn't shoot back."

"Should be a requirement for you guys," said Nick. "You ever been a bird watcher?"

"No."

Nick sighed. Led Cole through calf-deep snow toward the pines.

"Probably been storms through here since then."

"So?" said Cole, struggling to keep up.

They reached the trees. Cole thought of the tall sentinels looming in front of him as mostly Christmas trees. He felt ignorant for not knowing their true names.

"What's back here that's got those magpies so damn excited?" said Nick.

Thirty feet into the pines, they found out. The birds had been busy and the birds had been lucky. Every time snow covered their treasure, they beat away its powder with their wings to get their due. All the flesh had been picked off the corpse's face.

Nick said: "So this is what that message meant by 'clean up.' "

Footsteps trudged up behind Nick and Cole, but they kept their eyes on the birds' work.

"Jesus, Mary, and Joseph!" whispered the patrolman who had driven.

Nick held up his hand to keep the others where they were. Magpies screamed at him and flew away. Eternal optimists, they'd circle overhead until dark. The homicide detective snapped a pine branch off a tree, used it like a feather duster to brush snow away from the black-leather-clad corpse.

"His hands look frozen palm down in the ice," said Nick. "The skin was warm enough when he was dropped to melt the snow, then they iced over. The ice kept 'em from the birds."

The other highway patrolman and the senior FBI agent joined their colleagues. The state officer threw up between two pines.

His partner was more practical: "Who's this belong to?"

"FBI found him," said Cole. "It's ours."

"Murder's a local job," continued the patrolman. "Unless it's on Uncle Sam's turf—or something special."

"It's ours," repeated Cole.

"Hell," said the patrolman, "the sheriff won't bitch about that. If this turns out to be more than some fool who died natural, it'll be the second murder on his turf in less than two weeks."

The lawmen from Back East shot him with their eyes.

Soft light from table lamps filled the Idaho hotel room. Dalton Cole hung up the telephone, told Nick Sherman: "Our forensic team just landed. The autopsy will be done by dawn."

The body from the mountains lay on a funeral parlor slab. "I don't think we should dig up the other guy," said Nick.

"No," agreed Cole. "There's nothing he can tell us now."

The other guy's death and life were chronicled in the police reports and crime-scene photos stacked on Cole's bedspread:

Brian Luster: Thirty-nine years of life ended the day ATF intercepted the e-mail message. Cause of death: bullets acquired in a seedy motel. Two felony convictions, two incarcerations.

"California born and bred," said Nick. "Why did he come to Idaho to die?"

Cole checked his watch. "I've got agents scrambling to find out. Problem is, I had to order soft coverage of his known associates. If we roll up hard, pull them out of bed . . ."

"We might spook whoever's targeting Faron before we can smoke him out," said Nick. "So that means tomorrow before we get much."

"We're booked on the morning flight back to D.C."

"Sheriff and the reports say Luster isn't local. The John Doe in the trees? Nobody's missing, nobody around here fits his look."

"Why here?" asked Cole. "It's a long shot to Faron Sears."

"You certain Luster is tied to the bones in the woods?"

Sitting on the hotel bed, Cole frowned at the D.C. cop leaning on the bureau. The mirror hung behind Nick reflected Cole's answer.

"Yeah," said Nick, "me, too. Two murders within twenty miles of that phone booth equal too much."

"I'm not certain of any *much*," said Cole.

"This isn't going to be a 'reasonable certainty' thing."

"We got to out-think the clock, out-think—"

"We're hunting, Dalton. We ain't got time to just *think*."

"What do you think of our partner?" asked Cole.

"Think she's sharp," Nick said. "What about our bosses? Do you trust them?"

Cole shrugged. "We all know the rules."

"What about Faron Sears?"

"If I was sure I knew who he was . . ." Cole shook his head. "I don't know what to tell you about Faron."

Nick bored his eyes into Cole: "You know, whether he's a target, an innocent, or somebody who's set all this up as a weird political game, we've got to fuck him over."

Cole blinked.

"You and our partner are inside his machine," said Nick. "You're spying on him to catch whoever else is betraying him. Somewhere, somehow, you're going to cross a line Faron wouldn't want you to cross. You're going to have to fuck him."

"Yeah," said Cole. "But I'll try to be gentle."

The killer lay naked on his bed. No light glowed in that room. Night, day: made no difference. He was here. Now. And the coming *then*. *Before* meant all those years of waiting. Years of not enough. Before the awareness of the necessity of recognition. Power comes from presence: *I will be everywhere.*

He remembered it all like a magnificent movie, with the film rolling through his head and scenes projected into eternity by every wave of his hand, every blink of his eyes.

He was, of course, the star. The *auteur.* The artist.

That Chris played the Messenger was perfect. Lucky I'd let him live that time long ago, thought the killer. Chris Harvie, boy fuck-up. Recognized him the moment he got out of that tinny foreign car outside my house, shivering in his shiny black coat.

Come in, I'd said.

Watched our reflection in the dead green eye of the living room's TV. Me on the couch, Chris twisting in the easy chair. Letting me know what he knew. Letting me know that his buddy knew. And that his buddy knew when and where Chris was *right then*.

Come on, Chris had said. You're perfect for it. Made for it.

After that came the meeting.

Scene 2: Two A.M. on a many-weeks-ago Wednesday. The cafe outside a town thirty miles from my house. An open-all-night box. Bad food, bad service.

I showed up three hours early. Hid the car. Camo clothes, gloves, *ballackva* to cover my face. Binoculars. Circled in on the cafe from the trees. Nobody else waited outside in the night.

Binoculars let me zoom right through the cafe windows.

There was the waitress, gray sweatshirt and blue jeans, beehive dyed-blond hair. She was the only person at the counter, slumped on a stool, watching a flickering twelve-inch TV.

There was the cook. White T-shirt, spattered apron. Losing his hair.

Yellow booths, all empty.

In the winter trees it was cold and dark. Only the wind moved.

At twenty minutes to two, the Toyota turned off the highway—no headlights behind it. Chris wore his shiny black coat. His passenger filled the role: *a stranger.* Coat and pants that didn't belong out here. They entered the cafe. Took the booth farthest from the waitress. She brought them coffee. Went back to her stool.

Wait. Watch. No surprises seen. Walk with the shadows. Glide past the red car—nobody in the back seat. Take off the ballackva. Open the cafe door. The bell tinkles.

I burned as I walked back to the booth. Sat next to Chris, jammed him against the wall. I could feel his every move. Nothing the stranger did could escape me. The mail-order watch on my wrist didn't vibrate from a microphone's transmitting or recording.

Magnets in the stranger's eyes.

"And here he is!" said Chris. "My man, *the* man, dead on time!"

"Thank you for coming," said the stranger. "We need to talk."

And I said: "Only the weak *need.*"

"Good," the stranger said. "You're not just some money-stupid mechanic. I'd hoped, but I wasn't sure: it's not about money for you. So then why are you here?

"I'll tell you why," said the stranger, giving the true answer before I could supply a tactical lie. "You had to know if Chris posed a danger to you. If his buddy knows what Chris knows—and he does. That's our insurance policy."

"Brian, man," said Chris, "one bad mother—"

"Forget all that," the stranger told me. "I'm here with your chance to rise above everything. If you don't think you can handle what I've got for you, if you're not . . . able enough, then what we know about your past doesn't matter. We'll leave you alone."

"Hey," said Chris, "what—"

And I told them: "I can 'handle' whatever I wish."

"Yes, I imagine that in this nowhere corner of the universe, you've been able to do OK."

Couldn't stop my tremble, couldn't deny the truth.

"I hear you're a killer." The stranger shrugged. "Anybody can kill a nobody."

"I am not some 'anybody'! I am special, power—"

The stranger's words nailed my flesh to the cross: "Power is what power does."

"The question is," said Chris: "can you do the job?"

I sneered: "A *job*?"

"This isn't about a job," said the stranger. "Looking at you, knowing what Chris tells me, you don't want a job, and that's not what this is."

My lips were dry, breath hard to control. "What is it?"

"A mission."

"Yes." Warmth flooded me. Understanding. Relief. I saw it all in that moment of clarity: Finally, *when* was *now*! "Yes."

"What did Chris tell you?"

"Two missions," said I.

"Two to start. To see."

"See what?" said Chris. "You told me two big-time hits. That's the contract you're paying for—and you are paying."

"Everybody pays," I said.

"Yeah, well, the down payment just got us all here," Chris said. "And don't nobody forget, I'm, like, *the agent*. And Brian. Nobody fucks with our cut of the action, 'cause he is the baddest motherfucker in the world.

" 'Cept for maybe my man here," said Chris, playing salesman.

"How do I know?" said the stranger.

"How do you know what?" snapped Chris.

"I know who you *say* he is," the stranger told him.

"Hey," said Chris: "You calling me a liar? You calling Brian a liar? You came to us, man, and we—"

I said: "What have you touched?"

"Huh?" said Chris.

The stranger dipped a napkin in the dark liquid of a coffee mug, wiped the napkin over the counter, over its silver dispenser; wiped the cushion of the seat on that side of the counter.

Chris said: "What the hell?"

And I swung out of the booth, walked to the counter where the waitress sat. "Is the cook back there?"

"Hey, Matt! Wake up!" She snapped her cigarette lighter. "Matt! The man out here is hungry!"

The cook's head and shoulders filled the serving bay cut in the wall behind the counter.

"What do you want?" he mumbled. His eyes didn't catch the blur of my gloved hand.

Bam! The 9mm in my hand jumped. The cook staggered back from the serving bay, a red circle exploding in his chest. *Bam!* His breastbone shattered beneath a second crimson hole. *Bam!* A scarlet furrow ripped through the top of his bald skull.

I whirled to the waitress, saw her over my black barrel. Her cigarette bobbed in her lips as she whispered: "Oh shit."

Bam! I gave her a third eye. Crimson mist sprayed the window behind her. She crashed to the floor. The cigarette rolled onto her neck. Flesh seared as I walked through the swinging doors into the kitchen. Chris and the stranger heard my make-certain shot.

When I came back through the swinging doors, the stranger and Chris were on their feet.

"Oh shit!" said Chris, echoing the waitress. "Oh shit oh shit oh fuck oh shit! What the, why the hell—"

The cash register bell dinged when I hit NO SALE. I scooped all the bills in the slots, the twenties under the drawer, pushed the money into the pocket of Chris's shiny black coat. Told both of them: "Now it's the perfect picture of an official holdup."

To the trembling stranger, I said: "I am who I am."

"Yes," was the whispered answer. "You are."

"Oh shit!" muttered Chris. "Oh fuck me."

I couldn't stop my smile as I thought: *Everything comes in its time.*

Outside, Chris vomited his courage into the snow. The stranger turned to me: "What I'm offering is a chance to prove your power to the world. Not once, but twice. To—"

"To make those millions of eyes see! And bow!"

"Yes. Yes, that's right."

"I've been waiting for you," I said. "I didn't realize it, but, here you are. Finally."

The stranger handed me a thick envelope. I felt the bulk of what turned out to be the palm computer, manuals, pictures, as the stranger said: "Everything you need to know for now is in there. One thing you must choose tonight."

"What?"

Chris yelled from the car: "We gotta get outta here!"

"For communications, codes: what do I call you?"

"Call me *R*. Revenger. Ruler. Waiting to rise. And you are my Usher to what's mine that's waiting for me. You are *U*.

"They may never know our true names," I whispered, "but the world will tremble to my touch! Promise me that!"

Then—this was so sweet!—the Usher's hand floated to my face. Cupped me and covered my eyes and knelt me down in the snow. I felt the surge, my groin pounding, the power, the knowledge.

Then Chris honked the horn for them to leave.

Everything comes in its time.

Sallie sat where they'd put her.

After Monk ushered Dalton into the tower room, he turned Sallie over to a woman who with her husband had left their auto parts store, Cleveland Indians season tickets, and synagogue seats to move to D.C. and "work with Faron." The volunteer introduced Sallie to crusaders from Alabama and New Mexico and Oregon and "just simply everywhere," old and young, white, black, Asian, and Hispanic, there to "help Faron."

The volunteer didn't introduce her to the man with the crew cut who lingered near whatever room Sallie was in.

While Cole and Nick were in Idaho, she spent her second day wandering around Faron's headquarters. Often, Sallie went to a bathroom and wrote down data about Faron's staff for the Bureau to verify. And she started asking to meet Faron.

"Good idea," Jon Leibowitz told her. The ex-congressman smiled. "We'll have to arrange that as soon as we can."

At five o'clock that second day, Sallie went to the Shaker Heights matron, repeated her request for an audience with the man.

"Why, I'm not sure how to do that, dear," was the reply. When Sallie said she wasn't leaving until "that" was accomplished, the matron gave Sallie a container of raspberry yogurt: "Just in case it takes longer than you think."

The empty yogurt cup was in the trash and the matron had gone home when Jeff Wood found Sallie sitting on a couch in a waiting room by the main hall. Mr. Crew Cut yawned in the doorway.

"Why haven't you left?" Wood asked her.

"I haven't done my job yet. I haven't met Faron."

"Maybe tomorrow."

"I can wait." She patted the couch. "Right here."

"You're not very convenient, are you?" said Wood.

"I'm not paid to be convenient."

A grandfather's clock ticked in the foyer.

"Don't go away," he said.

"Don't worry," she told his departing back.

Seven minutes later, a phone buzzed in Mr. Crew Cut's blazer pocket. He answered it, escorted Sallie up two flights of stairs to where Monk stood in front of a closed door.

"Sit yourself," Monk told Sallie. To Crew Cut, he said: "When it's time for her to go in, you'll get the phone."

Monk said: "Sister, don't be all night at it—hear?"

He clumped down the stairs.

Day Eleven, she thought. And I'm only sitting here.

Mr. Crew Cut's phone buzzed. He answered, sent her inside.

This office was one floor below the sunlit meditation room. Both rooms had a church's dark wood paneling. A framed black ink calligraphy on rice paper filled one office wall. The print was simple: a big black circle on a pale universe. Three chairs sat in front of a desk with a computer work station off to one side. Night filled the windows. Behind the desk sat a black man wearing a soft, blue shirt. Faron Sears hit her with his eyes.

"So that's who you are," he said.

She felt the door shut behind her. "That's who I am?"

"I saw you from the window," said Faron. "This morning."

"I've been here all day." She sat across the desk from him. "Yesterday morning, too. Didn't you know?"

"I knew Dalton had a partner. I assumed she'd left with him."

"Your staff didn't tell you otherwise?"

"No."

"How . . . inconvenient," she said.

"I'm sorry," he said. "Such oversights won't happen again."

His smile is wistful, she thought, not sly.

"You're not the FBI I'm used to. Why do you pack their badge?"

"Our job is—"

"I'm not asking about your job. I'm asking about you."

"Then I don't have to answer."

"No, you don't." And he waited.

That damn, gentle smile, she thought. He doesn't seem so old. "You mean because I'm black? Why join the Bureau?"

He said nothing.

"Because I'm a woman?"

He said nothing.

"What do you think I am?" she asked. *Questions create responses. Responses allow you to shift the focus away from—*

"You're not a 'what,' " he said. Then he waited.

"It's no big thing," she finally told him.

"You didn't pledge your life *and* assume the authority to take a life because of 'no big thing,' " he said.

"The job requires—"

"You're talking in circles. Why are you afraid?"

"I'm not afraid of anything—and I know the trap you're going to spring next, about how, *'If you're not afraid, then—'* "

"Why is it a trap?"

Sweat trickled down her ribs, over the strap of the bra that somehow had become tight around her chest.

"What do you want?" *Why does my voice sound like a whisper?*

"I want to know," he answered.

"Because . . . cops . . . FBI is the biggest . . . because cops are the only ones who can do something about it every second."

"Do something *good*," he said. She nodded. "About what *it*?"

"Don't you smell the shit out there?" she whispered. "It's killing us. Suffocating everybody, kids, old people, everything my mom and dad worked for and . . . They're not gonna, nobody's gonna tell me what, do that to them, make me live in shit without my . . ."

You're leaning across the desk at him! She pulled back, sat straight, pressed her knees together under her full, demure skirt. "This isn't getting us anywhere."

"We're already here."

"And someone's trying to kill you."

"And that's part of the shit you're fighting."

She nodded yes.

"Is it just fighting the shit that matters," he asked, "or does what I stand for matter, too?"

The door behind her clicked open. Sallie whirled, her right hand crossing toward her—*empty hip.*

"Oh!" said the woman in the doorway. "I thought you were alone."

Lauren Kavenagh let her eyes measure Sallie, said: "So there you are. Long day. Late night."

Lauren wore a belted designer dress a decimal point beyond an FBI agent's budget. Lauren's shoulder-length hair was casually perfect. Her lipstick was smooth.

"Not too late," said Sallie. "I'm used to irregular hours."

"Really." Lauren circled around the desk: "Faron, you should check the projections from the new software project."

She moved beside him, one hand on his chair, tapping commands on the keys, pulling up a file. Faron glanced at the screen.

"For now, these things are your concern, Lauren," he told her.

"But it's your name on the bottom line."

He sighed. Studied the colored graphs and charts that scrolled through the screen. Lauren looked at the woman on the other side of the desk—a steady, controlled gaze. Sallie refused to look away.

"Everything seems fine," said Faron.

"Good." Lauren's arm brushed his shoulder. "Then I'll leave you two alone."

As she left, Lauren told Sallie: "Glad to see you're fitting in."

"I'll do my best."

"No doubt."

Silence filled the room after the door clicked shut.

"My job is to keep you alive," Sallie told the man behind the desk. *Re-establish the conversation. Their roles.*

"Will it be difficult?"

"Won't be easy. Tell me about Monk's people."

"He insists on having someone near me all the time. He says it's in case I need anything. I don't challenge his analysis."

"You might have to. We might have to. What about his people?"

"They're not 'his' any more than they're 'mine.' "

"How many does he have?"

"I don't know."

"Are they armed?" asked Sallie.

"I've never asked. He knows I wouldn't like that."

" 'Not liking' and 'forbidding' are two different things."

Faron smiled. "Your mind is quite good."

"What about the guns?"

"Necessity rules," said Faron. "Violence can sometimes be neutralized only by force. Do Monk's assistants have guns? I don't know. Do I trust Monk to make those decisions? Yes. Will I ask him about it? Insult my trust in him? Only under direst of circumstances—and with the FBI here, how dire can the circumstances be?"

"I hope you never find out," she said.

Faron said: " 'Miss' . . . 'Agent': What should I call you?"

"Call me Sallie."

"Your real name?"

"Yes," she said.

"I like it."

"Look," she said, "tell your staff that Dalton and I are to always know where you are, always be allowed by your side."

Faron shrugged, smiled. Nodded yes.

"There's nothing . . . Tonight, you should be OK. I'll go home."

"Sleep well," he said. "Don't be afraid."

12

***D**ream . . .*

Some part of Nick Sherman knew this was a dream, *the* dream, that he was in an Idaho hotel room and this was just—

. . . running. Cold, so cold. Snow. Trees. Gullies. Rocks. Pounding: feet, heart. Breathe, can't . . . Faster, run faster . . . Crushed snow. Packed trail mashed out in front of him. Hurry! Run! Crows drifting in gray sky. Cawing/no sound. Hungry. Stumble, fall, get up get up run. Red splotches on hills of white. Sound . . . run . . . behind me, behind . . . run! Listen! Hoofbeats.

Awake, he was suddenly awake. In bed. Flat on his back. The room was dark, the sheets wet under the blankets.

Catch your breath. Easy, easy. It was just a dream. Just *the* dream. His heart slowed.

Nick switched on the lamp. His gun was on the hotel bed table, a .45 automatic, not the 9mm Glock the department issued. The Glock held a shitload more bullets, but they lacked the stopping power of the weapon designed to help American soldiers survive sword-swinging charges by religiously fanatical Moro tribesmen.

A bang to beat God, thought Nick. *Why trust your life to anything less. What stops a dream?*

The bottle of Scotch and the glass he'd used were out of sight in the drawer. Right where he'd hid—*left* them. Nick had bought the bottle on the way to pick up files from the sheriff. Now the amber line on the bottle in the drawer was four fingers up from the bottom.

Still had the damn dream.

He closed his eyes. Imagined the tinkle of the bottle

against the glass as he slid open the drawer. Imagined running in crimson snow. Still hours until dawn. Get there, then work will take over. Be OK. Don't need to do it. Don't need to open the drawer with the bottle. Don't do it.

What the hell, won't hurt, long as you know you don't need—

That's right, he thought. Don't need to. Don't need to.

His hands curled into fists at his side, crumpling the soaked bottom sheet in a grip that could kill.

Cole refilled his coffee cup from the room-service decanter, then sat on the bed to put on his shoes. The world beyond the hotel room's window faded from black to gray. False dawn softened the yellow glare of the room's lamps. He looked around: *Not like my apartment back in D.C.*

Then he froze: *No, this hotel room is like what I call home.*

Cole rented a one-bedroom, high-rise apartment just over the Maryland line from Washington. He shook his head, thought: why do I live in an apartment that feels like a hotel room?

He told himself: *Tie your shoes.*

His cellular phone buzzed; he answered it. "Hello."

The woman's voice said: "You're a hard man to find for someone who said he was here to stay."

Lauren Kavenagh. Calling from Washington, D.C., a thousand miles away.

"I didn't expect you to call," said Cole.

"Your office told me you were out. When I insisted, they told me I could try this number."

"Sure," said Cole: She'd reached the safe house intercept number, and heard them answer with the phony PR firm's name.

Brring! The hotel-room telephone screamed.

"What's that?" said Lauren.

"Don't worry," he said as the bedside phone rang a second time. "It's just another phone."

"Where are you?"

He glanced at the cold fried eggs on the room-service tray. Crime-scene photos of the man murdered in the cabin lay on the bed.

"I'm in somebody else's place," said Cole.

"Well," she said. "Lucky her. How soon are you coming in?"

"I'm not sure I'm going to make it today."

"Uh-huh."

"Is that a problem?" he said. The hotel phone fell silent.

"Absence makes the heart wonder," she told him. "Wonder what you're doing—for us. Whether you're worth it."

"Miss Pickett is there, isn't she?"

"Oh yes, she's here. First thing, bright and early this morning. Late last night, too. She knows how to put in time."

"We've got a lot of research to do," he said.

"Ah. Research. Are you a stand-back-and-watch operation or more of a hands-on kind of guy?"

"I get the job done," he said. "Why did you call me?"

"I noticed you haven't been around the last couple days."

"Miss me?"

"Not yet. But there's something you should know."

"Why not tell Sallie? You can deal with either of us."

"You're the senior partner. That's the level I deal with." She told him the news she thought he needed to know, hung up without saying good-bye.

Cole went to the hotel phone, called Nick Sherman.

"You didn't answer when I called," mumbled the D.C. cop. "Why?"

"Busy," said Cole. He heard Nick sigh, said: "You sound awful. Your knee bothering you?"

"No big deal," said Nick. "We got a make on the throat-cut corpse in the woods: Christopher J. Harvie."

"Are your bags packed?"

"Always. Why?"

Cole said: "We need to change our plane reservations."

Newark's Military Park is a grassy triangle of open air wedged into a gritty New Jersey city. A bronze bust of John Fitzgerald Kennedy graces the park. Cannons point to the sky. Days, the park belongs to office workers and pigeons. Nights, the rats come out, sniff the rag-wrapped humans who huddle on the benches. That Friday afternoon, the park changed. By noon, a portable wooden stage stood next to JFK's bust. By three o'clock, 400, 450 people shuffled in front of the stage, their shoes soaking up the brown mush of yesterday's snow.

At precisely three o'clock, Faron Sears walked onto the stage. Applause echoed off the cold glass panes of the urban canyon. Faron's amplified voice cut through the winter air.

"Politics is not what they say it is on television," he said. "Television *is* politics."

Three camera crews filmed his words, their bright lights dissolving into the gray day.

"Not all of politics is television. But all of television is politics: Sitcoms teach us that stupidity is the heartbeat of fun. Laugh tracks train us like Pavlovian dogs. Cop shows flatten greed, violence and heroism for a twenty-one-inch frame. Talk shows divert us with strangers who lie about their sex lives. Videos transform music from a catalyst for imagination into a canvas for producers with product tie-in deals. Commercials define our dissatisfaction, showing us what we must have and do and obey."

Here and there in the crowd, heads nodded in agreement.

"TV news is whatever the reporters got to fill the gaps between commercials. With luck, truth dances through TV news. Reality doesn't define TV news. Reality does not define any news. News is what the politics and luck of the news givers say it is—and appearance beats reality with film at eleven."

Sallie stood close to the platform. *No counter-demonstrators, she thought. No rock throwers, no hecklers. No one with one hand tucked under his coat. What the hell could you do if you saw that somebody?* Her hip felt light, empty.

"Politics isn't what it used to be!" boomed Faron. "From the time people first banded together until Hiroshima flashed, politics meant something different than it does today.

"Back then, politics meant what we did in a public space. It meant there was a private space—perhaps only a lucky few could escape to there, but there was such a space. A frontier where you could live apart from the world. A door that could be locked. There were two realities, public and private, and though one always affected the other, they were separate dimensions.

"The atom bomb ended that. Our consumer society that must buy and sell planned obsolescence ended that. Television ended that. 'Cybertics' ended that."

Congressman—ex-Congressman—Jon Leibowitz stood across the street, talking into a portable telephone.

"If politics isn't what TV says it is," continued Faron. "If it isn't what it was before today, what is politics?"

Faron paused. Smiled. Shot his forefinger to the crowd.

"Politics is anything people do involving power. There is no 'private power.' No 'public power.' There is no more 'private' or 'public.' There is only one all-encompassing dimension of interlinked reality. A dimension that is an ever-evolving cosmos of galaxies called nations or corporations, solar systems called ethnic groups and economic classes, planets called jobs. Every shimmer of energy radiates out to every other shimmer of energy. In this cosmos, politics takes place every time we breathe.

"Think about it: in today's world, what can you do that is *not* political? Take a shit . . ."

Sallie felt the crowd wince: profanity from a political

speaker in public was not the way things should be. No: *not the way things used to be.*

". . . or say such a word? There are laws against defecating in public. Laws governing the toilet in your house.

"Stop brushing your teeth, and the American Dental Association and its lobbyists quiver. So do toothbrush companies, and zealots who believe that fluoride was a Communist plot. A lawyer can use the evidence of your unbrushed teeth to prove you are crazy and lock you up. If enough of us quit brushing our teeth, a toothpaste company would go out of business, its employees would hit welfare lines, and its stockholders would demand a tax-paid bailout!"

The crowd laughed.

"The words you utter—that's politics. We've always twisted to be 'politically correct' for whatever group can cause us trouble if we utter some sound that their censors hate. Words shape how we think: what is thought-shaping if not politics? As long as America's presidents thought of my mother as 'just colored,' they didn't have to worry about what happened to her."

There, thought Sallie: Lauren Kavenagh, walking toward Leibowitz. She's heard all this before. Does she still listen?

Vehicles flowed past Military Park, brake lights winking red in the day's gray air as drivers wondered what was happening, then drove on. Two blocks away, a sedan pulled to the curb. Dalton Cole and Nick Sherman rode in the back seat. The BuCar had picked them up at Newark Airport.

Cole handed his holstered Beretta, spare ammo magazines, Bureau ID, and handcuffs to Nick. "I'll walk from here."

"I don't like you walking around unarmed," said Nick.

"The e-mail to the killer still gives us more than two weeks."

"Yeah, and he's already given us two bodies."

"I'll see you," said Cole. He climbed out to the sidewalk. Faron's amplified voice reached Cole before the FBI Inspector's steps brought him to Military Park:

"So if politics has changed," Faron proclaimed, "then everyone's life has changed—everyone's. Mine. Yours."

Middle of the workday, yet here they are, thought Cole. People with jobs, rag-wearers, too. The crowd was half male, a racial and ethnic mix. That woman with cat's-eye glasses and blue hair had to be a grandmother. Two boys and a girl carried backpacks that screamed high school.

Cole passed behind the platform, caught the eye of Nguyen.

Faron's voice boomed through New Jersey: "So what does all this mean for us? For you?"

The FBI inspector strolled through the bystanders on the sidewalk across the street from the park.

"The new reality means *pay attention*.

"Now more than ever," continued Faron. "Pay attention to who you are and how much power you truly have. Don't trust yesterday's politicians to lead you tomorrow. They think that 'politics' is how they get you to vote so they can keep their horse-and-buggy jobs."

A clerk shivering in the open doorway of a shoe store ignored Cole as he walked past. The clerk's father had spent twenty-three years working on the line of a Cleveland shoe factory. Half the shoes in this store window had been made in Korea; twenty percent came from Mexico, where the factory that laid off his father had moved.

"If a politician doesn't understand that reality has changed, don't believe what he says. If he doesn't recognize that the Crips and Bloods and the Yakuza, the Triads and the Ghost Shadows, the Columbian Cartels, the Russian Mafia and America's Cosa Nostra are important *political* forces, then that politician is a fool."

Cole spotted Sallie standing near the platform. *Good agent,* he thought: Her eyes stayed on the people within striking distance of her subject. But she wouldn't have a gun, either.

"In our new world, is the person who's trying to be your leader paying attention? Does he or she know that fortress walls and private police squads encircle neighborhoods all over our 'melting pot' country?"

Cole walked past plywood-over-glass windows, past a boarded-over door with a chrome padlock hanging open in the cold wind.

"We are becoming less and less a nation, more and more a world of tribal clusters determined by ethnicity, geography, and wealth."

Next to the boarded-up store was a discount haircut factory that specialized in lunch-hour clip jobs.

"Issues and principles that have defined human beings since we crawled out of the swamp have not vanished, but how . . ."

Cole walked past a hole-in-the-wall carry-out-and-delivery pizza parlor: smells like cheese, pepperoni, and . . .

Remember: padlock gone.

". . . how we deal with what we want and need . . ."

There! Two buildings over, second floor of the boarded-up, unlocked building: an open window. The nearest cop was across the street in the park, his back turned to the could-be sniper's nest. The cop's ears rang with amplified oration.

Run. The door: no padlock. Slide inside. Slats of light fall through gaps in the plywood over the windows. Wind drifts through the dust and litter of the gutted store. Crumpled paper skitters across the floor. Empty room, one big box empty . . .

A door in the back. Push it open. Another room. A toilet stall. Stairs zig-zag up the wall. Muted light fills an open doorway on the second floor. Walk on the edges of the stairs so they won't creak. Up, slowly up. Top of the stairs . . .

Dalton eased his face around the edge of that doorjamb: At the end of a bare room, a man stood by the open window, his eyes on the park, his hip supporting the butt of a telescopic rifle.

Thirty-five, forty feet away, thought Cole. Slip around the edge and take one step. Don't disturb the air, *flow.*

Bolt-action rifle. With a bolt action, Lee Harvey Oswald got off what, three shots in seven or nine seconds? Whole world changed in ten seconds. Two shots, can get there in two . . .

Six silent steps closer. He's thirty feet away. White. Mid-thirties. Tall. Short hair. Ski jacket. Black sneakers.

Faron's voice filled the room: "Force *compels,* power *acts . . ."*

In the lower window's double-layered panes of glass, Cole saw his own reflection coming closer, closer. Don't look down! he telepathically ordered the rifleman. Don't look away from your target outside on the—

Rifleman turned toward the back of the room—

Cole charged, stuck out his right hand, cocked his thumb back, pointed his forefinger at the sniper, screamed: "BANG! BANG! BANG!"

The sniper flinched.

Cole pushed the rifle barrel away from his chest, but the rifle butt slammed into his ribs. Cole stumbled back, holding on to the barrel. He buried his knee in the sniper's stomach. And got pushed back. Cole crashed to the floor.

A foot slammed into Cole's groin. He jackknifed to a sitting position. The rifle butt stroked his cheek, knocked him to the floor. A cold steel tube pushed into his panting mouth. *Oil/ powder bitter-burning taste, gagging . . .*

"Power is created by circumstance and choice."

The *rattle-clack* of a rifle bolt sent a cartridge into the firing chamber.

Monk's voice said: "Don't kill him yet."

Dalton Cole sat in the back of the idling limousine. Monk, Jon Leibowitz, and Jeff Wood filled the seat facing him. Outside, the rifleman and Nguyen stood beside the limo. Nguyen's sunglasses reflected the crowd leaving Military Park.

Cole said: "So what should I have done?"

Ex-soldier Jeff Wood said: "What made you do what you did?"

"Instinct." Cole glared at the three men who'd "helped" him into this locked car. "Television."

"This life ain't no cop show, cous'," said Monk.

"I don't watch cop shows. But at least once a year, I see some news show that has old film clips of Dallas and an open window, and I watch Jack Ruby at work. And all the other 'shows' where somebody didn't do enough."

Leibowitz said: "We're grateful you were willing to risk your life for Faron, but we wonder why you went into that building in the first place. That's not the kind of thing a P.R. man does."

"He does if he sees a chance to get a different view of his client at work."

"Ah," said Leibowitz. "So *research* led you into an abandoned building?"

"Call it curiosity."

"You a cat?" said Monk.

"I'm on the team," said Cole, "and what I don't understand is why you people employ a sniper."

"Like you said," Monk told him, "we all seen those TV shows."

"So you've got armed guards? How many? Where and when and—"

"Knowing that isn't in your job description," said Jeff Wood.

"Has Faron received death threats?" asked Cole.

"Faron is point man for overdue change," answered Jeff Wood. "Danger is inevitable."

"But nothing we can't handle," said Monk.

Jeff Wood asked Leibowitz: "What do you think?"

The ex-congressman said: "I think that the only harm done is to Mr. Cole's ego and a few bruises that he's lucky aren't worse. I think that all of us have learned some lessons.

"Faron doesn't need to be burdened with your screw-up," he told Cole. "Don't tell him about this. No reports back to the James Group, either, or leaks to the press or public."

"Monk?" said Jeff Wood. "What about it?"

With a sweet smile, Monk said: "If Mr. Cole's gonna be a trouble man, he'll have to get hisself a whole lot tougher."

16

The train clackety-clacked toward Washington. Dalton Cole rode alone, the twilight world of refineries' gas-fire smokestacks and trackside ghettos slipping past his window. In the limo to Newark's depot, Jeff Wood had told him: "Faron likes to travel with the people." *With the people* meant that Faron, his lawyer, warlord, and security chief rode in the next train car back, along with a dozen *citizens,* some of whom recognized the VIP in their midst. Farther up in Cole's car were Nguyen and one of Monk's goons.

The *whoosh* of the train burrowing through the evening air changed: behind Cole, the door between cars slid open; closed.

A blur: gold suit, skirt flashing above a knee. Lauren dropped into the seat beside Cole, brushed strands of brown hair from her face, said: "If I sit here, promise not to attack me?"

"Hitting first isn't my style."

"I didn't think playing hero was your style. Why'd you do it?"

Look out the window, away from her eyes so she won't sense any lies: "Once I saw what had to be done, doing it . . ."

"Came naturally," she said. "Logical. But you had the guts to follow through, to actually do it."

Look back at her: "I didn't see a better choice."

The smile she gave him was soft. "Saw what was what, knew what you wanted, did what you had to. I know what that is like."

"Wasn't exactly a plan," he told her.

She brushed her hair back: "Plans aren't all they're cracked up to be. I planned on meeting a knight in shining armor."

"I thought you had."

"You mean Faron?"

Cole nodded.

"These days he's more Merlin the Magician than Sir Lancelot."

The train rumbled on. Cole said: "How did you meet him?"

"What are you, a history buff?"

"It's what we've got," he said.

"Really?" She let him feel humor in her cynicism. She stared out the train window. Not long to sunset.

"We were in the same training class. Multinational Business Devices, Santa Cruz. Affirmative-action hires. One weird woman. One black—not technically an ex-con because his conviction had been thrown out. For the first few months, he wore glasses. Faron has perfect eyes. Glasses hid the fire in them. But if you'd been around, you could smell the smoke."

"And you'd been around," said Cole.

"More than the pale MBD guys in button-down white shirts and perfect ties. They were afraid of his muscle, not his mind."

"What scared you?"

"Every damn thing about him," said Lauren. "Hell, he was *everything*: bad-ass black radical prison-sprung whizbang genius busting his way into big business."

She met Cole's eyes: "Do you know we were lovers?"

The train rhythm was like a heartbeat: *budda-bump, budda-bump.*

"If you're going to be a history buff," she said, "you gotta take the good with the gone."

"When did you stop being scared of him?" asked Cole.

"You tell me; then we'll both know."

"I doubt you're afraid of anything," he said.

"Fear is an amazing thing." She shrugged. "Put on the right mask, you'd be surprised what you can do, who you can be."

Tall poles lit the tracks as the train raced through warehouses and factory zones of blurred suburbs. Spotlights targeted the billboard wall of a brick building: "CONFIDENTIAL RECORDS GUARANTEED PERMANENTLY DESTROYED."

Lauren said: "I thought PR flacks did all the talking."

"I'm not perfect," said Cole. "Why were you weird?"

"California," she said. "Believe everything you've been told.

"Disco wasn't the only thing that sucked during the seventies," she said. "Once upon a time, I was young."

"You're not old now."

"We're about the same, and we're not fooling anybody."

"Maybe that's not so bad," he lied. "Were you a surfer girl?"

"Wrong side of the freeway. Mom died when I was ten—cigarettes and punching numbers all day into a Food Giant cash register. That was before us whiz kids came up with scanners and bar codes. Dad worked for the state—when he was sober. No time in my house for surfing. Or money for more than second-tier schools."

"Could have been worse."

"Don't I know it."

"Then came Faron."

"Then came Faron. I didn't even dare talk to him until . . . one day in the parking lot, he walked up and . . . put his hand on my arm. One innocent touch. Plus those eyes burning right through me. He said: 'Don't worry, we have better places to go.' "

"Looks like he was right," said Cole.

"Didn't seem like it at first. But I was still so young. Couldn't see all the moves he was playing. In ex-con versus cocky corporate, give me the con every time. Cons play like they're gonna eat steel in the showers if they don't cover all the angles.

"Faron set up the biggest racist in the building—who also happened to be a top executive. The creep busted all over Faron, called him nigger, told him how because he was black, he'd never get to be more than a keyboard tapper."

Cole said: "Faron taped him."

"You ever in prison?" asked Lauren.

"I've been around, too," he said. "How'd you and our leader get from corporate—"

"To this train? A hotshot rebel lawyer from San Francisco, Faron's tape, and MBD facing millions in lawsuits, picket lines . . .

"The payoff was a contract," explained Lauren. "Faron got

up-front dollars plus an exclusive twenty-year contract to write supplemental software for running all MBD's machines. It was one-way: MBD had to buy only from Faron, but he could sell to anyone. Give the 'boy' a few bucks and a bottom-level deal selling them 'supplemental' software they needed anyway. They figured they got rid of him cheap and got a deal at the same time."

"Then they realized that Faron's software controlled all their machines," said Cole.

"And everybody else's. He owns the gas for the information highway. And he sells it, one tank at time.

"Wasn't quite so easy," she said. "The settlement money ran out, the software wouldn't work on schedule, our warehouse burned down. Faron kept going. The fire-insurance money helped."

"And you were already with him," said Cole.

"How could I not be?" Her smile was wistful. "He needed someone to track the nuts and bolts while he created the grand programs. I needed someone who needed me that much, who was magnetic enough to hold me."

"And you're still with him."

"Not like before. Magnets lose their charge. But when it was gone, I was still Number Two in his empire, more powerful than I'd ever dreamed, richer, but . . . What do you do when you *get there* and you still got a lot of time left?"

"I don't know," said Cole. "What did you do?"

"Hold on," she answered. "Then all this started. Once, when he tried to make me understand why he was turning away from everything I—we—worked so hard for, he said it was like somebody booting up a master program in him. Turning him on so he could see.

"I told him I'd already done LSD," she said. "When the acid's gone, all you got are tracks in your mind."

"But you've stayed with him."

"Guess I want to see where this will all end up."

"Where will *you* end up?"

"Tell me when we get there, OK?"

The train rolled on.

"You owe me," she said.

"What?"

"You risked your life to save my ex-lover, my still boss, my whatever-he-is-becoming kind of guru leader. Of course, you're a complete screw-up, but you're still sweet."

"Sweet?"

She touched his swollen cheek: "Does it hurt?"

"That didn't." Her hand fell away, and he said: "I owe you?"

"You tried to project a major effect into my life. I didn't ask for it. So now you owe me. Plus, I told you my secrets. Faron's, too. You had legal obligation to keep them when you were just a hired hand. Since you chose to be a hero, too, now you've got a moral debt."

"What do I owe?" asked Dalton.

"Now you can never betray me."

Cole looked at her. She had brown eyes.

"If you do," she told him, "I'll haunt you forever. Plus, you owe me the truth about why a PR geek charges rifles and walks like a cougar. But now I've two hours of train ride left before I have to log on with the real world. Wake me up when we get there, OK?"

She closed her brown eyes without needing his reply.

The train clackety-clacked through the darkness. A lone watchlight lit a stand of trees beyond the tracks. Strands of Lauren's chestnut hair fell across her face, across her sleeping eyes and unpainted lips. Night roared past cold glass.

Sallie struggled to keep her balance. The train rocked as she walked down the aisle. *Cole had to be in the car up ahead.*

"There you are," said Faron Sears. A row of seats had been turned to face another. Faron sat facing the front. A laptop computer rested on his knees; its screen glowed blue.

"Here," he said, lifting his coat off the seat opposite him, putting it on the floor behind his legs. "Ride with me awhile."

The guard with the crew cut sat across the aisle from Faron.

"You're working," said Sallie. "I don't want to disturb you."

"I'm only surfing." He told the bodyguard: "We're OK."

With a nod, the crew cut stood, walked toward Monk. Gravity pulled from the empty seat in front of Faron.

"Come on," he said. "Keep me company. It's a long ride."

As many good reasons to stay as there were to walk. She

sat, her hands flattening the wrinkles out of her slacks, as if they were a too-short skirt she needed to pull over her knees.

"Surfing?" she said. "What ocean?"

Faron put his laptop computer aside. "Do you know what the Internet is?"

"I'd rather have you tell me."

"Internet is like a giant electronic cyber collective that anyone with a computer and a phone can be part of, a network of shared data. Alive, twenty-four hours a day. Growing, *being.*"

"Being what?"

"What it becomes," said Faron. "If George Orwell had written about the real 1984, he'd have reported that that was the year the Internet broke one thousand users, mostly in the U.S. Now, almost seventeen million people use it in a hundred countries: people, not 'Big Brother.' "

"And that's what you're . . . surfing. Here, now."

"I haven't hooked my laptop to a portable phone and dialed into the Net, but last time I did, I loaded mail."

"Electronic mail."

"Yes," he said. "We created the first 'political' Web site—a 'place' in cyberspace where you can log on to me and to the other people who log on to me. A bulletin board. A file of messages and questions from anybody who logs on, all interactive."

"How many people?"

"About one hundred forty-seven thousand."

"One hundred forty-seven thousand!"

"Not all at once. At any one time, my Web site has about two thousand entries. Comments and questions directed to me or about me."

"What do you do with that?"

"*Connect,*" said Faron. "I scroll through the messages. When I find one that's . . . inspirational, I type in a comment. The question and my answer are saved for anyone else to see."

"Which ones the computer *says* you've answered," said Sallie.

Faron smiled: "I set up Web site security that goes beyond my password. And my password: nobody knows it, not even Lauren."

"So you have one secret from her."

"As you have secrets from Cole." He nodded to the portable computer. "Every forty-five days, my site gets wiped. Keeps the take fresh, keeps users coming back. All my interactions flip into a permanent bulletin board and download as hard copy in a dozen university libraries working under grants from me."

"The sayings of Chairman Faron, preserved for all time."

"Do you think of me so harshly?"

"No, I . . . No. Just a joke."

His smile forgave her.

Don't do that! she thought; said: "You connect with your constituency one-to-one and at the same time it's like you're giving a nationwide speech."

"And whoever I interact with develops a personal stake in what evolves because of us."

"Jesus touching the masses," she whispered.

"An absurdly grandiose comparison," he told her.

"What?" Sallie shook her head, her mind racing. "The speech, the rally today in Newark: it didn't . . . it wasn't very big."

"How big was it?" he asked.

She stared at him.

"We announced it with real-world ads the day before. Only twenty-four hours' notice, yet we got a turnout of three hundred-plus—not counting cops and volunteers and paid staff and undercover FBI agents."

"Only two of us were there."

"Uh-huh."

"Why?"

"Traditional political rallies spend days organizing, hoping to make an impact, get noticed. Their success is judged by how many actual bodies attend the actual event. With the abruptness of what we did, that we got anybody there at all is news. And the news media was there. We'll be a how-did-they-pull-it-off? story.

"Plus," he said, "yesterday we announced on the Net that there would be a 'hard reality' in Newark. When Internet connectors see that, when they compare that data with what they find in traditional media, when they call up my speech from the Net . . ."

"Because you whispered, the world will strain to hear," said Sallie. "And with computers, the Internet, now they have ears."

"Some users can even download video of the event into their machines. 'Be there' whenever they want, free of any strictures of network newscasts."

"And now you've got someone who wants to stop you," she said.

"I don't worry about 'stopping me,' " he said. "It's too late. I'm here. That I *can-have-been* is the bottom-line importance."

"I think I understand," she said.

"Wish I could say the same," he said. "I know what some of all this means, but I don't grasp its totality—I can't: it's evolving beyond me. Today, evolution moves as fast as light."

"Where are you taking us?"

"No, the question is: Where are we now and where are we going?

"There had to be someone like me," he told her. "Better me than a Hitler or a Rasputin or a Charlie Manson. The Net's already become a political tool: Right-wing militias are on it; so are the 'declared' presidential candidates. Zapatista rebels in Mexico tie red kerchiefs around their faces, shoot up the government with M-16s—and organize their cadres on the Internet. The road never judges who walks on it. But me going down it my way might inoculate us against mind-twisting cyber-monsters."

"I don't understand how your mind works," she said.

"Me either."

"Where are you going with all this?" she whispered.

"I'm here, now." He smiled. "With you. On a train."

17

"We got two dead and nasty bad boys," Nick Sherman told Cole and Sallie in an FBI safe house in a quiet Washington neighborhood. Nick had taped photos of two dead men to their War Room wall.

"Christopher J. Harvie, age thirty-nine," he said, tapping the cluster of mug shot, prison, and death photos of the man in the black fake leather coat. "Bad checks at nineteen, did a year in Oregon. Moved to sunny California, lots of pick-shit arrests and nolo prosecutions, then got popped with a pocketful of pills. Did his second jolt at Folsom.

"Bad boy Number Two," said Nick, moving to the cluster of crime-scene photos from the Idaho cabin, prison-surveillance and mug shots of the tattooed bear. "Brian Luster, 46.

"Brian ran with Hell's Angels, pulled two hard-time stints, first for arson, second for amphetamines. His rap sheet shows a dozen assault arrests, two more for arson, one for armed robbery. A woman filed rape charges on him, dropped. LAPD thinks he was in on beating a Korean convenience store owner to death in a robbery."

"Our boys did time together," said Cole.

"University of Folsom," said Nick, "where they were both Aryan America."

"They're thugs under sheets," said Sallie.

"That's not their style," said Cole. "Bureau Intel says AA is seventy percent ex-cons. Bikers. Computer whizzes, skinhead hackers. Links to Europe."

"They're in cyberspace," said Sallie. "Just like Faron."

"Cyberspace?" Nick grinned: "Who you been talking to?"

"I've been doing my job!"

Dalton said: "Can we tie Luster and Harvie closer to AA? Backtrack what they've been doing before they died in Idaho?"

"You got twenty agents working on that," said Nick.

"They'll assassinate Faron because he's black," said Sallie.

"Don't name anything until you're certain," said Cole. "Once you name something, you ignore what else it could be. We've got to stay open on this until we close our hand on the killer."

Nick told Cole: "Maybe what the bosses lined up for you tonight will get us there faster."

The cocktail waitress yawned in a booth by the door. The bartender watched a late-night TV talk show with a state fish and game administrator in town to lobby Congress. Two men in a back booth ignored the TV and the beers on the table between them.

The man sitting across from Cole pushed the cold beer bottles farther apart: "I don't want your name; you don't want mine. I'm not wearing a wire, and you better not be either."

"We're federal employees of the same department," said Cole. "We have a legal right to talk to each other, share information."

"Maybe. But if a prosecutor makes one 'maybe' step, years of work can go down the toilet with one bang of a judge's gavel."

"What did our bosses tell you?" asked Cole.

"That you're a Justice department official investigating a possible threat to the civil rights of Faron Sears."

"Did they tell you what those rights were?"

"Only after I told them to get fucked if they didn't tell me more. Then they said somebody wants to kill him."

"Yes."

"And that's the scope of your investigation—*Agent?* Or are you looking for a way us good guys can be shut down internally on the pretext that we might be violating Faron Sears's civil rights?"

"You've worked in Washington a long time."

"No shit," said the stranger.

"I'm after murderers who've already killed two people."

"No bullshit?"

"I haven't got time for bullshit."

"Don't tell me about time. My wife thinks the only reason we're not divorced is because I'm never home enough to notice we don't have a marriage. The one night I try to leave the office on time, I get called up to the Fifth Floor, ordered to meet whoever-you-are in this nowhere place, and brief you on Justice's review of Faron Sears and his empire."

"I didn't know Justice was investigating Sears."

"Officially, we're not investigating. We're reviewing information as part of our ongoing oversight responsibilities."

"That's your public statement," said Cole.

"Our 'public statement' is no comment. You don't drop a bomb like 'the Justice department is investigating.' If you do, Wall Street bleeds. You especially don't do that after a federal judge rejects your bosses' attempt to cut a deal with your tar—with the affected private party."

"What division are you in?" asked Cole.

The stranger took a sip of beer: "My task force has some criminal attorneys on it, but most of us are antitrust."

"You're targeting Faron Sears for antitrust actions?"

"Listen, gumshoe," said the lawyer. "That me and my people are able to do more than answer the phones is a thrill. In the seventies and eighties, everybody was on the side of the big-money boys—and the big-money boys don't want antitrust problems. So we became part of those damn, nut-cut 'government regulators.'

"Now," he said, "after the savings and loans have been looted, the insurance companies' underwriting funds drained, midsize corporations crushed, we've been invited back to the table. At least we were for a while. Anyway, we're light-years behind in laws to handle everything from Japanese *keiretsus* to an octopus like Faron Sears who operates with products and processes that weren't around when our defining laws were written."

"You didn't lock onto Faron Sears just because he's there," said Cole. "Who sicced you onto him?"

The stranger looked at the gumshoe from the FBI.

"I've been around town awhile, too," said Cole.

"Then you know what it's like to be an overworked, under-resourced Fed. One day you get a package of legal cites, research material, and logical guidance; there's enough probable cause and already-done spadework to start an inves—a review rolling."

"Who dropped the package against Faron on you?"

"We received proper queries and direction from a variety of sources." The lawyer smiled. "The theory of antitrust laws is that if you can keep the markets free and open, when one guy tries to rip off more than his legal share, the other guys on the street have a chance to holler foul and make it stick."

"You got complaints and ammunition from his competitors."

"Some private queries, yes."

"I'll bet." Cole thought for a moment: "Did somebody on Capitol Hill sic you on Faron?"

"Members of the Judiciary Committee are concerned about new developments in antitrust issues, yes."

"And who pays for their election campaigns?"

"Be smarter than that: a senator who's concerned about a powerful force in our country isn't necessarily carrying dirty water for some special-interest group."

"Any one senator?"

"OK, maybe one, two of them care because certain long-time supporters of their political beliefs feel that *blah blah blah*, but the big push is coming from members who have legitimate fears."

Cole said: "Who's going after Faron Sears?"

"You become a billionaire by squashing millionaires."

"How and who?" said Cole.

"Off the books?"

"This is all off the books," said Cole. "Remember?"

"Uh-huh." The lawyer drained his beer. "Sears builds his empire like an extended tribal network. Or a computer net. Profit-sharing for all his employees is cut from their particular operation plus a share out of the umbrella corporation. He funds employees' outside ambitions with loans. They start up their own businesses—not just computer stuff: convenience stores, a laundromat, a private school, a gas station, whatever.

A loan from one of his companies or their pension funds
backs it.

"In return, Sears owns thirty percent of the entrepreneur's
business. Then Sears makes sure all his employees and pur-
chasing officers know that if they deal with that 'independent'
company, they'll sweeten their own wallets through the profit-
sharing plan. And the empire grows."

"Is that legitimate?"

"So far, so good," said the antitrust expert. "Horizontal
monopolies are an almost invisible entity in the regulatory
laws. They follow the rules enough to avoid any convictions."

"How does he push the rules?"

"FUD: 'Fear, Uncertainty, and Doubt.' A rival wants to market a competing product, Faron spreads the word that it might
not mesh with their system, and since their system powers
the main game, nobody wants to risk buying the competitor's
new toy.

"He strangles his competition with 'vaporware.' Faron's
software company announces products years before they're
ready to market, scares competitors off who can't risk developing their own version if Faron is going to beat them out of
the factories. But the announced software doesn't exist and
may never exist. It's a ghost that scares off competition.
Faron's lock with MBD means he's got them forcing his product on the world. If you're an inventor, you'll try to work with
Faron's people to make sure your invention fits the existing
market. There've been charges that Faron has stolen from
such 'information exchanges,' beat people out of their own
genius.

"Plus, if he decides he wants to compete with you, he'll
low-ball his products. His companies will take losses for
years, just to bankrupt the competition. The mother company
keeps the undercutting operation bankrolled, and when they
got the market cornered, the prices get jacked up."

"Who has he hurt—real bad?"

"He usually cripples, not kills. Leaves the competition
enough to keep going, preserve the myths of the free market."

"You've got a name," said Cole.

"I've got a tough victim with motive," said the lawyer.

Cole stared at him until the lawyer gave him the name.

"But it's a long shot," said the lawyer.

"Did the same guy get the package on Faron to you at Justice? Put the heat on the department to do something? Work the Hill."

"No."

The laugh track from the TV echoed through the bar.

"Do you know who put Faron in the barrel at Justice?"

"I got two former assistant attorney generals for antitrust, guys who 'went private' with downtown mega firms, each telling me they got separate clients. Plus I got congressmen, senators . . ."

"You've got no intention of telling me who," said Cole.

"The Fifth Floor urged me to exercise caution in that regard," said the lawyer. "We don't want to jeopardize our investigations."

"Uh-huh," said Cole.

"Look," said the lawyer, "people who can make Congress move, kick the Justice department into action, they don't hire gunmen."

"You got a lot of experience with people who hire gunmen?"

"Ask all my Harvard professors: corporations don't engage in the murder business." The antitrust lawyer looked into his empty glass. Then said: "Look. I don't know who's trying to kill Sears. A lot of people wouldn't mind seeing him dead. A lot of people would make a lot of money because of that.

"He's a nine-hundred-pound dragon. Who knows how much clout he buys with the millions of dollars he godfathers into political campaigns? Whether he's guilty of being a crook or just guilty of growing into a maverick political and economic dragon, I don't know."

"Do you know why our bosses steered me to you?" asked Cole.

"Gee, you mean they might have something in their hearts and minds besides a desire to serve law and justice?"

They both laughed.

"Look," said the lawyer, "if what I've been deducing in my work, plus the little they told me, and plus the little you've told me adds up to the truth, that's a package waiting to explode. Maybe our bosses' hearts told them that what I know might be helpful to you, so therefore I should tell you. But I don't think it's a question of their hearts or their minds. I think putting us together is them covering their asses. Now they can claim they did their best to be sure their response to this mess was 'fully co-ordinated,' or some other such PR b.s.

"But what I do know," said Cole's fellow federal worker as he slid out of the booth, "is if you let Faron Sears get killed, I want to be as far away from your shoes as I can."

According to the intercepted message to the assassin, in just fifteen days they entered the Free Fire Zone.

FBI agents had expended 3,112 hours piecing together the smarmy lives of Brian Luster and Christopher J. Harvie. They analyzed reports from the Drug Enforcement Agency, ATF, IRS, federal marshals and the Bureau of Prisons. Interviewed prison inmates, cops, corrections officers, a probation officer.

The full-court press indicated that both men operated in the commercial world of crank—illegal speed. Tattooed bear Luster was plastic-jacketed Harvie's mentor. They used other crooks as necessary. Luster paid a business tax to a Northern California Mafia connection. Harvie and Luster maintained apartments in Berkeley, both of which had been searched. Their phone records indicated nothing. Cash receipts stuffed in jeans and taken out of trash cans linked the men to truck stops and motels in California, Oregon, Washington state, Nevada, Montana, and Idaho.

Luster's motorcycle sat on blocks in a rented garage. Its gas tank contained a plastic bottle; tests revealed traces of crank inside the bottle. In his van, forensics found traces of narcotics, human blood, and Chris Harvie's fingerprints.

A sawed-off shotgun, a stolen 9mm automatic, a .44 Magnum derringer, a 30/06 rifle, ammunition, a brass-knuckle-handled Bowie knife, a lead pipe wrapped with black tape, incendiary chemicals, and timing devices were found in Luster's apartment. The search turned up a stack of Aryan America, Nazi, and Klan tracts against blacks, Jews, immigrants, traitor WASPs, Catholics, and Indians.

"Boy didn't like anybody," Nick said.

Sallie pointed to a search photo: the heap of racist literature had been covered with two moldy pizza boxes.

"I don't think Luster was much of a reader," she said. "Only one pile of hate stuff. Looks like he dumped it, forgot about it."

Luster's parents were dead. He had no siblings. An ex-common law wife expressed a desire to urinate on his grave.

A biker told agents: "Luster was a mean-assed son of a bitch. He'd do your deal, but you had to know that he was checking the angles, that he'd want a piece of you, too."

"AA was Luster's smart-money move," said a convict. "In the can, even the bad asses like a crew, and AA packs a wallop."

As for Harvie, a convict told agents: "Chris was a magnet for the big fuck-up. Chris wanted to have dudes suck in their nuts when he walked into the room. Always wolfin' about the bad ass he was and the bad asses he knew. So when Mr. True Bad Ass Brian let him tag along, Chris thought he'd died and gone to heaven."

Chris Harvie's kitchen chair was set squarely under its table, his clothes hung on hangers, and the five centerfold pinups were taped on the wall at precise angles. The screens on his three stolen TVs were dust-free. Letters from probation officers and a severely battered Montana high school yearbook were stored in a cardboard box in the apartment's lone closet, along with a bill of sale indicating he'd bought a used red Toyota.

"That old guy at the motel where Luster was killed said the two men who rented the cabin drove a red car," said Nick.

"The way he put it," said Sallie, "was 'some Jap thing.' "

"Where is it now?" Cole had asked.

Chris Harvie's Berkeley apartment yielded a box of .22 shells of the same make used to kill his idol, Brian Luster.

"The killer cuts Chris's throat in the mountains," said Cole, "takes Chris's gun, kills Luster . . ."

"Then plays Casper the Ghost and vanishes," said Nick.

"*R.*," said Cole. "His name is *R.*"

Chris Harvie's closest known associate was a prostitute who considered herself "kind of like a girlfriend," which she translated to mean that she took money from him as gifts, not fees.

"But, like, he was so freaked out about this stupid AIDS thing," she told interviewing agents. "Always *safe*, you know, and anyway, he never wanted me to, like, *really* do him, he was so scared of everything but Molly Five Fingers and head."

The agents persuaded the prostitute to give them a blood sample to determine if DNA traces on sheets in Harvie's apartment had come from someone other than her and the murdered man. She tested positive for HIV. When the agents broke the news to her, she called them lying sons of bitches, ran away to Berkeley's streets.

From the prostitute, agents learned that Chris Harvie's parents were dead. His only known relative was a sister who, the prostitute said, "never has nothing to do with Chris no more." Prison records indicated no contact between the sister and Harvie. A search for the sister found only an expired Nevada driver's license and an ex-neighbor who'd "heard she left town and started up drinking bad again."

At a nighttime meeting in the War Room, Cole told Nick and Sallie: "Everything leads to Idaho. They died there, they operated there, the phone booth linked to Faron was there. And finally, there's Robert Slawson."

Robert Slawson was a known associate of Brian Luster's who made the Bureau's Special Alert Index. Slawson's prison term at Folsom overlapped Luster's. Slawson lived an hour's hard drive from the mountains where Luster and Harvie died. Slawson was the National Commander for Aryan America.

On an ordinary Wednesday morning, eleven A.M., FBI Inspector Dalton Cole and D.C. Homicide Detective Nick Sherman sat in the back of a BuCar in Masonville, Idaho, Robert

Slawson's hometown. The BuCar idled on an American small-town street. Dirty snow, bare trees, houses that needed paint. A mangy white dog trotted down the chuckholed road.

Now or never, thought Cole. Kids at school, folks at work. The police got a call half an hour ago to stay away, maintain radio silence. If one of them is a spy, drops a dime, Bureau taps should pick it up. The court-approved Bureau wiretaps and audio-surveillance systems indicated that all targets were on site.

"This is a truly bad idea," said Nick.

"We can't wait for a better one," answered Cole.

"Just stay alive in there," Nick told Cole. Two agents sat in the front seat, parkas over their bulletproof vests. HK machine guns lay on the console.

"Do my best." Cole loaded a short-barreled hammerless revolver with Hydra-Shok bullets, pocketed the gun in his trench coat.

Then he got of that BuCar, walked to the empty sedan behind it, and drove away—alone.

On the south side of town waited a complex inside a ten-foot-high chain-link fence. An American flag fluttered on a steel pole in the compound. A cracked sidewalk ran from the gate to the front door of a three-story white wood house. Forty feet from the garage was a low brick building with a circular driveway and a garage door lowered over a shipping bay. The building had three steel doors, two labeled with signs:

DR. PETER SMITH
CHIROPRACTOR, HOLISTICISM AND HOMEOPATHY

AMERICAN VITAMIN AND PURITY
SUPPLEMENT SUPPLY CORPORATION

Cole stopped his car next to the fence's curbside speaker box.

"Good morning," said a woman's voice. "May I help you?"

"Dalton Cole, FBI. I'm here to see Robert Slawson."

Thirty seconds swept by on Cole's wristwatch. Four carloads of FBI agents rolled to hold points in Masonville.

A man's voice blared from the speaker box: "Who are you?"

"FBI Agent Dalton Cole. Tell Slawson—"

"You got a search warrant? An arrest warrant? A sub-poena?"

"No, I don't need—"

"Then you got no rights on our property."

"Don't bet on that. Tell Slawson I'm here to help."

"Fuck you."

"Wrong," Cole told the box. "It's you who's fucked if you don't cut this bullshit and get me in to see Slawson."

Two minutes passed. Exhaust from the idling car floated into Cole's open window. Another man's voice came through the speaker box: "What do you want?"

"I'm coming in. Where do you want me to park my car?"

"Write us a letter. Call and set up an appointment."

"You got one chance for me to help you, and this is it." The bulletproof vest under Cole's shirt and tie itched.

"You don't look like a nigger. Are you a Jew?"

"All you better care about is the badge in my pocket."

"You a faggot?"

"Why? Are you looking for a date?" Static crackled in the speaker box. The voice said: "Park your car with the others. Come back to this gate."

Cole parked the rental car on a vacant lot next to the chain-link border. Nine other vehicles with Idaho plates waited there.

The electronic lock on the front gate buzzed. Cole pushed it open, stepped onto private property. The Beretta rode on his hip. His unbuttoned trench coat was pocket-heavy with a revolver. The chiropractor's door opened. A gray-haired man in a parka limped toward the gate. He saw Cole, nodded politely.

Third floor window of the house: man with a rifle. Keep walking. They won't shoot you outside.

A man with a shaved scalp stepped out to the porch of the house. He wore a black leather jacket, British workman's steel-toed boots, jeans. He cradled a .44 Magnum revolver.

"This gun is righteous and legal, cop," said the skinhead. Close up, he looked nineteen, maybe twenty.

"Then what's it doing with you?" said Cole as he brushed past the skinhead, entered the living room that was furnished with a green couch, two threadbare chairs, end tables, and a Nazi banner on one wall. A second wall held a blue banner with boldly slashed red AA letters. White lightning bolts zig-zagged down from the letters to two red silhouetted figures, a muscular man and a thick-haired, voluptuous woman. Their hands stretched up to support lightning bolts. Across the bottom of the flag in white letters: PURITY / STRENGTH / PURPOSE.

Cole heard the door close behind him. The skinhead leaned against it, pistol heavy in his tattooed hand. A man with a beer gut and a pump shotgun stepped into the living room.

"You carrying a gun?" said Beer Gut.

"No shit," said Cole.

"Give it up," said Beer Gut. "Toss it on the couch."

"No."

Beer Gut racked the pump-action shotgun.

"You should have done that before I walked inside," said Cole. "Now where's Slawson?"

A voice boomed from the dining room to Cole's left: "What kind of wire you wearing?"

Robert Slawson leaned against the doorjamb, his black silk shirt unbuttoned to show the gold AA medallion on a chain around his neck, short-sleeved to show his weightlifter biceps. He had silver hair befitting his fifty-one years, a knife scar on his left cheek and black nickel eyes.

Seventeen years of prison under his belt, thought Cole: convictions that were the attainable shadows of greater horrors.

"I'm not recording or transmitting," said Cole.

"We'll check that out," said Slawson.

"Touching me is a ticket to hard time."

"If you ain't wearing a wire," said Slawson, "it's your word against ours. Might be hard for you to find the door."

The skinhead leaning against the entrance snickered.

"Did you see the TV from Waco?" said Cole. He thought: *The hell with the Bureau taps and bugs seeded in the house that would pick up his out-of-policy, potentially illegal threats.*

A sleek brunette with red lipstick, a leotard top, skin-tight

black jeans, and spike-heel shoes appeared behind Slawson:
"Bobby . . ."

"Leader!" he snapped.

"Yeah, sorry all to hell." Under the make-up, her cheek
looked bruised. *"Leader,* I phoned around. There's a van and a
car with three meats around the corner, and another Fed-
mobile with four guys by the Ford dealer."

Her eyes walked up and down Cole. Ruby lips opened and
curled up at the corners. Slow and easy, she waltzed to the
couch, sat down. Crossed her long legs and let her high-heeled
foot dangle.

A man stepped out from behind Slawson: "Show us your
credentials." That man wore a dark suit and tie, a blue shirt
and glasses that hooked behind his ears. "I'm Mr. Slawson's
attorney."

"Eiger," said Cole. With his left hand, he pulled his ID
folder from his inside suit coat pocket, held them out to be
read.

"Mister Eiger," said the lawyer.

Mr. Lawrence Eiger, thought Cole: B.A. from Idaho State,
law degree from Yale. Thirty-five, single. Solo practice in Masonville. Wills, real estate closings, drunk drivers. Attorney of
record for Aryan America, for Robert Slawson, for a hodge-
podge of vitamin and "health product" companies. Owner
with Slawson of the building next door where such companies
packaged and shipped products for everything from cancer to
impotence to baldness, and where twelve thousand dollars'
worth of computer hardware had been delivered. Also lawyer
for the chiropractor, who'd posted bail for AA members arrested around the country.

"Your credentials appear genuine," said Eiger. "But they
list you as *inspector,* not *agent.* That's a super grade."

"I have a certain command authority."

"So, Superman," said the woman on the couch. "You faster
than a speeding bullet? Stronger than a locomotive?"

"Where's your Siamese twin?" said Slawson. "You guys
never got the guts to go anywhere alone."

"Then one of you must be working for me," said Cole.

"No fucking way!" snapped the skinhead.

"I'm going to sit down," said Eiger, walking to a chair. "If

Mr. Slawson is so inclined, I have no objection to you explaining your visit to him."

"Convenient you were here." Cole took a padded armchair that put Eiger and the front door to his right, the couch with the woman in front of him, and Slawson on the left. As Cole sat, he felt the gun in his coat pocket *thunk* against the chair.

Slawson jerked his head. Beer Belly left the room. "What do you want, Fed?"

"I'm here to help," said Cole.

Slawson's laughter was forced. He swaggered to the couch, plopped down beside the woman, sniffed, and slapped his hand on her thigh. She didn't flinch. He rubbed his paw on her leg.

"Somehow I don't think you're volunteering to join Mr. Slawson's organization," said Eiger.

"Are you the one who does the thinking?" said Cole.

"Hey!" growled Slawson. "You're here to see me!"

"That's right."

"Yeah." The Leader sniffed. Rubbed the girl's leg harder. "So cough it up, cop."

Down the hall where Beer Gut had vanished, Cole saw the glow of a computer screen.

"Your people have been having some trouble lately," said Cole.

"Why is our trouble your business?" said Slawson.

"One of your members has been murdered."

"You here to confess?" Slawson sniffed. Moved his hand from the woman's leg to brush her long hair. She shook her head—an emotionally defensible gesture, but one that also led Slawson to stop caressing her and drape his arm on the couch behind her neck. She leaned back, rested her head on his muscle.

Slawson saw Cole's eyes on the woman. "Like her, don't you?"

Lawyer Eiger deliberately looked at no one.

I see that, thought Cole.

"Who you got in your bed, huh, Fed?" Slawson smiled like a shark smelling blood.

"You haven't asked me who's been killed," said Cole.

"You mean martyred," said Slawson. "We're prepared to die."

"Murder is not a federal issue," said Eiger. "And my client is involved in no crimes whatsoever."

"Don't you care about your people?" Cole asked the leader.

"I love all my Aryan America brothers and sisters."

"That must not leave you much energy for her," said Cole.

Slawson shook his head: "You laws been baiting me for forty years. Give it up. Accept the truth. Start doing what's right."

"Like you," said Cole.

"If you got the balls to go that far."

"Like Brian Luster. And Chris Harvie."

"Don't know as I recall those names."

"Want to see prison photos of the three of you together?"

"Oh, yeah," said Slawson. "Those guys. How the hell are they?"

"Brian Luster is still dead," said Cole.

"Life's a bitch, ain't it?" Slawson stroked the woman's hair. "And then you get one."

"Luster and Harvie were in AA."

Eiger said: "Membership in a private group such as AA is a protected—"

"You always let your lawyer do your stand-ups?"

"Get where you're going," said Slawson. "Then run."

"Heard you had some other trouble." Cole felt Eiger's eyes on him. "Mail problems."

"I fucking never had no trouble being a man in—"

Eiger cut Slawson off: "Are you referring to the postal inspectors' unlawful seizure of several thousand dollars' worth of legally shipped products from Mr. Slawson's corporation?"

"That happened yesterday, didn't it?" said Cole. "Think there could be any other kind of trouble coming your way tomorrow?"

"You have our attention, Inspector Cole," said Eiger. "As we will so note in any briefs that need be filed."

"You're one lawyer, Mr. Eiger. One hundred Justice department lawyers can generate mountains of briefs in a dozen courts. Lot of money to defend against that. One false step, the right petitions, property can be seized, ledger books sub-poenaed—"

"Harassment charges filed," countered Eiger. "Prosecutions thrown out the window."

"You know the damn government," said Cole. "They got more windows than you could break in a lifetime."

"What are you squeezing for?" Slawson's eyes had shrunk to black dots.

"Brian Luster. Chris Harvie."

"I read the papers," said Slawson. "Murder makes the news out here. Brian Luster was popped in some cheap motel. I figured his shadow did it. You got Chris's name, you figure so, too."

"Before we go any further," said Eiger. "I insist on defining the rules to cover this discussion."

Cole stared at him: "Waco rules, counselor. Waco rules."

"But you're not in Waco." Eiger smiled. "You're in the White Homeland—in 1986, Idaho, Montana, Wyoming, Washington and Oregon gained that new political identity. Therefore, the rules—"

"You and your pot-bellied storm troopers and BB-balled skinheads try to muscle these states, you'll find the people out here a lot tougher than you imagined."

"We'll see. Under the Constitution, we don't have to talk—"

"You want to play by constitutional rules when you think it's to your advantage," Cole told the man who was a member of the American Bar Association. "The rest of the time, you piss on the Constitution and the American flag and everybody else.

"But I'm here now," said Cole. "Waco rules."

"An *inspector*," said the lawyer. "You want something big."

"I get what I want."

"Do you?" whispered the woman.

"Shut up, bitch!" Slawson flexed his arm and her head bounced against it. She never lost her smile.

"Start with Luster and Harvie," said Cole, wondering if they knew the secret that Harvie was also dead. "Where the federal government goes from there depends on what you give us."

Slawson looked at his attorney. Eiger gave him a curt nod.

"Luster'd been with us since his first pop," said Slawson. "Nothing like prison to raise a man's consciousness. Chris came along later. We took our time with him, wanted to be sure they weren't a couple of infiltrating fags."

Slawson wiped a paw across his mouth, licked his lips. His hand trembled slightly as he put it on the arm of the couch.

"Get me something," he told the woman. "A beer or something."

Cole saw her eyes flick to Eiger, missed the lawyer's answering expression. The woman waltzed out of the living room.

"What were Luster and Harvie doing for you?" asked Cole.

"All members do their duty by living—"

"Don't give me the crap. What were they working on for AA?"

"They were doing zip for us since, I dunno, since the last time Luster got out of the joint," said Slawson.

"We've got three witnesses who say that Luster paid AA part of his take from the crank business," bluffed Cole.

Eiger said: "Mr. Luster sent contributions. We don't know the source of his funds, but like all nonprofit groups, we can and must assume their legality. And we assume he filed the correct forms with the IRS. We did."

"Sure," said Cole: "What were they doing for you?"

"Nothing!" said Slawson. "Shit, Harvie held colors only 'cause Luster told him to. We were just another crew for Luster to tag on to. He was with us when it worked for him."

The woman sashayed back with a can of beer for Slawson.

"Hey," said the skinhead by the door, "how about me?"

She sat on the arm of the couch, her slim legs stretched down to Slawson's, her fingers caressing his silver hair.

His forehead is wet, thought Cole. *His pupils are pulsing.*

"My client and his organization have had no contact with either of those individuals for six months," said Eiger.

"You just have that number lying around?" said Cole.

"When Mr. Luster made the Idaho papers, I advised my clients to review their records and come up with a best recollection," said Eiger. "So we could help relevant authorities, if queried."

"Just good American citizens," said Cole.

"Loyal citizens," said Slawson, "of the true Aryan America."

"What about the rest of the country?"

"History will show," said Eiger. Eyes behind the round lenses of his glasses were alive and bright.

"You really think history is going to work for you guys? Hell, Hitler was the baddest of your lot, and looked what happened to his thousand-year Reich."

"The Fuhrer made only one mistake." Eiger was calm, a teacher correcting students on multiplication tables. "The Fuhrer overestimated the political maturity of modern society.

"He was a great man tragically born too soon," added Eiger. "He let his kindness and faith overcome his practical genius."

Out of the chair, Beretta clear and sighted in two seconds. First shot, Eiger's forehead. Second shot takes out the skinhead. Slawson will be charging off the couch, backpedal shooting . . .

Stop it! Cole ordered himself: You're a law enforcement official. Not an avenging angel.

Don't be like them. Do your job. Say: "You think society is . . . 'mature' for you now?"

Eiger smiled: "Look at Bosnia. The mud people in Rwanda. Ethnic cleansing. The movements in Russia, in unified Germany. The Ukraine. This time we will not need to capture society in order to save it. This time society will come to us for salvation."

"And fuck the niggers and the kikes and all the rest," said Slawson. "Ain't nobody gonna tell me what's what and what to do."

He tilted his head back and drained the can of beer. The woman stroked his hair. Shot a glance toward Eiger.

Cole said: "The only question about your bullshit is whether you're all going to death row."

"You got no murder rap to pin on me!" yelled Slawson. "You—"

"On 'me'?" said Cole. "What happened to 'us'?"

"You want to hang Luster's murder on somebody," yelled Slawson, "you go find his sidekick Harvie!"

"Murder is not a federal offense," repeated Eiger.

"We've got two AA members targeting black leaders for—"

Slawson said: "Ain't no such thing as a 'black leader.' Even with the Jews behind 'em pulling the strings, they—"

"Congressmen," said Cole. "Scientists. Business—"

"Ah," said Eiger. "Congressmen. Now I understand why they sent an *inspector*."

"We got you on the run!" said Slawson.

"What my client means," said Eiger, "is that we have committed no crimes against any congressman, no matter who they are. We'll let the forces of history devour them."

"Trying to whack a nigger congressman." Slawson laughed. "Hell, who'd have thought Harvie had it in him?"

The BuCar followed the black road through snow-dusted foothills as fast as the law allowed. The driver was an Idaho field agent, the front-seat passenger was an agent assigned to the Hate Groups Intelligence Squad. Both had been cleared for the Faron Sears case. Nick and Cole sat in the back.

"The problem with AA," said Cole, "is that they love secret-society shit. They could have inner secret groups that do all the dirty work. Their membership overlaps other hate groups. Maybe they spun Luster and Harvie out to cults even we don't know about."

"But you don't think this is AA work," said Nick.

"Planting a man inside Faron's group, launching a hit man, wiping the slate by killing the two links back to AA—all that's too efficient for them."

"For now." Nick looked out the window at the snow-covered fields. *Running through snow, cold.* Nick shook himself free of the memory-feel of the dream. Not in daylight, too! He told himself: *Not while I'm awake!* He licked his lips: *Don't think about a drink. Can't have one. Can't get one while Cole and the Feds are around.*

Cole said: "Slawson might have grabbed AA in prison, but now Eiger calls the shots. Slawson probably doesn't even realize it, or won't admit it to himself. He's the front *and* the fall guy, wired on something, barely strung together. Eiger probably manipulates it."

"What now?" asked the Bureau's hate groups expert.

My question, thought Nick: *Should have been my question.* But he could only stare out at the fields of snow.

"If I was able to stir them up," said Cole, "if they don't know we got the bugs, undercovers watching them, if they react, maybe we can confirm that they're the ones. That'll give us a zeroed target, and then we can take them apart.

"Meanwhile," added Cole, "find a way to drop on the woman."

"We've got no evidence on her," said the local agent.

"You didn't hear me. Find something to nail her to the wall. She's one of Eiger's strings on Slawson. Eiger's probably doing her, too. Only a fool or a psycho would play that game. My bet is she's smart, which means she'll deal with whoever gives her the best offer. Right now, we don't have her price."

"Slawson will kill her if—"

"We don't have any 'if,' " said Cole. "Find one. Today."

The local agent shook his head: "In the old days, COIN-TELPRO, we'd have written anonymous letters to a couple hard-core A.A. freaks. Told them Eiger was a Jewish name. Maybe a letter to Slawson, telling him his lady was making it with a Jew traitor."

"Those were the old days," said Cole.

"Yeah," said the agent. Outside his window, snow-covered fields rolled to purple mountains' majesty. "Too bad."

Yellow headlights swung off the Wednesday-night highway, stopped in front of the roadhouse seventeen miles outside of Masonville, Idaho. The car was a cherry-red TransAm. The driver got out. Zippers on her leather jacket cut silver lines in the darkness. French jeans clung to her trim legs. She shook her thick, black hair and cat-walked into the roadhouse.

She blew into the lounge's amber fog, vapors of dried beer and stale pretzels, saw a rig jockey with his head burrowed into his arms. She put a ten spot on the bar, caught the eye of the 230-pound peroxided bartender reading a tabloid: "Hurt me, Irene."

The bartender slid a pack of cigarettes to the red nails of her customer, poured a shot of vodka. The TransAm driver knocked the shot back, set the empty glass on the wood, shuddered. The heavy lids of her eyes closed; opened.

Neon blue from a beer sign darkened the plastic dome of the juke box, showed her the reflection of the lone man sitting in a booth. With a slow shake of her head, the driver's slick red lips curled up. Her gaze on the wall in front of her, she said: "Hit me again, Irene."

The bartender reached for the vodka.

"Bring another glass; make it a pair."

The brunette plucked quarters from her change, strolled toward the juke box. She passed the drunk truck driver at the bar, gave him not a glance. Passed the guy in the booth, gave him not a glance. Saw nobody else in the bar to *not* look at. The bathroom doors down the hall were closed. She put her palms on the juke box dome. Her flesh looked translucent.

She fed the box all her quarters, punched the numbers for Hank Williams and Buddy Holly.

The drum roll from "Peggy Sue" made the drunk at the bar twitch in his dreams. She turned with the beat, shuffled back to the waiting shot glasses and cigarette pack. The cancer sticks dropped into her jacket pocket. The shot glasses dangled from parrot-beak grips of her strong fingers, not a drop spilling as she rock 'n' rolled over to the man in the booth.

She put a shot glass next to his beer, slid into the booth opposite him, parked her foot on the outside edge of his seat. Her long leg angled up between him and freedom.

"Hey, Superman," she said. "You looking for love in the lonely places?"

"I've found what I'm looking for," said Dalton Cole.

"Then you're a lucky man." The bar's blue light shaded her lips to black. "Didn't figure your surveillance was so tight.

"Unless." She arched her brow. "Naughty boy. Did you plant bugs in our happy home? I told Bobby I was going out, but not where I was headed."

"You come here three, four nights a week," said Cole.

"Naw. A hotshot Fed like you wouldn't gamble on that."

"Don't worry about me, Ricki."

The smile she gave him was long and sweet. "You have been a busy boy, haven't you?"

"It's been a long day."

"So you found out my name? Figured out this ambush?"

Cole shrugged.

"Don't be shy. Girl might think this was your first date. You had a lot of girls, Dalton? That is your name, right? The one on the ID you showed."

"It's the name I was born with."

"Bet the girls love it. Bet you love it when they whisper it real low and slow and sweet."

"Ricki Side," said Cole. "Why didn't you change it when you made those movies? If not legally, at least for the credits."

"I like who I am. Is there a law against that?"

"There are laws against child pornography, interstate transport of—"

"I was never in *the business*." She raised her shot glass in a toast: "I was just a star."

She poured half the vodka down her throat.

"You were seventeen in a couple of your pictures."

"So you know how to check driver's licenses, add and subtract. Got any other tricks, Dalton?"

Sixteen field offices and Headquarters had scrambled to Cole's crash command. Computers whirled, sources were pulled into "voluntary" interviews.

"At least two of your porno films can be linked to a New York organized crime family."

"Oh, gee, Mr. G-Man! Was I a bad girl? I thought America was built by family businesses! A punk out of law school could beat any case against me for child pornography. Hell, wasn't I the victim?"

Ricki drew a circle on the table with her red fingernail. "Got to find another stick to beat me with, honey. If that's what you want to do."

"I want to do my job."

"Oh, Dalton!" She shook her hair and let her jacket fall open. She wore a tight sweater. Even in that blue light, Cole knew she wore no bra. "You want a lot more than that."

Cole wondered if she smelled his sweat.

"Why did you set up this ambush?" asked Ricki. "Why not just have the Highway Patrol pull me over, drag me off to some cop shop where you had your buddies around for a gang bang? I mean, we can get away with this chat, you wouldn't be the first guy I played come-hither, get-lost with. Bobby digs those stories, so even if somebody sees us here, I'm cool. But why did you do this alone, just you and me?"

"What are you doing, Ricki?"

"I bought you a drink." She smiled. Ran her finger around the rim of her half-full glass. "I like it that you know my name."

"Which one?"

Her eyes were steady, but he felt more than heard her voice deepen: "What do you mean?"

"Those movies you made when you were seventeen, you—"

"You ever see any of my movies, Dalton?" Her red lips curled up. "I wonder what you'd think. But they're hard to find these days. The negatives burned. All over the country, the videos keep getting shoplifted or checked out and never returned."

"Is that Slawson's idea? Yours? Eiger's?"

She shrugged. "Just a coincidence."

"Cleaning up after yourself, Ricki? Changing your mind? Trying to reinvent yourself—again?"

But she just smiled.

"You've had a lot of practice at reinvention," said Cole.

"I was an actress."

"You were born Ricki Seidman," said Cole. "You're Jewish."

She blinked. Reached into her pocket for the cigarettes and a steel lighter with the insignia HAMC. Her hands were steady as she clicked the flame.

"You want to be friends, Dalton?"

"No. Your taste in friends sucks."

She shrugged. "Tastes change."

"What would your fuhrer say if he knew you were a Jew?"

"Bobby knows I'm the most phenomenal fuck he'll ever have. He's scared to death to lose that, even though he barely gets it up anymore. So why would he believe the lying Feds?"

"Then there's Eiger," said Cole. "He's not whacked on crank or whatever you're feeding Slawson. Eiger likes being shadow master. He's a lawyer. Knows how to read court records. How to believe them. He won't care if you're the best fuck he's ever had."

"Would you care?"

Cole shrugged. "Eiger seems like a reasonable guy."

"But a lousy lay. I have to wear a blindfold so he can do it. You'd want me to be able to see, wouldn't you, Dal—"

"I don't see how you could waltz with them. You changed your name, but you're still a Jew. They celebrate over six million Jews being killed. They think you should be killed."

"They don't know me. They never will."

"That's a stupid bet."

"Which is it, Dalton? Am I stupid, or am I crazy?"

He gave her hard eyes.

"Forget it," she said. "You're too straight to under—No, wait, take this into your square little FBI mind: The whole world is a concentration camp—dig it? Doesn't matter if they

gas you 'cause Mommy and Daddy were Jews or if they do it
to you because you like boys or if you buy the ticket on that
train 'cause you won't eat shit from self-righteous assholes
or . . ."

She ran out of breath, noticed the cigarette stub burning
her fingers. She flicked it to the shadowed floor, said: "So the
only choice you got is to run with the goons or run with the
sheep. Everybody gets the gas anyway."

Ricki raised her shot glass in a last toast, drained it.

"You are so amazingly full of shit," he told her.

"You're the one who came to me. Now, are you going to
tell my boys about me? That would be cool. America's White
Knight feeding a Jew to the Nazis to further his career."

She smiled: "I went to a Christian Sunday school to piss
off my folks. I was thirteen. Amateur days. The minister said
that thinking about doing a sin was almost as evil as doing it.
Tell me, Dalton Cole: are you thinking about selling out a Jew
to the Nazis?"

"Give me what I want," said Cole.

"Give you *all* that you want?" She smiled. "I could do that.
I know what you're thinking."

"Keep your sick damn life. Your suicide games with the
Nazi creeps. You hate their hands on you, don't you?"

"Got a better offer for me?" she snapped, but her tone was
brittle. "I could drive off into the night, and fuck you and fuck
them and fuck—"

"What do you get out of them?" said Cole.

"All the getting isn't over yet." She shrugged. "Nobody from
the wild movie days dares to fuck with me. I get a piece of the
skim. They don't know how stupid they are, how much I've
tricked . . .

"The money," she said. "I got a stash. And this is miles from
being the hardest acting job I've ever had. Might even be easier than my coming attractions, my next feature production
when I exit this scene. I could use a friend then. A real friend,
one who knows the truth, who's not afraid, who's—"

"Tell me," said Cole. "Tell me now. I got a pay phone quarter and a knife to slash your tires."

She gave him little girl eyes: "Are you that cold?"

"Sure."

Her lids dropped, she leaned across the table. Smiled straight to his heart: "My kind of man."

She whispered: "I'll tell you what you want. But it'll cost you."

"What?"

They were so close she filled his eyes. He smelled her musk perfume, her shampoo. Static electricity tangled a strand of her black hair on the stubble of his cheek. He could have reached across the table, brushed his fingers over her sweater. She kissed him—full on the lips, soft, hungry. Working. When she pulled back, her red lipstick was smudged.

"You should have gotten paid first," said Ricki. "Every whore knows that.

"*Der Minister* Eiger, Slawson: neither has a clue what you want. What those guys you asked about were into. They figured Luster for a user, not one of their fucking limp-dick Nazi 'brothers.' The other one . . . what's his name?"

"Chris Harvie," whispered Cole, his mind strobing, heart racing.

"Whatever, he was just another zip. And neither of them has been in touch with AA since prison, except for crank connections."

She smiled. "Was it as good for you as it was for me?"

"If you're lying to—"

Ricki stood, gathered her lighter and cigarette pack.

"You know I'm not," she said. "So, how you going to fuck me?"

"Not how, *if*. Only if you lie."

He let her nails brush the hair off his forehead.

"I like it true with you," she said. "But don't send any of your buddies around to work me. Try to use my little secret like a leash, and I'll burn everybody to hell."

"I'll do what I want," he told her.

"Like I said," she purred, walked away: "My kind of man."

Then she was gone. Hank Williams sang *crawfish pie, Billy-gumbo*. The juke fell silent. The bartender turned a page in the tabloid, read about aliens posing as Elvis impersonators. No one knew the aliens' home planet.

Outside, Cole circled around to the back of the roadhouse,

climbed in the empty BuCar. The surveillance team radioed him that the TransAm was roaring back to town.

A shadow walked toward the BuCar. The shape became a person: the drunk truck driver from the bar, fleece-lined denim jacket, jeans, and cowboy boots. He opened the passenger door, slid into the BuCar, said: "How do you figure someone like that?"

"You don't figure anybody beyond a certain point," said Cole. "People are who they are. Do you think she made you?"

"Doesn't matter," said Nick Sherman. "She's not the only actor around. I do a good job of playing a drunk."

"Yeah," said Cole, not thinking about it.

"She won't crack," said Nick. "Not to them, not because of us. She'll keep her cool, knows we won't rat her out."

"Then should we believe her?" Cole answered himself: "I say yes. She was guessing about the bugs, but she believes it's true."

"And you figure it's just coincidence, her being named Ricki and our assassin being code-named *R*."

"Happens," said Cole.

"Hate that," said Nick. "I like life better when everything means something."

They sat in the car for a moment, in the chill of the night.

Cole cranked the ignition key.

20

Thursday's dawn flight from Idaho got Cole and Nick to Washington before noon. They took cabs from the airport: Nick to the safe house, Cole to Faron's headquarters.

Sallie met Cole in the front hall. "The Man wants you."

She lowered her voice. "Finish with him fast, get to the Operations Room on the second floor."

"What—"

Sallie's glare stopped him.

Lauren's voice, behind Cole: "So, home is the hunter."

She wore a tan suit, her hair aglow with sunlight streaming through the old church's stained-glass window.

"I never thought of myself as a hunter," lied Cole.

"Lauren!" called a woman volunteer clerk from a doorway down the hall. "Can I see you for a sec?"

"Don't go away," Lauren told Cole. "I'll walk you up to Faron. He's been wondering about you, too."

Cole kept Lauren in his eyes as she met with the clerk. The casual words they exchanged were audible.

Sallie whispered: "Meet me there before one o'clock!"

And then Lauren came back for him: "Ready to come with me?"

They climbed the stairs. Her perfume smelled like spring. Her ankles were trim, smooth. He fingered the knot of his tie, flicked his gaze from her hips to his watch: 12:32.

"I'm out of breath," said Lauren. "I need exercise."

"Looks like you're in good shape to me," said Cole.

"Are you that easy to fool?" She knocked on a closed door. From beyond that portal, they heard Faron's muffled "Come in!" Cole left her alone in the hall, closed the door behind him.

"Where have you been?" said Faron from behind his desk.

"Checking out people who want you dead."

"And you're back already? These particular people, are they—"

"I don't think so," answered Cole. "Not this time."

"Well, tomorrow is another day."

"Something's bothering me," continued Faron. "About you."

"Hey, I'm the choice you made. Too late to—"

"No, personally you're fine. Even Lauren thinks so. Don't worry! She still doesn't know what you're really doing here."

"What does she know?"

"You amuse her," said Faron.

"That's not my ambition." Twenty-two minutes left. "What—"

"You and Sallie aren't the only ones covering me, are you?"

Cole paused. "No."

"*You* were who I agreed to. You insisted on bringing her in. I assume that you're also working with the rest of the FBI."

"Ninety-nine percent of them don't know the truth about our case," said Cole. "We've kept that part of our agreement."

And kept our crimes secret.

"But there's someone else, too," said Faron. "You and Sallie work inside. There's someone else out there."

"Why?"

Faron shrugged. "Because that's logical. Because you can."

"We have one street man. Only the three of us are in on the whole thing."

"I want to meet him."

Twenty minutes left. Cole sighed. "All right. I'll arrange—"

"I want to meet him now."

"No. We've got to keep him outside, undercover, in case."

"Fine, let's go outside—now."

"You don't order—"

"Be clear on this," said Faron. "I made a deal in the White House to let you do what they want. When you expanded that deal with Sallie, I did nothing. Now you've admitted that you and the men in the White House lied, have the entire FBI and CIA and who knows who else roped into my affairs despite our agreement, and—"

"We want to keep you out of a coffin. I can't do that with—"

"In one heartbeat, our deal can be off."

"Yeah, a heartbeat is how long it takes a bullet to work."

"Or for me to throw you out, reveal this deal to the press."

"That could get you killed."

"Or scare off the assassin. Have you thought of that?"

"The option was rejected as too risky," said Cole. *Risky to us with an illegal-wiretaps scandal.*

"Either you let me meet this third shadow hanging around my life *right now,* or I'll call the White House and—"

No other choice. Cole checked his watch: seventeen minutes. "OK."

Nick stood on a D.C. corner in the cold afternoon light. Capitol Hill's Eastern Market was to his left: a red brick barn of independent food stands. J. Edgar Hoover worked here as a grocery delivery boy.

Fucking FBI, thought Nick. How did Cole lose control of his man? What was Cole doing that was so important Nick had do this solo?

Nick licked his cold lips. Scotch from the bottle in his car burned his stomach. Three Wint-o-green Life Savers melted in his mouth. Nick spotted *him* when he was three blocks away, watched him walk closer. Saw no stalker behind him, no suspicious cars. But the homicide detective couldn't penetrate the expression of the man who came up to him and said: "You have to be Nick Sherman."

"If you say so."

"Nice to meet you." Faron Sears held out his hand.

Neither man squeezed with full strength, and both knew it.

"You should have checked my ID," said Nick.

"I ID'ed you as a cop two blocks away," said Faron.

"We shouldn't stand out here in the open," said Nick.

Faron said: "There are some bars around here we could—"

"We don't need to go to a bar!"

Faron blinked. "All right. I know a better place."

The Eastern Market resembles a long warehouse of vegetable, meat, and poultry stands. Tucked in the far corner is a lunch counter where Nick and Faron bought Styrofoam cups of coffee. Behind them, an old black man scraped charred onions off the grill and listened to jazz radio. A glassed-in butcher counter was to their left. In front of them was a fish stall, where, resting on ice, was a stack of gaping sea trout with cold black eyes.

"So you like Life Savers?" said Faron.

"What?"

"I've got a good nose," said Faron. "Got better in prison where my data sources were limited. I smell . . . mint?"

Nick looked away. "Been a long day. A long plane ride."

"You and Agent Cole: where were you?"

"If he wants you to know, he'll tell you."

Faron smiled. "What's the first thing you have against me?"

"Just like that?"

"Sure." Faron shrugged. "I felt it in your handshake, hear it in your voice. You'll die for me. Kill. But you don't like me."

Faron's eyes were as unblinking as those of the dead fish.

"Nothing personal," said Nick, "but you're a politician."

"True, but you've got more."

"What the hell. You really wanna know? I've been a cop close to thirty years. Now I'm putting my life on the line for a guy who once tried to whack out cops."

"So Cole tells you everything."

"He has to."

"Do you tell him everything?"

"Damn right," said the cop with a firm nod and a tough frown.

"No," said Faron, "I don't think so. You tell him everything you think he needs to know, but you don't tell him everything."

"We'll keep you alive."

"Those policemen I wanted to kill didn't wear their badges like you," said Faron.

"They would have been murdered just the same."

"Yes. And I'd have been damned for that. But they were no angels, and the times were different. I'm not like other—"

"Oh, don't start with 'relevant' alibis," snapped Nick. "My head hurts too much to hear that lame-ass shit today. Murder is murder is murder. And you aren't any different than me for that. That's why I'm here as a cop, because a person is a person."

"Back then, back there, I wasn't a person. I was a—"

"Save it for a talk show." Nick cupped his hand against his forehead, but still his brain thumped. "Spare me the rap about how our history of slavery and lynchings and rapes entitles you to special status as a killer now."

"Ahh," said Faron, "your problem is that I'm black."

"That ain't my problem," insisted Nick.

Faron told him: "Nor is it mine."

"Look, all you've got to worry about is whether I'll keep you safe. You got nothing to worry about, because killers and monsters who ride down on you are why I keep my gunsights polished."

"Monsters who ride down on you?" said Faron.

Nick waved that away. "The point is, for me, victim or killer, race doesn't matter."

"You're completely right. And completely wrong."

Behind them, the radio played big-band jazz that brushed Nick with yellow memories of a living room, a box radio on thin carpet, his mother in bare feet and her midnight hair floating around her shoulders as she twirled him by his small hands, said, *This is the music your father and I danced to when he was a soldier.* Nick picked up the foam cup, saw the black lake in there tremble.

"You *need* me to buy your rap, don't you?" said Nick. "Me agreeing. Hell, you're preaching from your heels because you flat-out need everyone on earth to buy your rap."

"You can't buy what I'm saying. You have to earn it. But yes, it's important that everyone—"

"Important to *you*," corrected Nick. "Personal."

"Life is personal."

"So you're in this *crusade* for yourself."

"Sure." Faron gave Nick three heartbeats to savor triumph. "Because I only have what the worst-off person has. These days, everybody from the top to the bottom is choking on blood from America's hacked-up soul. And our deepest cut is racism."

"Maybe, but what the hell: you got a whole lot more meat to cut than the guy working nine to five, Mr. Billionaire."

"I could lose all that tomorrow. I learned that the first time I heard my prison door slam."

"Now you own enough lawyers to keep out of prison," said Nick.

"What's in my pockets doesn't matter if the judgment line is based on my skin."

"That's not where I draw my lines. Race isn't my problem."

"Even if your heart were pure and your eyes blind, it would be your problem," said Faron. "You live in a world where racism pollutes the air."

"This air smells like fresh meat and sawdust and dead fish."

"And coffee you're not drinking," said Faron.

Nick blinked. Smiled coldly. "Listen, Mr. Messiah, you can't paint me with your 'racist honky' brush because—"

"I haven't painted you at—"

"Because," continued Nick, "I'm not white."

An El Salvadoran nanny lifted a blond, blue-eyed baby up high so he could watch the fishmonger scale a sea bass.

"I'm Indian," said Nick. "Not enough to be official. Grandma was half. I wouldn't make the roster."

"Which nation?" asked Faron.

Nick smiled: "You mean tribe? Northern Cheyenne.

"No big deal," he said. "Blue eyes. Light brown hair and I sunburn like a Swede. Hell, I don't think anybody knows."

"You don't tell anybody." A statement, not a question.

"Who I am is my business."

"Who are you?" said Faron.

"Uh-unh." Nick shook his head. "*My* business. All you need to know is that I couldn't be some closet Nazi, targeting anybody who isn't white like me—like *part* of me."

"Racism isn't a white sin; it's a human sin. I know light-skinned blacks who spit racist venom on darker-skinned blacks, blacks who hate Latins, Latins who are as anti-black as Klan members. I hear blacks scapegoating Jews like Nazis. Blacks, Jews, whites, Asians—everybody is somebody else's 'them.' "

"You brought me out here just to tell me that? Broke my cover so—"

"I wanted to know who I've trusted with my life."

"Then shoot me a sermon to nail me in my place," said Nick.

"Don't let me dictate your place. I don't know it—do you?"

"I can be any damn where I want!"

"Yes," said Faron, "that's what I think, too. So why are you angry? Why do you flash on my race? I don't think it's just me."

"Look, I'm sor—No, damn you! I won't apologize! I'm not some whip-swinging, sheet-wearing . . . I've never done one damn—OK, maybe I . . . I'm a pale-skinned cop in a city that's seventy-five percent black, so most of the creeps I've seen rape and murder are black; that's the way it is."

"So see the bad guys as evil, not black. . . ."

"I do, I do, but . . . but . . ."

The fishmonger hosed down the trout stacked on ice.

"Look," said Nick, "if you don't think I can—"

"I think you're a good man," said Faron.

Nick blinked.

"But you've got troubles. And it's not me. It's you."

Nick watched the water washing off the dead fish, said: "Yeah, well. Life. The job, stress." He raised the cup to his lips, drank. "Cold coffee."

A butcher carved up a lamb carcass.

"My troubles are my troubles," said Nick. "They won't get in the way of protecting you."

Faron put his hand on Nick's arm—a gentle touch, but firm. "I know you're undercover, but we can meet again."

"Why would I want to do that?"

Faron shrugged. "Maybe it would be a good idea."
Nick said: "The cemetery is full of good ideas."

No one saw Cole hurry down the stairs from Faron's third-floor office to the second-floor hall at five minutes after one o'clock—five minutes late. He found Sallie standing by an open door.

"Hurry!" she whispered. "Birthday lunch, but they'll be back in half an hour!"

She beckoned him inside the Operations Room, closed the door. This former choir room now housed twenty-five work-stations—desks with computers. Sallie led Cole to a wall of antique oak wardrobes that had been refashioned into shelved file cabinets.

"Yesterday I was here when they opened this." Sallie turned one of the two handles on the wardrobe. A door swung open.

"This is the first thing." She showed him five neatly stacked piles of eight-by-ten-inch photographs. "Crowd shots from Faron's rallies. If he's being stalked . . ."

"Maybe," said Cole. "There must be a thousand pictures. Put photo scanners on them . . ."

"*If* we get them out of here," said Sallie. "Look at this."

Sallie pushed down on the cabinet's other handle; couldn't move it. "This door is always locked."

"What's—?"

Cole saw her glance at her watch: "Twenty after one. They'll start trickling back in here before one-thirty."

There it is, thought Cole. *Here it is*: The integrity line he'd joked about with Nick, a legal line just like the one crossed by the rogue ATF agents who'd started all of this, the moral line drawn between "the right move to make" and what was "right."

Sallie whispered: "Call it!"

"Close the room door," he told her. "Block it."

As she obeyed, he lifted an aluminum letter opener off a work station. The opener was a double-edged dagger-like blade. Standard issue in this Operations Room, where old-fashioned hard-copy letters were slit open and "inputted to the system."

Cole slid the letter opener down the narrow gap to the lock's bolt. Metal blade scraped against solid metal bolt. Nothing moved. Sweat beaded on Cole's forehead. *Push . . . lever against—*

"The blade bent!" he muttered.

The Operations Room door *thunked* into Sallie's back and threw her forward. She whirled around.

"Monk!" she yelled.

Cole turned, leaned his back on the locked wardrobe door. The letter opener's handle jammed into his spine.

"Rooms ain't supposed to be shut up!" Monk stormed toward where Cole leaned against the wardrobe with one gaping, open door. "Specially ain't supposed to be shut when people like you—"

"Good, it's you," said Cole. "Look what we found!"

And Cole pointed to the open wardrobe door, the letter opener digging into his back as his gesture diverted Monk's attention.

"Look," Cole said. "Are these pictures from Faron's rallies?"

"That ain't the question," said Monk. "Question is, what are you doing poking around in here behind a closed door?"

"Since when are there laws against closing doors?" said Cole. "Hell, I don't remember if I . . . Did you close it, Sallie?"

Monk swung his eyes to Sallie. She saw Cole push his back against the steel shaft. *Up and down*, he was . . .

Sallie stammered: "I . . . When we came in, I don't know if

it was open. I went over there to . . . to open it. Get some fresh air. Then you busted in and knocked me—"

Clang!

Monk whirled, saw Cole rubbing his elbow, stepping away from the wardrobe where one door stood open, where the other door's surface was smooth and undisturbed.

Shit! thought Sallie: *Cole pushed the letter opener into the locked cabinet! Where Monk can't see it! Where we can't get it back!*

Cole rubbed his elbow. "Hit my crazy bone. We found this place empty."

Monk glared: "So you . . ."

"So I opened the damn cabinet door—the other one's locked tight. And I found a pile of pictures that if you're telling us the truth . . ."

"I don't need to lie to the likes of you!"

". . . then if you're *correct*," said Cole. "Somebody should have told us about these pictures. Our job is to assess Faron's campaign, study your constituencies, review your operation in—"

"That's got shit to do with sneaking open doors you got—"

"That has everything to do with *opening doors.* To do our job as best as it can be done, we need to analyze those pictures."

"You ain't lifting them off the shelf 'less I get the OK."

"Then let's get it," said Cole. "Let's go see our colleagues."

Monk closed the unlocked wardrobe door. Laughter from returning birthday revelers flowed down the hall as Monk shook the locked handle.

"Something wrong?" asked Cole.

Monk smiled. "Not as long as this is locked."

23

The killer lay on his bed of electric fire. The sun hung above the horizon outside his house. Sweat caked his naked arms (one hundred pushups), dried on his bare stomach (one hundred sit-ups).

Where are you now, Coach Wagoner? he thought. You and your fat-belly, junior-high-gym, laughing, come-on-girly-climb-the-rope mouth? Did you laugh on your vacation when you pushed the brake pedal in the mountains and it went down, down, down to nothing? Did you wonder about your mandatory auto mechanics class as revised art? You and your fat wife and bleached blond daughter with fat white thighs under her cheerleading skirt.

My legs are naked and strong, he thought (one hundred squats). I'm ready. My bed is electric, and all I need is here, on the bureau in front of the mirror, on the chairs-pulled-close palettes. What wasn't here was stashed or under the control of the Usher.

Crimson light glowed through the bedroom window.

Everything exists as you see it, he thought. And he felt his heartbeat. Coming, heartbeat was coming . . .

Outside, the sun was sinking. Outside was Faron Sears, his last moon rising. He was the first of two—who would be Mission Two? Usher would make that come, too. Usher was the link that had been missing all these years. Usher revealed that knowing what you are is not enough. Any nut case can grasp reality.

On his own, he'd learned certain truths: Define yourself by actions from your core: that's art. Prevail over that which fate would make greater than you: that's power. Dominate. Beat them all. Make them pay.

But for years, he'd known something was missing. Then in Chris Harvie's babble he'd heard the revelation.

Proof was the missing necessity. You must be acknowledged. There must be a witness. One witness so you know you're not crazy or deluding yourself. One witness that lets you carve your truth into the billion hearts of the world, hearts that then will be forced to bear witness, too. Fame equals dominion. If the world trembles from a masterpiece, whoever created that fear rules those hearts. All else is mere necessity. Or practice. Or pleasure.

Coach Wagoner and cheerleader thighs. College-boy hitchhiker who never saw the sniper in the trees. Elaine Roberts/ bitch spread her legs for everyone but . . . a hundred miles from home when her car died, sugar in the tank and *"Hey, hi! What are you doing here?"*

Come on, he'd said. Take a ride.

But there'd been no witnesses. Nothing had ever been big enough, grand enough, to scar the billion hearts. Until now.

Chris Harvie. He wasn't a true witness. He just knew what he knew. Fifth-grade commandant Mrs. Olson. Chris Harvie, reform school stamped on his forehead since kindergarten; she put him in the closet for pissing her off; nobody cared. Like nobody cared what she wrote to foster parents who got paid—*pay attention and don't make trouble on my time, kid*—or how she'd stand you in front of everybody and say look at the stain on the baby's pants.

Widowed, barren Mrs. Olson kept a clock radio in her bedroom. Liked to take baths, lay back and close her mean eyes, wrinkled flesh soaking in a steamy yellow room. Luckily, the radio had a long cord. Liked to have had a heart attack when she heard: "Catch!"

Must've got soap in her eyes and grabbed for a towel and what a shame, said the police. Must not have read the household-hazards booklet the volunteer firemen had her give to the kids every year.

Nobody wondered what the crone would have been listening to. Nobody asked Chris Harvie who he saw coming out of her bedroom window that night. Chris Harvie wasn't supposed to be in that alley either. He knew his score in town. Knew how much they believed him. Knew what could happen when you betrayed the wrong person.

Senior year, that boy finally get his JD go-to-jail card for a hot-wired car. Color him gone. But he came back, thus redeeming himself from being a full zero fuck-up. Good for him.

Heartbeat time. *See it!* Make it come! *This* was what he was; *that* was what he would be when everyone knew what he would make them know, and the bed comes trembling electric fire.

Night filled the streets outside the War Room. Dalton Cole, Sallie Pickett, Nick Sherman sat around the conference table.

"If what the ATF bozos intercepted is right," said Nick, "Faron is only the first target. Who's our killer's encore?"

His voice was controlled. He'd had a drink after meeting Faron, then a quick shot after he parked his car. He'd corked the bottle knowing he couldn't have another blast for who knew how long. Easy. So the hell with Mr. Smart Nose Faron Sears.

"Two weeks until Valentine's Day," said Sallie. "The start of the killing zone scheduled in that e-mail."

"But who's the killer's second target?" said Nick.

"We can't focus on that," said Cole. "Our known target is Faron Sears. We have one assassin out there, closing in. Plus, somewhere in Faron's organization is a spy.

"The AA bugs confirm what Ricki said," added Cole. "The most Eiger and Slawson are doing is figuring out how to take credit for whatever Harvie and Luster did and still avoid arrest."

"Ricki's been egging them on," said Nick.

"It's her drama," said Cole. "Eiger and Slawson don't know she's pulling their strings."

"The moment they do," said Nick, "she's dead."

Cole said: "If we get indications that she's in peril, order the Idaho team to get her out."

"What?" said Sallie.

"Any means necessary. Including a raid."

"You aren't rescuing a Girl Scout," said Nick.

"I'm interested in preventing another crime."

"At the risk of our objective?" asked Sallie.

The three law enforcement officers stared at each other.

"Order the team to cover her," said Cole.

"Yes, sir." Nick tapped a file folder. "Chris Harvie's sister. She's got no credit cards. No driver's license, phone, utility hookups, voter registration, civil cases, no death certificate. She has a dozen past arrests for intoxication."

"We don't think they've had contact in years," said Sallie.

"She's the last string on Harvie we haven't tied up," said Cole. "Find her."

Nick rubbed his forehead. Popped a Life Saver into his mouth. He held the pack toward his companions. They shook their heads no.

Dalton's eyes lingered on Nick—a touch they both felt. Cole shifted his gaze to Sallie.

"You're up." He shook his head. "I can't order you to do this. If you say yes, it's not just your career on the line."

"You're asking me to break the law," said Sallie.

"Yes. And if we're caught, I'll take the bullet for it, but you'll be put against the wall too. Or inside walls."

"Hell," she said, "we were trapped when we signed on."

"I can con help out of the Bureau," said Cole. "Set you up with Technical Services Division for the lock, and with CART."

CART is the FBI's Computer Analysis and Response Team.

"You've already made the calls. What if I'd said no?"

Cole shrugged. He handed her a slip of paper. "That's the name and number written on the cabinet door lock. TSD can use it to make you a successful thief."

"I already am." Sallie pulled a palm-sized computer disk from her pocket. "Staffers are issued these to program their laptops. Nobody bothers to lock the drawers where they keep them. CART might find something on here that'll help us."

"You did this before our adventure," said Cole. "Technically, you've pulled a black bag job without sanction."

Sallie shrugged.

"I shouldn't have worried about your sensitivity," said Cole.

"I can't stop worrying," said Sallie. "I give old timers hell for bugging and black bagging Dr. King. Now, here I am."

"Here *we* are," corrected Cole. "If someone opens that locked wardrobe door before you do your job, they'll find the letter opener. Won't take a genius to figure out why it's there."

Sallie said: "Let's say Monk and the others find the letter opener. If they sit a man on the door, I'll know."

"Be careful and be smart," said Cole. "Whatever's in there isn't worth blowing our cover."

"Or getting you hurt," said Nick.

The law enforcers gave a moment to silence.

"Concentrating on the assassin was our best choice while we settled inside Faron's group," said Cole. "Now we start down the find-the-traitor track."

"The Bureau deep-backgrounded all the volunteer and staff names I got them," said Sallie. "So far, nothing stands out."

Nick said: "What about the four at the top? The woman?"

"Lauren," said Cole.

"Wood, Monk, and Leibowitz," continued Nick.

"They probably have the most to lose if Faron is killed," said Cole. "Their crusade falls apart without its white knight."

"The inside man could have been a local Chicago volunteer," said Sallie. "A low-level snoop."

"That intercept is a command," argued Nick, "not data."

"So now Sallie and I go after Faron's commanders," said Cole. "Up close and personal. I'll take Leibowitz."

"And Lauren," said Sallie. "She gets along better with you."

"If you think so."

"That leaves me Wood and Monk," said Sallie.

"Be careful with Monk," said Cole.

"What about Faron?" asked Nick.

"What about him?" said Sallie.

"He's a smart guy," said Nick. "A gameplayer."

"He's not playing games!" snapped Sallie. "He's not like—"

"Sure he is." Nick watched her simmer. "He's an ex-con. Maybe he set all this up."

"What?" said Cole.

"Send an expendable assassin after you, use the FBI to catch him, become an unbloodied martyr, a certified hero."

"Faron's smart enough to have thought of a play like that," said Cole. "But he could never have counted on us finding out about it. He could never have planned on two ATF guys running illegal taps. So Faron setting this up doesn't wash."

"Not with what we know so far," said Nick. "Unless all his hobbles on us are to protect the scam and not his *politics*."

"What do you have against him?" asked Sallie. "He's—"

"I got nothing for or against the man. Do you?" Nick gave his colleagues a steady smile.

"Here." Jon Leibowitz handed Cole his briefcase as they got out of the taxi at the Dirksen Senate Office Building the next morning.

Cole said: "I'm here to help Faron. Not carry your bags."

Leibowitz put a gloved hand on Cole's shoulder. "I'm Faron's political general. Generals do not carry briefcases. If you carry the briefcase, you're obviously an aide—and I'm obviously a general. That's the perception, and perception creates power.

"Up here," he added, "we need all the power we can get."

A brass revolving door spun them inside the marble building. Leibowitz smiled at the policeman manning the security desk, called him by name and got a "Good morning, Congressman" reply as he walked through the metal detector. It buzzed.

"My folding-money days are gone," Leibowitz told the policeman. "I got pockets full of pennies. Want me to—"

"Nah, that's all right, Congressman," said the cop.

No gun on my hip to account for, thought Cole as he walked through the metal detector. Yet.

They entered a world of chessboard marble floors, mahogany walls, and arched ceilings. Echoes filled the corridors: voices, phones, footsteps.

"It's Friday," Leibowitz told Cole in a soft voice as he pulled off calf-skin gloves. "What does that mean?"

"General," said Cole, "I'm an aide, not a mind reader."

The ex-congressman smiled. "On Friday, the House is almost always out of session and the Senate tries to be. If you stay in D.C., your constituents think you don't care about them. If you go back to your state, you can't do the work here those same voters elected you to do. You're always doing two jobs simultaneously. You're doing the work you were elected to do and working to win the next election."

A man in a white shirt and a tie, suit jacket left at his desk, walked toward them carrying a paper cup. The scent of coffee wafted through the marble corridor.

"Are we up here for Faron's business empire or his political machine?" asked Cole.

"What's the difference?" said Leibowitz. "Faron employs thousands of people; they send senators and presidents and mayors to work every morning. Armies march on their stomachs; voters vote their paychecks. That makes the man who creates their paychecks very powerful—in politics as well as business."

"That's not the whole truth," argued Cole. Their footsteps echoed. "Americans put their lives on the line for—"

"For immortal principles in times of crisis," said Leibowitz. "Yeah, yeah, yeah. But day to day, what do you think they want their political servants taking care of?"

"The American dream," said Cole.

"You sound more like Faron every day. That's a compliment."

"Didn't sound like it."

"Then you're not listening," said Leibowitz. "Obviously, Faron convinced me that his *American dream* crusade was the best work I could do. But Faron isn't the one who has to drag that damn dream through these bloody trenches."

"You're getting well paid," said Cole.

"Less than I'm worth on the open market."

"If you're worth so much," said Cole, "why are we here on Friday if most of the senators have gone home?"

"Because armies are run by sergeants, not generals."

Leibowitz opened a door marked Subcommittee on Antitrust and Business Practices. Ten minutes later Cole was sitting beside Leibowitz and across a desk from a woman in her late thirties with razor-cut brown hair and eyes larger than Lauren's.

"So of course," Leibowitz told her, "your chairman's best interests and ours coincide."

"Really?" said the subcommittee's counsel. "How?"

"Naturally, we'll cooperate fully with the subcommittee."

"My boss will appreciate that. He hates issuing subpoenas."

"Yes," said Leibowitz, "mustering committee votes to do that uses up chips. But we foresee no need to ask for subpoenas."

"Witnesses seldom *ask* to be subpoenaed."

"We don't want to," said Leibowitz. "But you may have to issue them to us—and to the Attorney General—in order for . . ."

"The Attorney General?"

"In name, for the Justice department."

"Agencies usually don't get subpoenaed by Congress."

"Unfortunately, that might be the only way to address the chairman's concerns fairly, properly and fully."

"You lost me," said the Senate's expert on antitrust law, a position that made her more powerful and important than several thousand private attorneys, all of whom were paid far more than she. "Are you talking about Justice's task force investigating—"

"We are not being *'investigated,'*" said Leibowitz. "There is an industry review at Justice. That's why we're having trouble complying with your requests for documents. Justice's fishing expedition has tied up our lawyers and accountants at a cost that could impact lower-level employment within our companies."

"Forget that. I've seen the Wall Street analyses on Mr. Sears's companies. He can absorb a lot of legal costs. Besides, lawyers are tax-deductible."

"Thank God something makes us attorneys popular!"

Cole felt the woman behind the desk thaw a degree.

Leibowitz told her: "We're concerned that Justice is keeping your committee in the dark about what they're doing—as much in the dark as us. Add to that the sheer physical difficulty of having to prepare for hearings by your subcommittee at the same time we're trying to figure out how to satisfy whatever it is that Justice wants. All we're asking for is sufficient time for us to fairly and completely help you."

"Oh," she said. "Really? That's all?"

"Fairness is the core of your boss's concern," said Leibowitz. "And if we are to open our files and concerns and hearts—"

"I doubt the chairman will ask Faron to sing a love song."

"Whatever he asks us to sing, in fairness he should ask the Justice department to sing, too. If we put all our cards on the witness table, so should they."

"Ahh," she said. "I get it."

"But given everything—the work, the spring recess schedule announced by the leadership, other factors, waiting until a more judicious time to explore fully the need for hearings will—"

"What 'other factors'?"

Leibowitz smiled. "If the chairman and the administration launch investigations of Faron Sears just as he's winning thousands of hearts and minds to a new way of thinking . . . Well, the perception might be that politicians are trumping up trouble to discredit a good, successful, tax-paying, American-labor-employing leader whose personal leadership is a threat to them. The chairman doesn't want his legitimate work to be confused with political smear tactics."

"Wow," she dead-panned. "You just come right out and say it."

"That's the kind of guy my boss is."

"Spare me," she said. "While we're on investigations, I hear a grand jury in Chicago has targeted Mr. Sears's project there."

"There are hundreds of grand juries meeting everywhere," said Leibowitz. "Including some just down the Hill. I hear a panel in D.C. is looking into some members."

"Tell me about Chicago," she said.

"Neither Faron nor any of his companies have been issued any grand jury subpoenas," said Leibowitz. "Of course, a grand jury would take precedence over your committee's needs. That's not our choice; that's just the law."

"Coming or going, your case is for delay."

"For proper procedures in their proper time," said Leibowitz.

"I'll be sure to let the chairman know how helpful you've been," she said, standing.

"Give him my personal best, too," said Leibowitz. "Last time I saw him was at a public dinner."

"Gosh, I'm glad you didn't mention any activity with a checkbook. That might have been misconstrued."

"We're all good lawyers," said Leibowitz. "Except for my friend here. You ever meet Dalton Cole before?"

"No."

"I just wondered if you'd seen him around the Hill. Sooner or later, seems like everyone comes through your committee."

"Doesn't he work for you?" The counsel frowned.

"He's a consultant," said Leibowitz. "Brand new. The James Group. I'm sure that if you ask around, you'll hear about him. Let me know. I like hearing about our subcontractors."

In the hall, Cole steered Leibowitz into a dead-end turn above brass-railinged stairs: "What was that all about?"

"Buying time to find out who's doing what to us," answered the lobbyist.

"Not the business you did with her, the business you gave

me! You want to check my credentials, call the damn White House!"

"Understand me. Faron stuck us with you. You may have charmed Lauren, but you're an amateur stud in my stable."

Jon Leibowitz, ex-congressman, Harvard Law, lobbyist, met Cole's eyes with the steel of a hard-time con. "Now it's time to go."

Cole walked with him. "What about Chicago? If we have grand jury trouble there, to set up focus analysis, I need to know."

"Chicago isn't your—"

An office door swung open and two men strolled into the hall. The first man faced fifty, wore a double-breasted suit, had blond hair and a ruddy face. His companion hadn't seen forty yet, wore round-lens owl glasses.

"Chee. Never know who you're going to run into in these damn halls," said the man with the owl glasses.

Leibowitz turned on like a spotlight. "Hey, Joel! How are you? How's Mimi? Bet the senator is still mad at you for marrying her away from the staff."

"Nah, this way he figures he gets two of us for one salary."

The man in the double-breasted suit smiled at Leibowitz. Cole saw scales in that man's gaze.

"And how are you, Don?" Leibowitz said to the double-breasted suit. "I didn't expect to see you up here."

"Hi," said Joel, sticking his hand toward Cole. "Joel Johnson. Do I know you?"

"Ah, no," answered Cole. "I work with Mr. Leibowitz."

"We have to get going now." Leibowitz touched Cole's arm.

"Yo, Don," said Joel. "Let's roll. I'm a busy man."

"Go ahead, I'll catch up," said Don.

A farewell nod, then Joel strolled down the hall. Leibowitz touched Cole's elbow again.

Stand still. He wants to go. So stand still. Cole introduced himself to Don, got his full name.

"Some clients called me about your letter," Don told Leibowitz. "Nice job. Just the right tone, no direct pitch, an exploratory committee that complies with—"

"*Don,*" said Leibowitz. "I'll give you a call."

Cole turned so Don couldn't see that Leibowitz now had grabbed Cole's arm: *touch escalated to pull.*

Don lowered his voice so only Leibowitz and Cole could hear: "My guys need to know is if he's behind you or are you stepping out front for him or—"

"Everybody is on line with everybody else," said Leibowitz. He jerked Cole into motion. "I'll call you."

Leibowitz led Cole outside to the cold. "Don't ever do that! When I say it's time to go, when I turn you off, you—"

"I work with you, not for you—remember? And we both work for the same man—unless that whatever-the-hell exploratory committee you couldn't keep that guy from . . ."

"Wheels within wheels," said Leibowitz. "Faron has many projects simultaneously developing on different levels toward seemingly different ends. He has to compartmentalize, and—"

"I was hired to help with everything," said Cole.

Leibowitz shrugged. "If you want, I'll talk to Faron, tell him that you're insisting on breaking the system that he set up."

The ex-congressman waved to a trolling taxi.

"Oh, and by the way," he told Cole. "When you're talking about me or with me to someone else, you're correct to show respect and deference, but humanize your public approach.

"Call me *Jon*," he said. With a smile.

26

Early that Friday morning, Cole told Sallie: "If you can set him up, then we've got a chance."

"It should work," the computer hacker from the Bureau's CART team added. "Sit where you can see the screen. Second best, get where you can scope his hands. We need the exact number of key strokes, plus first stroke and last. Otherwise, we're screwed."

She said: "What if he—"

"Don't over-think," said Cole. "Do it."

"Don't worry," said the hacker: "If you blow it, nobody's going to kill you."

Not me, Sallie thought later that day as she sat in front of a computer in an office at Faron's headquarters. From the door, a man said: "Tell me again why we're doing this."

"Because Faron thinks it's a good idea," she answered Jeff Wood. He moved to the operator's chair beside her.

"Your access is limited," he told her. "Strictly."

"Too strictly. Unless we can access more of your records, we won't be able to help you." She softened her tone: "I know I'm a pain in the ass, but I'm not so bad to work with."

"At least you picked a nice perfume." His eyes stayed cold.

"I wore it for me, not you." True. False. Both. Cover.

"You have the proper attitude." Wood turned to the computer, flicked on the power switch. The machine whirred to life, booted up the system software. "Please step away from the desk."

"Excuse me?" she said, staying in her chair.

"Step away," he said.

"But then I won't be able to see!"

"You can move back—in a second."

Shake your head, like you *just now* get it. Sallie rolled her chair away from the desk. Out of view of the screen—but she could see the keyboard. Her cupped hands hid a ballpoint pen.

Let go, take it in, don't think . . .

Wood typed his personal password into the system . . .

Got first stroke: pen slash one mark on middle left finger. Missed second stroke; three is right thumb—mark it and keep counting strokes: four, five, six, seven is left forefinger—mark it . . .

Wood hit ENTER. The light from the screen flashed on his face.

"OK," he said, "come back. Our whole Movement is in here. Faron's speeches, staff, Internet data, bills. Tell me the search parameters you want, I'll see what passwords you need."

"But you won't give me a universal password. Not that I'd want one. I wouldn't want to accidentally pop into any of this 'open' Movement's secret files and end up getting shot at dawn."

"I wouldn't wait that long," he said.

"That's the first joke you've made since I met you," she said.

Then he smiled: "Could be."

"You have to trust people more," said Sallie.

"I trust people to be who they are."

"You know who I am," said Sallie.

"Sloppy security mocks your work. And I barely know you."

Sallie rattled off biographical highlights of her cover story. "That's me. Your turn."

"We're here on duty." Wood scrolled page after page of menus listing computer files as he talked. "Besides, for all I know, everything you've told me could be legend."

"Legend?" whispered Sallie, her heart pounding, pretending she didn't know.

"Espionage jargon for—"

"I get it, but . . . Why? Why me? Why anybody? Do you think someone would plant a spy on Faron?"

He shrugged. "Aggressive vigilance is necessary for survival. So is harsh discipline."

"Come on, Jeff: You're not a guy who believes in firing squads. You're a pacifist."

"Who told you that?"

"You were arrested for protesting the Vietnam War."

"I also fought it for two tours. 'Airborne, Ranger, Green Beret; this how we start our day.' I'm a good soldier."

"What does that mean?" she said.

"You must be unflinching in your commitments." His eyes glowed. "But life can deceive you. Leaders can betray you. Then perhaps you must choose the opposite of what you were. Green Beret to citizen soldier armed with revealed truth. Ultimately, everyone must seize his own destiny. Violence is just a tactical decision."

Screen after screen of data scrolled past their inattention. "There," he told her. "Now you know who I am."

Sallie kept her marked hands hidden, felt her head shake and heard herself whisper: "But what kind of ice cream do you like?"

Jeff Wood said: "I have to watch my weight."

As Cole neared an open office door on Faron's third floor headquarters, he heard Monk say: "Do they got any bombs?"

Two quick steps popped Cole into the room—Lauren's office. She sat behind her desk. Monk filled a chair.

"Whatever I've walked into," said Cole, "sounds more interesting than what I walked out of."

"Nobody invited you to walk in here," snapped Monk.

Cole shrugged: "What bombs?"

"Faron's been targeted by 'One Hour,'" said Lauren. "The sixty-minute network TV magazine show on Sundays that—"

"Everybody knows what 'One Hour' is. But 'bombs,' 'targeting': This is politics, not war."

"War is politics," said Lauren.

"What does 'One Hour' have on Faron?" asked Cole.

"We don't know." She looked at Monk. "Yet."

Monk said: "Their woman's been all over. Picked up court records in San Fran, been poking around in Chicago."

"You mean Kerri West?" asked Cole, naming the famous blond TV correspondent who co-anchored "One Hour."

"You think a TV star like her would be getting mud on her high heels?" Monk laughed.

"I wish it were Kerri West," said Lauren. "She's an actress, not an investigator. It's Katie Howard, a producer who does most of their investigative pieces. Who's she talking to, Monk?"

Monk glared at Cole.

Lauren said: "Either he's with us or it's too late."

"Word is that Howard woman was looking for Reverend Mike."

"Did she find him?"

"Don't know. But come to find out today, nobody's seen much of Reverend Mike for the last few weeks."

"Who's Reverend Mike?" asked Cole.

"The polite description would be street preacher," said Lauren. "Faron's Chicago project will create a new inner city out of poverty. Getting the project on line, dealing with that town's . . . traditional political power structures."

"The Machine," said Cole. "The Outfit."

"So you ain't wet behind the ears," said Monk.

"We dealt with a lot of people," said Lauren. "We had to—Faron calls it *revolutionize*—the old Chicago style. Reverend Mike is old style."

Monk said: "I get a crack at him, he's *outta* style."

"What did he get for Faron?" asked Cole.

"Out of the way," said Lauren. "That was enough."

"What did Faron give him?"

"Nothing bad, nothing big," said Monk.

"Nothing big enough," said Cole, "or he wouldn't maybe be the one who's talking about you to TV producers."

"We've got no shit on our shoes!" growled Monk.

"You walk in the street," said Lauren, "your shoes get dirty."

"How dirty?" asked Cole.

"Doesn't matter," she said. "What matters is what Reverend Mike sells to 'One Hour.' "

"They don't *buy* news."

"Not *that* show," she said. "Reverend Mike must figure that Faron is going to fail, so it's smart to desert us. Probably thinks that cutting Faron's throat and being anointed as a whistle-blowing hero will get him a better gig."

"I got a gig for him," said Monk.

"Just find out where he is," said Lauren. "Don't talk to him; don't let any of your people have any contact with him. Cross the street if you see him coming. Don't create any more *news*."

The former NFL crusher lumbered to his feet.

Lauren told him: "When you leave, close the door."

Monk looked at her. Looked at Dalton. Shook his head but shut the door behind him as he left.

Lauren tilted back in her executive's chair. "Mr. Dalton Cole. Learning all our dirty little secrets."

"Like you said, they're *our* secrets."

"Just you and me, huh?"

"It's Faron's operation."

"Yeah. Did you like giving Jon Leibowitz a hard time?"

"It brightened my day."

"Are you going to give me a hard time?"

"If I have to." Cole shrugged. "We've got a deal."

"I hope so. Of course, we had a deal with Reverend Mike."

"What was it?"

She shook her head. "No, he's not your business."

Shoot blind: "Have you worked a deal with 'One Hour'?"

"Dalton! 'One Hour' is the most honored journalism institution in America! Objective investigative reporting at its finest! To think that in their unflinching quest for truth, justice and—"

"How'd you do it?"

She smiled at him. He smiled at her.

"The show needs Faron," she said. "He's the picture. They're doing a segment on him because he'll get big ratings. So getting him on the air is crucial. Faron boxed them in. Called the show's star anchor. Got him to agree that it would be 'great' and 'more honest' TV for Faron to appear live and answer all questions from the show's whole damn herd of correspondents.

"Which means the show's producer got handed a format she couldn't change without Faron being able to prove that 'One Hour' broke its promise. The interview has to accommodate egos of four talking-head 'correspondents,' each of whom will insist on delivering at least one nationally televised question to the hottest political and social figure in the country.

"So it doesn't matter what Katie Howard, who's actually

reporting the story, finds out. Her questions have to be parceled out to the stars. Makes it hard to set up an ambush. Hard to keep a strong line of questions. Faron will be the lone cowboy hero facing down the lynch mob—even if they claim he's riding a stolen horse."

"Is he?" asked Cole.

"Not in real life. And not on TV. And since they can't edit a live interview, cut out all the pauses and questions that didn't zing anything . . . I can't believe they'd devote the whole show to him, but even if they do, sixty minutes minus commercials is all the time they have."

"Could be enough," said Cole.

Lauren smiled. "Don't worry. One thing I've learned: Faron Sears takes care of himself just fine."

The cellular phone in Cole's suit pocket buzzed, cut the office air and vibrated the bones above his heart.

"Somebody wants you," she said.

"Sorry," he said, reaching for the phone.

"Happens all the time," she said.

"This is Cole," he said into the unfolded phone.

Into his ear came Nick Sherman's voice: "We've got Chris Harvie's sister!"

That afternoon in the War Room, two ponytailed, special-hired hackers from CART screamed at Sallie when she deciphered the ink scratches on her finger: "We are totally fucked!"

"Why?" asked Cole as he packed his briefcase for the road.

"Because," said the first hacker, "if who she 'observed' is a normal keyboarder, she has him using his damn thumb!"

"She must have blown it," said his buddy.

Sallie snapped: "*She* is standing right here. *She* didn't blow it! I got what I could! And I got the first and last key strokes!"

"Big whoop," said Hacker Number One.

"Double big whoop," said his partner. "You say he used his thumb. Do you—"

"The space bar," interrupted Nick.

"See?" said Hacker One. "*He* gets it. The—"

"—space bar," finished his buddy. "That means that your guy's one snaky dude. He doesn't use one code word. He uses two."

"You brought home the big weenie," said Hacker One.

"Don't believe us?" said Hacker Two. "Call the National Security Agency. Tell them you have a seven-stroke code to break."

"No problem, normally," said Hacker One. "Most people encrypt with a real word. If you're right, our first letter is 'D' and our last letter is 'G.' Run them, in two minutes we'd have maybe fifty possible code words. If you get access to the machine, you'd only need three minutes to find the right word."

"But," said Hacker Two, "your guy threw in a space. If he's using American, first word starts with 'D.' It's probably 'do.' "

"But a guy this cagey," said Hacker One, "he probably used, like, *Klingon*! Or babble. The super crunchers will spit out—"

"Say three million possible combinations," said Hacker Two.

Hacker One said: "Could be '*do ring.*' Could be '*do sing.*' "

"Could be 'do-wah-dilly dilly dum dilly do.' "

"That's not how the song goes," said Hacker Two.

"Shut up!" said Cole.

The room froze. Cole went to the window, stared through the slats at an ordinary winter Friday afternoon.

"The key to every investigation is to remember that people are who they are," said Cole. "What they've done . . . their dreams."

Hacker One said: "Ah, OK, keemo-sabe, but—"

Cole ignored him, said to Sallie: "Remember who our man is."

Then he told her his guess for the password that would unlock Faron's entire computer system. The two hackers shrugged: *could be*.

"What if you're wrong?" said Sallie.

"You can shoot me when we get back," said Cole.

"On the cool side," Hacker One told Sallie, "the training disk you copped before, like, clued us in. Normally, an operation like Faron's, we could suck their system dry on six mega disks."

"Like a total glide, man," said Hacker Two.

"But with Faron's, we got varies up the ying-yang."

"Varies?" asked Sallie.

"Variables," said Hacker One.

"Numero Uno," said Hacker Two. "Faron's band of merry bro's rock 'n' roll on the Internet and everybody out there sings back."

"That take is probably as big as most corp's annual feed."

"But, Numero Duo: Faron's using his own software."

"So?" said Sallie.

"History," said Hacker One. "Faron made bucks because his software has the primo fail safe. You had to work hard to crash."

"So?"

"So Numero Trio," said Hacker Two. "Even when they delete files, most likely there are ghosts. Layers of buried—"

"You can get whatever's been through Faron's computers!"

"Only whatever was once saved," said Hacker Two.

"Like, that's the theory," said Hacker One.

"You've got me betting my ass on theories," muttered Sallie.

"Well, we *know* we can copy everything current," said Hacker One. "And we *hear* that NSA's got super boxes and software to upgrade our take from Faron. You execute the right copy commands on these mega disks NSA let Inspector Cole borrow."

"How'd you get them?" asked Hacker Two. "We knew the spooks had super-sensitive, big-load disks in R&D, but when we told him that we, like, never expected—"

"Never dreamed, man!"

"Trust me," said Cole. "Knowing would be your nightmare."

"How long will it take?" asked Sallie.

"Figure three minutes a disk," said Hacker One.

"Four." Hacker Two shrugged. "This ain't the future, man. We got different state-of-the-art components, varies . . ."

"Yeah, OK, four minutes. And figure . . . ten disks. Twelve."

"Forty-eight minutes!" Sallie's yell rang through the safe house. "You want me to be exposed for—"

"Hey!" said Hacker One. "It ain't what *I* want, now is it?"

"Besides," said Hacker Two, "all you got to do is get in, pick a machine that's on line, boot up, insert a command disk we'll program, enter it, switch to a data disk when the machine beeps—"

"And keep switching disks every time one fills up."

"That's all?"

The hackers looked at each other; nodded yes.

Sallie glared at Cole: "Have a real nice trip."

That night Sallie smelled everything in the back of the parked van. Dry heat. Electric dust from radios and computers. Wet rubber, wool, drying shoe leather from the men huddled around her. She smelled their sweat, their nerves, their gun oil.

The radio crackled: "Lion and Leopard just got a table at Jeanne Louis's. He's giving her hell about something."

In the van, Control radioed back: "Copy. Maintain."

Lion: Jon Leibowitz. *Leopard:* Lauren Kavenagh.

Jeanne Louis's restaurant was nine minutes from Faron Sears's headquarters on Capitol Hill where a blue van sat parked in the night. In the van, Control thumbed his mike: "Report Three."

"We got a clear angle from a roof across the street," answered a radio voice, "through big windows, lots of lettering. Lynx's kicking the crap out of college-age guy."

Lynx: Jeff Wood. Agents had followed him to a kung fu studio. A driving time to Faron's headquarters of 20 minutes.

Control looked at the black woman agent he didn't know. She wore a black blazer tailored with Velcro pouches sewn inside like a hidden belt. Black turtleneck, its bulky collar rolled up over a throat mike. Black pants. Black running shoes. Her black hair was combed over the radio earpiece in her left ear.

"My people didn't get put on the targets soon enough," Control told her. "We have no guaranteed location on Lizard and Loco. Assume they are on site. We have no reliable estimate of bodies on site, though twenty-one people have vacated since seventeen-hundred hours."

"The place empties out after six," said Sallie. "Almost."

" 'Almost' is not a stable green code."

"Yeah, well, almost is what we've got."

"Eight-zero-one, street time," said Control. Two troublemen huddled near the front of the van's cargo bay. The two hackers from CART adjusted their earphones and mike headsets, pretended not to be excited to be in the field. Control whispered to the woman he didn't need to know: "Command activated this op. My team assumes paperwork is in process. Haven't seen it. Must be misplaced."

"I'm not here to comment," said Sallie.

Control winked: "It's the good old days again."

"Let's go," said Sallie.

Control said, "Stand by." A troubleman grabbed the door handle, whispered: "Ready." Control flipped switches. Darkness filled the van. Sallie heard a click in her earpiece.

"We are green light," Control radioed. "I say again: green light."

The snap of his fingers cracked through the van. The

troubleman slid the well-oiled back door open. Sallie swung down to the street. The van door clunked shut.

Exhale, she ordered herself. Breathe in, breathe out. Faron's turf began six car lengths up the icy brick sidewalk. *Walk it steady. OK to hurry; it's truly cold.*

Four car lengths from the van, she whispered: "Check."

Control's voice in her left ear: "You're loud and clear."

"You, too. Stay that way."

She tapped the access code into the former church's gate keypad. The lock buzzed.

"I'm on the grounds," she whispered. She walked up the stairs. Pushed the door buzzer.

Mr. Crew Cut opened the door: "Were you sent for?"

"I'm no volunteer," she said, and stepped past him: *Inside!* The door closed behind her. "Where's Jeff working?"

"Mr. Wood is not here."

If you're on the door, Nguyen is probably on Faron. Maybe with Monk. Maybe not.

"Damn," she said. "OK." She started upstairs.

Don't volunteer justifications, the trainers always stressed. *Don't vomit your cover story. Your lies will trap you, not cover you. Besides, if you're real, you don't need to justify yourself. And everyone in the penetration must buy your bona fides.*

"Didn't know you were coming back tonight," said the guard.

"That makes two of us. Since Jeff's not here after all, maybe three of us." She sighed. "I'll just have to do what I can."

Climb one step at a time. Don't look back. She followed the hall past open doors, dark offices, past the Operations Room—open and dark. Down the hall, up the back stairs.

Lights were off in the cubicle assigned to Sallie and Cole. So far, she'd seen only the door guard. Faron could be in his rooms. Monk could be anywhere. She turned on the lights in her office, turned on the computer. *Has the guard told anyone that I'm here?* She called up one of the permitted files with a password issued by Wood. Scrolled down to a random page. Moved the desk chair out.

Been here, she thought as she stared at the scene she'd manufactured: Just stepped away for a moment.

She snuck down to the second floor. Sallie slipped inside the dark Operations Room, pressed her back against the wall so she was out of sight of the open door, whispered: "On target!"

"All clear," said Control in her earpiece.

She took a pen flashlight from inside her blazer, snapped it on. The bulb felt warm, but she saw no light until she put on the hook-bowed "sunglasses": infrared light. Infrared glasses. Everywhere she swung the light, desks and chairs and computers shimmered out of the darkness as eerie green silhouettes.

She hurried to the desk farthest from the open doorway and turned on the computer. She dialed the screen down low.

ENTER ACCESS CODE WORD: _____

"Cole better be right," she whispered.

That night, alone and unauthorized in Faron's Operations Room, Sallie typed "D." Then "A." Then hit the space bar. Four key strokes later, she'd entered Cole's deduced code word.

The computer flashed: ACCESS ALL LEVELS/FILES GRANTED *DA NANG.*

Sallie whispered: "We're in!"

In her earpiece, she heard the van's jubilation. Hacker One's voice replaced Control's: "Remember the drill."

Working by feel, Sallie unpacked twenty computer data disks from the pockets sewn into her blazer. In the shadows of the dark room that night, Sallie inserted the hackers' command disk, pushed ENTER. The desktop computer *beeped,* chugged.

"It ate your command disk," Sallie whispered into the mike taped to the hollow of her throat. Two minutes later, the computer *beeped* again. Sallie popped out the command disk, inserted a data disk, hit the ENTER key . . . Lines of data burned down the screen.

"It's working." She glanced to the doorway of light, dialed down the computer screen's minimal glow to full blackout. Work in the dark. Work with the infrareds. Work by sound. *Work fast.*

Infrared light led her to the wardrobe door. She played the

light along the cracks looking for hairs that would fall off, for alarm wires, for anything designed to foil or detect an intruder. Scratches Cole had made on the door lock were unpolished.

The computer *beeped*. She hurried back in the darkness, changed data disks. Returned to the wardrobe. *Try the handle first:* luckier things had happened. The handle was locked solid.

The Bureau's Technical Services Division had checked the lock manufacturer's code book, cross-referenced the lock face number Cole had memorized, machine-tooled the matching key. They also cut four extra keys, each a slight variation from what the lock should accept: *shoulds* and *woulds* are two different realities. The primary key was taped in her blazer's right side pocket. The extra keys were taped inside her blazer's left side pocket.

Slide the primary key in the lock. Turn it . . . *If there's a booby trap or alarm, this is when it'll blow.*

Sallie swung the wardrobe door open. She aimed the cone of infrared light inside the yawning gap. . . .

"Holy shit," she whispered.

Control's voice: "Report!"

"It's money!" She played the invisible light over shelves stacked with bills. "Piles of ones, bunch of stacks of fives, tens . . . twenties. Smaller stacks of fifties . . . hundreds."

"What else?"

Top shelf empty. Second one down—the same. Third shelf down held the stacks of denominations running up to the twenties; fourth shelf down had the fifties, the hundreds. Below that . . . empty space, no shelves, floor. . . .

"No letter opener!" she hissed. "Somebody found it!"

The computer *beeped*.

Run back—*No*: shut the wardrobe door first, lock it. Better to lose a minute of copying than to leave the wardrobe door jutting open to be seen by anyone passing by. A dark eternity later, she was crouched behind the computer, inserting the thirteenth disk and hitting the ENTER key when she felt her skin tingle.

Sallie dropped behind the desk. *Light* exploded through the room. Sallie peered around the edge of the computer:

Monk stood in the room's entrance.

He's coming in here! She crouched behind the desk. Heard the rattle of the locked wardrobe door. Monk's "Humph." The lights are still on, she thought. He's looking around, senses something. Heavy footsteps walked deeper into the room along the far wall, closer to Sallie. She dropped flat to the floor. Through the gap between the bottom of the desk where she hid and the floor, Sallie saw Monk's size 13 Italian loafers . . . moving closer.

OhGodOhnoOh!

Time it. Time it just right or . . . *Wait! On the desk! Is . . .*

Good burglar: everything is picked up. The computer was chugging along on its appointed chore. Screen was black, but a red light glowed near the disk portal. What if the disk filled up and the machine beeped?

Four rows away coming he's only four rows away his angle . . .

Sallie flowed beneath another desk and . . . *curl inside there/bless the worker who hadn't pushed the chair all the way in.*

Monk stared out the big window at the night. She heard him standing there, then heard his footsteps walk back the other way.

Light died in the room. Sallie freed her breath.

The door slammed shut.

The computer *beeped.*

She made her way back to the working computer, switched the full data disk for an empty, hit the ENTER command. Sallie followed the infrared beam to the front of the room, pressed her ear against the closed door and listened: Nothing. Relief flooded over her, flowed out of her, bearing the crushing weight of—*Why did Monk close the door?*

Her fingers curled around the cold brass knob: Locked.

The infrared showed her a keyhole, not a dead-bolt handle.

"Control," she whispered. "We've got a problem."

She had neither lock-picking tools nor lock-picking training.

"Don't panic!" Control's voice shook.

She flashed the light around the room: nothing. The computer *beeped*. Early. She dialed its screen to full light, saw: COPYING HARD DRIVE COMMAND COMPLETED.

She automatically holstered the disk in a Velcro pocket, turned off the computer. Swung her infrared light around the room.

"Control! What's outside the window?"

"Say again?"

But she knew he'd heard her. She went to the glass. Technically, she was on the second floor. But the old church's first floor had a twenty-five-foot ceiling—and that was above a five-step walk-up entrance.

"I'm going out."

"*Negative!* You got nowhere to go! The external sill—"

"It's a good six inches wide. Each corner's got a funky old hand sized gargoyle like at Notre Dame. I can ease out, stick against the wall, ease the window back down . . ."

"Shit!"

". . . slide down to my ass . . . crouch down . . . grab a gargoyle and drop, then . . ."

"You will die."

"Figure I can dangle down six feet. Only leaves what, twenty-four feet to drop?"

"Half your window is over the raised lawn, half is a concrete parking slab cut lower to be level with the drop of the street. I say again: Do not go out the window. I say again: You will die."

"I can swing out and drop on the grass."

"Assume you'll make it. Assume you won't be ripped up scraping down the outside bricks. Assume you don't break a dozen bones and stay conscious. Assuming all that luck, you'll still be trapped *outside* the building and *inside* their security fence!"

"Worry about the fence when I'm down. Monk is on the prowl. My bet is he found out I'm in the building. When he can't find me, he'll tear this place apart and the next time he comes into this room he locked, he *will* find me!"

"But—"

"I'd rather figure out a lie about how I got out of the building without being seen than get trapped with loaded disks."

Control's voice softened: "You don't have to do this. Nothing is worth it."

"*I'm* worth it," she said.

Sallie opened the window. Cold air rolled in. The hungry night roared. *Don't listen to it.* She climbed out on the ledge. *Don't look down; keep your head, back pressed against the wall, legs spread; ease up, up . . . Standing.* Felt nothing below her toes.

"Out," she whispered.

"OK, you're OK. You can—"

"Quiet. Need to . . . quiet."

The wind picked up, whispered.

Like practicing blocks and strikes and kicks on the balance beam in the dojang, the black belt told herself. *So what if that six-foot-long, four-inch-wide balance beam was only half a foot off the Tae Kwon Do school's floor?*

Slowly, carefully, she shifted all her weight into her right foot. With her fingers clutching—not too hard!—the top ledge of the window, she pressed her left foot back against the glass.

Eased her foot down. Closed the window. No way she could open it again.

I'm standing on a six-inch ledge thirty feet above solid concrete on a freezing dark night. Can't go back; can't get caught. Can't get any worse.

"Hey!" yelled a man in the street below: A citizen in a ski coat, glasses, rottweiler straining on his leash.

"Holy shit!" she heard the citizen say. Saw him run, dog loping at his side, running toward a phone, any phone, house phone, pay phone, 911 phone about a burglar or a suicide leaper.

"Spotted!" she hissed into her microphone. "Citizen. He's headed up Sixth Street!"

In her ear, she heard Control frantically working radios and cell phones with the surveillance teams, agents on foot and in cars close to the running man and dog.

"We can't interdict a citizen!" Control said. "And with that dog, we'd have to put him down! Can't—"

"Oh fuck!" she said. "Fuck me!"

There was a pay phone half a block away the direction the citizen had run. She imagined the 911 call. Heard the dispatcher responding. *God please let crime be exploding every-where in D.C. no cars to dispatch to a citizen's weird call!* Control would be scrambling to contact the Bureau's liaison with the D.C. police, to get the liaison to tell the cops not to respond to an undercover operation blown and reported by a citizen. She knew that would never happen in time. Knew that if Nick Sherman had been there with his D.C. police radio and D.C. cop talk, Nick could have shut that down. And she knew Nick was with Cole on a plane.

On any damn plane flying high through this damn dark damned night was where she ached to be as she looked up from the street . . .

A black steel fire escape jutted out from the bricks fifteen feet to her right, bottom steel rails level with her waist. The ladder down to the street was rolled up on the far side of the fire escape's platform—too far to reach.

But the platform . . .

Worth it, you're worth it. Can do it. Like a flying kick. Strong legs; they had surprised the mere men at the Academy who'd snickered at her before obstacle course day. Got real strong legs.

What was the average police response time to a 911 call? Two minutes? More, maybe four. But not much more.

They wouldn't roll an ambulance with them. *Don't need it. Won't need it.* Angles, inertia, physics, fall-rate versus forward velocity. *Don't over-think: Do!*

She coiled her energy down into her left leg as much as she could, sank her weight into her left foot, then quickly poured all her power into her right foot and pushed off . . .

Jumped. For an eternity, she flew, fell. Her hands slammed on round steel, her arms jerked in their sockets as she gripped the bottom rail of the fire escape. Her dive swung her body back and forth as she hung over concrete in the night.

Yes!

Pull yourself up! She ordered. *Just one pull up. Ten before you could eat in the Academy cafeteria; one is nothing, pull* . . .

Her elbows took her weight on the fire escape's steel plat-form, she bent and pulled herself between railings, curled to a ball on the safe, solid, steel-poled floor.

"You're OK! You did it!" Control shouted triumphs relayed to him in the van from the surveillance teams.

A police siren sang to the night. Coming closer. *Move. Get up. Move.* Roll the ladder down—and be trapped inside the fence as the cops pull up.

Control said: "Advise you have units on way from—"

"Shut up!"

Somewhere in the dark sky: a helicopter, chopping closer. Police helicopter. With search lights.

Motion shimmered in the glass of the window leading into the dimly lit second-floor hall. Sallie whirled away from that pane, climbed the fire escape to the third-floor landing: through the glass, she saw another dimly lit hall. The window was locked.

Sirens, four blocks away, less, coming closer . . .

Sallie ripped the first strip of clear tape off her throat mike, stuck that six-inch-wide strip on the glass just above the window lock, ripped out the other strip.

Tires cried around a corner. The helicopter chopped closer.

She held her fist flat like a wedge in front of taped glass: Focus, focus, believe . . .

Pap! Her knuckle punch cracked a hole in the taped window.

She ripped the tape off, stuck her fingers in that jagged gap. Pain burned her middle finger, but she flipped the lock free. She raised the window, tumbled inside to the floor and was back on her feet, pulling the window down, jumping back from the glass and pressing against the wall as the helicopter dropped a white cone of light onto the building and the glass flared, looked solid and closed tight, and she was safe.

But she had no time, no time. When the lights played on the outer wall, she used tape ripped from her pocket to seal the hole in the window, stem the draft: *was a hall; supposed to be drafty.*

Sirens screamed to a halt outside. Blood rolled down her finger. Tape from a second pocket sealed the gash, but she felt a pulse throbbing against the adhesive.

Go! Get out! Her throat mike dangled under her sweater collar. *Fuck them. They'll know when I'm there.*

The helicopter chopped the night.

Slow, easy: walk down the hall, around the corner. Empty hall. The lights still on in her office. Her finger throbbed. Panting, stop panting. Five steps to—

Behind her, the man's voice said: "Stop!"

30

Sallie turned: "What's all the excitement?"

Faron smiled: "I thought excitement was your expertise."

Monk rounded the corner behind his boss. He stabbed a finger toward Sallie. "I been looking for you!"

"I've been with Faron," she said; thought: *Something moved in Monk's eyes.*

The helicopter spotlight flashed through the outside windows.

"Faron, they's cops all over outside!" said Monk.

"You better find out what's going on."

Monk looked at both of them: "I can't leave you alone."

"I'm not alone; I'm OK with her."

"I ain't sure 'bout that."

Faron laughed: "Don't worry. She's safer than the cops."

Monk shook his head. Ran downstairs.

"Are you OK?" asked Faron when Monk was gone.

"Why? What's . . . why?"

"You look . . ."

"Been a rough week," she said. Her finger throbbed. *Don't let him see you bleeding.*

"What are you doing here?" he said.

"My job."

"Which one?"

"Doesn't matter, does it?" she said, fighting exhaustion, fighting fear, barely able to talk. "It all ends up being for you."

"I'm not that lucky."

The helicopter chopped away.

"Whatever it was out there," he said, "it's all over now."

Don't let him see you bleed.

Monk loomed beside them: "Cops said somebody thought they saw a burglar casing our place. Nobody out there now."

Control got through to the D.C. cops, thought Sallie.

"The streets are rough out there," said Faron.

"Shit happens," intoned Monk. "Guess even around us."

He stared at Sallie. "You wasn't in your office."

She said: "Huh? I'm right here."

"No, *before.* I saw your office lights on, checked."

"Oh, well, then. Faron . . ."

"I was with him 'fore I went by your office."

"I had to go somewhere," she said.

Monk's eyes pressed. Wouldn't yield. *Keep your hand hidden.*

"The bathroom," she said.

Monk shook his head. "I checked the one 'cross from your office—knocked first, ain't no savage. Nobody home."

She turned her voice cold: "It didn't have what I needed. So I've been looking around for . . . Do I have to spell it out for—"

"Never mind," ordered Faron. "Sorry, it's . . . Sorry."

"Yeah," said Monk. "Sorry."

Faron said: "There's a bathroom here Lauren uses some-times." He steered her into a wood-paneled room. "I'll wait here."

She closed the bathroom door, turned the lock.

Breathe, can't. Sallie ripped the throat mike off her flesh. She stuffed the mike in her pocket, pulled the receiver out of her ear, stuffed it in there, too. *It'll make feedback static . . . good they won't hear.* She threw up in the toilet.

When she could breathe again, the mirror showed her hud-dled on the floor, tears rolling down her cheeks. Sallie crawled to the sink. Dragged herself to her feet. Rinsed her mouth. Filled the sink with water, stuck her face in it. When she raised her dripping face, opened her eyes, the water in the bowl was pink.

Her finger. She peeled the tape off, rinsed the gash. The medicine cabinet held a bottle of mouthwash, a box of Tampax, some loose Band-Aids and a vial of Chanel Number 5. They wouldn't know when she put the Band-Aid on. She covered the cut. Used the mouthwash. Looked at the perfume.

Sallie reeked of exertion. *I won't wear that woman's scent.* She looked in the mirror. Brushed her hair with her hands and waited until her image stopped trembling.

Walk out of here. Walk tall. Walk cool. *Run.*

"I'm going home now," she told Faron.

He walked her downstairs. "Have you eaten? We can go—"

"Need to go home."

"I'll walk you to your car. These streets . . ."

"Cops all over out there. Didn't bring my car, I'll—I'll go to Union Station, only four blocks. Subway."

"I'll drive you. Or call you a cab."

"No! You can't come with me."

"Whatever you want," he said.

"I want that damn sidewalk under my feet!"

Saturday morning, Cole and Nick paced around the Las Vegas police headquarters interview room.

"She jumped across fifteen feet of *nothing,*" mumbled Cole.

The interview room loudspeaker crackled: "They're bringing her in now."

"After that jump," Nick told Cole as they stared at the door into the interview room. "No retreat, no surrender: we *nail* this."

The door opened: A whiff of lemon ammonia from mopped tiles. A matron pushed a woman inside and then slammed the door shut.

"Come in, Valerie," said Cole.

She was scrawny. Gray-streaked matted hair, sunken cheeks, nervous eyes. She wore a faded Jackson Browne T-shirt. Salvation Army slacks. Blue slippers from the jail. She shuffled to her place at the table and the men took theirs. Cole put a pack of cigarettes and matches on the table. Gave her a nod. She got a cigarette to her thin lips, but her hands trembled too much to strike a match.

Nick lit it: "Not doing so well this morning, Valerie?"

She stared at him through a cloud of smoke. "Guess you know 'bout how I'm doing."

Nick blinked.

"Are you Valerie Jeanne Harvie?" said Cole.

"Used to be."

"The jail forms say you were married," said Nick: "Where's your husband?"

"Which son of a bitch do you mean?" She sucked the cigarette until the glowing coal touched her fingers.

"Why are you in Las Vegas?" asked Cole.

"Shit if I know." She stubbed out the cigarette. When nobody said no, she pulled another out of the pack. Her hands still shook so much Nick had to work the match.

"One day I woke up, and here I was. Guess the place you stop crawling is home." She smiled: "Did I really try to run through a plate-glass door?"

"After you stole a bag of potato chips," said Cole. "Convenience store has it on film. Grabbed, ran, hit the door, dropped like stone."

"Potato chips. They'd've gone good with beer. Don't think we had any more beer."

Nick said: "Who 'we'?"

"I don't know. Some guys at the flop." She smacked her lips. "You guys got any breath mints?"

"I don't need to carry that shit," said Nick.

Cole glanced at his partner, told Valerie: "You know you're under arrest. You have rights, can ask for a lawyer."

"Call Perry Mason; he can bang my bones for his fee when he gets me out of here. Ask him to bring a bottle in his briefcase."

"You can also do yourself a world of good," said Cole.

"I been wondering about that. I'm a drunk, but I ain't pure stupid. Right now, I'm somewhere's between blasted and bouncing off the walls, so I can see what I see and think straight enough.

"Know what I mean?" she said, looking at Nick.

"What I can't figure," she said, "is why I got two Las Vegas detectives lighting my cigarettes. Shit, I should be in the drunk tank or county detox or wherever in the hell they truck you in Neon Town nowdays. Potato chips: hell, that beef ain't worth court money to the blue boys, and you guys wear suits.

"Less'n I broke that glass door, too." She touched her head. "Didn't find no blood on me."

"You didn't break the door," said Cole.

"So why you knocking on mine?"

"Help us," said Nick, "we'll help you."

"You got a bottle on your belt?"

"Cut the crap!" snapped Nick.

"Shit!" said Valerie. "What's eating him? I ain't no hard guy! I ain't gonna take no punching out 'fore I do what I gotta do!"

"You tell us every damn thing you know!" yelled Nick.

"Shit, Babe, I'm sorry! All you gotta do is ask."

Nick leaned back: "Don't call me babe."

"You're the Man; you tell me the words."

Cole handed her another cigarette. Lit it for her while she kept her eyes on Nick. He was sweating, glassy eyed.

"We're here about your brother," said Cole.

"Chris?"

She waited, but they said nothing. "Hell, I ain't seen him in . . . a dozen years. He pull some shit here in Vegas?"

"What would he pull?" asked Cole. *Come on, Nick,* thought Dalton: *Pull it together. Kick in.*

"No big shit, that's for sure. Not that I know what he did, but . . . hell, I'm his big sister. I gotta stick up for the squirt.

"What you want me to tell you?" she said. "You name it; I'll say it; I'll say I said it. Then you'll cut me loose, right? No damn rubber room or . . . hell, you should toss in a few bucks! Give some to the potato chip guy, reward me out the rest!"

She drew on the cigarette. "Hell, give me the bucks, ride back to wherever that store was, I'll pay the man myself. Give him some more business. I'll be happy, he'll be happy, you'll be—"

"Who does your brother run with that's real bad," said Cole.

"Nightmare bad," said Nick. "Not just mean-guy tough."

"Chris?" She shook her head. "I might be nothing, but he's only nickel-and-dime. That's something, but it ain't big-time evil.

"Last time I saw him, he'd been, I don't know, prison days, California. Said he had some steel-dicked buddies, but hell, they'd of just been hard-luck cons, too. I know he was doing crimes, but what he was into was all nickel-and-dimes, and he weren't headed nowhere nobody couldn't guess."

Her hands trembled as she tried to lower the cigarette to the ashtray; couldn't do it. She got the cigarette back to her lips. Ashes fell all over her front.

"What about before?" asked Nick.

"Before what? What the hell do you mean? Yesterday? When we were—"

And she stopped. Stared at them as she fell away inside herself. A minute passed, then she whispered: "Damn."

Cole and Nick let her ride. Fought their nerves.

"I'll be damned," she said.

"You belong to us," whispered Nick.

"You ain't after my brother. You're after the Mr. Evil he knows."

"What do you—"

"Oh no!" she said. "I'm a drunk, not a fool. One time in my life, I got two suits smoking me for something I got. You can't get Chris to tell you . . . hell, maybe you don't even have him locked up. Call me a lawyer, detectives. Him and me, we gonna deal with you for all the reward money in this town."

Nick threw the table across the room. "Listen to me, you bitch drunk! You are locked in my hell! You sit on that chair with your damn mouth shut, I'll throw you in a paddy wagon and drive you around the desert while the snakes come out of the hotbox walls! I'll dump you on a P.D.'s lap and—"

"Nick." Cole's whisper froze the room.

The D.C. detective walked to an empty concrete wall. Cole plucked the burning cigarette off the woman's thigh. Her body shook; her face was blank.

"Valerie," he whispered.

Her eyes blinked, saw him.

"It is very important that you tell us what you know."

Cole barely heard her response: "Important to who?"

"We're not playing you for a game," he told her.

"You can't do nothing to me ain't gonna happen anyway."

They all knew that this, at least, was the truth.

"Valerie," said Cole. "He killed Chris."

She saw certainty in the lean cop's steady eyes. Said: "You're a cold-hearted son of a bitch."

The silence on the videotape timed out at two minutes. The tape showed Nick walk back to his chair, sit down.

"You think I ain't worth spit," Valerie finally said. "You're right. But that still wasn't justice to trick me with my brother. Shit. Juice washed out all my tears years ago. I'm an empty bottle. 'Nother dead soldier in the weeds. I remember when Mom had him and . . . The son of a bitch killed my Chris, didn't he?"

"Yes," said Cole.

"Finally." She shook her head.

Nick picked the cigarette pack off the floor. Gave her one and lit it.

"I'm sorry," he said, but his words didn't touch her.

"Us Harvies weren't the all-American family," she said, speaking as much to her memories as to the men who faced her. "We were the white trash in the back of the class."

"They sent other people there, too," said Nick.

"Don't be my friend now, OK? Don't play that one on me."

"I'm not," said Nick. "I won't."

"Moved around a lot," she said. "Last stop we all made together was in Montana."

"I was born there," said Nick.

"Hooray for you. We were the weeds the wind blew in. Last

stop we was all together, Mom and Chris and me, small-town Montana. I took off in high school; Chris took a few years coming up behind me 'fore he hit the road, too. Mom died in Salt Lake.

"After he got out of there, whenever I'd see Chris, most likely to all his buddies, too, he'd brag about how he knew the baddest, smartest, most whacked-out stone-cold killer in the world. Said nobody else knew but him. Said the killer knew Chris knew.

"He told me who," said Valerie. "I remembered him from when he was a kid and I was still there. Weird little fucking son of a . . ."

Cole said: "If Chris knew who he was, why wasn't Chris killed?"

"Maybe the sicko liked the idea that he was big time for somebody. Chris, hell, he never knew good luck from bad. Chris told me this guy, when he was in fifth grade, he murdered his teacher and got clean away with it—'cept Chris saw something. Chris was sure there was others, too."

"Fifth grade?" said Cole. "Could Chris have made this up to—"

"Yeah, Chris was a bullshit artist. But he was bad at it. You could always tell when he was puttin' on. Poor dumb bastard."

"Where?" said Nick.

"Who?" said Cole.

"Choteau, Montana," said Valerie. "The son of a bitch is Kurt Vance. Little Kurt Vance. Kill him for me."

"We have a primary suspect," Cole told the D.C. safe house team over the phone. He ordered them to locate Kurt Vance. Las Vegas police had let Cole use the captain's office to make the call that couldn't wait. Nick Sherman sat inside that glass-walled cubicle with him. Valerie Jeanne Harvie had been whisked away to an Air Force hospital as a protected federal witness.

"You believe her, don't you?" said Nick Sherman.

"She told the truth about what her brother said."

Nick shook his head: "No—you *believe* her."

"Fits," said Cole. "Idaho is far enough away from that town to set up his schemes and not be recognized, close enough to get there. The connection to Chris Harvie . . . Well, if you assume that a fifth grader can be a murderer . . ."

"No problem." Nick leaned forward in his chair to leave, but Cole didn't move, so Nick settled back. His partner stared at him.

"You're the best partner I've ever had," said Cole. "A good friend. And the best damn homicide detective I've ever heard of."

"Why do all these hugs and kisses make me feel like I should put my back against the wall and my hand on my piece?"

"I'm your friend, not your enemy."

"Then let's go, friend. We got work to do."

But neither man moved.

"These couple years . . ." Cole shook his head: "I've watched, seen. But never really looked."

"At what?"

"At you. At what you're doing."

" 'What I'm doing' is sitting on my ass in a Las Vegas cop shop while *my partner and friend* plays touchy-feely with me while there's a killer—"

"You saw what happened to her."

Nick blinked.

"Valerie didn't start out that way."

"People are who they are."

"There's more to it than that."

"Get where you're going. Then we gotta get out of here—*boss.*"

"You've got a problem with liquor, Nick."

"Are you asking?"

"No."

"*So, your honor,* has the accused ever not done his job?"

"That's not the—"

"No, that's the total of it. For you, for my badge."

"You're more than a badge."

"Used to think so. At least, far as you were concerned."

"Nick . . ."

"Fuck you . . . *Dalton.*"

"We both know that you're there, and now is when you gotta beat it. You can do it, you're tougher than—"

"You think I'm tough, huh?"

"Yes."

"You ever bury the woman you love?" said Nick.

Dalton Cole said no.

"Then don't tell me about tough," said Nick. "Don't talk to me about what I do to keep going, 'cause you don't know enough."

"Your wife isn't all of it," said Cole. "That cancer must have been hell, but you can't use her as *the* reason any more than you can use your banged-up leg. Death is your business. She's been dead more than a decade, and when I first came on Cold Case with you, you weren't this—"

"You've never seen me drunk on the job!"

"You didn't used to be this haunted."

Nick looked away. Drifted away. Somehow Dalton was standing over him: "Nick? Are you OK?"

Truth ripped a bullet-hole whisper out of him: "No."

The phone *buzzed* inside Dalton's jacket pocket. He answered while Nick gasped, got his breath back. The voice of the Deputy Assistant Attorney General crackled through Cole's cell phone.

"Cole! Hell of a job! Congratulations!" said the DAAG.

"How the hell did—"

"You got your man."

"No! We've got a lead on a suspect!"

"You told your housekeeper team that he was a primary, that he was hot, and that's good enough for—"

"You son of a bitch! They work for me!"

"We all work for Uncle, Inspector Cole. And this time tomorrow, we'll be on to bigger and better things."

"What are you talking about?"

"Kurt Vance. Domiciled in Choteau, Montana. Warrants being cut now."

"Warrants? For what? Cut why? We don't have enough probable cause to do more than ring his doorbell and question him!"

"You're running behind your own ball, Cole. Your team at the safe house went through the inventory of documents we pulled out of Chris Harvie's domicile, found a recent receipt for gas from a station in Choteau, Montana, which—"

"Which proves nothing! And why the hell is my team reporting to you?"

"We're all on the same team, Inspector. You just hadn't
gotten the call yet."

"What else haven't I been told," said Cole.

"Don't worry about filling in the blanks on this one. We'll
be able to cover our ass without revealing anything about
Faron Sears or—"

"What have you done?"

"We've scrambled the Hostage Rescue Team from the
Provo field office. They'll land south of Choteau in what . . .
oh, Great Falls. Figure two hours after that."

"Don't! Don't do it!"

"It's a done deal, Cole. Congratu—"

"Call them off! Stand them down!"

"No way. We want this over."

"I thought we learned our lessons after Waco, after the
Ruby Ridge fiasco, the congressional hearings. I thought we
learned—"

"We learned to get the target clean and quick, Cole. And
that's what we're going to do."

"I thought you wanted the assassination stopped. I thought
you wanted whoever set up Faron caught. This is bigger than
Kurt Vance—even if he's guilty! We got murders, we got conspiracies, we got crimes to solve and prevent. I thought you
wanted—"

"We don't want the mess we have, Cole. You should know
that."

"Yeah. I guess should." Cole rubbed his brow: "Order the
HRT guys to hold until I arrive and take command."

"Not necessary."

"Listen," said Cole, "Vance is just a primary suspect. I *think*
it might be him, but I don't *know.* Sending the Bazooka Boys
in to take him dead or alive won't solve your problem."

"That's one opinion."

"Look, if something goes wrong out there, somebody will
take the fall for it. Right now, the only person on that line is
whoever blew charge for the cavalry."

Silence filled the air between Washington and Las Vegas.

"HRT will hold until you arrive to take command," said the

DAAG. "But be very clear, Inspector Cole. Your orders are to arrest and neutralize Kurt Vance *soonest*. Understood?"

"Oh, yeah," said Cole. He folded the phone and looked at Nick.

Nick said: "I can make it."

That Saturday afternoon, clumps of snow dotted the quiet yards of Choteau, Montana. By three o'clock, all the neighbors of 111 Guthrie Street, the second house from the edge of town, had left their homes on mysterious errands: mothers with crying babies, old people tapping canes, young couples looking straight ahead as they drove away from homes in which they had no hope of ever living free of a mortgage. By 3:15, snipers in camouflage fatigues lay in the gully behind 111 Guthrie Street. Men with HK assault machine guns and black assault fatigues pressed against the far walls of the two homes flanking 111 Guthrie Street.

When Cole and Nick drove up to the command post van around the corner from the target house, the sun hung low on the horizon. The FBI Hostage Reserve Team commander told Cole: "Ready to hit it, sir."

"Order your men to hold their positions," said Cole.

"Sir, we've been holding. In twenty-seven minutes, the sun's going to set. I don't want to have frozen men breach a house in the dark."

"Me either. Do you have extra vests?"

The commander's aide jogged toward an equipment van. The commander said: "We've covertly evacuated all the civilians in the probable fields of fire."

"Town like this," said Nick Sherman, "you do anything 'covertly,' you're a miracle worker."

"How do you know he's in there?" asked Cole.

"His car's in his driveway. We had a woman agent call Vance's number. He answered; she said, 'Shit, wrong number. Sorry.' Hung up."

"His voice?" said Cole.

"Yes, sir," said a local policeman. "Nobody's been in or out of there since. Hell, nobody ever goes in there. Kurt Vance ain't a sociable guy."

Cole said: "Do we have a picture?"

"We're having a problem with that," said the commander. "Kurt Vance doesn't have a driver's license."

The cop said: "Hell, he drives all the time."

Nick said: "Small town. Everyone assumes; nobody checks."

"What about insurance? Registration?"

"The bank handles that. Trust fund," said the cop. "Kurt was orphaned when was five. His folks had some farmland. Not rich, but enough to support him just fine. Different foster families around here until he was eighteen."

"Went away to college, didn't he?" asked another cop.

"I always thought so," said the first cop. He shrugged. "Now, who the hell knows where he went?"

"What *do* you have on him?" said Cole.

"Lives alone, always. Keeps to himself. Weird."

"Nothing," said the second cop. "When he came back from some college, I heard he had a stomach problem that wouldn't let him work. He'd take off, travel a lot. Nobody ever knew where. Home here one day, gone for a month or two the next. But damn, I can't believe he's a hit man for drug cartels!"

Cole asked the HRT Commander: "What's your brief?"

"That Vance is a hard target. That was personally sanctioned for me by a Deputy Assistant Director as we were flying in."

"What charges?"

"I was told that mission commander Inspector Cole would elaborate on that. My understanding is Vance is a multiple killer engaged in interstate flight. Armed, highly dangerous.

"Like they told me," he added, enunciating each word:

"Under our rules of engagement, Vance has been designated a hard target."

"I want him alive, not dead," said Cole.

"We take on a guy like that, my men come first—that's my only guarantee. That doesn't run counter to Bureau policy. Or our job description, *Inspector.*"

He leaned close to Dalton, whispered: "And my men and I shoot our conscience, *Mister* Cole. We're not assassins."

The HRT deputy commander ran over with armored vests. "We're losing daylight fast. Are we go?"

"Inspector Cole wants our man guaranteed alive."

"Are you crazy? What are we going to do? Walk in there and ask him to come out for a chat?"

"Yeah," said Cole, unbuttoning his overcoat. Nick shed his coat, too. They strapped on the vests.

"Due respect for sheer guts, Inspector," said the HRT commander, "but if you two go up there, ring his bell—"

"He's not expecting us," said Cole. "He'll answer the door."

Nick handed Cole the same five-shot hammerless revolver he'd given him to penetrate the AA. Cole cradled the gun in his bare fist, stuck his fist in his topcoat pocket.

Nick said: "You got a civilian car for me? Automatic transmission?"

The deputy commander nodded.

Nick shoved his .45 up his left sleeve until the hammer lay against the palm of his left hand. Big as Nick's hands were, the gun butt protruded below the bottom of his left hand. Nick clasped his hands across his stomach like a Buddha.

"Can't see it," said the HRT commander, "but you can't stay like that."

"I can stand and wait for the door to open like this."

"Then what?"

"Hell, I don't know," said Nick.

"Here it is," Cole told the HRT commander. "We get inside, set up physical interview control, we'll call you with our cell phone. Write your command number on my hand. You don't hear from us in fifteen minutes, figure two agents down. My direct orders are this: no matter what, Vance gets stopped. Hard target first, save us second."

"That's against—"

"Bureau policy?" Cole smiled. "Today I am Bureau policy."

"You got some balls to do this." The commander inked a phone number on the back of Cole's left hand.

"Balls aren't necessary," said Cole. "And this isn't much compared to jumping over nothing."

They left the HRT commander scratching his head as they walked to the car.

"What do you think?" Cole asked Nick as the cold earth crunched under their feet.

"Everything they say fits with the kind of guy we're looking for," said Nick. "Lone wolf. This place, small town where nobody asks too many of the right questions because they assume they know the true answers. Perfect lair, perfect safe hole. The seminar I took about serial killers down at the FBI Academy profiles a lot of those guys as roving hunters, like sharks, wolves."

"We're after a political assassin," said Cole as he climbed into the car, "not a serial-murderer-type maniac."

"Oh, yeah, that work on the boys in Idaho looked real political and sane." Nick ground the car engine to life. "If Vance is our guy, and I think he is, your experts will have to write a whole new textbook just about him."

As the sun sank behind the distant mountains, a blue Ford cruised down Guthrie Street to the two story house near the edge of town. Two men got out of the car. The man in an overcoat led the way up the sidewalk to the porch. His buddy wore cowboy boots, kept his hands crossed over his belly. They climbed onto the porch. The man in the overcoat reached to ring—

The house exploded. Windows shattered. The front door buckled and the roar threw the two men backwards through the air.

Sunset bled the light from the stand of trees a quarter mile from Choteau's city limits. From those trees, you could hear sirens in the town, see flames eating a house on Guthrie Street, black smoke billowing up to the big indigo sky.

Kurt Vance lay on his stomach, binoculars resting on aspen deadfall in those trees visible from the porch of his parents' house. The 70-foot tunnel from his basement to the coulee had taken three years to dig, line with aluminum sheeting torn off deserted buildings, shore up with lumber bought in anonymous lumber yards. He scattered the dirt on night drives. He kept the tunnel's aluminum door opening into the coulee buried under six inches of earth. Only a few boys ever crossed that scrub land, and they were looking for gophers to shoot, not hidden tunnels.

Small-time fools, thought Vance. A town of small-time fools. Small-time cops who felt like TV heroes chatting over their car radios, never thinking about who might own a police scanner.

The first radio warning came at ten A.M.: "Cal, get over to Burt's house right away and pick him up! The FBI just called! They got a big bust coming down right here today! Over."

Cal radioed the other cruiser back, asked when.

"An FBI SWAT team's flying to Great Falls now! Over!"

"Bust who for what?" Cal had asked. And he'd been answered.

Everything had been planned for. Vance grabbed his evacuation duffel, checked charges he'd wired years before as the police scanner said: "Them SWAT guys just landed in Great

Falls, but they got an agent flying in special to take charge. We don't do shit until an FBI guy named Dalton Cole says so."

Vance forwarded his house phone to his cellular phone, crawled out of the tunnel long before the HRT unit rolled into Choteau. Plenty of time to rebury the tunnel door under dirt and rocks. Plenty of time to scurry to the trees. Plenty of time to hike to the metal shed the town thought was owned by a wildcat oil driller. Plenty of time to drive away unnoticed in the pickup locked in that shed that Vance had titled in a phony name in another county.

But why leave a victory untasted? So he took cover in the trees. Watched his neighbors leave, one by one. Saw HRT snipers sneak around the coulee, their eyes so intent on his house they never noticed the camouflaged tunnel.

Look behind you, fools. When his portable phone buzzed, he answered the call forwarded from his house, some bogus bitch checking to see if he was there. *Oh, yeah. I'm here.*

Took forever for that Dalton Cole, FBI, to get there. Vance's plan had been to let them walk up, ring the bell. They'd wait, try the handle. Find it open. They'd go inside . . .

Then a vision shimmered in Vance's eyes, a beautiful new vision blowing through the plan and rewriting *what could be.* So before the raiders entered his house, Vance flicked the switch on his radio transmitter and blew the two guys off the front porch. The fireball lit the world. Smoke covered the stars.

So they know Kurt Vance, he thought. So what. Already, I am more than that. I am invisible. I am smoke. I cover the stars.

Saturday night, the Montana Highway Patrol whisked Cole and Nick out of Choteau to their plane. They left the special agent in charge of Montana to explain the disastrous raid by the FBI on a suspected felon's house in Choteau. The SAC lied to TV cameras without knowing the truth. He never mentioned Inspector Cole or whatever investigation that hotshot had really been mismanaging.

By the time Cole and Nick fled, searchers in the rubble had found computers, guns, a Japanese sword, books—including a catalog for weapons and a biography of a presidential assassin by a former president. They found a framed newspaper article about a missing Wyoming teenage girl, the crumpled police scanner.

Cole's chest was sore where a chunk of door had lodged in the armored vest. Nick's face was bruised, and he dragged his leg. As Choteau's volunteer firemen hosed water on the burning house, a sheriff's deputy offered the two Feds a swig of Bourbon. Cole declined. Nick lied: "Thanks, but I don't need it."

"Hell, if this ain't a time for a drink, when is?"

As Cole watched, Nick told the deputy: "If I don't need it now, I won't ever need it, will I?"

"Suit yourself," said the deputy, taking a swig and chalking up the Fed's shaking hands to damn near getting blown to hell.

"Inspector," said an ordinance expert from Malstrom Air Force Base. "I found a radio trigger."

Cole said: "You mean he picked when to set it off?"

When the search team found the tunnel, Cole knew.

"Kurt Vance," said Cole during the flight back to D.C. "He kills with a knife, a gun, a bomb, electrocution. He knows computers, cop procedure. Plans way, *way* ahead. Waits for his enemies to come into his kill zone, not caring that he's got a shitload of cops a gunshot away. How do you stop a guy like that?"

"Kill him first," said Nick.

The last photograph Montana authorities found of Kurt Vance showed a pimply-faced, shaggy-haired high school sophomore.

"After that," said the sheriff, "he must have been absent whenever it was picture day."

"By then he'd figured out who he was," said Nick. "He didn't need a picture. Didn't want anybody else to see."

"So years later, Chris Harvie ropes him into assassinating Faron?" added Cole. "What's in it for Kurt Vance?"

"I'm not sure," said Nick. "Yet."

They faxed the high school photo to FBI headquarters, where a computer team "aged" the image to become a likeness of an older Kurt Vance. They then altered it with beards, mustaches, fake glasses, creating a portfolio of possible faces for a wanted man:

White male, approximately 5'10" tall, 165 lbs., 38 years old, short brown hair, tan. No known marks, tattoos, or distinguishing characteristics. Armed and extremely dangerous. Wanted for assault on special agents of the FBI and related homicide charges.

Every FBI field office got a copy of the portfolio by Monday. Every local and state police agency had a copy by Tuesday.

"I wish your computer pictures gave better likenesses," said Nick. "What they came up with could be almost anybody."

"But at least now we can go all out on a legitimate manhunt," said Cole. "We don't have to be careful about what we're hiding."

The DAAG called Cole on the airplane. "You blew it!"

"The plan fell apart before I got there." Cole told him about the police-band scanner, how the overeager local police had violated radio silence procedure.

"Is that true? Can anybody refute that spin? Can we sell it?"

"I don't care."

"You weren't brought on to fail, Inspector Cole."

"I didn't sign on to get fucked, either."

"Your job—"

"Is Faron Sears still alive?" said Cole.

The jet engines droned eastward through the night.

"Don't blow it again, Cole." The DAAG hung up.

Sunday morning in the War Room, Nick told Cole and Sallie: "The bosses fucked us once. They'll do it again."

Sallie refilled her coffee cup from a thermos. She refilled Nick's cup, too; his hands trembled. *Almost dying can do that to you,* she thought.

"Which housekeeper do you figure for a Headquarters fink?" asked Nick. "Hell, they probably even got this place bugged."

"Doesn't matter," answered Cole. "We need them.

"You did a hell of job," Cole told Sallie.

"Here's what we got," she said, ignoring the praise. "Item one, money. The stacks of cash in the wardrobe. Faron gets a ton of mail every week. And every week, people send him cash."

"Donating cash to a billionaire," said Nick. "I love America."

"Not to *him*," said Sallie, "to his Movement. Personal commitment. People being sincere in their—"

"So what?" said Cole.

"So a white-collar crime team at Headquarters graphed out the donations. Based on statistics and Faron's records, at least a dozen times in the last seven months the weekly cash tallies have come up short by several thousand dollars."

"So he's got an embezzler and a traitor and an assassin," mumbled Nick. "You make a lot trouble, you get it back. An embezzler wouldn't try to kill his own cash cow."

"But conspiracies need untraceable cash," said Sallie. "So maybe the embezzler and the traitor are the same person."

"How much of a shortfall are you talking about?" said Cole.

"About $74,000."

"That's enough to notice," said Cole.

"Not if you're used to dealing in billions," said Sallie.

"What else?" said Cole.

"Jeff Wood has a $200,000 debit item transferred out from the Movement for an unspecified project. Jon Leibowitz got $94,000 in unitemized expense money. Last year, Lauren took two straight cash draws, first $500, then two weeks later $11,000. No justification or payback."

Cole drained his coffee. "Faron put up $20 million of his own money for his crusade. What else did you get out of his computer?"

"The hackers are still working." Sallie looked at her notes: "We've gone through 204,369 past Internet messages to Faron. We don't need to worry about the current flow; Wood and Faron gave us access. We're checking every time he got flamed."

"Flamed?" said Nick and Cole together.

"Netspeak for . . . attacked, insulted, weirded."

"Wood's code was strong enough to let us suck up the files, but many files have an individual code that prevents us from reading them." She smiled: "Our hackers loved turning that over to NSA, *directing* them to start code-breaking into the files."

Cole said: "Somebody e-mailed our assassin Vance from Faron's Chicago place. Maybe Vance and the inside man are also using the Internet to—"

"If the inside man lets Vance know we're there undercover as well as on his trail . . ."

"What about that Chicago project?" said Nick.

"Faron's not our target," said Sallie. "We're looking for who wants him murdered."

"Leave Chicago alone," said Cole. "Sounds like we'll find out about it on TV. If we go poking around there, keeping our cover from Faron's people, his enemies, *and* a bunch of reporters will be impossible. Besides, we might draw heat on Faron that he doesn't deserve."

Sallie lifted a folder off the table. "CIA photo interpreters came up with something from those shots of Faron's rallies. They used computers to digitalize every picture, then programmed a run for approximate matches. Of all their hits, these caught my eye."

The first photograph was a blowup of an Asian man in a business suit. A second Asian man in sunglasses was partially visible over his shoulder.

"He's standing at the edge of a crowd in Tucson," she said. "Here he is in the auditorium in Kansas City. Different suit."

"Expensive suit," said Nick. "Not your average stalker."

"And here he is at the rally in Newark," she said. This third photo showed the Asian standing beside a man in his twenties who wore a conservative business suit and descended from a Nordic gene pool. The two men leaned on the trunk of a car.

"We pulled up the license plate," said Sallie. "A rental car. The credit card slip for the rental belongs to Fine, Heifitz, and Miller. A major D.C. law firm."

"The CIA can do that with computers—that fast?" asked Nick.

"We can take your picture, digitalize it, put you in any other photograph. In five years, you'll do that on your home PC."

"Another measure of reality down the tubes," said Cole.

"But here's the big find." Sallie showed them a photograph of the same Asian man bundled in a topcoat. The photo had been blown up and cropped to zoom in on his face. She laid out sequential shots: first the close-up of the Asian man's face, then a wide-angle photo showing him standing at the edge of a crowd, then a long shot of the crowd filling a street in front of a mansion.

Sallie said: "He was in Chicago at Faron's noontime rally the same hour that the e-mail message was fired off to Vance in Idaho. This guy was just outside the building where that call was made."

"Rendezvous," whispered Nick. "Maybe a pass-off contact."

"Who the hell is he?" said Cole.

"All we know is that he might be tied to that D.C. law firm that rented the car in Newark."

Cole rubbed his eyes. "Everybody who's had more than three hours sleep a night in the last few days raise your hand."

The air above them stayed unbroken.

"Law firms are hell to mess with," said Sallie.

"Hell, they're all crooks," said Nick.

"Bunch of them are our bosses," said Cole.

"You mean crooks or lawyers?" asked Sallie.

"OK," said Cole. "We've got Kurt Vance. I say he's our shooter. We got him running against the whole damn system. And we got this man: call him a stalker, call him a groupie; he's real interested in Faron. But our only possible link to Mr. Asian Stalker is a D.C. law firm, which means we have to tip-toe around things like client privilege. This afternoon, all field offices will get a medium-priority query about any matters they're investigating in which anyone of Asian heritage is represented by—what was that law firm?"

Sallie read: "Fine, Heifitz—"

"All those usual suspects," said Cole.

"You'll end up with a hundred faxes on your desk," said Sallie. "That's a big law firm. Lot of clients needing help with the law. Plus he could be one of the lawyers, not a client."

"Odds are," said Nick, "messing with a big D.C. law firm that has college friends and wanna-work-theres scattered through the Justice department will make our bosses nervous."

"That's why I'm touching this with a soft hand. And to keep them happy, tomorrow we follow their hunch about a murderous business rival."

Nick said: "Everybody who truly cares if the bosses are happy, raise their hands."

The air above the three of them stayed unbroken.

Cole unlocked his apartment Sunday night and kicked the pile of newspapers inside. The air was close and dead.

He draped his trench coat over his suitcase full of dirty clothes. His mailbox downstairs was jammed. His answering machine showed nine calls. He ignored the playback button. He tossed his suit coat toward a dinette chair. Missed. Left it on the floor. Flopped on the couch. His head sank into the back of the sofa as his eyes closed. A bed waited in the other room. Firm. Empty.

Shit! Hadn't checked the surveillance on AA Nazis in—No, OK: there'd have been an alert if anything . . .

If I die tonight, Ricki Side will be the last woman I kissed.

Hell, the first woman who's kissed me in . . . nine months? Since Diane the lawyer who only came when she was on top walked out with her briefcase looking for somebody who cared about houses in the right neighborhoods and *real careers.*

The phone rang.

"Cole!" said the DAAG on the line. "I need a report! What are you—"

"Sir, this is not a secure line—"

"Wha—"

"Afraid I can't let you precipitate a breach of secure communications."

"*Precipitate* your ass!"

"I'll call you." Cole hung up. Felt nothing.

Brinnng!

Dalton lifted the receiver, mumbled: "So who are you?"

"That's always the question, isn't it?" she said.

"Lauren! I . . . what . . . Are you at work now?"

"Working for Faron for some of us is not a nine-to-five job." She sighed. "OK, I'm in my new apartment staring at my rented furniture and my not-unpacked boxes, but yeah, I'm working."

"Is that why you called?"

Silence.

"Lauren, are you . . ."

"I've been calling you since this morning."

"How come?" He sat on the floor like a yogi.

"On 'One Hour' tonight they did a promo for the show about Faron. I knew they would, so, this morning, I thought you might like to . . . probably should watch it. So . . . I called."

"I wasn't here."

"I know." Her voice softened. "If you didn't see the spot, you didn't miss much. A 'next week on' mention by the anchor. They're going with the tag-line title of 'Who is Faron Sears?' "

"That's the question."

"Look, I'm sorry I bothered you; go back to what you were doing. Sunday shouldn't be a work—"

"What do you have in all those unpacked boxes?"

"A whole lot of not much."

"I got a lot of that over here, too."

They didn't say anything for a long time.

"I better let you go," she said.

"I'm fine right here." Cross-legged on the floor, head bowed, phone pressed against his ear, world on his shoulders.

"You sound tired."

"You've got great ears."

She laughed. "No one's ever told me *that* before."

"Maybe you just never heard them."

"No, I've been listening hard."

"Maybe," he said. "Maybe . . . hell, I don't know maybe what."

"Look, you're tired, you should go to—get some rest."

"OK."

"I'll see you when you get in tomorrow," she said.

"Ah . . . I might not get in tomorrow." He closed his eyes to lie. "Faron's got me . . . You know: different planets, same sun."

"I don't really give a damn what Faron has you doing."

"Good." He felt his truth ring in her ears.

They said good night. He sat on the floor. Reached up to the phone table, pushed the playback button on the answering machine, and listened to her taped voice calling him.

Sallie took a bath, put on flannel pajamas, changed the Band-Aid on her finger, called her mother.

"Hey, baby!" said the old lady into a phone three miles across the city from Sallie's apartment. "You finally get home?"

"Yeah, Mom," said Sallie, lying back on her bed. "I'm OK."

"I know that! We got ourselves a deal, right? You just working a gove'ment job. You never gonna be doing no dangerous thing."

"That's right, Mama. That's our deal."

"Girl, you lying through your pearly white teeth."

The two of them laughed.

"You OK, chil'?"

"Yeah, Mama."

"Don't you go thinking you're taking it easy on my old bones. You tell me the truth. I already bore up more'n you seen."

"You got nothing to worry about, Mama. I work with good people. They take care of me."

"You gots to take care of yourself! You know that!"

"Yes . . ."

"That was our deal." The old lady grumbled. "But you home now, right? You got no hurts on you, and I can stop waking up every time one of them damn news bulletins interrupts my programs."

"You can turn the TV off, Mama."

"Hell, then who'd come to visit me?" She laughed. "All them shows, they mighty full of kind of folks I never knowed, but they can make you laugh. Or least sleep."

"I know, Mama. I miss you, too."

"You know, I seen Roma from your high school class the

other day. Got two kids. She says nobody sees much of you these days."

"You don't even get to see much of me. This job . . . It takes everything I got to do it right. Doesn't leave me much time."

"But you *do* got friends."

"Sure, Mom. Lots of friends; good people at work, too."

"You work with a lot of white folks, don't you?"

"Mostly."

"Seems like everywhere I look, there's more white faces. You friends with them? Hang out together? Go to each other's houses, over for dinner and such?"

"I . . . No. Guess not. Not much, anyway.

"I mean," said Sallie, "we're friends, treat each other right, and there's no . . . But . . . seems like we're all . . . There's work parties and events, weddings, and such, but . . . When we want to get comfortable, relax, seems like it's all black or all white."

"Huh. I wondered 'bout that. Thought so. Kinda makes me wonder. And sad."

"I know. Me, too."

"You know I'm proud of you, girl."

"Yeah, Mom . . ."

"God-damn spitting proud; forgive me, Jesus."

"You'd be prouder of me if you had a couple grandkids."

"Be happier for you, yes. But couldn't be no prouder of you."

"Maybe someday."

"Oh. Well now. You got something you want to tell me? Some name you want to whisper?"

"Mother!" Sallie crawled under the bedcovers.

The older woman laughed.

"There's nobody," said Sallie. "Nobody at all."

"Nobody at all is better than that jerk Clive you brung—"

"Mother! That was in college! He was on the way out my door before you tricked me into bringing him visiting through yours!"

"Girl, if I didn't see who you was going to throw back, how was I supposed to worry about who you was going to keep?"

"You might have let me know I was going to dump him!"

"I knew you'd figure it out in your own time."

They laughed.

"There just aren't many good men out there," said Sallie. "Men who are . . . there just aren't."

"Uh-huh."

"What's you uh-huhing me about?"

"Why nothing, chil'. You doing all the talking."

"Never learn, do I." She paused: "Mom, what was it like when you met Daddy?"

"Girl, you are keeping too many secrets from your mother!"

The daughter said nothing, waited.

"Your dad made my bones shake the first time he looked at me."

"Wish he were still—"

"Me, too, chil'. Your granddaddy picked tobacco, and tobacco picked his seed," said the woman widowed young. "If I want all this sighing and nostalgia, I can volunteer at some old folks' home. When do I get to see you?"

"Soon, Mom. I hope soon." The daughter said good night. Hung up. Stared at the pistol in the holster on her bed stand.

The bottle of Scotch stared right through the cabinet wood at Nick as he sat at the kitchen table in his suburban Virginia house. He knew the damn bottle was right there, easily half full.

Easy. His hands kept their grip on the edge of the table. Made it gonna make it gonna do it doing it . . .

Got through that damn sweet damn explosion *oh Christ! it hurts,* and my leg, knee swollen like a cantaloupe, hurts and . . .

Gonna make it. Gonna show Cole who's right; he's right. I'm right; I'm going be right, going be all right.

Damn bright yellow light in damn faded yellow kitchen should have repainted it years ago didn't need to keep it . . .

Oh, it hurt. And he laughed. Damn, it *always* hurt. Woke up walking hurt every damn morning. Picking rock, gandy dancing, football. *Being a man meant waking up and walking hurt.*

The last damn bottle. Deserved a proper burial. Respectful farewell. Just a little, one, just a—

Faron. *Think about work.* Vance'd be running, where

would he run to, he'd know how he was going; running with the wind to leave no scent, loping toward Faron—son of a bitch, Faron, who's he think he is? Fuckin' cop killer snake-oil—

Nick heard the faint hum of cars on the interstate a quarter mile beyond winter-bare trees. Suburban silence. The creak of his kitchen table. Cabinet, in the damn cabinet . . . The last damn bottle. An amber pool in a clear shaft. Lapping up against the glass. A tremble. Little damn fucking lapping waves laughing and staring right through the damn wood.

What the hell happened to the damn horses?

Just the waves in the thirsty, lapping waves in the last damn bottle, thirst—

Nick blasted the cabinet with all seven rounds in his .45.

Gun smoke filled the kitchen as shell casings rolled off the table, his ears too full of the gunshots to hear the brass clink on the linoleum. Jagged holes dotted his genuine oak cabinet; its splintered door gaped open.

Cop lore: The .45 slugs would have punched through the kitchen wall behind the cabinet, slammed into the far wall of the living room. If the neighbors heard, they'd think it was TV. They'd want to believe it was TV. They wouldn't dial 911, make him explain badge to badge why he'd shot the shit out of his house.

One slug had bull's-eyed for sure: slowly, steadily, amber liquid dripped out the cabinet door. Like blood.

The shark locked on Kurt Vance as soon as Vance stepped out of the hotel in Fargo that Sunday night. Vance spotted the shark. The hotel was at the edge of downtown in this North Dakota city of 50,000 people. *That many people, there had to be at least one would-be "professional" shark.*

The shark wore a ski jacket and blue jeans, Dingo boots. A ski cap. He paced in front of a closed store across the street from the hotel like a window shopper. The glass worked as a hunting mirror—but the shark's image was reflected, too.

Vance strolled down the hotel steps. Checked his watch, touched his back pocket. Walked up the street. He'd driven around this hotel until he'd been certain of the geography.

Now he walked toward the feeble glow of a serious drinkers'
bar. Heard the dingo boots cross the street behind him.

Vance reached the alley, "glanced" down it, "saw" the neon
glow of another bar sign, scarlet neon tubing swirled in the
shape of a woman and a cocktail glass. Vance paused to *show
decision,* then hurried down the alley.

That night, the only light in the alley came from a single
bulb above a door fifty feet away from the entrance. Halfway
there, Vance whirled, doubled-back, and startled the man
who'd been closing the gap between them.

Vance smiled. "So glad you could make it."

The man was puzzling over what he'd heard when Vance
sprayed him with tear gas bought at a truck stop.

Vance kicked the blinded, gasping man in the stomach,
threw him down the stairs to a boarded-up Chinese restaurant. Slapped him until his eyes cleared. Slapped him a few
more times. Slammed the heel of his palm into the mugger's
forehead when he tried to move. Cut a line with his knife
across the fool's pale forehead. Stifled the mugger's scream
with a gloved hand over his mouth.

Vance said: "It's your lucky day."

"Hey, man, I don't know what you—"

Vance flicked the knife across the man's nose. "*I* know.
That's enough. Have you been in prison?"

"Whatever you want, man, I'll—I did one year, OK? But
this tonight was just a . . . a few times thing. Pass by the hotel,
hang around, see if there's any cops, see if anybody comes
out . . ."

"*I* came out," said Vance. "*I* came out."

"Oh, shit, I'm sorry, mister. I didn't know."

"That's what we're going to talk about. *What you know.* Are
you from around here?"

"Got paroled back. Lived here all my life."

"You're doing really well," said Vance.

In the winter darkness, the knife was cold and bright.

"Now," said Vance, "tell me about Fargo's bad boys."

"If I need a lawyer," Peter Elmore told the two Feds who'd ruined his Monday morning by showing up at his Baltimore office, "there's one on my staff right down the hall."

The senior agent—something Cole—said: "That's your choice, Mr. Elmore."

The agent who limped said: "We're just doing our job."

"Is that supposed to make me happy?"

"You should be a happy guy," said Nick. "Big office, company out there's got a couple dozen people . . ."

"Seventeen."

"Must be worth a few million dollars."

"I'll save you the trouble. We're rated at $21 million."

Cole said: "Were you once Faron Sears's partner?"

Peter Elmore wore a sportshirt and cords, no tie, no jacket. His thinning hair was brushed flat. "So now that black son of a bitch's got the FBI for a goon squad, too."

"Too?" said Nick.

Elmore said nothing.

Cole said: "You threatened to kill him once, didn't you?"

"No," said Elmore. "I *promised* to kill him. Big difference. Once upon a time, promises meant something. Promises he made to me, promises I made to him. I kept mine, all except that last one. He gutted that out of me, too. I don't make promises anymore."

"So you never tried to—"

"I lunged across a table. Faron just sat there. Monk—he's—"

"We know," said Cole.

"Monk slammed me down on that wood like I was a fish. Man to man, I'd rip Faron's sorry ass. But Faron's not just a man, he's an army: Monk and Wood. Lauren with her cold heart, smooth tongue, and smart hands. And now you FBI flatfoots."

"We don't work for Faron Sears," said Cole.

"Then we have something in common."

Cole said: "The settlement gave you—"

"After Faron stabs you in the back, he keeps his hand around the knife so he's got you right where he wants you.

"We were partners! Fourteen years ago, I was on my way to being as big as he is! I believed that ex-con's con, believed that signing with him to develop my ideas would make us both stronger.

"Took him three years, but when he and his gang were done, all my software was 'updated' and thus 'coauthored' and thus 'joint ventured' but contracted to his companies on an exclusive basis to be purchased and used at their discretion.

"All he had to do was decide not to use my stuff. Whatever *I* owned had been subsumed into what *we* owned, so *I* couldn't sell it without his permission, and *we* had an exclusive deal with *him*. Next thing I know, I get a buyout offer. If I say no, every product I own becomes worthless, because my *partner* won't use it, and nobody else can. Even if I tried to walk clean, the bastard had me. My lawyers called it a steel blue-sky: if I broke with Faron, any software I developed for five years would be deemed to have been 'seminally generated' by our association. I could create it—but he'd own half.

"The guy cut my balls off with my own hand," said Elmore. "Cost me six years and $9 million out of my pocket, not my business ledger, because that was a 'partnership property' in dispute."

"You put a lot into that fight," said Cole.

"When I had to move my family into a trailer park, my balls stopped being worth it," said Elmore.

"You settled."

"I kissed the mat. I got the 'right' to develop all this—as long as I dropped my claims and sell whatever I develop to Faron at my lowest price. If I make money, he makes money. Hell, his 'settlement' even *generously* loaned me two million dollars in start-up costs for my 'freestanding' company. What else was I going to do? Flip burgers at McDonald's? Be a drone for MBD? Work for the Japanese?"

"Do you still hate him?" asked Cole.

"You don't get it, do you? Some stranger didn't do this to me. I expect that; that's the way of the world. But my *partner* did it to me; my *friend* did it to me. *Faron* did it."

"So you want to kill him."

"I want a hot fudge sundae for lunch, but I won't have one because it's bad for me. Yeah, I want to kill him."

"Because he's a *'black'* son of a bitch?" said Nick.

Elmore spread his arms: "What was I supposed to call him? An *Irish* son of a bitch? What are you, the free-speech police?"

"Didn't your wife leave you after that failure?" said Cole.

Elmore looked away. "He fucked me so good I couldn't . . . You read the divorce papers she filed before you came here. You know he fucked me and then I couldn't fuck her and then it got ugly. Then she left. Won't come back, even though . . .

"What do you want?" said Elmore. "I let you drop your lines in my water. I thought you might be with that task force from the Justice department. I've been a good, cooperative citizen."

"You're a smart man," said Cole. "Creative. Lots of resources. Victimized. Mad as hell."

Nick said: "You've got a cousin in organized crime."

Elmore shook his head. "Vinnie? You guys say he's in the Mob. You put him away once, selling bootleg cigarettes in New York. Wow. My cousin makes dimes dodging taxes to sell people drugs Uncle Sam backs with farm subsidies, and you act like he's the Godfather. Hell, even if he is, we haven't talked in eight years."

Cousin Vinnie ran a crew for the Gambino family. The Bureau was sure he'd ice-picked a Colombian interloper in the Bronx.

"And Vinnie wouldn't help you settle a score?" said Nick.

"Tell me what you're setting me up for or get out."

Risk it, thought Cole: "Someone has hired a hit man to—"

Elmore laughed, pumped his fist once: *"Yes!"*

Cole and Nick glanced at each other.

"What's the matter?" Elmore grinned. "You think I'm the only guy out there with good reason to notch a gun for Faron?"

"Aren't you worried about being a prime suspect?" said Nick.

"Nah. Since Faron, every step I take is spanking clean and accounted for, videotaped, notarized, and lawyered. I'm so damn innocent you couldn't nail a frame on me!"

"Looks like you got something else useful out of being in business with Faron," said Nick.

"Yeah: the brains to not give him a bullet to shoot at me."

"You're not surprised somebody else wants to shoot at him?"

"Are you really from the FBI? Don't you remember BCCI? Do you really think that Fortune 500 companies—or the guys who sit on their thrones—that they're above violence? You're walking in the billion-dollar league, with egos to match.

"Countries are falling apart. Companies are taking their place. Corporate feudalism. I hate unions—hell, look at Hoffa and the Mob—but what did America's tycoons do to unions when our folks were kids? How many starry-eyed lefty labor organizers ended up under a swamp or dangling from a light post?"

"Who besides you would be mad enough and big enough to hire a hit on your ex-partner?" said Nick.

Elmore smiled: "I wouldn't speculate on that even if I could."

"You said 'goon squad, too.' Why?"

Elmore studied the men sitting on the other side of his desk. He said: "Everything in this room is videotaped."

Cole and Nick froze, then Cole said: "We can get a search warrant to check out any tapes we want."

"You wouldn't find what you're looking for," said Elmore. "That happened before I got cameras set up everywhere. That's one reason I set up the cameras."

"Don't make us guess it out of you," said Nick.

Elmore spoke to the walls: "Hear that, you scum-sucking lawyers working for Faron? If you subpoenaed this, suck on it. I'm co-operating with a request from an official FBI investigation.

"Seven months ago," Elmore told the cops. "I got some visitors. In the parking lot. Three business suits. They told me that I was lucky. That 'security' for my business looked pretty good. That they represented 'commingled and parallel financial interests,' and that as long as I had nothing to worry about, I had nothing to worry about. They'd keep an eye on me."

"Did they mention Faron?" said Cole.

"Gosh, no, they didn't. They didn't give me any names. They wriggled back in their car and drove away."

"And you think—"

"The witness declines to speculate for the record."

"Off the record," said Cole.

"No such thing. I learned that from Faron."

"You got more to tell us," said Nick.

Elmore smiled. "You're here, the Justice guys were here . . . Looks like my old friend Faron is in trouble. I'm glad to help."

He took a computer disk from inside his pocket, booted it up on his desktop machine, called up a file.

"The license plate of that car." Elmore stroked a few keys. Printed a hard-copy page with that data.

Cole took the paper, stood. "Thank you for your time."

"Oh, no problem! I've been waiting *a long time* for *right now.*"

Fargo has a shopping mall. That winter morning, Vance stood alone by the pay phones near the mall entrance as he made his call.

"Federal Bureau of Investigation," said the bored agent

working the walk-in, phone-in desk across town. "Good morning."

"Yeah," said Vance, "like, I'm from out of town . . ."

"This is the FBI, not the—"

"Hey, I'm looking for one of youse guys who worked a deal with me once. Dude's name was Cole, Dalton Cole."

"Sir, no agent by that name—"

"I know he don't work in this bum-fuck place!"

"*I* work here, *sir.*"

"Yeah, and you got caller ID, right? Cole helped me cut a deal out of a jam, and . . . see, I'm from out of town."

"What do want?"

"Call Cole. Tell him—No, ain't gonna give you no name-check shit, nail my ass 'fore—you get Cole's phone number, where he's working now, so the con he helped with a knife scar on his forehead, so I can call him."

"Now why would I do that?"

" 'Cause you know I'm for real. 'Cause you know a local yokel bad guy named Wally Burdett; ask the cops if you don't. He's the one what's trying to sell me on a dope-for-hot-cars deal."

"The Drug Enforcement Agency and the local police have—"

"Get Cole's number for me, man; I call you back. He gives me the word; I'll walk it in for you. Tell him the cars are coming from Chicago, the dope down from Canada, and if you don't know that's interstate FBI crime, get a map."

No one noticed Vance hang up the pay phone, clump over the snow-plowed parking lot to a car with North Dakota plates that didn't match its registration.

No one in the neighborhood across from the mall paid any attention to the car that parked on a winter-morning street where most people were at work or watching TV or cleaning house. Vance got out, lifted the hood and listened to his engine. He stood where he could see his motor—and the mall.

Eleven minutes later, a Fargo city police cruiser slowly drove past the mall, brake lights red as it crept past the pay phones.

Next time, they'll co-ordinate faster, thought Vance. He

waited until the police car left the mall, closed the hood of his car, drove away.

Fargo has a hospital. Vance called from the pay phones outside the surgical unit and kept his voice low.

"Federal Bureau of—"

"It's been an hour, Jack. You gots what we want?"

"If you come in—"

"You get me Cole's number, I call him, he says to see you; you and I work it out. I'm running out of quarters, Jack."

"Agent Cole is difficult to link up with today."

"Then I'm—"

"Wait! What about the stolen cars?"

"If I'm fucked, fuck them. Fuck you, too, Jack."

"You called us, we can—"

"Give me Cole. I don't know you."

"Agent Cole transferred out of Washington's field office."

"Tell me what I don't know. Where can I call him?"

"He's currently assigned through Headquarters, and I cannot release a number for him."

"Well, shit, Jack, then I guess I just have to work my best deal with you. Hang around."

The receiver clicked down in the Fargo agent's ear. Vance strolled out the emergency room entrance before a city squad car and an FBI sedan pulled into the hospital's parking lot.

Dalton Cole, thought Vance as he climbed into his car: *An FBI agent from D.C. who's important enough to fly all over the world.*

What an interesting guy.

"**P**avement time," said Nick, but that Monday afternoon, he and Cole never left the War Room, seldom put down a phone.

The Pennsylvania license plate number from Peter Elmore was registered to a Delaware corporation called Phoenix Enterprises.

Phoenix Enterprises was a "public relations, security, investment, and research company" owned by American Investors, Inc.

American Investors, Inc., was a limited partnership formed in Gary, Indiana, between two local lawyers and an L.A. corporation with a mailbox and no tangible assets beyond a bank account.

Sole owner of the L.A. corporate shell: Jeff Wood.

Records on file with state regulatory agencies showed Phoenix's $200,000 initial capitalization had mushroomed into a "corporate headquarters" near the Pennsylvania-Maryland border and a half-million-dollar "security contract" with the nonprofit group founded by Faron Sears to revitalize inner-city Chicago.

"I thought Monk ran the heavies," said Nick.

"Evidently Wood has a private army, too," said Cole.

"So maybe he was the one after machine guns in Chicago," said Wood. "Wood'll get rich via a nonprofit he's helping command. Sweet. Long as nobody knows."

"Think he's a front man?"

"For who?" Nick shrugged.

Cole scrambled surveillance of Phoenix's "corporate headquarters."

The forensics team sifting through Vance's fire-gutted house linked him to three deaths: a girl in Wyoming, a John Doe rifle-shot along a Montana highway, and his fifth-grade teacher. From Seattle to Sioux Falls, from Calgary to Carson City, homicide squads bombarded the FBI-Choteau police command post, asking if Vance could be the Unknown Subject who'd done their local horror.

"The good cops want to know the truth," said Nick. "The others want to hang an open file on our boy, get themselves off the hook."

"Nick, we never got to talk. About—"

Phone rang. Nick grabbed it, started uh-huhing. Cole waited. When Nick's call didn't end, Cole phoned Montana to check on cars stolen within a hundred miles of Choteau. Nick heard him ask the agent in the field about airports close to Choteau. Nick's phone had been buzzing a disconnect for a minute. He put the receiver down, picked up the growing stack of FBI 202 Interview Forms, statements about Kurt Vance.

Vance's neighbors knew little about him. He was odd, said one of them, but, hell, everybody out here is. But he was a neighbor, this is Montana, and we don't have "those kinds of people" like they do Back East and in California. The county librarian said Vance came in more than most people do— "damn TV." She said he looked at books about history and cosmic forces. She remembered he'd checked out books on President Reagan.

Nick felt it start to happen as he stared at the report pages in his hands: the tingling along his spine, the *sinking in*, falling in step, loping along in a natural glide.

Kurt Vance. *R.* Who liked to kill. Who could do more than anybody around him imagined, who laughed at all of *them*. Who roamed probably far and wide from his isolated small-town lair, orchestrating who knew what horrors. Secret keeper, secret maker, stone soul, convinced he was somebody special.

Wasn't Reagan you were reading about, thought Nick. It was the glory hound son of a bitch who shot him.

Through the pounding in his head, the shaking in his

hands, Nick felt the tingle, the knowing. Through the achy yearning *thirst,* he felt it: *I've got your scent, you son of a bitch.*

Cole skimmed a stack of messages and held his phone while an agent in Missoula, Montana, retrieved the passenger manifest for that day's eastbound plane.

Pink phone slip, the DAAG: Status report. *When I'm ready.*

Pink phone slip, Headquarters relayed message from the commander of D.C.'s Cold Case Squad: Please call re: possible contact from one of your previous informers. *Haven't got the time for mere crime.*

As the Montana agent came back on the line, Cole glanced across the War Room to Nick's back, thought: *Gotta find the time.*

39

Night held the city by the time Cole drove home alone. Snow fell. Brake lights winked in his windshield, and Cole sent the same flash to the headlights floating in his mirror.

Didn't lie to Lauren, he thought. Never made it in today. Wonder if she called my machine?

Vance. Kurt Vance. *R.* Faron. Who was *U.*? Who was supposed to be Vance's Number Two? Vance'll run *toward* something, not *away* from us. The e-mail said wait until after Valentine's Day. Nine more days. Time to buy a card, roses. Like I've got someone to give them to. No way Vance had been spooked off making the hit.

The traffic light turned orange. Cole pumped his brakes, flicked his gaze to the headlights in his mirror: that driver was smart, stayed back. As the light turned green, Cole thought: How much does Kurt Vance think we know?

Cole eased his car forward. A van cut between Cole and the car behind him. The car came out from behind the van. At the next intersection, Cole turned left just as the green arrow turned orange—yellow headlights in the mirror slid with him: Busting an orange arrow in snow storm, thought Cole: bold.

Two blocks later, Cole pulled into his building's underground parking garage. Snow floated down to the street behind him.

Mail crammed into his box filled his trench-coat pockets. Ninety percent junk, but maybe an early Valentine's Day card. *Yeah, right.* He was careful not to drop any envelopes as he pushed the elevator button. His briefcase filled his left hand. The elevator he rode was empty. He held his keys in his right hand with the mail. At his door, he fumbled, got the dead bolt key in. *Click.* Turned the door knob, pushed his door open.

A man stood inside Cole's apartment, pointing straight at him: "If I wanted you dead, you would be."

40

*G*un's on my hip . . . hand full of . . . mail—don't drop it and trigger . . .

"Don't do it!" The man inside Cole's apartment was big, beefy, suit coat unbuttoned. "You don't need to! If I wanted you dead—"

"I heard you the first time."

"We can't do our business in the hall." The man beckoned. Cole stood his ground.

"Don't worry." Again he beckoned. Strong hands, steady eyes. Fifty-something. "Your apartment's not bugged."

"Are you the exterminator?"

"Lucky for you, I'm not."

Cole set the briefcase down against the inside wall. That motion covered his right hand. *Get him used to you not taking the chance.* Cole tossed the mail and keys onto a table.

"OK," said the man in Cole's apartment. "Left hand— creds."

"We know who I am," said Cole.

"Life's not always about you." The stranger reached inside his suit jacket, brought out an ID folder that flipped open with years of practice: "P.J. Toker. Special Agent, FBI."

Cole stepped closer for a better look. His door shut. "If they aren't real, they're excellent forgeries."

"Oh, they're real." The beefy man transferred the credentials to his right hand, used his left to lift his lapel. "Just like—"

Cole kicked him in the stomach.

The big man *oomphed*, doubled over and staggered back.

Black steel flashed as Cole drew his Beretta, racked the slide. The safety was already off, and now a bullet was chambered to fire in a technique/set-up sometimes called *the Israeli condition.*

"Don't fucking fuck with me!" Cole swung the gun to the open bedroom door. No one there. "Turn around! Grab the wall!"

Wheezing, gasping, the intruder complied: "Easy, Cole, easy!"

Cole jammed the Beretta into the spread-eagled man's spine: "Show me how fucking quick you are and it'll be your last act."

A fast pat found a gun on the guy's right hip: .357 Magnum, not the new .40-caliber auto Bureau issue, but *could be.* Cole slid it across the floor toward the front—*the door's not locked!* Kept searching the man, found cuffs, lock picks, a very-out-of-policy .25 automatic ankle gun he slid toward the Magnum.

"Get off the wall! Cuff your right wrist. Back over here!"

The big man obeyed Cole's commands. Cole cuffed the man's arms behind him and around a room-dividing pole near the kitchen.

"Don't fucking move!" Cole nodded toward the bedroom.
"If you got a buddy—"

"It's you and me, pal."

"Better be, asshole!"

"Call me P.J."

Cole shrugged out of his trench coat, threw the billowing
garment through his bedroom door, charged behind it, gun
flicking from side to side.

Closet, *empty*. Bathroom, *empty*.

The big guy was still cuffed. Cole locked his front door.
Got the guns, dropped the magazine out of the .25, emptied
the chamber.

"Like your style," said the man as Cole shook the shells out
of the bear-stopper .357 Magnum revolver. "Keep your anger;
it'll keep you alive."

Cole lowered his gun to his side: "Who the fuck are you?"

"P.J. Toker. You sent a notice out, 'bout a law firm."

"Burglary is a hell of a response."

"You get screwed enough, you get tricky. When your notice
got posted, I made some calls. One of my trainees is one of
your housekeepers."

"You should have taught him to keep his mouth shut."

"I taught him to uphold justice and be true to his friends."
The man shrugged. "He's a good agent. Tried to help me sort
out whether I could help *Inspector* Dalton Cole with a Fine,
Heifitz, and Miller case connected to Asian nationals."

"So you broke into my home."

"Look on your coffee table. I borrowed a bug box from
TSD; detects frequency transmissions and current flows. Says
you're clean, but I unplugged your phones anyway. They can
dial somebody up, turn the phone into a mike."

"Who they?"

"You tell me, bro. Mind uncuffing me? If I wanted you
dead—"

"Yeah, yeah," said Cole. "But people change their mind."

"Life's a gamble."

Cole thought about it. Uncuffed him.

P.J. rubbed his stomach. "Glad you didn't kick my balls:
they're old but they're useful."

"Your belly was closer."

"Bigger, too." P.J. obeyed Cole's nod, sat at the dinette table. "You know you got a squat team on you?"

Cole frowned.

"You can see them parked down in the street. Your binoculars are by the window."

"You searched my place!"

"Just until I found what I needed. Blue Ford parked on the side street; good angle on your door and your parking garage."

Cole kept the Beretta in his right hand. Scanned the street with his binoculars. *Line of parked cars, no blue Ford—*

Dark-maroon Ford. Snow on the cars parked in front of it and behind it; no snow on its hood or windshield.

Shift change: there'd been a tail on him; the blue Ford pulled out of its parking spot when the maroon job showed up.

"Who are they?" said Cole.

"If they work for Uncle Sam," said P.J., "they could be OPR."

OPR: Office of Professional Responsibility, the FBI unit charged with policing its own agents.

"They're here for you, brother," said P.J.

"Are you Washington field office?"

"No. Organized Crime—Special Desk on Asian Groups."

Cole holstered the Beretta, put the photographs from Faron's rallies on the table in front of P.J. "You know this man?"

P.J. bowed to the picture: "*Konbanwa*, Yoshio Chobei.

"We've never met. Mr. Yoshio Chobei, personal secretary to the vice president of Sugamo Industries, a company tied as Japan's second-largest producer of computer products. A company that is a major client for Fine, Heifitz, and Miller."

"Chobei is Yakuza," said Cole.

"His uncle in Tokyo, his *oyabun*, was one of the inner circle in the Kanto-kai, the Japanese policeman's nightmare, a formal coalition of major Yakuza groups. Luckily, Kanto-kai self-imploded in 1965.

"Chobei tested into Tokyo University: business and English. Graduated in 1980. In 1982, he showed up as a junior staffer for the Liberal Democratic Party—Japan's been their show since '55. In 1987, the National Police Agency heard that Chobei had become boss of the Rengo-kai Yakuza group, which is amazing, since Rengo-kai officially disbanded a while ago."

"No gang boss takes a job as a junior political aide or a personal secretary in a computer company," said Cole.

P.J. laughed. "Yeah, that's what the geniuses over at the Treasury department said. They also said to lay off Chobei."

"Why?"

"His corporate boss is a bigwig in international-cooperation and trade groups. Powers that be who work with our bosses work with Chobei's associates. Therefore, Chobei can't be Yakuza. And me? Hell, I was 'racist' for raising the issue."

"You got backed off. The Yakuza—"

"Don't assume you know the Yak," said P.J. "Yakuza are a republic unto themselves. Nine major groups, a hundred thousand members, biker gang affiliates. Spring 1994, Yakuza groups held a summit with Mafia families in a Paris hotel. They also work with the Chinese Triads. Do you know about *sokaiya?*"

"I don't even remember my high school French," said Cole.

"You'd know it if you worked on Wall Street. *Sokaiya* are blackmail artists. They buy stock, show up at a corporation's annual meeting, and unless they're bribed, they ask embarrassing questions about executives' personal scandals or business failures. Sometimes they start a brawl. In America, they've made runs at AT&T, IBM, General Motors, Dow Chemical, Bank of America, and nearly took over City Bank of Honolulu in 1978.

"In 1994, about a thousand Japanese corporations got together to break the *sokaiya,* held their annual meetings on one day, cooperated with the Japanese cops."

"Did it—"

P.J. ignored Cole: "But the peculiar thing about the *sokaiya* is that Sugamo Corporation stopped having trouble with them in 1992—two years before the crackdown. Five years *after* Chobei became a gang boss. That same year, Chobei was hired by Sugamo."

"Tell me," said Cole.

"My guess is that Chobei 'evolved' *sokaiya* tactics, used Yak money, bought into Sugamo. Got himself legitimate business power, political clout. A Tokyo left-wing newspaper claims that Chobei has become a *kuromaku*—that means black curtain in Kabuki theater, power broker in politics."

"Not bad for a personal secretary."

"Never been convicted of a crime, never been arrested. Got all his fingers and no visible tattoos."

"How did you focus on Chobei?"

"Three years ago he went through Customs in Honolulu. He had a . . . the English translates as 'helper.' That helper accidentally flashed tattoos. Customs Intelligence snapped photos, logged the passports, sent us a routine notice."

Snow fell outside Cole's window.

"That's all you've got?"

P.J. slammed his fist on the table: "All that took me three damn years! Four trips to Tokyo! More damn polite asking and bowing and connecting dots! How the hell did *you* focus on him?"

"You don't need to know."

"Fuck you, *Inspector*. I put my ass on the line with this number, and—"

"Why?" said Cole. "You could have figured a way to—"

"What I figured is that the Yakuza don't play amateur ball when they're colonizing new turf."

Cole shook his head. "Not enough. You're an old pro: *Why?*"

"I don't want my grandkids to end up *ronin* in our own damn country."

The glow of the lights in Cole's apartment was soft, warm.

"I can guess what you mean," he said.

"Where'd you take those photos? Our section has a right—"

"You don't work for your section anymore," said Cole.

"Bigger hands than yours have tried to cut off my balls."

"Your balls work for me, as of now." Cole rubbed his brow. "Go to your office—now. Make copies of everything you've got on Chobei and whatever else you think you'll need. I'll give you a couple hours, then the authorizing calls will start."

"You taking me to the cutting pen?"

"I don't know where we're going," said Cole. "Can you get back out of here without those guys seeing you?"

Their gaze between the two men was steady. P.J. picked his Magnum off the coffee table and turned his palm up to Cole.

Cole dumped the cartridges into P.J.'s hand.

The older agent geared up. Cole waited. P.J. hefted the attaché case that held the electronic eavesdropping detectors.

"One more thing," Cole told him. "Next time you ambush me, I'll shoot you cold."

"Hell, *boss:* next time, you won't *see* me." Then he was gone.

Cole locked his door.

No messages on the answering machine. Had there been any when P.J. arrived? He plugged his phones back in.

Cole got what he needed out of his briefcase, opened the sliding glass door to his narrow balcony. The air was cold; snowflakes melted on him like frozen tears. In the street below, he saw the maroon Ford. Dalton unfolded his cellular phone.

Snow fell softly on Washington's suburbs. Two men sat in the maroon Ford, the engine off.

"He's down for tonight," said the man slouched behind the steering wheel.

"Lucky guy," said the passenger. "You want the first shift?"

The driver sighed: "You got the jug?"

"Forget it!" snapped his partner as a van crept past them down the one-way street's slippery slope.

"Look," said the Ford's driver, "it ain't my fault."

"You drank too damn much coffee!"

A homeless man wrapped in a blanket materialized out of falling snow two blocks in front of where they were parked.

He held his bare hand over a grate. Snowflakes kissed his knuckles.

"I need the jug," said the driver.

"And I said you drank too damn much coffee!"

"I was cold!" The driver took his eyes off the homeless man: "I didn't ask for this prostate, and I need the jug now!"

"And I don't need to sit in this damn car all night smelling a plastic milk jug of your cold piss!"

"The jug is for you, too!"

"Yeah," said the passenger as the homeless man shuffled across the street to their sidewalk. "Right."

"Look, what am I supposed to do?"

"Hold it."

"*You* hold it!"

"Sorry, I'm married."

"Oh," the driver winced. "Don't do that! Don't make me laugh!"

"When are you going to go the doctor?"

"You know what he's going to *do* to me?" The driver glanced in the rear-view mirror: Another van creeping down the road's slope, wet with melting snow. "I'll go *tomorrow*, OK? Now, I gotta go—"

"Use that tree."

The driver looked to his left. The sidewalk waited outside his window. Beyond the sidewalk was a landscaped strip of grass.

"That's a damn *bush*! That ain't tall enough to—"

"Hell, nobody's gonna see you! Nobody cares anyway!"

"What about him?" The driver pointed to the homeless man who was now six car lengths from them, shuffling closer, clearly drunk.

"Like he's gonna care."

The driver tumbled from the car. Bent over, he hurried toward an evergreen shrub near a slight knoll. Made it, got his pants unzipped. In their Ford, his partner looked away—

Saw Dalton Cole standing in the golden glow flowing out his apartment building's glass doors.

"Shit!" The passenger grabbed the binoculars off the dash, zeroed them past the homeless man: No question: Cole, like he was waiting for a taxi or pickup car.

The passenger turned the key in the ignition, pushed the button that slid the driver's side window down.

"Hey!" he hissed to his partner.

Who whirled to look over his shoulder, panic on his face.

"We got to go!"

"I'm still—"

Red lights and sirens exploded in the night. The homeless man leaped beside the Ford's passenger, brandishing a .45 and yelling: "Police! Don't you fucking move! Police!"

By the evergreen shrub, the driver turned, jaw open, staring back at his partner. Before he could adjust his clothing, *man with a shotgun* bounced over the knoll, that cannon pointing straight at the driver, and yelled: "Freeze! Drop it!"

The night became a kaleidoscope: police cars; whirling red and blue lights; the bum with a .45, yelling; Cole, eyes blazing; cops with blue jackets, gold letters reading MONTGOMERY COUNTY POLICE who bent the men from the Ford over the hood of their own car.

"You can't do this to us!" yelled the passenger.

"I just did," said Cole.

"You don't know who—" said the driver, then he shut up.

The Montgomery County police lieutenant showed Cole and Nick the leather ID cases and badges taken from the men in the Ford: "United States Marshal's Service."

"Gotta tell you," said the lieutenant. "Badges look real."

Cole said: "Real marshals wouldn't harass an FBI inspector."

"Uh-huh," said the lieutenant.

"I'll sign papers," said Cole. "Your ass will be covered."

"What are we supposed to charge them with?"

"Interfering with an FBI agent in performance of his duty."

"That bullshit won't walk. Besides, we're local law, not—"

"Lock them up for indecent exposure," said Nick.

"Nick, you burned up all my IOUs," said the officer, who commanded cops just across the map line from where Nick's badge ruled. "These *bandidos* have badges and a legal right to be where they were. I'm not going to bet my pension on your bullshit."

"You've got a big Bureau chit now," said Cole.

"Won't do me any good if you lose your creds tomorrow."

"Tomorrow is tomorrow. Tonight, you can legitimately haul their ass to your shop, verify who they are."

The lieutenant shook his head. "Come on, amigos. We're all going to sort this out together." The lieutenant shouted orders. His men led the two handcuffed marshals to squad cars.

Nick picked up the blanket from where he'd dropped it. "Well, at least tonight's drama proves one thing."

Cole looked at the homicide cop: His cheeks had the pallor for the bum's role, his bloodshot eyes were in character.

"Drunk or sober," said Nick, "I can cover your ass."

Through the cop's grin, Cole smelled Wint-o-green.

"**G**ive it up," Cole ordered the three men who sat across from him in a fifth-floor office of the Justice department. Outside, dawn had yet to break the darkness on that Tuesday morning.

The trio's authority flowed from the man with the grayest hair: the Assistant Attorney General, the AAG. He stared past Cole. The FBI's Assistant Director for the Criminal Investigation Division, the AD/CID, also could not meet Cole's eyes. But the Deputy Assistant Attorney General, the DAAG, glared at the FBI agent: "Last night—"

"I did my job. I stopped getting fucked last night."

"For what it's worth," said the FBI executive, "the Bureau and I didn't know you were under surveillance."

"Completely appropriate!" snapped the DAAG. "Especially after Cole's debacle in Montana, the—"

"Whose debacle?" shouted Cole.

"We're not here to apportion blame," said the DAAG.

"Of course we are," said Cole.

The DAAG said: "That surveillance was appropriate and prudent! For your own protection! What if our prime suspect targets—"

"Bullshit," said Cole. "When did you put the marshals on me? After I put out the query on that law firm?"

The AD/CID sighed, said: "Yes."

"You're protecting Yoshio Chobei," said Cole.

"No!" snapped the DAAG.

"The Japanese got you to start the antitrust probe against Faron," said Cole. "They're the ones who dropped the package on your guys at Justice, goaded the Hill. Got you guys to—"

The AAG cleared his throat: "Your perspective is flawed."

"I see just fine."

"But that's not enough," answered the AAG. "Nothing unethical or unwarranted has been done by this department or by anyone in this room regarding Mr. Faron Sears."

"There was that illegal bugging," said Cole.

"Unauthorized," said the law-and-order chief.

"But you're carrying water for—"

"Faron Sears's enterprises were troublesome for antitrust regulators and investigators long before . . ."

"Before what? Before the Yakuza came into the picture?"

"Faron Sears *is* a legitimate problem," said the presidentially appointed AAG.

"What kind of problem? Economic? Legal? Political?"

"Yes," said the AAG. "And yes, lawyers working for various Japanese interests were among those bringing evidence to our—"

"Lawyers for Sugamo Corporation," said Cole. "They manufacture the same computer products that Faron—"

"I believe," said the AAG, "that they were among the interested and affected parties who communicated and assisted—"

"You guys," said Cole. "Don't ever work the street. Can't you smell a rat burn? A crook snitching out some guy he hates?"

The DAAG said: "With maybe real stuff, real crimes. You brick agents lock up people with rat burns all the time."

"How convenient for you and your political party that the Japanese dropped the dime."

"Don't ever imply that again!" said the AAG.

"What'll you do? Have Chobei's soldiers take care of—"

The executive from the FBI said: "You're out of line, Cole!"

"Who put me there?"

"You're right," said the AAG. "This is more than casual antitrust enforcement. But Japanese interests were not our only catalysts. American sources also dimed out Faron Sears."

"What did you get for loosing the dogs on Faron?" asked Cole.

"The satisfaction of doing our job."

"Keeping him from being assassinated is my job," said Cole. "Keeping the Yakuza from increasing their clout in—"

"What are you?" snapped the DAAG. "Some kind of modern yellow-peril racist? Sugamo is a legitimate international—"

"Then why does Chobei run their show?"

"He works for Sugamo, not the other way around," said the DAAG. "And since you broke cover last night, I've read the reports, and except for alarmist knee-jerk rumors from your Bureau—"

The AAG held up his hand, said to Cole: "Do you suspect any of these elements in the plot to assassinate Faron Sears?"

"Damned if I know," said Cole. "But we have a link."

"You're damned if you fuck with—"

A glance from the man with gray hair silenced the DAAG.

"You have the authority to investigate and resolve any direct threat to the life of Faron Sears," said the AAG, "regardless of its origin, whatever or whoever may be involved. Do it."

"Not good enough," said Cole.

"*Excuse me?*" said the AAG.

"I had that after we met," said Cole. "I had that the moment I swore my oath and was accepted into the Bureau. You fucked with me once. You'll fuck with me again."

As if it were his own, Cole walked behind the AAG's desk and collected sheets of paper and a pen. He smiled at the DAAG, then told that man's boss: "I want your lap dog's head."

"Wait a minute!" cried the DAAG. He held up his hands to the gray-haired man who'd preceded him through Harvard. "I'm not—"

"You're the price," said Cole.

"For what?" asked the AAG.

"For shafting me once," said Cole. "And for me not dropping dimes on all your dirty little secrets now."

"Stop this!" shouted the DAAG. "I'm not a piece of—"

The AAG cut off his right-hand man: "Scott!"

Mentor and protégé stared at each other. The younger man blinked. Choked. Cole gave him the pen and paper.

"Write," said Cole, his voice for the DAAG, his eyes on the gray-haired man as the FBI executive kept silent and watched:

"Address it to the attorney general. Don't date it. Write: 'Because of my unprofessional conduct in multiple incidents regarding the sensitive investigation carried out under the highest directive from this department and the White House by Inspector Dalton Cole, FBI, as conveyed to you by . . .' "

And Cole named the AAG and the AD/CID sitting in the room.

". . . I hereby tender my resignation, effective upon receipt."

The DAAG choked, but his pen scratched his fate onto the paper. When the pen was silent, Cole said: "Sign it."

Cole walked to the table, read the paper over the trembling man's shoulder. He dropped an envelope on the wood.

"Put it in here. Don't seal it."

The DAAG moved like a zombie. Cole put the envelope inside his suit pocket, then glared into the DAAG's broken eyes:

"Keep your fancy title. But you don't work for them now; you work for me. You helped them fuck me. Don't let them do it again. Remember they hung you out to dry. Remember who's got your balls in his pocket—letterhead stationery, fingerprints, handwriting. Your balls, and their by-name, ratted-out ass."

Cole faced the two senior men. The office windows brightened with gray light.

"Excuse me, *gentlemen*," said Cole, "I've got a job to do."

43

Taxis in New York turned their lights on early that Tuesday afternoon. The doorman at a Fifth Avenue hotel touched his hat as three Asian businessmen drew near. The oldest of them carried a thin attaché case. His black coat hung open, as if the cold wind no longer mattered. The youngest strode ahead of his two companions. He was also the largest, barrel-chested in his topcoat, close-cropped hair and beefy cheeks. His hands were empty. Between them was a middle-aged, smooth-skinned man with carefully trimmed hair. As the old man stepped into the hotel lobby, a concierge bowed, led him toward her desk. The revolving door spun the middle man inside. He saw the old man being led away, frowned.

Cole confronted the middle man, bowed deeply, and recited the words he'd memorized and practiced with P.J. Toker on the flight from Washington: *"Konnichiwa, Chobei-san. Sumimasen ga—"*

Yoshio Chobei stared at the unknown American: *"Hai?"*

Over Chobei's shoulder, Cole saw the bodyguard spin through the revolving door. The bodyguard hesitated just long enough for P.J. to badge him. Chobei saw that transaction. When Chobei turned back to Cole, his eyes said he knew.

"Meishi o dozo." Cole offered his business card to Chobei with both hands, the card held so Chobei could read it. Chobei scanned the Japanese characters and embossed seal.

"Gomennasai," said Cole, hoping the phrases were still appropriate. *"Nihon go wa, hon no sukoshi shika shirimasen."*

"That is all right, Inspector Cole," said Chobei. "I speak a great deal of English."

"Domo," said Cole.

Chobei nodded at the bodyguard, who then followed P.J. to two chairs by the door. Chobei pocketed Cole's card.

"Perhaps you would be kind enough to join me for coffee or tea, a drink?" Cole gestured to two lobby chairs.

"Mochiron," said Chobei. *"Yorokonde."*

When Cole didn't respond, Chobei smiled: "Ahh. Your Japanese truly is limited. I apologize. I would be honored to join you."

Chobei abruptly strode past Cole to one of the chairs, sat. He smiled as Cole followed, sat across from him.

"If I may," said Chobei, "my principal—my employer—is elderly. If he could be . . . released to go to his room to rest . . ."

"This is America," said Cole. "He can go where he wants."

Chobei nodded to the old man sitting at the desk across the lobby. The old man paid his respects to the woman who had detained him, walked to the elevators, disappeared into the clouds.

"Your *teppodama* can go, too," said Cole.

"My . . . 'bullet'?" said Chobei. "I am sorry, but I must correct your Japanese. My associate is a Sugamo logistical officer."

"My slang must be imperfect."

Chobei waved his hand. "No matter. My associate waits well."

A woman took their order for coffee. When she walked away, Cole said: "Would you like to see more formal credentials?"

"Your identity has been clearly established," answered Chobei.

"As has yours."

"Then what can a mere vice president of Sugamo Industries do to assist the famous FBI?"

"It is we who may be able to assist you."

"Ahh," said Chobei. The waitress put china cups of coffee and a steaming silver pot on the table. "How might you do that?"

"You have a great interest in American politics and government—as well as commerce," said Cole.

"It would be impolite to ignore the culture of a country

that is ally and friend to my homeland. To be ignorant of the government that manages the marketplace where Sugamo participates."

"I'm not here to help you make money."

Chobei smiled. "How unfortunate."

"And I'm not here about Sugamo—not directly."

"Then . . . directly, what business do we have together?"

"Faron Sears."

"Mr. Sears is a most honored colleague in both our countries. A major and respected businessman in areas that Sugamo also—"

"Lot of people hate his guts," said Cole.

Chobei shrugged.

"Why are you stalking around the country after Faron Sears?"

"Stalking? I am not certain what that word might mean, but . . . as you said, this is a free country, a man can go where he wants."

"I said this was *America.* I didn't say it was *free.*"

Chobei sipped his coffee. "America has many things that I like. Coffee drinking—a cheap and pleasant stimulant."

"And legal. Not like some 'awakening drugs,' " said Cole, translating the slang term for the amphetamines that the Yakuza have made Japan's leading illegal-drug problem.

"I like Elvis Presley and Marilyn Monroe, too," said Chobei.

"You got a thing for dead Americans?"

"Sometimes it takes death to make us appreciate what we have."

Cole met the steady gaze of the brown eyes across from him. "What about Faron Sears?"

"Why does the FBI care? Perhaps this is a part of your American culture I misunderstand. Should I consult with one of my company's attorneys to clarify my understanding?"

"Who would have thought that Yoshio Chobei needs to run to a *gaijun* lawyer to help him talk over coffee."

"You said that the FBI might be able to assist me," said Chobei. "Your coffee has been wonderful, but my hour is late."

"I hope not too late," said Cole. "It is well known that Faron Sears's companies are business rivals of Sugamo."

"American companies control fifty-four percent of Japan's software business," said Chobei. "That means Mr. Sears's software companies are rivals of my company even in our country. As are IBM, MBD, Microsoft, Lotus, many others. Of course, their presidents have never made slanderous anti-Japanese speeches."

"He's issued a warning to his country about the Yakuza. Does that concern you?"

"What concerns me is what concerns me. And my organization."

"Do you mean Sugamo International?"

"Faron Sears peddles unfounded negative sentiments about my country. He funds political and economic groups to foster anti-Japanese sentiment. He has an ex-congressman lobbying against us on Capitol Hill, creating a political machine so *Mister* Sears can become *President* Sears, or so *Mister* Sears will have a puppet government to do his bidding. It would be irresponsible for a man in my position to ignore Mr. Sears. Such a man could be neither timid in his assessing responsibilities nor a fool in . . . executing them.

"I hope my English is correct," added Chobei—with a smile.

"Oh, I understand you. What concerns the FBI is that rivals of Mr. Sears may resort to violence."

"Yours is the world's most violent country," said Chobei.

"That's why I'm here. If Faron is harmed, trouble will target anyone who's been stalking him. Anyone who's been a rival. Anyone he's warned about. Anyone by any name."

"I see. And so your 'assistance' is . . . ?"

"Sugamo's business is welcome here," said Cole. "But."

"But what?"

Cole smiled. Then, a minute later, he said: "I hope I've made my point."

"We all have our hopes." Chobei shook his head. "So you are the famous G-men. You look much bigger and stronger in movies."

"We're tough enough in real life."

"Cool," purred Chobei.

"*Domo.*" Cole stood first, said: "The coffee's on your tab."

Chobei laughed. "Cool."

As Cole spun out the revolving door, P.J. following, he heard Chobei's fading laugh, again heard "Cool."

"Cole," said P.J. Toker as they hurried down Fifth Avenue, "whatever you're working better be worth what you've just done. Now Chobei knows we know him. Knows we're watching him and Sugamo. Makes it ten times harder to bust him and the Yak."

"We've been having *so much* luck doing that so far," said Cole.

"Can I listen to the tape?"

"Maybe someday," said Cole.

The agent riding shotgun in the BuCar bounded out as Cole and P.J. approached, opened the back door for the inspector.

"How justifiable is your intelligence on that warehouse in L.A. that you told me about?" Cole asked P.J. as the BuCar honked and nudged into traffic.

"We could maybe get a warrant," said P.J., "if the U.S. attorney promised his first-born to the judge."

"We've got a three-hour edge on the West Coast. I'll arrange a warrant. You can be in L.A. to execute it before midnight."

"Knocking over a warehouse leased in part to Sugamo Industries is a major risk," said P.J. "Diplomats and Fifth Floor at Justice . . . If we don't find ammunition and amphetamines from Mexico . . ."

"Sugamo won't complain," said Cole. "If they do, they'll get dragged into the spotlight. Chobei doesn't want that; neither does whoever's still legitimate in Sugamo.

"Listen to me, P.J.," added Cole. "On this bust, the operative word is 'bust.' Do you understand?"

They rode in silence for a moment, then P.J. said: "Guess I'm not the only one you want to understand that there are new rules."

Cole ordered lights and siren. The whirling red light added little speed to the BuCar's progress toward the airport.

Cole told P.J.: "From now until I get reverted back to special agent, aggressively pursue any and all Yakuza matters, especially Yoshio Chobei. Whatever you've got on your wish

list, call that number I gave you, you'll get it. The only rule
is, before anybody sees your intelligence product, it comes
to me."

Their driver whipped the BuCar around a slow truck and
into FDR Drive traffic.

P.J. whispered: "What the hell did you two talk about?"

Cole said: "Movies."

44

The eight o'clock shuttle from New York brought Cole back
to Washington. He climbed into the back of a waiting BuCar.

"Eight days until Valentine's Day," muttered Cole.

"Ah . . . yes, sir," said the driver, who'd been ordered to
pick up the inspector, do what he said, and ask no questions.

Cole flipped through faxes, phone messages, reports.

Checks of commercial airports in Montana and 102 passenger rosters had turned up nothing. None of the sixty-three
small private plane fields in that state had reported any flights
linked to anyone like Kurt Vance. Amtrak ran passenger trains
along the northern edge of the state. Conductors and ticket
agents remembered no one like him. Bus station canvasses
had turned up only negatives.

A motor vehicle is stolen every nineteen seconds in
America. Every stolen car report in Montana, the Dakotas,
Wyoming, and Idaho was being scrutinized to determine if its
thief could be Cole's target. Cole had even ordered missing
license plates in those six states reviewed and any unac-
counted-for numbers put on the hot sheet.

Border Patrol checkpoints from Seattle to Sault Sainte

Marie stopped every vehicle, checked every face that crossed into Canada. Mounties watched for a new man on their soil.

Each long-distance call made from Kurt Vance's number in the last three years was scrutinized. He had called mail-order houses for computer equipment, underground books on everything from creating a new identity to knife fighting and Special Forces manuals. Hours of calls from him were logged onto a Montana gateway to the Internet. The ponytailed hackers hunted Vance in cyberspace.

Every credit card registered to Kurt Vance was keyed into an alert system: the FBI would know where and when they were used two minutes after a clerk electronically scanned the card.

Hunting fugitives means tracking their connections to the real world. Normal crooks call relatives, contact friends, slip into patterns of purchases and associations that searchers can keep checking until they find their quarry's trail.

But you're not normal, Vance, thought Cole. No family, no friends, no known associates.

You're supposed to kill him here, thought Cole, staring out the BuCar window at the night-lit Capitol dome. Supposed to do it close. Supposed to do Faron *before* somebody else. *Why?*

Forensics experts lifted enough fingerprints from un-charred surfaces and broken cups in the Choteau house to build a set that "in all probability" matched the digits on Kurt Vance's hands.

Touch something, Vance. Something that some cop in Anywhere, America, will print and run through the FBI.

Six hundred thousand local, state, and federal law enforcement officers were on alert for Kurt Vance. *So many hunters chasing one running phantom. There'll be a thousand false stops. And each mistake will make the hunters less likely to risk the hassle of another citizen wrongly detained. Each mistake will clog the system while it gets checked out.*

You need money, thought Cole, *cash. Hold up a 7-Eleven, get shot by a quick-trigger state trooper. Mug some black belt like Sallie, end up handcuffed to an emergency-room gurney. Step into the open. Just for a moment. Enough time, all these resources targeted for a hit, nobody could escape. If we have enough time.*

The BuCar driver let Cole out two blocks from Faron's headquarters. Inside that fortress, the door to Faron's office was shut. Lauren's door was open, and Cole looked in.

A lamp dropped white light to the polished wood of her desk. She sat facing the window of night, and her eyes were closed.

Softly, he said: "Am I disturbing you?"

Lauren's eyes flicked open and she smiled: "The traditional way to break the spell is with a kiss."

"These days that could get you sued."

"Maybe," she said as he sat across from her desk.

"Why are you here so late?"

"Waiting to be awakened." They laughed. She said: "Where have you been?"

"New York."

"Did Faron send you there?"

"Yeah," lied Cole.

"You two and your secrets."

"All of us seem to have them." Cole shifted in his chair. "Everywhere I go, I get tossed questions about what you're doing."

"Me?"

"In the corporate sense."

"Glad you're not discussing my personal life."

"I don't know much about your personal life."

She held her palms up to the ceiling. "It's all right here."

"No, you've got a new apartment—"

"Filled with boxes—"

"With not much in them."

"Good memory," she said. "What else can you do?"

"I thought I was the one who knew how to ask questions."

"You just need practice."

"What are you, some kind of expert?"

She shrugged. "My father was a kind of cop."

"What kind?"

"The asshole kind. Made it easy to write him off."

"You wouldn't do that," said Cole.

Lauren shrugged. "Call it stepping back. I let him have his life; he did what he could for mine."

"Doesn't sound so bad."

"Bad depends on where you start from. He's gone now; I let him rest in peace. What questions do you keep hearing that you want me to answer?"

"What about Faron's Chicago project? He bought a whole ghetto."

"Not a whole ghetto: only seven square blocks—not counting the schools, a few public buildings, a public park."

"His deal is . . . ?"

"Busting poverty from the inside out. He's the landlord for eleven hundred adults. He made his tenants 'investment partners.' They can buy their homes from him. Most don't have jobs, so he's building a computer factory in the heart of their dead zone. Employee-owned, managed by his company. Skilled and educated labor required. All employees must be 'investment partners'—which means they must live in the neighborhood. 'Investment partners' can sign up for adult education and training programs he's put in the local school. We figure it will take three years to train the average resident: reading, writing, and 'rithmetic, plus computers, government, law, logic, philosophy, history, health, consumer smarts. Lots of tutors, but if they don't pass, they don't qualify to work. Their future will be up to them, and attainable by them."

"With a little help from Faron."

"Corner stores, neighborhood businesses, we own them. Entrepreneurs who want their own thing need only apply, come up with the plan, come up with the money—which our credit union will loan them. And, of course, be an 'investment partner.' "

"Who lives in the ghetto."

"Residency checked back to before Faron announced his plan. No carpetbaggers allowed. No invisible landlords or bosses. He's moved in medical programs, counseling, home improvement squads for the old public housing—"

"His own cops."

"Local residents, trained by us, augmented by our security people, riding with Chicago police and deputized by Cook County: community police controlled by resident participation. Paid for by the rent roll or mortgage payments. No more outside occupying force. Straight out of the ancient history Black Panther manual."

"Guys with guns who owe their loyalty to . . . ?"

Lauren shook her head: "What's your problem here?"

"I worry about guys with guns."

"They're reputable professionals subcontracted from a reputable firm. There to keep the peace, like any cop. When you put on a badge, you're a peace officer, not an angel of justice."

"Faron must have made a lot of enemies doing this."

"The Machine is trying to eat at the trough; plus they're worried about power shifts, but basically, who would hate a man who's bringing billions in business into town?"

"That street preacher, for one. Did Monk find him yet?"

She smiled. "What else is on your mind tonight?"

"Leibowitz: Do you know what he's doing?"

"Keeping the Feds off our back. Competition legislation. Technical issues. Coordinating Faron's crus—our Movement, working with the mainline politicians. Why?"

"I heard him accused of Jap-bashing."

"Who?" she said. "Leibowitz or Faron?"

"Where does one man's plans end and another man's ambitions begin?"

"Leibowitz won't fuck Faron," said Lauren.

"So everything he's doing . . ."

"Don't ask me about everything. I only know what I know. Faron decides that. We're all free-wheeling planets around his sun."

"You're no computerized satellite."

"Gee, thanks." Lauren flicked her gaze past Cole.

"What about the Japanese?"

"Faron's got nothing special against them. He's out to change everybody, regardless of race, creed, or color."

"They cut into your—into his—business market."

"They try." Her eyes measured him. "Tell me your secrets. Tell me what you're doing for us."

"That's coming together," said Cole.

"Yeah, I've noticed how diligent that Sallie is about being at work. More so than others in her firm."

"I'll be around more."

"Look forward to it."

Cole quickly said: "Do you really think he can turn things around in Chicago? Especially for the kids?"

"He did it for himself. You get to kids early, who knows what they can grow up to be."

"You think about kids much?" he asked.

"No," she said. "I don't."

Cole said: "Me either."

45

Monk drove D.C.'s streets. Sallie rode with him.

"Check it out." Monk nodded toward three boys huddled on the street: "Wednesday, not even ten A.M. They 'bout sixteen. This is their school. See the bro in the car across the street? He gives the nod to OK the customer; one of the runners goes to the stash. Takes the fall if it's a bust, a short count for a juvie."

"You know a lot about the dope business," said Sallie.

"It ain't a business; it's a way of life."

"It's the end of life," answered Sallie.

"Guess you been listening to Faron."

"Can't you give me credit for anything?" she said.

Monk stared out the windshield at the road he drove. "I give you more credit than you know, girl."

"Then stop calling me 'girl.' "

The giant behind the wheel looked at her. "Bad habit. Sorry."

"OK," said Sallie. *Opening, he's open. Start easy, innocent.* "How come you call yourself 'Monk' instead of your real name?"

He smiled: "*Arthur James* sounds like some kinda English butler."

"Before football, were you going to be a priest?"

He laughed and they turned a corner. "Hell, before football, I was just another skinny parish boy with Coca-Cola skin and eggshell eyes. White boys where I had to walk to catch the school bus, they'd throw rocks, call me *Monkey*. 'Here comes da Monk!' Took that name, made it my own. Now I'm kind of used to it."

"Why are we driving in circles?" she asked.

"Check the neighborhood. Make sure it's cool."

"You think someone will try to hurt Faron?"

"I did," whispered Monk.

The car cruised past the high school.

"What do you mean?" said Sallie.

"This ain't something I talk about."

"Bullshit. You're too smart to let that slip out if you didn't want me to ask."

He glanced at her. "All the time you been spending with Faron, he never told you 'bout him 'n' me?"

"No."

"Guess he's respecting my privacy."

"That's the kind of man he is."

Monk's eyes touched her as he turned the car right: "Yeah."

"Tell me," she said, knowing that every request creates a debt. *This is my job; this is what Cole requires.*

"When I stopped being a football jersey, I signed up to be a junkie. That needle gives you the 'no more's': no more money, no more knee pain, no more regrets, no more terrifying tomorrows. From linebacker to mugger, quick trip. Edge of the Quarter one night, saw a dude who looked like he had cash that *belonged* in my arm."

Tires cried as the car skidded round a corner. Inertia pulled Sallie to one side.

"Faron looked right through me. Nobody has eyes like that."

Monk didn't see Sallie nod; she didn't realize she did.

"Like I was a pane of glass," continued Monk. "He said, *'You can have what you can't steal.'* Then he walked away, and those eyes made me let him go. But he looked back. Waited for me."

"You followed him," said Sallie.

"That ain't the heart of it: I found *my* way. He just helped. Then . . . now, I help him so maybe somebody else, those kids . . ."

"You're not so tough after all," she said.

"Got to be tougher now than I was on the field. That was just pain and sweat. Out here is real. Alone."

"I know," she said.

A red light stopped the car.

"You do," he said. "You do."

Green light. The car rolled forward. The air was thick.

"Are we going there now?" asked Sallie. "I mean, straight?"

"We got time." Monk drew a breath to say something, but then had to concentrate on a car jumping out from the curb.

"What you've done," said Sallie. "You should be proud."

"That's not important now," he said as he eased off the brake.

"Amazing," she said.

"What?"

"Faron," said Sallie.

Monk held the steering wheel straight.

She said: "What he can do to you with just a look. Get you to . . . move. Follow. Go where you . . . Amazing."

She heard herself; quickly looked away. Monk lowered his window. Cold air rushed into the car.

"Yeah," he said. Then he whispered: "Oh, well."

A block later, he parked the car in front of a high school. As they shut their doors on opposite sides of the vehicle, Sallie said: "Are you worried about someone trying to hurt Faron?"

Monk snapped: "Look around you, girl. Name this country."

"No," she said. "Something in particular has you worried."

"My business is taking care of business," he said as they walked toward the school doors. "Making sure what's what and whatever is supposed to be is where it belongs."

"This is a school," said Sallie as she pulled open the front door. "Try telling me that in English."

"Not your business, *Ms.* Pickett. Don't worry about it. Don't worry about a thing." He nodded to metal detectors mounted in the hall: " 'Less you carrying a weapon I don't know about."

"Not today," said Sallie.

Sallie followed him through the metal detectors, turned down the deserted corridor toward the auditorium—

And saw *Mrs. Sparrow* walking toward them. Sophomore English, *made me do extra credit for an A,* must have transferred here from Duke Ellington High. *She never forgot a face.* Coming closer—Sallie grabbed Monk's arm, snuggled her forehead into his massive, tensing bicep as she turned her face away from the woman whose heels clicked by them on the ammoniaed school tiles. Sallie held on until the echoes faded. Only then did she feel Monk trembling.

"Monk, I . . . I had something in my eye, couldn't see. I didn't mean to grab you like that."

"Let go."

She felt him swallow. And hated herself for her grip.

Briinggg! Doors banged open, voices clamored, teenagers swarmed into the hall and swept Sallie and Monk into their midst.

Sallie hid backstage among the volunteers and security people as the high school principal introduced Faron. She applauded with the crowd when he said that he was creating a college scholarship for each of the school's top twenty graduates.

Faron took a drink from the water glass on the podium, took the microphone to the edge of the stage, and sat down.

"When I was in high school," he told the students, "I had bad answers to the right questions. You've had the benefit of watching my generation screw up, of walking through doorways where there used to be bars. I hear how smart and cool and together you are. So I figure this is my chance to hear today's high school questions—straight from you."

The auditorium was silent. Someone giggled, then so did others. Then came silence. Coughing. Seats creaking. Backstage, the principal stepped toward the curtain, only to be stopped by Monk's hand. "He's paid for the time."

Silence and more silence until, from the sea of all black teenage faces, a boy called out: "How much money you got, man?"

Laughter rang through the crowd.

"Doesn't matter," said Faron.

"That's easy for you to say; you got it!"

"And you know what that makes me to a lot of this world?"

Nobody answered.

"A rich nigger," said Faron.

"When you all talk about me, you call me nigger. I know it. You know it. Be smarter than that. I hear you bitching about how white people keep you down. Yet, all the time, I hear you using a slave owner word for people with skin like us. You talk about 'disrespecting' and 'pride' out of one side of your mouth, then, out of the other side, you disrespect yourself and your parents and seventeen thousand people lynched down South and Dr. King and Malcolm—all by calling somebody, anybody, nigger.

"If you call me nigger," said Faron. "Be sure you're sitting out there and I'm way up here."

Again laughter rippled through the crowd. Sallie felt electricity in that ripple. She peeked around the curtain at the sea of teenagers: *Where was Mrs. Sparrow?*

A girl's voice spoke from the audience: "It's just, you know."

"No, I don't know. Do you?"

"It's like our thing, man! Our Black Thing!"

"Justifying slavers and racists and lynchers is your idea of 'a Black Thing'? Language is power! If you brand the racist term on yourself, on your friends, or even on your enemies, then you help the racists."

"What the hell you call yourself?!"

"Faron Sears. And that means what I make it mean, every day."

"We're African Americans!"

Scattered applause sounded from the teenagers.

"Hell," said Faron, "I'm from Chicago. I'm a full-blooded native American."

The crowd laughed.

"My ancestors were stolen from Africa. Whipped and chained, treated like cattle. Who they were is part of me—but just part.

"THIS IS MY COUNTRY!" Faron's outburst shook the audience. "I will not surrender my birthright! America is as much mine as it was JFK's!"

Someone in the audience hissed: "Damn!"

"Be proud of where you came from, of what your people had to endure to survive. But don't chase after some mystical identity from somewhere else so that the nation you were born in can be stolen out from under your feet—again!"

The kids glanced at each other, their faces conflicted.

Faron said: "There's something I don't understand. I was in an L.A. high school, talked to a girl. Black girl. Smart, wants to be a lawyer like the woman who served in Congress and helped break up the Watergate crew. You know what this girl told me?"

The audience hung on Faron's words.

"She said that every time she got A's, every time she carried books outside the classroom, her 'sisters' would bust on her, ask her why she was trying to be white.

"What are you going to tell her?" Faron demanded. "You going to tell her that being black means being uneducated? That all black women are good for is making babies and bottom-dollar checks? You going to tell her she's a bitch or a whore or a nigger—not a person? That her brothers are only good for shooting hoops or beefing with guns over dope that kills and money that don't care? That being smart and doing well in our world where there are a hundred colors of skin is something that only white people can do? You going to tell her that? That's what the white Nazi Klan racists tell her. Whose side are you on?"

"Yo, man, chill!"

But before the audience's laughter could crest, Faron yelled: "I'll chill when I die!"

Faron shook his head: "One of the best musicians in this world is black. The man plays jazz out of our black streets that'll make your bones shake. Plays Mozart and makes the world sigh.

"But his heart's broken—just like that girl's. He goes into schools, works with people like you who front out that they want to be musicians. But they tell him they won't practice scales and chords because that's how white people do it— never mind him or Duke Ellington. So what comes out of their horns is lame, but they figure hey, boom boxes will give them a beat. Boxes made in Hong Kong, programmed by Singapore technocrats. Black people invented that beat—why surrender it now?"

Sallie glanced around the curtain: Mrs. Sparrow was walking down the side aisle, toward the stairs leading backstage.

"Being smart isn't being white or Chinese. It's being smart. You can be whoever you've got the guts, brains, talent, luck, and sweat work to be: doctor, mechanic, lawyer, mayor, corporate boss, cop, president, nurse, opera star, sales clerk, mechanic, mother, father.

"I came here to help those of you who put it on the line and do the best you can with what you got. But I got this sick feeling that too many of you are sitting out there being cool, busting on our brothers and sisters who use their brains to plug into the universe. If that's you, you're working with the Klan.

"Don't let someone put you in a box. Doesn't matter if it's a prison cell with bars or a jive-sell that's built with words—a box is a coffin. And the next time anyone tells you that being successful or being smart is being white, they're putting you in a box. They ain't your brothers or sisters, they're assholes. And they're shitting all over you."

Backstage, the principal hissed: "We spend our days trying to get them not to talk like that, then he comes along . . ."

"Maybe them getting it rough will help them get it right," said Monk.

"Where you get off telling us what to do?" yelled a voice in the audience. "You ain't us!"

Faron sat in their glare for almost a minute. Then he stood, walked to the podium. Turned back to the audience. "That's true."

The mike clunked as he set it on the podium. He picked up the water glass, flung the water out to the stage.

The principal said: "What the—"

Faron broke the polished top off the glass in his right hand and with its jagged rim slashed his left palm.

Screams cut through the audience. Scores of kids bolted out of their chairs. Sallie's stomach collapsed.

Faron held his bloody palm out to the crowd. A crimson line trickled down his wrist, dripped to the stage. "This blood flows through you!"

The audience trembled in silence.

"Our blood binds us together. As unique and separate as we are, white, black, Chinese, man, woman, young, old, our blood runs the same, looks the same, works the same, needs the same."

Everyone in the auditorium saw the steady crimson drip, drip, drip on the stage.

"How can any man speak for another man? Any man speak for a woman? Any black speak for a Chicano or an Irishman? I can't speak *for* you, and speaking *to* you is arrogant power. But our blood is the same, and we can and must speak *with* each other. I can't tell you what to do. I'm just laying out what you already know so you can see it through another set of eyes.

"America is our country, but if we're black—and most of you are . . ."

The crowd laughed—nervously, eyes on the dripping blood.

". . . you got a harder time staying alive in it and walking where you want to than some blonde from Sweden. That's not fair, that's not right, but that's the truth—or am I wrong?"

A chorus of voices sang out: "No!"

"I don't have to tell you about racism. The 'Whites Only' bathrooms when I was a boy are gone now, but walk down a Georgetown street some summer night, you can feel and hear and see racism!"

"Yeah!" yelled a dozen young men in the audience.

"But do you know what the two leading killers of young black men are today? Murder and AIDS. They don't come from just white men. They come from us, too. And if the only thing we blame for that is white people, then we're saying, 'We just poor, ignorant, black folks'—always victims, never victors."

The audience was silent.

"I will never lose my anger at the racism I have seen and I have suffered in this country. I will never forget the horrors people have suffered and still suffer today because of the color of their skin. I will never forget my anger, because if I do, that means I've surrendered to the evils that created my anger, and as long as this blood flows through me, I will never surrender!"

The audience roared.

"But . . . I learned something from people who were smarter than me and paid for that wisdom with their lives. We have got to stop letting the racists make us think like them. Dr. King knew that. Malcolm knew that. You know it, too.

"We've got no choice. If we embrace racism, racism embraces us. If we forget the rainbows in our blood, we will lose our blood. If we hate or disrespect something or someone by calling it honky or chink or wop or whatever, then we're tattooing 'nigger' on our foreheads. If we don't use every affirmative means at our disposal to be our best, than we deny who were truly are. If we let racists define us, then they win. If they win today, bad as it was when Mississippi trees hung with bitter fruit, it will be nothing compared to the hell to come."

He turned his back to the audience, started to walk off stage. Someone clapped, but as other hands joined the applause, Faron whirled back: "You asked about my money."

The audience snapped to attention.

"I'm richer than I imagined possible in high school. But not because of the money. I'm rich because I'm free—inside and out. I'm rich because I'm nobody's nigger."

Then he snapped off the mike, walked backstage before the applause filled the auditorium. Sallie pulled a scarf off her neck, wrapped it around his bleeding hand.

"Thank you," said Faron as his blood darkened the silk.

"You were . . ." What, she couldn't say. Sallie saw Monk watching, saw him look away.

"Ah, Mr. Sears," said the principal, "our nurse is—"

"This is nothing." He closed his hand around Sallie's scarf.

"I know you must leave," said the principal, "but some of the teachers waiting by the door out there would like to . . . Well, maybe not shake your hand, but thank you."

"Other way around," he said.

"You funded the excellence awards for them."

"They're the ones who have to earn it."

The clamor of departing students filtered through the curtain. Faron looked at Sallie. "Would you come with me?"

"Go on," she said as Nguyen materialized at Faron's side. *Safe enough with Nguyen, safe enough here. Don't have my gun. And Mrs. Sparrow* . . . "I've got work to do back at the office."

Faron smiled: "Monk? Will you make sure she gets back OK?"

Monk let her fill his eyes. "Sure. No problem."

In the War Room across town, Nick told Cole: "Ricki's gone."

"What?" said Cole, putting down his briefcase.

Nick dropped the faxed report on the table between them. He rubbed the bridge of his nose, popped another Life Saver.

"Last night. Surveillance team followed her to the roadhouse. Come eleven P.M., the bartender starts to leave. Ricki's car ain't moved. Your two FBI guys badge their way inside. Bar is dark. Juke box playing. Nobody there, nobody in the bathroom. By the time they run back outside, her TransAm is gone. She back-doored them."

Cole said: "What about the bugs?"

"After midnight, Slawson boils over. Calls Eiger, screams 'bout how he knows what the bitch is doing. Eiger races over to the compound. Slawson is mad dog pissed off. The tapes sound like he swung on Eiger but was too wired to connect. He and Eiger stayed up all night yelling and waiting. Come morning, they drove 'round town together looking for her. By the time they got back to the compound, they'd started to worry that we'd picked her up."

"Did they go to the bar?"

"Soon as it opened. From what we picked up, Eiger and

Slawson bought the story your boys hammered the bartender into selling: that she'd been there, but that she'd left alone.

"In the bar," said Nick, "Ricki changed a twenty for quarters, fed the juke box and tipped the bartender to let it run out that night. The same song playing over and over."

"What song?"

"Buddy Holly: 'Rave On.' "

"What?"

"Something 'bout: 'saving your love for me.' "

"I know the song," said Cole.

"Oh yeah? Who do you suppose she was playing it for?"

"I don't care," said Cole.

"Sure," said Nick. He needed a shave. Smelled. "What do you want to do about your girlfriend? APB?"

"Let her run. She's got nothing to do with us. If we look for her, we'll stir up dust for Eiger and Slawson to follow. Ricki's got enough shadows chasing her."

"Wonder where she'll go." Sarcasm sharpened Nick's words.

"What is this, Nick?"

"We call it work where I come from." He shoved a file from his side of the table to Cole's. "That security company that Jeff Wood owns. Surveillance photos of the Pennsylvania site. Driving track, shooting ranges, barracks, classrooms. Plans filed with the county showed a lot of electrical customizing. Your TSD deduces a shitload of computers in there. Our ex-soldier's building himself a brand new army: high-tech *and* hand grenades."

"I'm not worried about Jeff Wood right now."

"Come on, Cole. Come on, *partner.* Spit it out."

"You're drunk."

"Not now. Not on duty. Or do you mean '*a* drunk'?"

"What are you trying to prove, Nick?"

"I got nothing to prove to nobody as long as I do my job."

"And where's all this *doing* taking you?"

"Long as I get there," said Nick, "it ain't your problem."

Cole picked up his briefcase to leave. "You know what, Detective Sherman? You're right."

Sallie and Faron were in his office that afternoon when a volunteer knocked on his door: "Faron, there's trouble downstairs with a guy who says he knows you!"

"Coming," said Faron, moving from behind his desk.

"No!" Sallie stayed him with her hand. "My job. You stay . . ."

Faron said: "I didn't come to Washington to hide."

"That's not what this is about."

"Sure it is." He smiled. "I'll be—"

"You'll be two steps straight behind me."

As they strode toward the stairs, he told her: "I like following you."

Her heart pounded. She dried her palms on her slacks. *With no gun, you've got two choices: get close to the threat fast, or put your body between Faron and . . .*

They saw the tableau in the entryway hall from the stairs: Monk, Nguyen, and the guard with a crew cut made an electric circle around a disheveled Nick Sherman. Nick's eyes burned. He held Monk's bulk in the corners of his grin, said: "Never happen. You ain't fast enough. None of you . . . fast enough.

"Well damn me all to hell," said Nick when he spotted Faron coming down the stairs. "It's the great man himself."

Faron stepped around Sallie: "He's OK. He's a friend of mine."

"See?" With a sweep of his arms, Nick stepped toward Faron. The electric circle flowed with him. The stench of Scotch filled the room. "Been telling 'em that, but your boys don't know how to listen. They think they got brawn *and* brains."

Monk's eyes rode Nick. Monk told Faron: "Say the word."

"I'm glad you're here," Faron told Nick. "Glad you came."

"Don't shit a shitter." Nick laughed alone. "Why would you be glad I came? You think *I'm* glad I came? You think I want to be here, you son of a bitch?"

"Yes, you want to be here."

"Why the hell I wanna be a dumb-ass son-of-a-bitching, blow-my-life-away thing like that, huh?"

"Because you've started winning."

Nick staggered. Nguyen and Monk stepped closer . . . froze when Nick rooted, shot a finger at them: "You ain't got me dead yet, you can't touch me."

Please, God, prayed Sallie, *this isn't happening, snatch me away, don't let—*

"You think this looks like I'm *winning?*" Nick told Faron.

"This looks like you're drunk as hell."

"Wow," said Nick. "You should be a detective. Save the world with a piece of tin . . . fuck up real good, 'stead of just being Jesus."

"Jesus forgives sins. I don't."

"So what the hell good are you?"

Faron said: "You came here to find out. And you're not as drunk as you think."

"You got no idea what I think!"

"Yes, I do."

"Put up or shut up, bro," said Nick. "You ain't got—"

"Come on." Faron turned, nodded toward the stairs. "You're here to see me put up or shut up. So do the same. Come on."

Faron turned his back to Nick, started up the stairs. Nick blinked. Flicked his eyes at Sallie, then stumbled after Faron. Monk dodged in front of Sallie, marched behind Nick. She took the middle of the stairs, blocked the other two bodyguards. Their procession climbed the stairs to Faron's meditation room.

"No," said Monk. "You ain't going in there alone with him."

"It's OK, Monk," said Faron.

"Yeah . . . *Monk.*"

Sallie sensed the ex-linebacker's muscles tighten.

"He ain't going nowhere with you unless I pat him down first!"

"Try, and I'll blow you a kiss!" said Nick. "I'll blow you the hardest kiss in the world before your hands—"

"The room's empty," Faron told Nick. "Are you going to talk about being tough, or are you going to lead me through that door?"

Through the open door, Sallie saw afternoon sunlight prismed by the stained-glass skylight into a rainbow of blue and pink.

Nick said: "You don't tell me where to go."

"The door's open," said Faron. "Your choice."

Something flashed on Nick's face, a haunted look, fear, the eyes of a deer flashing where had been the eyes of a wolf. Nick shook himself. Forced a smile. "Long as we got that straight."

As Nick shuffled into the room, Faron turned to Sallie. His touch on her arm was light, gentle.

"It's OK." He smiled just for her. "Come see me tonight."

"*OK*," she said. "*Yes,*" she said.

Faron stepped into the room, shut the door.

The *clunk* of the shutting door shook Nick, but he kept his eyes on the far wall and the rainbow shaft of sunlight.

"She did good, didn't she?" Nick muttered to the wall. "Sallie. Held her mud. Rolled with the play and did her job. I used to be like that."

"What are you now?" Faron said behind him.

"Showing up here, now, drunk—that kind of says it all."

"That doesn't say much. It's like the bang from a gun. The sound is just the sound."

"What do you know about guns?" With a blur, Nick filled his hand with his .45.

Faron told him: "John Dillinger said never trust a woman or an automatic pistol."

"Yeah, well, we dropped him in Chicago 'fore you were born."

"Before *we* were born. So what's special about your steel?"

"It's mine," said Nick.

"Can I see it?"

"You can see it from back there."

"Why did you take it out if you didn't want me to have it?"

"My gun, my piece, my pistol, my . . . Almost 30 years, most every day I strapped on steel."

"And a badge." Faron stepped beside the man who wouldn't face him. "I know about you."

"You don't know nothing about me."

"I know you're a great cop. I know you're a drunk."

Nick cocked the pistol. Slowly, so slowly, Nick rolled his head to look at Faron. "You were right about one thing. You being black didn't warm my heart."

"Me being black isn't supposed to touch your heart at all."

"You always got an answer, don't you?" The gun hung in Nick's grip. "Then tell me, how many people can you be at the same time?"

"I'm always just me."

"You talk about 'always' like you know something about it. Day I met my wife, knew I'd always love her. But she's dead, Jack, dead and gone—*that's* always."

"That's now, not always. She's just dead. It's not like she never was."

Nick waved the cocked gun: "You think I'm afraid of dying?"

"Nobody in this room is."

Nick rolled his gaze around the closed room. "Got a world of nothing in here. Don't even have a chair for a man to sit down."

"A man can stand in here. You're doing just fine."

The gun wiggled between them.

"Don't tell me how I'm doing," said Nick. "You don't know."

Faron asked: "How many people can you be at the same time?"

Nick scowled, shuffled closer. "What do you—"

"It's your question. You answer it."

Nick looked away.

"Start where it starts," said Faron.

Nick rubbed his brow with his empty hand. "God, I need to sit down, rest, stop . . ."

"Later. Soon."

"Do you hear anything?" asked Nick. "I don't now, but . . . Grandma died in the old folks' home on the reservation. Mom kept Dad moving around so we wouldn't, so I wouldn't have to be a *breed*. Grandma was supposed to die when she was little, same year Edison made electricity work in houses. Trail of Tears, running with Little Wolf's band . . . Oklahoma, Nebraska, north, snow. She told me about terror, hearing horses chasing her and . . . men in blue suits who hunted good people to kill them."

"That's not what you do," said Faron.

Nick looked at him.

"Show me your gun."

And Nick raised it between them.

"That's not the correct way to pass a weapon."

With schooled habit, Nick put the safety on. Faron took the gun. Nick gave no sign he noticed, his eyes far away as he mumbled: "Sometimes . . . I hear the horses and I'm running, sometimes I'm on the horse and screaming and *hungry to get them* and . . ."

"OK, you're OK."

"I'm on that killing ride. Doesn't matter which, who I am, Cheyenne or white, on the horse or running, terrible blood screaming . . . I can't keep living that killer ride."

"You are the runner in the snow," said Faron, "and you are the hunter on horseback."

"That's tearing me apart!"

"Booze won't help. Lying about it won't help." Faron held the gun between them. "A bullet won't help."

Nick whispered: "You can't help either."

"That's right. The world will chase you, shoot you, hurt you. Don't hide—from them, from horses pulling a hundred different ways inside you. Booze won't hide you; neither will hiding from ghosts. We're all crazy; we're all scared. Sometimes, we're all faking it. The trick is to know that, and to keep going."

Nick Sherman blinked, turned round and round in that room where invisible sunlight split into colors. Tears cut his cheeks.

"Worked all my life to get here," said Nick, "to be able to do something this important . . . to be able to fuck it up, stumble in here and . . . fuck myself out of it real good so I wouldn't be . . ."

He shook his head. "I got nowhere to go, nothing left."

Faron aimed the gun between Nick's eyes—

Nick stumbled away from the .45's bore.

And Faron smiled: "But you stepped back."

Faron slid the ammunition magazine out of the gun, jerked the slide back and snapped a cartridge through the air. The shell clattered on wood. Faron let the slide *clack* home, picked the bullet off the floor, weighed it in his hand. He put that bullet in his pocket. Then slapped the magazine back in the gun, reached inside Nick's suit coat and snapped the weapon in its holster.

"If you've got nothing left," said Faron, "you get to start all over."

As soon as Sherry stepped into the Chicago hotel room, she knew this would be a hard trick. Guy looked out the blood-sky window instead of paying attention to the business he bought.

"Honey," she said, "I'm over here. Ain't nothing coming out there but the big dark."

"Do you know what day it is?" he says, looking at the glass.

"Honey, we don't get down to business, that sun's gonna set all the way come up again and then, trust me, sugar, it will be Thursday. Right now, we be wasting time."

"In one week it will be Valentine's Day." He smiled.

"Hey, babe: you wanna make a V-Day date, pay me an advance. Sherry's a popular girl, and, like, cards and flowers and candy are nice, but cash makes me burn all over."

"Would you please lock the door?"

Sherry rolled her eyes, but fastened the chain, slid the old-fashioned bolt through its catch, too.

"Don't worry," she told her customer. "Vice would need twenty minutes to bust the door. Gives us plenty of time."

"Time is completely on my side."

"Yeah, well, time is what you pay for, and . . . sugar, what's this on the table? Some weird typewriter?"

"It's a portable laptop computer."

"Still in its plastic—like a rubber." Her customer didn't laugh, but, like, who cared: "Speakin' o' which, everybody gots to wear safes. I ain't got no problem, but we just met. Maybe a couple more dates, you can freewheel it, but now, safe is safe, right?"

"My motto exactly."

"Damn right . . . honey, what the hell is this! You got this thing handcuffed to the table! You think it's gonna run away?"

Finally, he turned around: "You never know."

"Where'd you get it?"

"At a mall. You can buy many, many things at a mall."

"Speaking of buying, I got a purse over there."

"Yes, I saw you carrying it when you drove up and parked, got out to work the street." He walked toward her. Smiled. "I like your earrings—big, shiny, gold. They catch the eye."

"How'd you know Carmen? You date her?"

"No, she's too short for me. But I saw you talking to her, and when she walked around the block, I paid her five dollars for your name."

Sherry stepped back to check him out again, eyeball to eyeball. "She really say I'd do you like you want?"

"For five dollars, Carmen would probably say anything."

"No shit, but just so we's straight, I ain't into no freak. Least, nothing cheap."

"I have enough cash. You do, too."

"Whach you mean?"

"You've had a busy day."

"My manager, Magic, the Mob-connected guy? You been around town, you'd heard of him . . ."

"I'm not from around here."

"Yeah, some cowboy plate on your car."

"Wisconsin isn't a cowboy state. It's east of there."

"Whatever. My guy Magic, he won't take no shit on him or us from nobody nowhere."

"He hasn't been by to pick up your take for what, two tricks?"

"My business . . . *my business*. Now what you want?"

"Everything I need."

"You got the right girl. And save up for Valentine's Day. If I like a guy, I get sentimental . . . know what I mean?"

"Sentiment is expensive."

Hurry him up, she thought, walked closer: "Honey, what did you say your name was?"

Her world exploded with black fire. When she could think again, see, she realized the creep had handcuffed her to the bed, her hands up behind her around the bedposts' steel. Handcuffs bit each of her ankles and chained her feet spread wide toward the foot the bed. Duct tape over her mouth trapped her scream.

"Shh," he said, "it's OK. You don't need to worry."

Sherry rattled the handcuffs, bounced on the bed, couldn't scream. Creep's going through my purse! Taking the cash! All my important papers! Fucking take-off artist, Magic'll beat my ass . . .

No, OK, just that. Just a take-off fuck. He'll do me, walk. OK, I'll be OK, he'll uncuff me, push me out . . .

OK, OK. No street talk about no psychos: wouldn't be me.

Never be me, this shit, yeah, comes with—not me. Never me. Opening a new briefcase, he's taking out—oh shit oh shit shit shit *straight razor*!

"But I'm afraid your dress just won't work." He leaned over the bed, the razor—

Slit her dress. Cut it off. Cut off her bra—oh shit the razor steel's *cold*; it's touching my—cut off her panties.

Don't look at the bright steel razor.

"I like your earrings." He took them off. Undressed and Sherry saw he was *ready*. From a paper sack, he took an ugly orange jumpsuit, baby powder, doctor's gloves.

Look out the window, just *look out the window*; turn your eyes out the window, night swallowing the burning red-cloud sky—*THIS ISN'T HAPPENING TO ME!*

The creep put on the orange jump suit, the doctor's gloves,

climbed on the bed and straddled Sherry's thighs: *God, he's heavy!*

"You asked me my name . . ."

Sherry couldn't take her eyes off his rubber-sheathed hand that held the razor.

"Let's see if we can't create a *fascinating* answer."

"Forget about what you might have done," Cole told Sallie when she scrambled a rendezvous at Union Station. "Do you know what they said or did? Do you know where Nick went?"

"No," she told him. "They were alone about an hour. Then I saw Nick walk downstairs alone. When I looked for Faron, Monk told me he was unavailable."

"Nick's not answering his beeper or cell phone," said Cole.

"Are you afraid that he . . ."

"There's too much to be afraid of."

They sat at a cafe table in Union Station's vast main hall. Commuters streamed inside to catch trains home where it was safe and they were happy and they were loved.

"Do you think Nick blew our cover?" asked Cole.

"No. At least, not yet. Vance's inside man will figure that Nick was just another one of Faron's lost souls."

"What are you going to do about him?" she asked. "About this?"

"I don't know."

"I like him," she'd said. "I like him a lot."

"Me, too."

"That doesn't matter, does it?"

"Yes," said Cole. "That makes it terrible."

Cole insisted on ordering her a burger: *You have to stay strong*. Then he pushed himself to his feet. "I gotta go."

"Do you think you'll find him?" she'd asked.

"Relax for awhile," he'd told her. "You're working tonight. Did Faron say why he wanted you to come back, what he wants?"

"No. We were just talking when—"

"Yeah," said Cole. "You better go see him."

"If you think so," she said.

She went home to her apartment. Stared at her window: Don't think. Relax. Sallie rolled her head. Her neck cracked. Stiff, out of shape, still sore from the jump night.

One by one, she undid the buttons on her blouse. Her bra was black. Her blouse floated over to her bed. Shoes flicked off her feet toward the closet. She unzipped her slacks, tossed them on the bed. God it felt good to peel off that damn panty hose! They crackled as they flew to the bed. Her panties were black.

She stretched her arms wide like a cruciform and arched her head back, closed her eyes. So stiff. Antsy. She folded herself down to touch the rug. Lay face down in her bra and panties.

Sallie pointed her fingers in at her shoulder, straightened her arms to raise herself in the panther, her breasts and stomach off the floor, her legs stretched long and loose out behind her, her face toward heaven with her lips parted and her eyes closed. She held it until rivulets of sweat trickled down her sides.

On her feet, she moved through *koryo*, a choreographed black-belt form of blocks and strikes, kicks. Toward the end, the martial ballet evolved into a soft dance.

Enough, she thought. Got to hurry. But she moved slowly as she unfastened her bra, shrugged it away. Her breasts felt tender. Too soon for her period. She peeled off her panties.

The light in her bathroom was bright. Sallie filled the sink with hot water, snapped a new blade in her razor, soaped her underarms, shaved them. Washed and soaped her legs. Usually she hated shaving her legs, the bizarre dictates of fashion. But that night, with the merciless world outside her locked door, to do something unnecessary and self-indulgent seemed liberating.

She laughed at herself: *Girl, have you changed!*

Don't think about it. Don't think about anything. About killers and friends crashing and Faron and work and Faron. She turned on the shower, stepped inside and pulled the clear plastic curtain down the length of the tub.

Water beads drummed on her back. Steam rose. Merely breathing was hot and wet and good. She felt the curls she'd refused to process relax with the water. Her shampoo smelled like roses. Steam filled the shower stall. She glanced through the plastic curtain to the mirror above her sink. Saw her dark body in the misted glass.

She chose a pair of clean jeans, a simple blouse, sensible shoes, a blazer. She brushed her hair in the bureau mirror.

A little lip gloss wouldn't hurt. Would be OK. Would help. She told the mirror: This is OK. You're just going to work.

Don't need to bring my gun, she thought. Besides, carrying it could blow our cover.

Cold night air invigorated her after she parked her car and walked toward the gate at Faron's headquarters, yet she felt . . . lethargic. Like she was moving in molasses.

Her codes got her through the locked gate and front door. No one sat at the security desk inside the foyer.

Sometimes Faron sealed his home and sent everyone away so he could be alone—so Nguyen had told Sallie. Times like that, said Nguyen, Monk hovered nearby, but he kept out of sight. Sallie's footsteps on the carpeted stairs were quiet. On the second floor, she hurried down the hall toward a set of back stairs, past offices, past the Operations Room . . .

Where Monk sat working at a computer. Two quick steps carried her past that open door.

Shit! She stopped in the hall. Even if he didn't see me, he'll find out anyway. Can't disrespect him, can't—don't want to see his sad eyes. Gotta do what you should do.

She stepped inside that room—shot her eyes to the back wall past where he sat, looking his way but avoiding seeing him.

"Hey," she said, "didn't expect to see you here. I mean, working in here. Not tonight, not that . . . you know."

Monk let her stammer.

"Look," she said, turning to face the wall to her left, "you heard Faron ask me to come to . . ."

The wardrobe door she'd burgled was open. The massive man stared into the glowing VDT at the work station where he sat.

"Monk?"

Computer burn filled his eyes. He wouldn't look at Sallie as she walked toward him, alongside him—

Saw the letter opener driven up into the base of his skull.

Lights on parked police cruisers flicked red and blue veins through the night outside Faron Sears's headquarters. Yellow crime-scene tape stretched around the old church's black iron pole fence. A siren wailed to a stop as an ambulance pulled up.

Cole double-parked behind the ambulance, found Sallie in the back seat of a cruiser.

"I had to show the responding cops my creds," she told him.

"It's OK," he told her. "Are you OK?"

"Shit, no."

"Did you see anything? Do you know anything?"

"No. The homicide detectives noticed scratches on the wardrobe lock. I didn't confess they might be ours. I wouldn't explain what I was doing here.

"What was I doing here?" she whispered.

"Your job, and this isn't your fault."

"If I hadn't taken so much time at home . . ."

"Stop it." After she blinked, he said: "Where's Faron?"

"Upstairs, cops with him. Faron was in there while Monk was getting killed. On the third floor. Wouldn't have heard anything. Monk . . . Right where his spine met his skull; he died quick."

Footsteps crunched frozen gravel in the gutter. Cole turned and found Nick Sherman, his face ashen, his topcoat buttoned.

"You don't have time for this," he told Cole, his words clearly meant for Sallie, too. "But I don't have a choice. I'm sorry. I fucked up as bad as an asshole could. I'm a drunk. I'm fighting it. That's not an excuse; it's the truth. Just the damn truth. Your call. You should pull my badge. I'll walk away wherever you want. You want to shoot me; tell me where to stand."

A police cruiser tore away from their scene, siren screaming and party lights flashing: crime loves the Washington night.

"What do you want, Nick?" asked Cole.

"I'm a guy who catches killers. I don't want to lose that."

Cole said: "Will there be a next time?"

"If there is, you won't have to shoot me."

Three partners stared at each other as the siren faded away.

Nick said: "I want to stay alive."

"Can you stay straight and handle all this, too?" asked Cole.

"Yes," whispered Nick.

"You're a senior D.C. homicide detective," Cole told him. "Grab the detectives who caught this call. They now work for you, but keep it looking like standard operating procedure. Your chief will get a call in five minutes. Keep the lid on about Vance."

"I don't think this was him," said Nick.

"Me either," said Cole. "Work it like a clean case."

"Like maybe a burglar did it," said Nick.

"Oh, sure," said Sallie. "One amazing burglar who—"

"Play that up in reports to protect us from leaks," said Cole. "But we all know that somehow, this belongs to us.

"One more thing," said Cole. "Where have you been?"

"Took a few personal hours." Nick smiled. "Then I followed a hunch, turned your boys loose Out West. They found a plane reservation made two days before our Choteau raid. For a flight from Missoula, Montana, to Washington, D.C., on Monday, February 12. A reservation for Chris Harvie."

"By then he'd been dead—"

"Smart work," Cole told Nick over Sallie's words.

"Do you think Vance will show up for that flight?" she asked.

"No," said Nick, "but if he does, he'll run into an army."

Sallie said: "Are we blown here?"

Cole looked around. "No TV vans, no reporters, not yet. Did the police radio mention FBI agents or federal officers on scene?"

"No," said Sallie. "Just the squeal address. No radio mention of Faron Sears either."

"Go," Cole ordered Nick. "Lock your uniforms up—no radio traffic, no phone calls, no leaks. Same with the ambulance crew."

Nick hurried away as a taxi turned the corner, stopped.

"Are we blown?" Sallie asked again as she stood beside Cole.

A car stopped behind the taxi just as the fare opened the cab's back door. Jeff Wood got out of the car; Lauren climbed out of the cab. Faron Sears's executives saw their *consultants,* and with unspoken agreement, hurried toward them.

Lauren's face was wet with tears, her eyes bloodshot but wide. "Dalton, what are you . . . Monk . . . do you know—What . . . ?"

No time, no easy way, thought Cole. His hand held the cell phone he was desperate to use.

"Why are you here?" Lauren asked him, her eyes wide and heavy with frozen tears, Wood fighter-faced and flexing hands beside her.

Cole said: "Because I'm in charge."

51

"Tell me," whispered Lauren, her cheeks flushed and shiny with dried tears, "which of you is the biggest son of a bitch?"

She sat opposite Cole at a round conference table in the second-floor meeting room of the remodeled church. Jeff Wood sat on her right. On her left was Jon Leibowitz. Farther around the curve sat Faron; her words were aimed at him and at Cole, who sat across from her, with Sallie and Nick.

Pink shimmered in the dark windows as the last flare stuck in the street outside died. The police cruisers were gone; the ambulance was loaded and gone; the yellow tape in the steel fence was gone. Only ashes of flares remained to clue commuters who traversed these streets that something had happened here.

"Doesn't matter," said Lauren. "You're all sons of bitches."

"Why weren't we told that some lunatic is planning to kill Faron?" asked Jon Leibowitz.

"Why didn't *you* tell us?" Lauren's soft question hit Faron. "You let these people come in and you all lied to us? Why?"

Cole said: "The Bureau felt that the best way to interdict the killer would be—"

"Oh, bullshit," said Lauren. "Bullshit, bullshit, bull—"

Leibowitz said: "Lauren's right. You say you're acting on information received. What kind of information? From whom?"

"A confidential source." Cole looked at Faron: *Don't! Remember what I made you promise in the hall a few minutes ago!*

Wood said: "You must have more."

"We're chasing the suspect now," said Cole. "Last report, he was a thousand miles from here."

"A suspect?" said Leibowitz. "Or a conspiracy?"

"As far as we know," lied Cole, "the suspect is acting alone."

"Then how did you get a source on him?"

Cole shook his head. "Sources and methods are confidential."

"You're the guy who was here today," Lauren told Nick. "When I was coming back in, I saw you, then I heard about you."

Cole said: "Detective Sherman was assigned as liaison to us from the D.C. police, and he needed to eyeball these facilities."

Lauren said: "Do you have an answer for everything?"

She shook her head. "If you'd have told us who you were and that a killer was out there, Monk wouldn't have had to die."

"We know no connection between our original investigation and this murder," said Cole: the most minimal of truths.

Nick said: "A few nights ago, a citizen phoned 911 with a burglar casing this building. Cruisers rolled, but found nobody and you all reported nothing missing. Maybe the bad guy who got away then came back to finish what—"

"The scratches on the wardrobe lock," said Leibowitz.

"You want us to believe that somebody broke in here," said Wood, "and picked the lock like a pro. Before or after they snuck up on Monk *as he was sitting down*? Monk was paranoid, quicker—"

"We don't know what happened or how," said Nick. "That's why we're investigating. What was in that cabinet?"

"Money," said Wood. "Cash that comes in through the mail."

"The cabinet is empty now." Nick's shrug spoke by implication.

"Wouldn't have been," said Lauren. "Shouldn't have been."

"Who had a key?" asked Nick.

Wood shook his head: "If it's a burglary, why do you—"

"Because *I'm* in charge of investigating a homicide!"

The ex-soldier glared back. "I have a key. So does . . . did

Monk. So does Lauren. Jon. Faron. Our accountant. Our volunteer chief, our head operations—"

"We need a list," said Nick. "I know you've all had a shock, it's late, but we need to interview each—"

"We?" said Leibowitz. "I thought that *you* were the local police officer in charge of a local burglary murder."

"Whatever happens here," said Cole, "happens on my watch. I'm in on everything."

"Oh, really?" said the lawyer.

Lauren stared at Faron. "Why haven't you said anything?"

"What would you have me say?" was his answer.

"You could say you were fucking sorry!" Lauren yelled. Her tears broke free.

Sallie said: "Lauren, I know how you feel, but—"

"The hell you do," said Lauren. "Monk was my friend for . . . The hell you *know*. You're just a sneaky, back-door, FBI bitch."

The sorrow and pain in the room froze.

"And let me tell you something else, Ms. Pickett," said Lauren. "Don't worry about defending Faron. He always wins in the clinches. But, hell, I suppose you know about that by—"

Beep beep beep beep beep!

Cole, Nick, and Sallie flinched as the beepers they carried went off. Dalton checked the number flashing on his beeper's screen: the War Room. Nick showed Cole his beeper: the same number. Cole turned his beeper for Sallie to read; she nodded.

Cole said: "Leave us and handle that—please."

Without a word or a glance, she left the room.

"Monk is dead." Faron's voice drew all their eyes to him. The smile he gave Lauren was gentle, sad. "Next to you, Monk was my oldest friend. You know that I think life and death are mere changes. We should treasure what we have when we have it, and—"

"You're not the one who's dead," said Lauren. "You want to treasure death; be my guest. Ask Monk how he feels."

"When I could, I did. Then, he felt glad to finally be alive."

"Did he tell you, 'Oh, thank you!'?" snapped Lauren.

Wood put his hand on her shoulder: "Hey, Laur, it's—"

"It is not OK!"

"No, it's not," said Faron. "It's beyond OK. I wish Monk

had had more time here. I miss him; I mourn him. But my sorrow can't help him, and it's mine to bear, not to justify."

"How convenient." Lauren shrank in her chair: "Give it up! All this! Monk is dead because you and I came here, and . . . Just give it up! Go back to California. Let go, go . . . Give it up."

"I can't," said Faron. "It's too late."

Lauren's words flowed out with the last of her anger: "Guess you're right. It's too late, too damn late."

Sallie came back in the room. Her face was hard, her eyes wide. She caught Cole's eye and angled her head toward the hall, but he turned to the people sitting across from him.

"Whatever happens," Cole told them, "reveal nothing of what you've learned in here, what you learn about Monk's death. Not to anyone. Not to your coworkers, your family, the press."

"You have no power over the First Amendment," said Leibowitz.

"Speech is only free if it does no deliberate, unjustified, reckless, malicious harm," said Cole. "Otherwise, we're all liable for what we do and say."

"You can yell fire in a crowded theater," countered the lawyer, "if there is a fire."

Sallie leaned against the door, her eyes closed.

"This isn't theater. This is a homicide investigation and a federal investigation, *counselor*. I'm sure you can inform us about impeding criminal investigations and obstruction of justice."

"You don't want to meet me in court," said Leibowitz.

"You're right," said Cole as he stood. "Too easy a victory."

He walked to Sallie, bent to hear her whisper: "Kurt Vance just butchered a woman in Chicago."

Yellow tape wrapped the room where Monk died. Inside that web, techs fingerprinted and photographed with shades drawn to the night. Upstairs, a conference table supported notebooks for Nick and Cole. Sallie monitored a tape recorder.

First came Jon Leibowitz, attorney at law. The log showed his interview began at 9:47 P.M., Wednesday, February 7.

"I should thank you," he told Cole. "Faron should, too. You've defeated any antitrust actions the Justice department initiates against us."

"How do you figure?" said Cole.

"Your undercover operation put you, an agent of the Justice department's FBI, alongside me, the counsel for Faron *et al*, during which time I conducted business protected by client privilege. You being with me under fraudulent credentials violates that privilege, victimizes me and my client so much that any court will throw out the government's case."

Leibowitz smiled. "Couldn't have worked out better if I'd planned it. Once your bosses realize how they've screwed up, they'll drop their briefcases and run for cover."

The tape recorded eleven seconds of silence.

"We're here about murder," said Nick.

"Not guilty," said Leibowitz. "And if you think I'm a suspect in a criminal act, I have rights to counsel."

"Why would we think you're a suspect?" said Nick.

"Don't insult me with a baited question."

"What do you think happened?" asked Cole.

"I don't speculate," said Leibowitz.

Cole took him straight on: "In the last year, you've si-phoned ninety-four thousand dollars out of Faron's political movement in unaccounted for ex—"

"Our financial information is confidential!"

"We can get a subpoena," said Nick.

"Based on already illegally obtained information? Fruit of the poisoned tree."

"Forget about who'd have to prove what in court," said Cole. "While you're posturing for a judge, the press could get wind of unethical—"

"I was spinning reporters when you were still learning how to load your guns."

"Then we're all ready," said Cole.

"Monk told me something wasn't where it was supposed to be," said Sallie. "Maybe he was talking about the Movement's money. Forget about the chump change missing tonight from the wardrobe, you've lifted ninety-four thousand dollars."

Nick said: "Motive, means and opportunity. Your alibi for opportunity sucks—at home watching videos of news shows. As for means, you had the codes to get in, the letter opener was there, Monk would trust you enough to let you get behind him."

The homicide cop added: "Money is murder's big motive."

"You can ask questions," said Leibowitz, "but you can not force me to answer. Continuing this interview is futile. But before I go, let me assist you by clarifying what appears to be illegally obtained information on your part.

"Yes, I've drawn out ninety-four thousand dollars. That money has gone into researching political districts, especially in New Jersey, where there's a governor's race opening up. Also, several New Jersey House seats are on the line as well as one of the Senate seats."

Leibowitz smiled. "I've also been heartened by the re-sponse to my query to selected parties about forming and funding a campaign committee to find an appropriate reform candidate."

"Who?" said Cole. "Faron?"

"At this stage, he has deliberately distanced himself from . . ."

"He doesn't know what you're doing," said Cole.

"He knows the job he asked me to do, and he trusts me."

"You're building a political machine," said Cole, "but he might not be the candidate."

"His ideas drive the machine, but—"

"And his money built it," said Cole. "For you to take over."

Leibowitz shrugged: "An honorable man would never ignore the call of the people."

"Faron won't run," said Sallie. "If he chose politics as usual, he'd start with the presidency, not New Jersey."

"First steps first," said Leibowitz.

"You," repeated Cole.

"Part of my duties are to help Faron explore all his options."

"You created this option. For you."

"Faron will understand that allowing the committee to draft me for office will bolster his political power. He'll see it as a chance that's too good to pass up."

"What if he tells you no?" said Sallie. "Or what if he says he wants to run?"

"That's up to him. And the committee. And the voters of New Jersey. My legal residence has always been there. Faron's—"

"Damn, you're slick," said Nick.

"No," said Leibowitz, standing. "I'm gone."

When the door closed behind the lawyer and the tape recorder was turned off, Nick said: "I don't figure him for Monk.

"Even as wimpy as he is," continued the homicide cop, "he could have rammed that dagger through Monk's spine and up into his brain. But Leibowitz is a button pusher, a string puller."

"We've got one remote-control killer out there now," said Sallie. "Why not Leibowitz pulling two strings?"

"Maybe," said Nick. "But even if Leibowitz killed Monk for some reason, why would he have turned Vance loose on Faron? Sallie's right: Faron won't run in New Jersey. Why would Jon Boy want to kill the man whose endorsement could get him elected?"

"A murdered mentor can't call you a traitor," said Cole. He sighed. "Who's next?"

*   *   *

The tape recorder rolled at 10:14.

Jeff Wood said: "I hear you've penetrated our security in more ways than mere infiltration."

Nick said: "I thought Monk was in charge of security."

"Monk was a superb tactical officer and close-work man. Or so I thought. Apparently, he was too trusting."

"Not a problem of yours, I guess," said Nick.

Wood said nothing.

"So . . . security?" repeated Nick.

"I am the strategic coordinator for that and other needs."

"Guess that makes you a general," said Cole.

"What I don't understand, *General*," said Nick, "is why you don't seem fazed by your friend and 'tactical officer's' murder right here in the middle of your strategic security."

"Every war demands its dead," said Wood. "I've seen more death than you can imagine. I learned to embrace it. I loved Monk, I'll honor him and miss him, but he's not the first. Or the last."

"That's a refreshing attitude," said Cole.

"That's true reality."

"What's also true is that you've diverted two hundred grand into your pocket," said Nick. "Formed your own private army that got the contract you oversaw for the Chicago project."

"Of course," said Wood.

"What would Monk have thought about that?" asked Nick.

"He knew."

"Too bad we can't ask him exactly *when* he found out," said Nick. "Does Faron know what you've done with his money?"

"It's not 'his' money. It belongs to the cause."

"And what did you use it for?" asked Cole.

"You already know. I created a new, elite security force, a backbone and vanguard for our organization."

"A goon squad," said Sallie.

"Mindless goons would do me . . . *us* no good. The best strategy is to be prepared while seeming to be indifferent. To win your enemy over, not fight him. To defeat your opponents in the void without them even realizing they've been engaged in battle."

"*Mein General,*" said Nick, "you talk a lot about enemies."

"I don't belittle you. When you belittle me, the effect ricochets off to hit you."

"Occupational hazard," said Nick.

"What enemies?" asked Cole.

"The same enemies I've been fighting since 1967. Apathy. Exploiters. Manipulators. Betrayers."

"Your enemies," asked Cole. "Or Faron's?"

"Faron is the best leader to change what must be changed. His is the most honest, purest vision."

"Why does anything have to be changed?" asked Sallie.

"I've seen too many people die who shouldn't have," said Wood. "I've seen too many people betrayed and tricked and led into being their own worst enemies."

"What about the money?" said Nick. "What about your army?"

"The money and the army serve the cause."

"Faron's . . . or yours?" said Cole.

"There is no difference."

"Yeah, but you're getting rich."

"The veils over my force strengthen it against compromise. Its strength protects our Movement. Any profits in my name plow back into our work."

Cole said: "Did you try to buy machine guns for your 'elite force'?"

"I'm not in charge of procurement," said Wood. "And if I were, why would I attempt to buy automatic weapons? They're illegal. Besides, *Agent Cole*, investigating machine-gun sales is the job of the ATF, not the FBI."

"My job is murder," said Nick. "Who do you think killed Monk?"

"If I knew, that would cease to be a problem."

When Wood had left, Nick said: "What a warm and charming guy."

Sallie shook her head: "Listening to him . . . did anybody else hear strains of Eiger and Slawson and the AA crap?"

"Wood is a purist," said Cole, "not a racist."

"He's a zealot," said Sallie.

"Is that another way of saying he's a stand-up guy?" asked Nick. He looked at Cole. "Do you believe him?"

"Every word."

"Me too," said Nick. "If he thought Faron was deviating from the true course, do you think Wood could rationalize arranging Faron's assassination and picking up the cross himself?"

"In a heartbeat."

Lauren glared at the three cops. Her chin trembled, her voice quavered, and her hands were white, knuckled fists. Her red eyes focused on Dalton. "What lies are you going to tell me now?"

"Lauren . . ."

"*Ms.* Kavenagh to you, *Agent* Cole!"

"I'm sorry it was necessary to deceive you," he said.

"You guys are always sorry—afterwards. Tell me: did you get what you wanted?"

Nick said: "All we want is the truth."

"Is that all you want, too, Agent Pickett?"

Sallie didn't answer.

"This isn't easy for any of us," said Nick, taking her heat for both his comrades. "But we have to go through it, and if you care about finding who killed Monk . . ."

"Faron killed Monk," said Lauren.

Sallie said: "What?"

"This is how it happens. You follow the guy, he takes you where you never dreamed you'd go, then you get cut down."

"You're talking about Monk and Faron?" said Nick.

"Oh, yeah. Sure. Monk believed him, Faron led us all here . . . You guys showed up. Now Monk's dead."

"But," said Nick, "do you think Faron stabbed Monk?"

"No," she whispered. "There are more efficient ways to kill somebody."

Sallie said: "If you're so mad at Faron, blame him. Why—"

"You tell me why." Lauren shook her head. "*Why* isn't what your tape recorder wants. It wants to know what. *Who.*"

Cole said: "Do you know what? Who?"

"I don't even know what I can do tomorrow morning except come back here and keep coming until—oh, Monk!" She wiped away tears.

The homicide detective said: "Where were you tonight?"

"Same place I was last night." Her voice grew hollow. "Same place I'll be tomorrow night. Home. Alone. No . . . witnesses."

Only got a few more minutes before she blows, thought Nick: "Ms. Kavenagh, eleven months ago, you drew eleven thousand, five hundred dollars out of this movement's operating funds. No vouchers, no reasons given."

Lauren blinked.

"One five hundred dollar draw," said Nick, "then a few weeks later, eleven—"

"You people," she said. They watched her. "You want it all, don't you?"

"Yes," said Nick.

"Yeah," said Lauren, "I took—what was it? Eleven thousand, five hundred dollars from Faron's precious Movement."

She shook her head: "I did it so no one would ever know. Pretty silly, huh? Why wasn't I smart enough to plan for a trio of cops chasing a killer?

"All of us—Faron, Jon, Monk and Jeff and me—our health insurance files are in the system. Most everybody who works here is a hacker. I've been with Faron so long, my personal books can be accessed. If I filed a health claim or took what I needed from my savings or . . . I didn't want anybody to know.

"Now, I've got to tell you. For the damn record, right? The surest way to lose privacy is to fight for it."

Lauren stood. "How . . . stupid of me to want to keep it secret."

She pulled her blouse out of her skirt. Unbuttoned the lower three buttons as Cole and Nick and Sallie stared, transfixed.

"I had a hysterectomy." Lauren's voice was monotone, her red eyes were dry. She pulled her blouse up and the waist of her skirt down. "See?"

A white scar curved in a four inch smile below her navel.

"They told me the scar would fade with time. Guess I'm lucky it hasn't."

Lauren's eyes focused on nothing as she lowered her blouse, readjusted her skirt. She left the room.

The tape recorder logged a minute of silence. Then Nick's voice said: "Interview terminated at eleven-oh-nine P.M."

Nick Sherman stared at the crimson-smeared bed in the Chicago hotel room. Beyond the grimy window, an el train clattered through a gray Thursday morning. Three Chicago police SWAT team members crowded against the wall behind him. The Chicago homicide detective beside Nick said: "Fucking animal butchered her."

"I saw your photographs," said Nick.

The beefy woman working the registration desk downstairs wore a Bulls sweatshirt over her armored vest. She had a 9mm tucked by her spine, and a Chicago badge in her pocket. Smoke snaked to the hotel ceiling fan from her cigarette. The shabbily dressed man on the couch was the city karate champion. A shotgun waited under the cushions of the couch. A sign taped to the elevator lied: OUT OF ORDER. Cops waited at the top of each landing. Sniper teams covered each side of the hotel.

Inside the murder room, the Chicago detective told Nick: "All the desk clerk remembers is that the guy is white. When he comes back, he's ours."

"What if he doesn't come back?" said Nick. "It's been all night. The body he left is the kind of mess you run away from."

"He left two shirts, pants, cold pills, three hundred and seventy-five dollars, and car keys in the dresser. He tucked her in with a sheet. Textbook freak. The fax we got from your behavioral science boys says he's the kind of creep who likes to . . . ghoul over his work. He'll be back."

"There's something wrong," said Nick.

"Not from where I'm standing," snapped the Chicago cop. "Why did you find the body?"

"An anonymous call, a woman, said she heard screams in a room here. We figure it was some whore tricking up here who heard bad business, dropped a dime. Our unit was slow to respond, but . . ."

"And besides her, hacked-up and throat-slashed on the bed, you found *that*." Nick pointed to a chalk circle on the yellow wallpaper near the bed. The chalk circled a bloody handprint. Four of the crimson fingerprints showed distinctive whorls and clear points.

"We photo'd it, shot it to the Bureau hoping for a quick ID. Knocked us over when we got a call back so pronto."

"You're sure Kurt Vance didn't spot your cars, bolt?"

"We aren't certain, but we aren't fools. First officers on the scene figured a psycho, got a description from the manager, set up a plainclothes team at each end of the street. Nobody got close to the hotel who matched the perp's description."

"You said your vice squad had videotapes of her."

"Sherry on the stroll. I'll get you a tape."

Nick stared at the bloody sheet that had soaked through to the mattress, the stains on the floor. Projected the image of the naked woman with her gaping wounds. He blinked, looked away, looked at the dusty yellow wallpaper and the bloody handprint.

Nick whirled to the Chicago detective. "The body, you took it away, but everything else . . ."

"Like he left it. We even left her empty purse on the table."

"This," said Nick, pointing to the bloody handprint. "You didn't type it, did you?"

"It would be stupid to destroy a great piece of evidence and a clear fingerprint just so the lab boys could get a sample when the whole damn bed was soaked and her body was . . ."

But Nick had already run into the bathroom, his eyes darting from the stained toilet to the grimy tub to the sink: gray-smudged porcelain around—shiny handles. The bowl of the sink was cracked, but white. Sparkling clean.

"What did the autopsy say killed her?" he yelled.

"You're as nuts as this guy!" the Windy City cop told Nick as he came back to the murder room. "She's chopped up sixty ways from Sunday, and you're worried about an autopsy report?"

"It's not done—not even scheduled, is it?"

"The priority is finding *who*, not *what* killed—"

Nick pointed to the bloody handprint: "That's not *her* blood, it's *his*."

"What?"

"If he butchered her alive, he'd have hit an artery. The blood spray would have covered this room. Those walls are bare. He probably strangled her, did the cutting only after her heart stopped pumping."

The Chicago cop blinked.

"Kurt's a careful boy," said Nick. "He wouldn't have wanted a prostitute's blood on him. He bled himself in the sink. Coated his hand, left us that. He staged a horror show, made sure his fingerprints would get spotted and checked right away."

"Why?"

"So we'd drop everything else and come running with all our cavalry," said Nick.

Sunday at 7:30 P.M., half an hour before show time. Two cars parked in front of a black glass building in Washington, D.C. The passengers were silent as they climbed out to the sidewalk. Cole led the way to the building and opened the door to the TV world for everyone. Lauren went through first.

She's said nothing to me since our interview, thought Cole. Didn't speak to any of the mourners at Monk's cremation on

Friday either, not even to Faron, who gave a eulogy about Monk, love, loyalty, and joy, and had the decency to never once say "I."

News reports had concentrated on Monk's evolution from the gridiron to politics. A *Washington Post* source linked Monk's murder to a suspect in five Capitol Hill break-ins and one homicide. A TV station reported that police were showing neighbors that man's mug shot. No press reports mentioned conspiracy or assassins. No one knew that the "burglary suspect" had been in federal protective custody for two weeks as he ratted on a crack crew.

Faron followed Lauren into the black glass building, with Wood and Nguyen on each elbow, their eyes scanning the deserted street. The presence of FBI agents working undercover at Faron's had been revealed only to key security people on Faron's staff and explained with a story about Faron as a victim of financial fraud.

Three days to Valentine's Day, thought Cole.

Lawyer Jon Leibowitz followed his client into the building that produced a TV news magazine show trusted by 41 million Americans. He carried letters and faxes that had negotiated the rules for that night's show. Leibowitz's alibi for Monk's murder was inconclusive—as were Lauren's and Wood's. Cole had ordered covert surveillance of all three executives.

In a conference call from Chicago Saturday night, Nick had told Sallie and Cole: "From the start, we knew that finding the spy would be harder than stopping the assassin."

"Is anybody running Vance?" asked Sallie. "Or is he running wild? What he did in Chicago, you think just to divert us . . ."

"Whoever found him pulled his trigger," said Cole. "Now . . . they may not even be in contact anymore. They may not have to be."

"The chain goes from Kurt Vance to Chris Harvie and Brian Luster to whoever's running the show," said Nick.

"And we have no link between our dead ex-cons and anybody who works for Faron." Cole rubbed his brow. "Or to AA, the Yakuza, any business rivals . . . anybody."

"So you want to wiretap Faron's executives?" Nick asked.

Cole nodded. "Not legal, but I don't care."

"You never asked them about the seventy-four thousand dollars missing from the money that passed through that wardrobe," Sallie had said.

"None of them brought it up, either," Cole said. "Don't you think one of them should have noticed?"

"Monk noticed," said Sallie. "Monk thought he was after a simple embezzler, so he let the wrong person get behind him."

That Sunday night, Cole followed her inside the TV castle. They rode the elevator to the third floor. Nick was flying back from Chicago, where a steel ambush still waited for Vance at a flophouse hotel, while an army of FBI agents were interviewing airline employees, train station workers, bus agents, verifying the identities of hundreds of thousands of passengers who'd caught flights out of Chicago's two airports since Wednesday afternoon. A call from Justice's Fifth Floor mentioned the millions of dollars spent to come up with only yet another murder victim.

"What do you care?" Cole replied. "Your ass is still covered."

An e-mail message linked to the Chicago hotel murder room had showed up in Faron's Internet site:

Are you quite prepared to die? R.

"Don't respond," Cole had told Faron. "Maybe that'll goad him into communicating again. Give us more to work with."

"Doesn't matter," Nick had said in the conference call. "He doesn't care what anybody says."

The elevator carrying Cole and Sallie into TV land chimed.

"Wow," said a young woman in the hall as they stepped out of the elevator. "You guys are like a clown car. I'm sorry, but, like, it's just elevator after elevator of Mr. Sears's aides. The Green Room is already like, bursting!"

"My associate will join the others," said Cole. "I'll wander around."

"The other men have already, like, checked us out."

Cole smiled. "I just want to, *like*, see how America's reality factory looks from the inside."

He stepped past her clipboard and Velcroed smile, walked down the corridor of white walls and cubicle offices to the heart of the factory floor: a sound stage of cables, lights, cameras, and monitors orbiting a center set, where a lone chair faced a half-moon quartet of empty seats. Men and women with headsets and clipboards scurried over a floor covered by black cable mambas.

When the cameras came on, Faron sat alone opposite four famous TV journalists.

"Good evening," the oldest of the four told the camera. "I'm Jim Carrol. Welcome to 'One Hour.' Tonight, we're live, trying to answer the question that's on every American's mind: *Who is Faron Sears?* We're asking Faron Sears the questions you want answered . . . with maybe a few surprises of our own."

Theme music swelled. Monitors showed the commercials broadcast to the national audience. Across the stage, off camera, Cole saw Sallie and Lauren, Wood and Leibowitz, felt the chill that "maybe a few surprises" had brought them.

Cole saw a ladder to a catwalk that circled the outer wall of the sound stage. He climbed steel rungs. Theme music swelled.

Jim Carrol introduced Faron, told the camera, "We'll start with history." The monitors showed photos from Faron's youth as Carrol's voice narrated. From the catwalk, Cole saw *the past* in the monitors, saw Carrol patting his hair and listening to his own voice.

"So, Faron Sears," said Carrol when the cameras went live. "Who are you?"

"Thanks to you, I'm now important."

"I'm not sure I understand."

"Success in America means being on television." Faron smiled. "More than fame, it's validation. Life beyond flesh and gravity. If you're important enough to be on TV, you're worth something."

"Most of our audience might think that's a little shallow."

"Most of your audience understands. And agrees. My hope is that they also see that the path to virtual reality through your cameras is a more dangerous illusion than other realities."

"Are you saying TV is dangerous? This from a man who owns a cable channel and a software empire? Why?"

"TV today enforces the idea that everything is OK, that passivity in front of a screen instead of journeying in the world or in your mind or your soul is OK. Because if every-thing's OK, then you can feel OK about buying what's in the commercials."

Cole saw a man on the catwalk, tool box in his hands. Kneeling, opening . . . the technician taped a cable to a light.

The blond anchorwoman was telling Faron: ". . . a disdain for politics and politicians, yet you appear to be running for office and regularly slug it out on Capitol Hill and in the White House."

Faron said nothing.

"I thought you agreed to answer all our questions," she said.

"You didn't ask a question." Faron smiled.

"What about politics?"

"Politics is how things get done. Sometimes it's negotiating to get the garbage picked up, sometimes it's wearing the right tie when you read news on TV so people won't change channels."

The director cued Anthony Drane, the dark-haired, two-time Emmy winner and legendary dragon slayer of the show. Drane spoke to the cyclops eye of the machine: "Speaking of politics, we want to focus on your Chicago Resurrection Project."

On cue, Carrol told the world: "First, we've compiled a film report on the project."

Monitors filled with film clips and voice-overs. Lauren drifted away from her companions. She followed an invisible path around the set, as though centrifugal force had cast her on a trajectory spinning out from the center she circled. On the catwalk, Cole walked above her, with her.

On live TV beamed to the world a stone's throw from their journey, Drane was saying: ". . . have a man known as Rever-end Mike, who says he paid out, for your Chicago Resurrec-tion Project, hundreds of thousands of dollars in bribes to city, county, and state officials. That he even saw to it that some members of what he calls 'the Outfit'—the Chicago Mafia—received bribes."

On film tape, a heavy-set black man in a suit and tie re-peated Drane's charges in more colloquial English.

Lauren walked through a forest of arc lights beneath the

catwalk. Looking down, Cole could see her the part of her hair, the slope of her breasts.

Faron told the camera: "He may be right."

"On national television, you admit to paying bribes?"

"We gave Mike more than a hundred thousand dollars. Every election, he gets walking-around money from the Democrats and Republicans to help them get out the vote. My guess is that he skims most of it for himself. We paid him so none of our opponents could."

"This is incredible!" said Drane.

"And legal." Faron smiled. "We told him to obey the law. In writing, on videotapes which we'll release to all the press."

"All the press?" yelled Drane. "But we have an exclusive . . ."

"Plus, our lawyer mailed copies of this information to city, county, and state government ethics committees. If they allow us to, we'll forward the same material to the FBI.

"If we're lucky," said Faron, "our sting will help reform the way business and politics are done."

Lauren stopped. She cupped her forehead with her hands. Looking down, Cole thought she might be crying.

Reporter Carrol spoke to the camera as if it were Faron: "How does America know that all your crusades aren't a tactic to increase your personal fortune?"

"All my private assets are being reorganized," said Faron. "My companies will eventually become employee-owned and -operated . . . including the Chicago project."

Carrol said: "What does 'eventually' mean?"

"I thought you knew," said Faron.

On camera, the fourth journalist, a fortyish black man, blinked: "Critics say your project's private police force will turn the ghettos into an armed camp."

"The ghettos are already an armed camp," said Faron. "We hope to change that force from self-destruction to self-protection."

"We should add," Carrol told the camera, "that violence hit your crusade here in Washington, with the murder of your associate in a burglary at your headquarters. Our condolences. But given that incident: Do you feel like you're the target of a conspiracy?"

On the catwalk, Cole froze.

Faron shrugged. "I've been a target all my life."

The woman journalist asked: "What do you do about that?"

Faron spread his arms. "I'm here."

Theme music swelled as the director gestured thumbs-up. Cole found a staircase, walked down the catwalk as commercials filled the monitors. Lauren heard him coming, turned.

"Don't ask me for Preacher Mike stuff, Mr. G-Man. Was my idea to make it into a sting after we found out these people . . . But don't ask me. Ask Leibowitz. He still cares."

"What I came to say—"

"Back in two minutes!" yelled the floor manager.

Her eyes are bloodshot, hair brushed like she didn't use a mirror, lip trembling. Could reach out and . . .

Don't. Cole told her: "I'm sorry. About having to lie to you, pretend to be somebody I wasn't. About Monk. The interview, what we had to know, what you . . . I'm sorry about your scar."

"That's an awful lot to be sorry for."

"I've been around a long time."

Theme music swelled. "Quiet on the set!"

Lauren gave Cole a faint smile. Walked away while millions of viewers watched something else.

55

I'm invisible, thought Vance. And it was so ridiculously *easy!*

He'd driven from Chicago to Detroit, abandoned the car at an airport long-term lot, flew to Lexington, Kentucky, early Monday afternoon. Vance spotted the extra uniformed cops at the Lexington airport, the undercover cops hawking the waiting areas. A janitor waltzed with a broom in the same hall over and over and over again.

My suit and tie say *salesman*, but to cop eyes, *I am invisible.*

The reservation clerk at the hotel blinked when he checked in, but Vance knew that pause came from his cloak of invisibility, not because of the blurry computerized sketch taped behind the registration counter: *That's how I might look . . . if I weren't who I am.*

"Will you be staying with us long?" the clerk asked, his eyes on Vance's snappy city Stetson and light-changing, clear glasses.

"If I'm lucky, be here through Thursday."

"And how will you be paying, Mr. . . . . Lawdos?"

Vance handed him a credit card from a same-day-service Chicago bank based on a $500 deposit, a fake driver's license and a mail-drop address. Lee Lawdos: *Genius creates artistic conveniences.*

"Enjoy your stay in Lexington, Mr. Lawdos."

Tuesday it rained. That was dangerous. Vance wore a hat, turned up his coat collar, waved to the desk clerk, left. He drove around all morning so the hotel staff would think he was working, hurried back inside under an umbrella, coat collar up, hat on, made it through the lobby and past two FBI types watching the front desk: still invisible. From his room, he phoned places that would call him back, perpetuating his cover as a salesman for the hotel switchboard. He stayed in his room all afternoon. From his window, he saw them arrive. Two cars of Lexington cops. Five rental sedans in a parade.

Welcome to Lexington, Mr. Sears. Call me Mr. Invisible.

The rain stopped and made his mission safer. He ate an early room service dinner, donned his cloak of invisibility, and left to see the man who would die.

That evening the hotel elevators had two operators who wore suits and smiles and should have had sunglasses over their blind eyes. The lobby had six . . . no, seven sentries trying to blend into the anxious *is-he-here* crowd.

The arena was next door to the hotel, an easy walk over damp, harmless streets. Everywhere Vance looked, there was a uniformed cop or a plainclothes watcher, some with ear tubes.

Nothing for you to hear. I am invisible. And silent. I wear a perfect bow tie.

What a crowd of losers, he thought. Mothers and fathers dragging kids who want to be home watching TV. Rednecks with caps and bankers who'd gussied up with fresh suits and second wives. Must be a thousand faces descended out of slave chains—and the progeny of the guys who once held the whips being careful to mix among them, careful to show that this was natural and all right.

Metal detectors guarded all the doorways. He knew they wouldn't sense the plastic containers taped inside his shirt to his back. But the arch he passed through buzzed.

"Excuse me, sir," said the state trooper. "What are you carrying?"

"Is this all right?" Vance showed the trooper a flat silver pocket knife he'd bought in a Chicago antique store. Its only blade was less than two inches long.

"That's nothing," said the trooper with a Magnum on his belt.

"Was my father's."

"No offense, sir. Hope you get a good seat."

Why else would I risk coming so early? he thought. *I can't be invisible forever.*

Vance took an aisle seat twenty rows from the stage: close enough to see, not too close to be studied. The crowd filled the arena named after a local basketball legend, but it was winter, and the air didn't get hot and clammy too fast. That's good, he thought.

Well. Materializing down front just before show time: one of the men from the explosion in Montana. Had to be Dalton Cole, FBI. And who's that with you? Pretty black woman, sensible shoes and slacks and a jacket over a gun. Dalton talked with a state trooper who wore silver bars on his collar, had a Smokey Bear at his heels. Looking ragged, Agent Cole. Like you're so tired it's hard to see straight. Maybe I can rough you up even more. Black bitch stood by the stairs at one end of the stage as Cole walked off.

A moment later, entering to applause, shouts: There he is,

the man himself. The dead man. Faron Sears. Shit-eating smile, gentle wave, makes the crowd sit down.

Vance wanted to scream: *The power in this room is mine!*

A Chinaman slipped from behind the curtain to guard the stairs on the other side from where the bitch waits.

Don't get too excited, over-heated/sweat/stirring . . .

You're mine, Faron Sears. Wonder if I would have come for you without Usher showing . . . Of course I would have! I rule, not Usher. I need no one. And tonight, *I am invisible.*

The man on the stage cracked a couple of jokes and the crowd laughed. *Look,* thought Vance: Gun Girl's got a smile on her face. She's aimed her eyes on the crowd, but she's riding Faron's spiel and loving it. *Interesting.*

Words rolled out of the dead man's mouth: ". . . corruption" and "walking through it, not with it" and "what goes on in Washington works its way there from Main—"

Vance felt his invisibility slipping away.

Go! Wait. Don't bolt. Don't draw attention to yourself! He shifted in his chair. Looked uncomfortable, needy.

The crowd laughed, many stood to applaud. Vance stood with them. He turned to let the cops see that his back was to the stage, hurried up the aisle to the exit, through the double doors.

A huge cop intercepted him: "You got a problem?"

"If I don't get there fast . . ."

"Up the stairs, either direction."

Vance obeyed, gave the cop no cause to wonder. Faron's amplified voice followed him into the bright, big men's room with its twenty urinals, half a dozen stalls, and mirrors that showed Vance emerging from his invisibility.

Applause pounded on the closed bathroom door, sustained and thunderous. From outside, Vance heard: "I gotta go now, Mom!"

He ducked inside a stall, locked the door, sat on the toilet. Heard the boy come in. Heard him pee. Heard the crowd filling the corridor. Other men came in, shoes seen from under the silver door.

I'm far from invisible now, he knew. But I'm behind a locked door. Faron will leave. Cole and the security and the cops will go with him. No one will check the bathrooms if Faron isn't here.

He waited. Twenty-five minutes after the last person to pee left, all the lights clicked off.

Silence surrounded him. He opened the stall door, felt his way through the darkness to the wall switch. He flipped it on, over-rode the automatic shutoff and filled the room with a yellow glow. Light shimmered in the mirror.

Nothing to worry about. You can always break *out* of a public building. As for getting into the hotel, I can be invisible enough for that. It's night. *God, I look good in the mirror!*

The door swung open and a man yelled: "Hey!"

The mirror showed Vance a uniformed security guard who carried a club but no gun. The guard was more surprised than Vance. Unafraid, the guard walked toward the stranger who stared at the mirror, the stranger whose hands were empty.

"Y'all ain't supposed to be here! Everybody's gone home!" The guard's voice was country Kentucky, fifty years in big-time Lexington but still stuck in his roots and his small-town, uniform-makes-me-boss beliefs. "Hell, what happened to you?"

Very slowly, Vance turned and gave him a big smile.

Nobody can get to us *but* us, thought Cole as he rode the elevator up in the Lexington, Kentucky, hotel. Billionaire Faron had rented two entire floors. No hotel guest fit Kurt Vance's description. A half dozen guards secured the lobby.

"How was his speech?" asked one of the two elevator guards.

"Tell you truth," said Cole, "I didn't listen to it."

"Mind on other things, huh? Don't worry. Up here is safe."

The computerized elevator music mimicked old Beatles songs as the doors slid open to the eighth floor: security team's rooms, the command post. Two state troopers stood watch inside each stairwell. The ninth floor held executive suites—Faron's, Cole's, Lauren's, Sallie's, Wood's. Leibowitz had stayed in Washington. So had Nick. When the elevator doors slid open on nine, one of Wood's men was waiting.

Cole asked him: "Are they still at the governor's reception?"

"Everyone but Ms. Kavenagh. She's in her room."

That e-mail ordered Vance to kill Faron in Washington, D.C., thought Cole, to wait until after Valentine's Day—after tomorrow. The message had been intercepted before Kurt Vance's house exploded, before he butchered a woman in Chicago.

Cole knocked on Lauren's door. No answer. *Could be a dozen OK reasons.* The guard in the hall looked bored, but he wouldn't have left his post. Cole used his master key, let himself into her room.

She sat at a table in front of the glass door to the balcony. A silhouette lit only by a fluorescent lamp above the kitchen sink and the light twinkling through the balcony door from the night.

Cole let the door close behind him, lock. "I knocked. Twice."

"I wondered who that was."

"Do you want me to go?" he said.

"Do you want some wine?" A bottle stood on the table in front of her. "Or are you on duty?"

Cole stepped deeper into the room. "I'm always working."

"If you're here working, I withdraw my offer."

"Do you have another glass?"

She told him where to find one. On his way with it to the table, he passed the bed. Saw her discarded panty hose. The wine she poured him was white and cold.

"Californian," she said. "But that's what we've got."

"It's good enough."

They sat in shadows. Her reflection clouded the French door glass. Her blouse was ivory.

"Why didn't you go to the governor's reception?"

She drank her wine. "I've been to that reception enough, thank you. The wine here is just as good."

"How's the company?" he asked.

"Well, you showed up. Why didn't you go?"

"One more gun there wouldn't make much difference."

She raised her glass. "Here's to duty done."

They drank. Warm air from the furnace vent blew through her hair.

"Before," he said, "I told you I was sorry about—"

"Lying to me? Back then, I was just starting to trust you."

"I never meant to betray your trust."

"Of course you did."

"Not that much. Just . . ."

She glared at him. "How much betrayal is too much?"

"Never mind." She shook her head. "I don't want to hear what you think you know."

She lifted her wine glass. "Here's to men with answers." She drank alone. Stared out the window.

The furnace shut off, and her hair floated still. She poured more wine in her glass. Leaned across the table and filled his hotel goblet. He saw a glint of light in the bottle, in her eyes.

"Aren't you afraid to be here alone with me?" she asked.

"Why?"

"I might be the killer. The one who killed Monk."

"I'm not afraid of that."

The wine bottle trembled on the lip of his glass. She set the open bottle on the carpet. "What are you afraid of?"

"You can hurt me worse than that."

She said nothing. Wouldn't look at him.

"Who you are is dangerous enough to me," he said.

Her eyes stayed on the floor.

"Now you know my secret." He leaned across the table but her hands stayed in her lap. "Now I can't betray you."

"You'd be surprised," she whispered. Wouldn't look at him.

He moved around the table, took her face in his hands and her cheeks were warm. A tear wet his finger.

"I'll take that risk." Her eyes shone. "But not alone."

She pressed his hand against her cheek. "We're not kids anymore."

"Good."

He kissed her, and she kissed him back, her lips softening, opening. His fingers tangled her hair, felt the silk of her blouse, her back, her breasts: Jesus, her breasts were soft. She shrugged out of her blouse, wore a chemise and no bra. His jacket dropped to the floor. He pulled his tie off, his shirt. His gun weighed down his pants as he dropped them, pushed off his shoes. Cole pulled her hips close. Unzipped her skirt over the silk of her chemise, the cotton of her panties.

Lauren pushed away from him. She crossed her arms and the silk chemise rose over her head, flew away.

"You're beauti—"

She touched her fingers to his lips.

Cole wrapped her in his arms, kissed her a million times. Her nipples were tangy and hard. He picked her up and laid her down across the table. She put her bare heels on the edge of the wood, raised her hips so he could peel her panties off. She lay open to him as he knelt before her.

After Faron's speech, Sallie and his entourage attended a reception in a mansion she was certain had once been a slave owner's castle. She met the governor, one senator, two congressmen, county and city officials, millionaires, a newspaper publisher, a bunch of lawyers, and doctors, and college professors. All but a self-conscious handful of them were white.

Faron introduced her to everyone as though she were someone else. Someone real. She smiled, felt guilty each time she let someone grasp her gun hand that she was supposed to keep empty. She lied, told them the consultant cover, that yes, she was working with Faron in Washington.

Only forty years ago, Faron and I would have been kept out of here, she thought as she moved through the crowd. Or ordered in to pour the champagne or scrub the floors. Or worse. Part of her wanted to draw her weapon and blast a round into that magnolia-haunted air: *I'm here, we're here, nobody will ever . . .*

Don't be stupid, she'd told herself; smiled at yet another face. *You can't shoot yesterday.*

The hosts scheduled the reception for two hours. Faron spent thirty-one minutes gliding through the crowd, shaking hands, never letting himself get buttonholed or glad-armed into this caucus of power mongers or that social clique.

As they drove to the hotel, he sat in the back seat between Jeff Wood and Sallie. Nguyen rode shotgun, a uniformed state trooper drove the rented sedan. They had a scout car and a trooper's cruiser out front, a chase car and another cruiser behind. Four minutes from the hotel and safety, Faron said: "Tell the other cars to go on without us."

"What!" yelled Sallie and Wood together. Nothing they said dissuaded Faron. He told his driver where to go.

A dozen school buses and five times as many cars waited outside a sagging gymnasium on the edge of town. Wood and Sallie insisted on going in with him. Sleeping bags covered the gym floor like furrows on a plowed field. When Faron entered, the first person to see him was a red-haired college girl carrying her toothbrush and towel to the locker room. She said, "Oh, my God!" and bit her lower lip, started to cry. Faron hugged her, said "Thanks for coming," and surfed into the crowd on the murmur of his name.

He spent two hours in the gym, moving from one awestruck cluster of college kids to another. Touching, not shaking hands. Talking with, not lecturing to. He listened more than he spoke, praised more than he pronounced. Sallie and Wood let him walk alone among strangers. When the crowd noticed Faron, a hundred cheap cameras flashed. Within fifteen minutes, cameras were forgotten. Everyone cared more about being there than capturing an image.

On the way to the hotel, he told Sallie: "People who will ride a bus a hundred miles and sleep on the floor together for something that profits them *nothing personal* are more important than whoever shows up at a party."

The hotel elevator whisked Faron, Sallie, Nguyen, and two guards to their suites. As they passed the fourth floor, the elevator music murdered another song.

"I hear a symphony," said Faron.

"What?" said Sallie.

"That song is supposed to be, 'I Hear A Symphony.' The Supremes."

"They broke up before I . . ." She cut her words off. By the sixth floor, her legs felt weak.

On the hotel's ninth floor, the elevator doors slid open. Sallie stepped out first, saw the hall guard, knew him. He nodded OK. Nguyen stayed in the elevator, said: "You got him now."

Faron thanked the elevator guards and Nguyen. The doors closed and they were gone.

"He was supposed to check your room!" Sallie told Faron.

"That's OK," said Faron. "No need to."

She walked down the hall with him. The hall guard looked away. "Let me go first. Wait."

And he does it, what I said.

She found the suite's lights on, the sitting room empty. On the table, his laptop modem was hooked to a phone. The windows were dark, but no building outside was this high, so the open curtains didn't matter. Sniper team on the roof had checked in OK. She swept the suite: Bedroom: king-size bed, suitcases, empty closet. Bathroom: nobody. She went back and opened the door for him: "OK."

"I thought you didn't have to worry until tomorrow," he said as he entered. He shook his head. "I never liked Valentine's Day."

"We've had to worry from the start." She had to ask: "Why don't you like Valentine's Day?"

"I never got the perfect card. I never had one to give."

"You had lovers when I was still just a little . . ." Again, she chopped her sentence short.

He finished for her: "A girl." He smiled. "There must have been a million hearts drawn for you."

"No."

Then the words exploded out of her: "I'm not going to be another one for you! I can't be another woman in your hotel room!"

"You're the only woman here."

"There must have been—"

"What must have been is what was. As a Panther, after prison for a while, starting out . . . Then for years it was just Lauren."

"Devil's fever," whispered Sallie.

"My mama used to say that." He shook his head. "Lauren was Lauren, not a trophy white woman. That lasted far longer than it should have. Sometimes when someone you care

about has needs, you go further than is right, you do the easy
thing that also feels OK for you. But we've been over for a long
time. One way we knew was when there was a hotel room
again, all there *was* was a hotel room."

"Since Lauren . . ."

"Since Lauren there's been nobody. Over a year." He took
a step toward her.

She couldn't move. "Must have been a hundred groupies
who . . ."

"Thousands of great women out there are desperate for a
man who won't use them and walk out leaving a kid behind. I
never left any kids behind me, and after prison, after starting
this, I don't dare risk that. Plus I can't just use somebody. And
yes, there are women who don't care who lies between their
sheets if he has fame like mine, or money like mine, or power
like mine. But they don't care about *me*."

When he was so close she felt the warmth of his breath, he
said: "There are a thousand reasons why not to be here."

She whispered: "A million."

"There are only two reasons for us to do this," he said. "I
want you."

"For what? Why?"

"For everything good we can have."

"That's too smooth, too easy, too . . ."

"No it isn't, and you know that."

"What . . . what's the other reason?"

"You want me, too." His hands slid up her sides, his fingers
brushed her breasts, he cupped her face and . . .

Kissing me, he's . . . Kiss him, *oh, God, kiss him!*

Wednesday morning, February 14, 7:16 A.M. A state trooper paced the ninth floor hall of the Lexington hotel.

Inspector Dalton Cole, FBI, opened his room door, stepped into the hall, clearly ready for work.

At the other end of the corridor, Lauren Kavenagh opened her door. She wore a casual dress suitable for traveling.

Before Lauren's door closed, Special Agent Sallie Pickett, FBI, entered the hall from her room.

In that heartbeat, Faron Sears walked out of his room.

The trooper swiveled his head each time a door opened.

"Hell," he finally told the four people trapped on the hall carpet: "Just one big, 'Good morning!' to all of you."

"Good morning," they all replied. The trooper pushed the elevator button. They broke the nails that held them to the floor, met in front of that machine. "Good morning," each one said to all the others. *Good morning.*

The elevator chimed. Cole and Sallie moved in front to catch any bullets. The doors slid open: two of Wood's security guards. Sallie and Cole insisted that Faron and Lauren get in first. They stood in front of the guards, faced the doors as Sallie and Cole entered, turned to the front.

"Hey!" yelled the state trooper.

Cole hit the rubber emergency strip and the doors bounced open.

"I almost forgot!" said the trooper. "Happy Valentine's Day!"

The elevator started down. At the eighth floor, a security guard cleared his throat. Faron turned to Lauren, his oldest friend: her neck was crimson, her eyes locked on the indicator panel above the doors. At the seventh, Faron looked at Cole's back, sensed the tension. At the sixth, Faron saw Sallie's eyes lowered so she couldn't see any reflections in the elevator doors. At the fourth, Faron began to hum along with the lobotomized music:

" . . . must be sure, *ba-da da* . . ."

The elevator passed the second floor. Faron felt all his companions praying for it to *get there fast*. He smiled, and kept singing:

" . . . than just, hold-ing hands . . ."

Elevator stopped, chimed; doors slid open. Cole and Sallie stepped out, saw Wood's man, and a trooper give the OK nod. Behind them Faron laughed. The three people who'd ridden the elevator with Faron stared at him.

"Happy, *happy* Valentine's Day!" said Faron.

The lobby team swept them toward the coffee shop. Wood looked up from his breakfast, said hello, sent a guard to stand outside the plate-glass windows as a human shield.

"How many?" asked the hostess, who gave Faron a shy smile of recognition. "Are you all together?"

"Apparently so," answered Faron. "More or less."

"So it's four then?"

"Two two's," said Faron as they followed her to a table with a good but protectable view. "We'll see how it goes."

Service was immediate: coffee, water, menus.

"I'm starved!" said Faron. "How about all of you?"

Spinning red light on a police cruiser rolling into the parking lot caught Cole's eye: The escort to the plane? A photographer for the *Herald* snapped pictures of the quartet.

"Down here," said the waitress, "we do eggs right."

"How's that?" said Faron.

Cole watched a huddled conference near the hotel entrance between a uniformed cop and a local FBI agent.

"Sunny side up. Over easy. Any way you want."

The local FBI agent hurried to the hostess. Glared at the oblivious newspaper photographer, nodded to the inspector from D.C.

Cole stood. "Would you excuse me? I'll be right back."

*   *   *

A camera flash ricocheted off white tile walls and a mirror to blind Cole with stars for a moment, then he could see again.

Like any public men's room, he thought: a damp scent of ammonia and urine, aluminum stalls, urinals, wall sinks, a mirror. Except this men's room in the arena where Faron held a rally reeked of death. A sticky brown smear covered the gray tiled floor. In that crusted lake lay a battered, slashed corpse.

"Just like the morning-shift man found him," said the captain of homicide, Lexington, Kentucky, Police Department.

A criminologist fingerprinted the towel dispenser. A technician took two more pictures. Hurried out.

"Figure your boy sucker-punched him," the captain told Cole. "Beat him to death with his own nightstick. What he did then . . . Answer me why he did what he did then."

On the mirror, smeared, rusty letters, stretched by gravity: HAppy VALEntinE's Day! DaLton CoLE FbI!

"Used the man's tie for a brush," said the captain. "Cut his throat to get the . . . Tell me why he did all this."

"Captain, your questions impinge on a classified federal—"

"Fuck federal! I know this old boy, and he got bushwhacked on my damn turf! Whoever did it left a dedication to a fucking federal cop who comes into my town with a politician and gets every Bureau badge off its federal butt playing bodyguard or hunting some guy you missed in Montana!"

"Who knows about this?"

"My murder squad and you. You're about to cough it all up."

"If we have to go to a judge—"

"Even your damn federal judges here gotta live here! Besides, you go to court, I'll have every damn newspaper and TV station and network stringer and . . ."

Cole pressed his hands to his legs to keep from trembling: "I don't want to do this the hard way."

"I don't care," said the captain. "I don't like Washington."

"Me either. But the only way to catch this monster is by working with Washington rules."

"I want a name."

"Try Kurt Vance, but he won't be using—" *Remember Nick, the Chris Harvie reservation.* "Captain: this man's wallet—"

"Missing. No money in his—"

"Get on the radio! Airport, bus station, hotels—anybody who buys a ticket using this victim's credit—"

The assisting detective ran the order out of the bathroom, left his captain and Cole alone with the dead.

"What about a picture of your guy?" said the captain.

"We all had one last night. Didn't do any good."

"Why?"

"I don't know," said Cole.

"Now, tell me *what*. Or do I start calling reporters?"

"Don't dime this out. You can close the murder, but it's—"

"I'm going to count to five."

"Count the seven agents I've got here. You're not locking me down while you set your play. I can't stop you, but you can't stop me either. You got a dime; I got a pocketful of change.

"Last five years, the Bureau's been all over this state. Wiretaps, stings. A lot of public officials and big shots caught corruption beefs. Plus, you know we raked in a ton of shit on major players that we didn't use. While you're dialing reporters, we'll be calling big-timers, explaining that because of you, we're going to have to pursue their shit trail that we found dormant in our files, that maybe we won't be able to indict them, but—"

"You're bluffing."

"You got to live out here, Captain. Not me."

The restroom door swung open. A morgue attendant said: "Hey, Captain! Can we take him?

"Captain?" the man repeated to the silence a moment later.

"Ask the damn FBI," said the local lawman.

"If the captain and his people are through, do what you do."

"Ahh . . . I'll get a gurney." The door closed.

"Thank you," Cole told the captain. "We'll co-operate as—"

"You sticking around?"

"No. I've got to . . . I think our perp's already—"

"Next time you come to town, I believe I'll shoot you." The captain left Cole reflected alone in the lettered glass.

Vance saw them as his jetliner taxied down the runway: four sedans, three cruisers spinning red lights, pulled up to the private jet that had been backed away from the terminal.

Look: there's the black bitch, hand against her thigh. *Your gun is out, darling.* There he is! A blur hustled into the chartered private jet. Oh, my, you are protective of him, aren't you, dear?

The jetliner shuddered under Vance.

I'm invisible again. It's a short hop, I can stay invisible.

Look! Dalton, that's you, getting into that jet, too! Good boy, always stay with the Man. I'm gonna beat you out of town.

Vance's plane roared down the runway. As he was pulled back into his seat, he stifled his laughter.

Happy Valentine's Day!

Wednesday, it was Wednesday. They killed Jesus on a Friday.

Late that Wednesday afternoon, Nick sat in the War Room, staring at four names and addresses on a yellow legal pad, four men who'd flown out of Lexington with addresses or identities deemed suspicious by the army of investigators Cole had scrambled into action. Nick stared at the names, at the slight tremble in his hands on the table beside the yellow legal pad.

Break away, think about something else, come back refocused. Think about the good days. Nick remembered his wife, the way she made him laugh, a kaleidoscope of a thousand ordinary days, a frozen vision of him fresh from some homicide scene where he had ruled to a chair beside her in the hospital room, impotently sitting through the hours until cancer would devour her. Together, they worked crossword puzzles and . . . *The first one to die was Chris* . . .

Four names on a yellow legal pad stared at him.

Cole and Sallie and the other agents working phones and studying reports paid no attention as Nick's pencil furiously scribbled on the pad.

Nick yelled: "He's using the name Lee Lawdos!"

"What?" It was Cole. The room fell silent.

" 'Lee Lawdos' is a we-don't-got-a-description man with a mail drop Chicago 'home' address who caught a plane yesterday from Lexington to Baltimore!" said Nick. "He's Kurt Vance!"

"How do you—"

" 'Lawdos' is an anagram for 'Oswald'—Lee Oswald."

Cole stared at his partner.

"Trust me," said Nick, "I know."

"It's just sick enough," said Cole. "We've got both Washington airports covered."

"He assumed that. But from Baltimore, he could take a train, a bus, rent a car . . . hell, almost walk here."

"The Fifth Floor called," said Cole. "We've run out of extra bodies. Double shifting, pulling in DEA, marshals . . ."

Cole drifted off, blinked back, said: "Lee Harvey Oswald?"

Nick rubbed his throbbing head. "Our boy isn't just hunting or running from us. He's mind-fucking us, too. Laughing. He's making some . . . masterwork triumph. And he's entered his killing zone."

"How come no one spotted him in Kentucky?"

"I don't know," said Nick. "Will Faron let us lock him down?"

"Funny you should use that term. He told me that nobody is going to put him in a prison again, least of all some creep who wants to kill him or some traitor who wants to stop him."

"Still got no idea who that is," said Cole. "Or who Vance is supposed to kill next, like it says in the message."

"Maybe that's another feint to throw us off," said Nick.

Cole shook his head. "Nobody knew we would intercept that e-mail."

"The Chicago police sent their surveillance tapes of the

prostitute Vance killed," said Nick. "Kurt Vance *picked* her. Maybe we can see why, maybe—"

The phone rang. Nick grabbed it, listened for a moment, then stared at Cole.

Cole and Nick entered a basement room at FBI Headquarters with a steel door and a shatterproof window. FBI agents, including the SAC for the Washington field office, waited in that sealed room, along with a technician who sat at the control board for a robot in the chamber on the other side of the shatterproof window. The DAAG smiled when Cole entered—a triumphant smile.

"The cost of your case is challenging its assumed benefit," he told Cole. "Who's worth what is a constantly shifting score."

"You keep it." Cole stared through the window.

On a table in the other room lay a book-size, padded mailer.

"Our first thought was that somebody mailed you a bomb," said the technician. "Twice the stamps needed to get here from San Francisco. Mailed Thursday. No return address. The dog said no, external scans said no, but prudence says take care. It rattles. X-rays show low metal content, a mass inside a cardboard box."

"When the 'suspicious parcel' alert came through for you," said the SAC for the Washington field office, "I checked with Cold Case. You should answer your messages. Supposedly, an informant looked for you by name in Fargo, North Dakota, nine days ago."

"Vance," said Nick.

"Find out everything that happened in Fargo around the day the contact about me was made," said Cole.

An agent reached toward a phone . . . it rang. He answered it, told Cole: "They're patching a call through for you."

Cole took the phone, nodded at the package: "Open it."

Into the phone, he said: "This is Cole."

The technician flipped switches, put his hands inside rubber gloves wired to a control console.

Over the phone, Cole heard Lauren: "Dalton? Can you talk?"

"Limited," he told her.

On the other side of the window, robot, claw-like hands on the end of jointed, cabled poles came to life.

"Do you have men following me?" asked Lauren.

Robot hands swung over the table.

"Yes," answered Cole.

Everyone in the basement room watched the robot.

Lauren said: "I thought . . . Don't you—"

"Security is the primary concern," Cole told her.

The technician said: "Whatever it is, it's stable enough to endure the U.S. mail."

Lauren's voice grew cold. "Nobody wants to kill me."

"You have to understand . . ."

"I thought I understood. I thought you were perfectly clear. You're my 'primary concern.' "

Steel hands capable of microsurgery plucked the package off the table, carried it to the glass for the men to read the address.

"This isn't the time to talk about this."

"Because it's Faron's time. Like always, all I am is part of—"

"No, that's . . . no."

The technician looked at Cole. He held up his hand: Wait.

"So was Kentucky hard work or simple pleasure?"

"You . . ."

"I'm sorry! I just . . . I'm being ripped apart! I knew what was what, what I was doing, but that was . . . Can you see me tonight?"

"I . . . no."

"When?"

Nick stared at Cole. Cole shook his head.

"I don't know," he told Lauren. "I have to go."

He hung up. Moved to the window.

Nick nodded to the package. "Recognize the handwriting?"

Cole stared at his name, the Headquarters address. "No."

The robot ferried the mailer back to the table, sliced a precise line through the manila mailer with a scalpel.

"No readings of released gas or vapors."

Robot fingers reached inside the slit. Lifted out a video cassette movie box.

"The mass is in there."

"Bring it close first," said Cole.

Metal hands swooped the cassette box next to the glass.

" 'The FBI Story,' " Nick read on the box. Smack on the movie box's still photo of the Eagle Scout good-guy pre-Watergate actor was a bright red lipstick kiss.

"Get it open!" ordered Cole.

As the robot moved the box back to the table, Nick said: "A $3.99 sticker from Wal–Mart, a close-out bin in Anywhere, U.S.A."

Out of the box, the robot shook four computer disks held together by a rubber band. A gloved technician brought the disks into the control room, booted one into a PC. The computer matched the disks' software, flashed a contents menu on the screen.

"Most of the files are encoded. Couple hours, we can crack them, but . . . Here, an uncoded one: 'NWSLTR.' "

The screen filled with a desktop publishing program, the front page of a newsletter emblazoned "PURE EYES ONLY—SECRET."

"Aryan America," whispered the technician.

"Ricki," said Nick.

"She sent you their computer files," said the DAAG, who'd read all the reports. "You must have had to fuck her good to get—"

Cole slammed him against a wall.

"Dalton!" Nick grabbed Cole as he pushed the DAAG's face against the reinforced plaster. Cole let him go, walked out.

"That's Strike Two, *Inspector* Cole!" the DAAG yelled after the man who'd left the room. "Next time . . ."

Nick smoothed wrinkles on the DAAG's suit. "Sir, you're confused. Inspector Cole isn't at bat, he's pitching."

Time rewound itself for Nick, and again a black Chicago prostitute named Sherry Ward was alive, prancing in platform heels down a sidewalk in the greenish tinge of an undercover, night-shot video. The time was forever, the season summer. She wore a micro dress, her purse slung over her shoulder. Sherry laughed and said something to a white woman who wore hot pants and black boots, then she sashayed to a side street. Nick saw her unlock a car, get in, drive away. Gone until he rewound the tape and her life played out again.

Time for Nick meant night, Wednesday, late. No one sat with him in the War Room. Only he watched the video of a butchered woman over and over again. He felt as alone and vulnerable as a whore driving a car toward certain death.

Earlier, over tasteless Chinese carry-out, he and Cole and Sallie had watched the videotape of Sherry Ward.

"Turn it off," Cole had said. "There's nothing there."

"Maybe," Nick had said. But what he thought was: *Yes, there is.*

Cole told them: "Valentine's Day is gone, we're sure Vance is in town, and it's too late."

"He won't get Faron." Sallie shook her head. "He won't."

"One man can't stand this much heat forever," said Nick.

"We don't have forever," answered Cole.

The Lexington team had nothing. The Chicago team had nothing. Fargo reported two criminal deaths, one of an ex-con who, after he was murdered, had his only legitimate charge card used to gas up a car with stolen North Dakota plates in Wisconsin. The team on Aryan America had nothing.

P.J. and his squad on the Yakuza had turned up nothing more linking the Yakuza, Yoshio Chobei or the law firm to Faron. The bust of the L.A. warehouse yielded a handful of untraceable amphetamines, as though the pills had been deliberately left there to be found, a gracious concession—and an insulting wink.

The surveillance of Faron's business rival reported nothing.

An FBI-D.C. police team canvassed every public lodging in the Washington area with Kurt Vance's computerized likeness and a list of possible aliases: Lee Lawdos, the Fargo murder victim, the man killed in Lexington, Brian Luster, Chris Harvie.

That likeness had been released to local media and TV crime-stopper programs: Armed and dangerous federal fugitive responsible for two murders, believed hiding in D.C. area. Reporters who asked questions received careful lies.

Wood put as many guards around Faron as he could. Wood had spotted the surveillance team on him. He ditched them, then called Cole. "You interfere with me only as I allow." Then waited where he was so Cole could direct the surveillance team to him.

Leibowitz stayed close to his apartment, and, according to the agents watching him, stayed there alone.

"He's not making any calls on his land line phone," reported Sallie, "but they've all got cellulars we can't scoop up."

Lauren was in her apartment, too. The tape of her phone call to Cole had been delivered to the War Room. Conscience made Cole put the tape in the case file.

I'm already on the cross, he thought. *What's a few more nails.*

Cole offered Sallie a ride home.

Nick told them: "I'll stick here tonight, use the cot."

In the War Room, Nick thought: *Every time I don't focus on work, I remember I'm not drinking.* The urge was there, but that was something he knew how to fight. Yet he'd never realized how much he'd organized his life around *the next drink.* What he felt was thirst, yes. Ache, yes. But mostly, loss. Not knowing what to do. Except work. And *not drink.*

He rubbed his throbbing head: too much coffee, too little sleep, no familiar anesthetic, too many screaming nerves hungry for the old habit. *Concentrate, got to concentrate.*

Because Nick had a secret. He knew he knew *something.* But he didn't know what. Didn't have a "what" to tell Cole.

Relax, got to relax, let it come, let . . . Get it here in time! Nick closed his eyes. Let go. Listened. *No hoofbeats. This would have been the time to take a short one to relax so . . .*

He picked up the TV/VCR remote, turned the machines on and filled his eyes with the tape of a woman walking and laughing and driving toward certain death: *What are you trying to tell me?*

Sallie sat in Cole's car outside her apartment building. Every breath spun her further into the swirl of a dark river.

"Tell me I blew it," she said, her eyes lost in the fogged windshield. "Tell my I threw away all professionalism. Jeopardized our mission. Endangered Faron. Violated Bureau regulations and street rules. Destroyed a career I've given my life to. Betrayed you and Nick and everybody and everything."

"Are we that powerful?" said Cole.

"What do you want me to do?" she asked him.

"We're in the same car." He shook his head. "No, that's wrong. At least you didn't compromise yourself with a suspect."

"I'm sorry."

"Me, too. But we're not totally sorry."

A car bathed them in headlights, drove by.

"What's the best that could happen?" asked Sallie.

"Right now, us sitting here, Kurt Vance could cross a cop, get his heart shot out. And some insider on Faron's staff we don't personally know could write a confession that ties up all the loose ends, videotape himself doing it, and end with a bang, blow his brains out."

"Do we get to live happily ever after then?"

"Sure. Why not."

They sat for a long time.

Cole said: "You're the finest agent I could have gotten. You got it all, do it all. Thank you."

The lone tear that escaped to run down her cheek answered him.

"Get some sleep," said Cole. "Don't let him catch us crying."

"We can't lose now," she whispered.

"You're right. We can't."

She opened the car . . . closed the door and pressed her forehead against Cole's shoulder. Then she got out, knew he watched her walk away down the long, empty sidewalk alone.

59

Thursday morning, the killer woke in his Washington, D.C., hotel bed. The "Do Not Disturb" sign hung on his door. Even if the maid blundered in, she'd see nothing suspicious, nothing that hadn't passed airport security: clothes, toiletries. His laptop computer and beeper.

If the FBI hadn't somehow realized he existed, thought Vance, *U.* would have been there to facilitate and validate: best-laid plans. Then he laughed. Improvisation is the measure of an artist. He would choose when and where to announce his reality.

What will be Number Two? Who else for *U.*? Wouldn't have needed *U.* Insist that *the big they* don't assume that.

He turned on the local TV news: Cloudy, seasonally cool, with temperatures near freezing all day. Chance of precipitation today near zero, tomorrow only 10 percent.

Perfect weather for invisibility. Two hours later, he stood in front of the security desk at the national headquarters of the Daughters of the American Revolution, a marble castle a quarter mile from the White House. He wore an old Army coat, blue jeans, a stocking cap, a beeper on his belt. *But I'm invisible.*

The guard behind the desk and a visiting colleague both frowned when he walked in. The desk guard said: "Can I help you?"

"Supposed to go to the museum."

"Down there," she said, watched him walk away.

Then she said to the tall black woman guard standing beside her: "So you down here permanent after tomorrow?"

Put your eyes on the framed picture of women in sashes. Watch reflections in the glass. Make sure the desk guard doesn't grab a phone.

"No way. Mostly, I'm over to Greenbelt, NASA. Making sure nobody walks out with a rocket ship."

Walk to the next picture, check them before you move.

"Hate this special stuff," the tall woman said.

"Ain't that the truth? Gotta wear special picture IDs and all. You got more of your people coming down with you?"

"Nah. You be the only one I'll know here in the morning."

"Forget it, girl. Tomorrow, I'm on maternity leave."

"Get outta here! Good for you! When you due? Your first?"

A woman peering through bifocals at documents in her hand walked out of an office as two uniformed women at the door machine-gunned each other with child data. The bifocal woman raised her gaze . . .

Turn to read the card in that display case.

The soon-to-be-mother in uniform told her colleague: "Go down that hall to get all what shit you need for tomorrow. Find anybody at our table, they'll snap you a face badge for you. Madhouse down there. They still got people phoning in to register, and now we gotta name tag everybody."

That was your idea, wasn't it, Dalton?

"Just so I get out of here before the damn meter maids show up. I got three whole days with the kids at their dad's, and I don't wanna start it with no twenty-dollar ticket."

"I hear that. Take you 'bout thirty minutes."

An arrow pointed down the corridor to the DAR's opera-house auditorium: Constitution Hall. Vance followed the zigzagging corridors leading from the museum and administrative offices to the street entrance of the hall. Standing in an alcove, he watched policemen supervising the installation of metal detectors, security desks. He grabbed a broom and immediately *belonged* here, stayed invisible as he walked through the side door to the stage.

Constitution Hall was a vast horseshoe auditorium with rows of blue padded chairs and gold stars and scarred mahogany. White columns flanked the stage where technicians bolted steel plates inside a lectern. A policeman led a German shepherd along each of the thousand rows of seats: bomb dog.

Fire roared in Vance's eyes, and he saw the vision.

The bomb cop turned toward the stage. Kurt swept the broom across that bare wood and walked out the stage door on the other side into a corridor crowded with massive breaker boxes, lighting and sound panels, curtain controls. He spotted a solid door and opened it: a humid furnace room. He couldn't go in there. A flight of steps led him back the way he'd come. The pregnant security guard sat at her station alone. As he passed her desk, he saw a computerized image of himself, *before*, taped next to her red phone.

But now I am invisible.

Outside was cold, gray. The wind picked up. Cars stood in front of every parking meter along the curb. He shared the sidewalk only with a gray man pushing a shopping cart full of bundles.

Improvisation is the measure of an artist.

Friday morning, 7:09, Cole stood in his kitchen making instant coffee. The milk in his refrigerator had long since gone sour. He thought: *This is no way to live.*

Someone knocked on his door.

Cole wore his blue shirt, pants, but not his shoes and socks. His hair was damp from the shower. His Beretta was in the bedroom.

"Who is it?" said Cole as he stood clear of the door.

A muffled female voice said: "Dalton! It's me!"

Sallie? Dalton kept the chain on, stood back from the door as he opened it. *Lauren* stood in the hall, shivering in a trench coat, a giant black purse slung over her shoulder.

"I'm not here," she said as he let her in.

"What do you mean?"

"Your men watching my place think I'm still there. I gave twenty dollars to the old lady across the hall to let me go down her fire escape, come back the same way. I feel like one of your secret agents."

"Why?"

"To give you a chance to be with me. No one knows I'm here. I caught a cab to your corner, walked in with the three maids. My collar up, hair in this bun . . . Did your men out front warn you?"

"No."

"Aren't you glad I came? Don't you care?"

Her cheeks and mouth were cold to his kiss. Cole leaned back, told her sad smile: "I have to—"

"Shhh." She shook her hair free and stroked his freshly shaved cheek. "It's Friday. Early. There's nothing you can do about Faron now. Except handcuff a suspect who's right here."

"I wish . . . Listen, he's still going to make that speech today."

"Faron only cares about the voices inside him."

"Sometimes I think he is crazy."

"You make *me* crazy. You make me forget everything." She tried to kiss him. "This is what you're supposed to do. This is safe."

"Faron—"

"Is speaking to the National Coalition of Black Women at ten. He may not be safe with them, but none of them are assassins."

"Sallie's on him." He reminded himself more than told her.

"I bet." Lauren traced the furrow of Cole's brow.

He swallowed. "Cops there, too. My agents. Wood's people, the DAR's security service."

"One more gun there won't make any difference." She ran a finger along his side, up his chest. "You don't even have one."

"It's in the bedroom."

"Ahh!"

"We can't. I have to go."

"Where?" she said. "To follow orders from your bosses or the heartless Mr. Should? Where's better than here and now?"

"I'm responsible for—"

"For yourself," she said. "The hell with Faron. You got an army protecting him, nobody doing anything for you. What more can you personally do right now to stop anybody from killing him?"

"Besides," she untied the belt of her trench coat, "if he cared about dying, he wouldn't be where he is."

The trench coat fell off her shoulders. She was naked.

"I always wanted to do that," she said, stepping out of low shoes. "But it's so cold out there."

Barefoot, she walked toward his bedroom.

"Don't go," she said. They lay in his bed, a sheet over their nakedness. Gray light filled his window. "We can stay here forever. We can put our dark glasses on and nobody will be able to see us and it will all be OK if we just stay here."

His clock radio showed 8:27. At 7:30, the alarm he'd set the night before as a fail-safe turned the radio on. Dave Brubeck's "Take Five" filled the room, but they hadn't cared.

"No," he told her. "I have to go."

"Did you mean what you kept yourself from saying?" she asked.

He looked in her eyes: "Yes."

She whispered: "I meant it when I didn't say it, too."

They kissed, hard.

"Don't go," she said. "Don't leave me."

"If I don't do what I should, I'm no good to you. Or me."

"Then promise me you'll stay away from Faron. You won't run away with me and my million dollars. So OK. Chase your killer. But stay away from Faron."

"Why?"

"Because Faron's killer might miss his target, and I don't want you nearby."

"He might miss, but I won't."

Her eyes bored into him: "Promise me that you won't miss. That you'll shoot first and won't miss."

"Lauren . . ."

"That's the only way I'll let you go."

"I'll do my job."

"Damn your job! Kill him so you'll come back to me alive!"

"I'm not a . . . I've only killed once and I don't—"

"It only takes once to kill you."

He said: "I can't die now. But I have to go."

"Will you drive me to our headquarters?"

"That's on the Hill. I was going to Constitution Hall."

"Won't take long. If you do, I promise I won't make your men look bad again."

Cole smiled. "Interfering with a federal officer in performance of his duty is a felony."

She smiled. "I'd say your performance was superb."

Nick heard hoofbeats. *Surging, pounding, horse tight between his thighs, mini dress high-heeled Sherry screaming/running for her car charge past her like wind, volcano eyes . . .*

"Sir?"

"Huh, wha—" Nick opened his eyes.

A housekeeper agent stood above him.

Blink. *I'm in the War Room. A blizzard fills the TV.*

"You fell asleep," said the agent. He turned off the TV, raised the window shade on a gray day.

"When?" Nick stirred on the sofa. "What time is it?"

"Nine thirty-one," said the agent. "You want some coffee?"

Nick swung his shoes to the floor. His knee was stiff and his neck cramped. The room was cold, but his clothes were clammy. "Yeah, I'd love coffee. I'll go down—"

"I'll get it. And a towel for the shower. There's some clean Bureau sweats you can wear."

"You don't have to do that."

"Believe me," said the agent, sniffing as he left Nick's atmosphere. "My pleasure."

The dream, thought Nick: *What was it?* All night long, he'd reread files, looking for what it was in them that he felt but didn't see. The tape of Sherry pulled him; he watched her timeless walk and driveaway to forever dead. He had fallen asleep on the couch, woke charging in a dream toward . . . toward what?

"This morning," said the agent as he carried two foam cups into the War Room, "you drink it black."

Hot, with a metallic taste. Caffeine hit Nick's—*Blink.* He whispered: "Where would you stay if you came to Washington to kill somebody important?"

The agent saw Nick's face: "What do you—"

Nick grabbed the phone on his desk, dialed the number.

"Homicide, Detective Mizell."

"Lou, it's Nick! Fast: What hotel did John Hinckley stay at when he came to shoot Reagan?"

An instant after he got the answer, Nick slammed down the receiver, grabbed the phone book. He ripped out the page with the hotel's address and phone number. The housekeeper agent yelled to his colleagues downstairs: "We're hot!"

A desk clerk answered Nick's call, then obeyed his shouted order to move to a phone where no one could see him. Nick told the agent who stood beside him: "Patch us into the Bureau's records division and make sure they know we're running!"

He pointed to the hotel's name on the torn page: "Roll undercover teams to cover that hotel! Scramble a SWAT squad to a hold point out of sight of the hotel!"

The agent punched numbers into another phone. Other agents crowded into the War Room doorway.

"Sir," said the desk clerk when he came back on the phone, "we've been checked by the FBI. None of our guests match that computer picture, and frankly, all this is becoming a major—"

Nick yelled: "Make me happy or I'll register you in a major cell!"

A third voice entered the phone conversation before the desk clerk recovered: "CID patched in."

"Mr. Clerk, read every person registered in your hotel to this guy. CID, run them against your data base, not just our case logs. Verify home addresses with the phone companies; that's not enough, but do it first and do it now!"

"Affirmative."

"Get me through our main number; I'm mobile!" Nick hung up, grabbed his sport jacket, his gun.

The agent who'd awakened him said: "Shouldn't we wait for—"

"I'm through waiting!" Bad knee, bad leg, bad thirst, he charged outside.

Nick got the call in the car five blocks from the safe house.

"We got a hit!" said an agent at CID. "Lone male registered as 'Ray E. James!' Room 734! His registered L.A. phone is bogus, he left a cash deposit, and—"

"Repeat that name!" said Nick.

"I say again: 'Ray E. James.' Los Angeles addr—"

"Anagram!" yelled Nick. "Flip it: James Earl Ray! King's assassin!"

Nick ended the call, told the agent driving: "Hit it!"

He dialed Cole's cell phone as the BuCar surged forward, its red lights and siren cutting the quiet residential morning air.

The Capitol dome filled Cole's rear-view mirror. He swerved the undercover sedan to the nearest curb. Lauren held on in the seat beside him. Cole shouted into his phone: "I'm almost at Faron's! No siren. Take me fifteen minutes to get there! Don't wait!"

He snapped the phone shut, turned to Lauren.

"No!" she said.

"Get out, walk to . . . Please!"

"No!" She clutched the big purse that had held her clothes. "I'm not going to let you go die!"

He glared at her.

"You don't have time!" she said.

He tore away from the curb in a tire-crying U-turn.

The door exploded into Room 734. Two SWAT cops burst inside, shotguns ready. On their heels charged a beefy man brandishing a .45. Forty seconds later, as a SWAT team member muttered "shaky probable cause; no warrant" to his partner, Nick punched Cole's cell-phone number: "He's not here."

"Shit!" Cole stepped on the brake, didn't run the red light. Lauren's face was ashen.

Nick swept the hotel room with his eyes: laptop computer, shoe box, the SWAT team dumping a suitcase on the bed. Cops crowding into the room. Nick beckoned a SWAT team member out of the bathroom, went in there alone for quieter conversation.

"We'll set up an ambush," he told the phone, "but he's out there."

Nick looked around the bathroom. Used towels hung neatly over the shower rod. A long black hair lay coiled in the sink.

In Nick's earpiece, Cole said: "I'll alert Sallie at Constitution Hall, but unless Faron—"

"Wait one," said Nick. Cole parked in front of a fire hydrant. Nick picked the hair out of the sink, held it up to the light. Laid it back on the white porcelain. Somewhere, he heard *hoofbeats*. Nick slid open the medicine chest: a safety razor, shaving cream. Two flat white plastic disks. One sponge sat on top of the disks, a bag of sponges waited on the floor.

"Are you there?" said Cole.

Nick unscrewed the top of a disk. A fine dark powder filled the open disk. The powder was soft, and it stained his pale Indian skin a shade of night. He rubbed his fingertip on his hand that held the phone. *Sherry getting into car, driving . . . crime scene, her purse empty, no ID, no driver's . . .*

Through the phone, Cole heard Nick whisper: "Oh, shit!"

"All answers come down to one word."

Faron's amplified voice rolled from the shielded lectern to the packed main floor and balconies of Constitution Hall's opera house.

"Love."

Standing in the wings to Faron's left, Sallie felt warmth flow through her jagged nerves. You promised, she whispered to him with her mind, you promised you'd stay behind the lectern.

Faron's words reached out to the sea of black faces:

"Love that is true, not cheap. Love that is tough. Love that does not look away. You do not love your oppressor; you love life, and that love puts you in a pitched battle for yourself."

Don't listen to him, don't be lulled by his words: stay ready.

"The sword that love puts in your hand must be different from the whip that your oppressor holds. You do not fight him on his terms for his crown, you fight him to free everyone from any whip, a fight that becomes your own victory."

I belong here, thought Sallie as she looked out at the black women who filled the auditorium. Racists once kept an opera singer from performing in this hall dedicated to freedom because she was black. But we refused to be denied. Black women, white women, other freedom rebels fought back, and today I stand everywhere. Anywhere. I—we—will not be denied.

"Love requires more courage than facing death. Ask a woman who's risked bearing a child. Love opens you to unbearable loss. All friends die, all lovers die, every child dies. That terrible price is exceeded by only one pain: to deny love is to deny the moments that brighten eternity. Without the light of love, never will we have more than the dark burning rain of fate."

From where she stood in the wings with a uniformed D.C. policeman and one of Constitution Hall's unarmed security guards, Sallie scanned the balcony, hunting for the barrel of—

Beep beep beep!

Hers, not the security guard's beeper. Sallie checked the number, used her cell phone to call the War Room. The agent who answered could barely contain his excitement: "We may have acquired the target! I'll report!"

Sallie closed the phone. Relief washed away her tension.

On the stage, Faron held his open hand, palm out, to the audience: "Five killers stalk us today.

"Five crises bleed America every day:

"Fear. Despair. Ignorance. Poverty. Racism.

"Any one of those killers can shatter imperfect America and its dreams. Those five killers hunt together, strengthen each other. Their rampage from sea to shining sea breeds corruption, crime, violence, jealousy, hatred, self-destruction, slavery, soulless death. They wear a million disguises. TV commercials for products that promise happiness but deliver trinkets. Crack dealers who promise heaven and hand children hell."

Sallie's cell phone buzzed. "This is Control. We missed him. Stand by." Her stomach churned. She made her hand stop trembling.

"Our best weapon against the five killers is love. Love fights the servants of death. A billion dollars spent fighting crime with a heart full of hate is a billion dollars spent toward failure, a billion dollars spent replacing vicious criminals' hate with our own. Even if we lock up the crooks, the hate stays free to haunt us and slay us as we sleep.

Again her phone buzzed. "It's Nick! Vance is there with you!"

"What! How, he—"

"What I say is not important. What we do is. No leader can stop those five killers. The most any leader can do is shine light on us or shoot a flare into the darkness. You and I and America can be saved only by each other: white, black, brown, red, yellow, man, woman, sick, healthy, old, young."

"Listen! He's there as Sherry, the prostitute he—"

"What?"

"The secret of existence is that everything we do affects the universe. We can't control our effect. A billion times, we get zero justice for our choices. But we know that how we act shapes what we do. If we serve the five killers, then they will rule our lives."

". . . skin stained black, a black wig. The convention registration desk says Sherry picked up her name tag this morning! He used her driver's license for ID. He's there as a convention-eer! He's in the audience! As a black woman!"

"Let me tell you about fear."

A dozen policemen burst through a door at the back of the auditorium. First one, then twelve, then a hundred women in the audience saw them. A faceless murmur overpowered Faron's words.

Sallie yelled to the cop and security guard: "Come on!"

They ran on stage as a dozen women in the balcony hurried down the stairs. Two women on the main floor dashed for exits. A policeman yelled: "Stop those people!" The crowd surged with invisible terror.

"What are you doing?" Faron yelled to her, his words broadcast by the microphone to the panicking crowd.

A scream shot from the audience. Sallie lunged between Faron and the mass of humanity, her eyes scanning the faces for *the threat*, her gun in her hand.

The roar of the crowd filled the air. Frightened faces crowded against the stage. A dozen women stampeded up the stairs and out the stage exit where Sallie had been standing.

Press Faron between the city cop and me, pull the security cop with no damn gun and minimum-wage guts up behind Faron.

She saw it the same time as the security cop with the stupid glasses and ugly earrings: the exit on the other side of the stage.

Phalanx around Faron, thought Sallie. Get him there, turn . . . Corridor, breaker boxes . . . the hall ahead goes where? Doesn't matter; a hundred running people fill it. The security guard tried a door opposite the breaker boxes; it opened: Yellow walls, pipes, steel stairs down to a cement floor.

"Go!" Sallie pushed the D.C. cop into the basement room, pushed Faron in behind the cop, ignored his protest. She swung her gun to the crowd, backed through the door, then told the anxious unarmed woman guard: "Close it!"

Sallie turned, saw Faron going down the stairs, heard the click of the steel door closing. The city cop was on last ste—

The security guard kicked Sallie in the kidneys. Sallie's head snapped back—a fist grabbed Sallie's hair and slammed her head into the wall, then pushed her body down the stairs into Faron. Faron crashed into the cop. The cop turned—

The guard shot the cop three times with the .25-caliber automatic built into a beeper. The first shot hit the cop's bulletproof vest. The second slug cut his arm as he drew his Glock. The third tore through his cheek. The impact spun him around. He tried not to fall . . .

A spit-shined shoe kicked Faron to the cement floor. The guard pressed the muzzle of the beeper against the cop's head, squeezed off the fourth round.

Faron rolled over on the cement, saw Sallie crumpled at the bottom of the steps; saw the dead policeman; saw the guard, the murdered cop's blood dripping from her cheeks and the crooked hair and glasses she was pulling off as she grabbed the cop's Glock and said in a man's voice: "Loved your speech."

*   *   *

Cole swerved the car around a woman running in the street as he skidded and double-parked in front of Constitution Hall. Women poured out of the main doors.

"Stay here!" he yelled to Lauren.

"No!" She jumped out of the car to follow him. Her shoulder bag bounced off a fat woman wobbling in high heels.

Cole ran to the side of the building: women fled the museum. He fought his way inside. Behind him he heard Lauren: "Dalton!" Turning, he saw her white face amidst the rush of backs, her hand reaching toward him. Then the crowd swarmed and she was gone.

The crowd propelled three women helping a feeble grandmother toward Cole, a solid wall of humanity that would sweep him back outside. He saw a doorway, fought his way through it, bouncing off running women, fighting the opposite direction they were going. He staggered onto a wooden floor to face a gilded cavern of fear.

A coffee-skinned woman in a yellow suit vaulted onto the stage, ran past Cole. Women filled the aisles. Uniformed policemen tried to calm them. The roar of voices was deafening. He could have fired his Beretta and not been heard twenty feet away.

"Wait!" he yelled to a forty-something woman in a lawyer's suit as she ran past him. He held out his hand—

She punched him in the face, recoiled, tried . . . couldn't speak to Cole. Ran. What she feared was consumed in her eyes by the horror of what she'd done.

Faron said: "You don't need to kill her!"

The thing turned from the stairs where it stood above Sallie's crumpled form. Stared at him with colorless eyes. Its wig was askew, ruby lipstick smeared, white uniform shirt fouled with blood. The beeper that transmitted bullets was clipped on its belt; the Glock taken from the executed policeman filled its hand and swung toward Sallie's head.

"She didn't see you!" cried Faron.

"Of course she didn't." A man's voice. "I was *invisible*."

"So she can't identify you!"

"But is that valuable? Or not?"

Faron licked his lips. "You have the power to decide that."

"That's all the bargaining you can come up with? You were supposed to be sort of smart."

Faron didn't move his feet or drop his hands. "Once you kill her, you lose power over her."

"Now *that's* smart." Vance smiled. Locked his arms, both hands on the gun zeroing Sallie's—

"No!" yelled Faron.

The gun swung back to nail Faron to the concrete, and the thing laughed. "Gotcha!"

"I'm all you want! All you need!"

"Wrong, wrong, wrong. So typically wrong, wrong, wrong. Let's see how smart you are. Convince me that we have a lot of time together, time so she can live longer. Maybe, who knows? Live to put flowers on your coffin!"

"You're in charge of time," was all Faron said.

"Not bad," said the killer. "Not great, but . . . Figure you're under a little stress. Face the other way."

Do it, thought Faron: He'd want you to see him shoot her. He heard muffled sounds. Two ratchety clicks. Clanging, what . . . ?

"Turn around!"

Sallie hung face down, her hands cuffed behind her back, looped around the steel railing.

"Look at all the wonderful things she carried!" The killer put Sallie's FBI credentials in his pocket, along with her phone. Her gun was in his belt. "Step back three giant steps."

The gun thrust at Faron the instant he moved to comply. "Ah-ah! I didn't say 'Mother May I'!"

Vance laughed, then walked over to a wood cabinet mounted on the yellow cinder-block wall.

"Oh, look!" He held up a roll of silver tape. "Improvisation is the measure of an artist."

The killer took the dead policeman's handcuffs. "Let's see what's down that way."

Faron obeyed the gestured command to walk down a muggy corridor where thick pipes for steam, water, and gas followed the walls and ceilings.

"What's the bitch's name?" asked the killer behind him.

"The woman's name is Sallie."

"Is she any fun?"

Water puddles on the floor splashed with their steps.

Where are you, Cole? Nick? Where are Wood and Nguyen and—

"How much time do you think we have?" asked the killer.

"That's up to you."

"Mmmmn, no. Not entirely. But no one saw us come in here; we can't hear what looked like a swell riot outside, so they can't hear us. Besides, everyone knows you're safe with *Sallie.*"

"Do I turn left or right?"

"Tell you what: you choose."

Left. Wider passageway, maybe fifteen feet. Big pipes on each side. But that choice dead-ended forty feet beyond where they turned.

"Well, you chose it. Go down there."

Hot. Dank. Bright yellow walls. Light from bare bulbs screwed between pipes in the ceiling.

"Turn around." Ten feet away, he stared at Faron. Took off the black wig: a shaved, dark skin-melting head. A head of a bald black man, a human being painted invisible with a cliché of color.

"Now you get another choice." He tossed handcuffs to Faron. "You can snap the cuffs on one wrist, stick your hands around that pipe over our heads, cuff your other wrist. Or not do it. Or try to fake me out, attack me. Then, as a consequence of your choice, what do we think will happen to the bitch?"

Faron stood on his toes to cuff himself over the pipe. When he let the cuffs take his weight, the steel bit into his wrists, the concrete floor scraped the soles of his shoes.

"Don't you love freedom of choice?" The killer kicked Faron in the groin.

Gasping, wheezing, Faron forced out the words: "You can only kill me, not save your—"

Gray tape pressed over Faron's mouth.

"I'm already saved." The killer smiled. Faron couldn't take his eyes off that face, the beads of sweat tracing black furrows down the cheeks from the shaved head. Mascara and pancake makeup clotted and ran with the furnace room's humidity. Even the color of the killer's hands was smearing.

"Do you like my earrings? Catch the eye so you don't notice

much else." The killer squeezed his chest: "How 'bout my breasts? Are they as nice as Sallie's?"

He snaked the tie off Faron's neck, ripped Faron's shirt open and pressed his sticky, melting palm over Faron's naked chest. "This is the only heart you have."

The killer pulled lipstick out of the uniform shirt he had acquired from the woman who normally protected NASA, the woman he had stalked and stuffed into her car after she had emerged from Constitution Hall. He had altered her picture ID to show his cosmeticized image with a thirty-dollar self-developing camera and a one-dollar laminating machine in a drugstore. He ran the bright red lipstick over his lips . . . kissed Faron's breastbone.

Buzzing! What the . . . ?

The killer took Sallie's cell phone from his pocket. Held his finger to his smeared lips: "Shhh!" Opened the phone and listened. Mouthed: "It's for you!" Held the phone to Faron's ear: Crackling, underground static: "'ther—'n't—ere—u—ole—"

Snap! The phone closed by Faron's ear.

"I guess cellular phones don't work in Hell." Kurt put the phone away: "Let's make it an even dozen."

The killer measured paces down the passageway away from where Faron hung.

One. "The Usher is supposed to be here, but . . . Best laid plans and artist's improvisations."

Two. "Oh, don't worry, I'll get away! I'll wipe off my old *invisibility,* put on the policeman's clothes, carry your Sallie to safety. In the pandemonium, everyone will focus on the wounded FBI woman. See me as a rescuing, heroic cop. Then color me gone."

Three. "I wish we had more time to share. We're so alike!"

Four. "They think both of us are weird. Crazy. Geniuses, but bad."

Five. "We both know the big truth."

Six. "Power is everything."

Seven. "But bottom line, score me perfect, score you a loser."

Eight. "Because you're afraid of power. You think giving it away will keep you safe and free. Guys like Agent Cole think they can control power. You're both wrong."

Nine. "I embrace power. So I become power. And that makes you just another log in my fire."

Ten. "Wonder what the Usher has in mind for me after you."

Eleven. "But don't let the Usher confuse you. Just so you know . . ."

Twelve. The killer aimed his gun at the lipstick kiss: "I am the brightest shining—"

They heard the sudden *roar* of the crowd outside. A moment later came the metal *clunk* of the boiler room door closing, then silence. The killer looked back the way they'd come.

On the stage, Dalton snapped his cell phone shut. Where are you, Sallie? You answered, but all I heard was static. An old woman sat down in the front row. Think! Where would she go, where would she take him? *If you lose control, take cover.*

"What are you standing up there for?" the old woman yelled.

Cole ran to the other side of the stage. Ahead of him was a hall, cable and breaker boxes. And a door. Something smeared the knob, something dark, dried, not blood, but . . .

Dalton put the universe in the V-sight of his drawn Beretta. He threw open the door. The roar of the crowd followed him in, died when the door clunked shut behind him. He saw stairs leading down. Passageways. Pipes everywhere.

Sallie, God Sallie cuffed up . . . Cop, Jesus! Head gore, dead!

He followed the Beretta down the stairs toward the policeman who'd been shot through the head. *Risk a glance:* Sallie, handcuffed, slumped, blood on the stairs. But her back moves, eyes shut, but she's breathing! Who else is still alive?

Static on the phone: who'd answered? Can't make a call, wouldn't get through, *no time:* Don't die dialing for help.

Hot, wet: pipes. Why is it so damn quiet? The corridor junctions in a T: right or left? Go right, toward most people's strong side.

Crouch low . . . Lunge out! Dead end ten feet away. Lunge back. Go left fast. This time, go out high . . . Jump—

Beyond the sights the Beretta, Faron dangled from a pipe.

A security guard lay face down over a pipe running on the wall at knee height. Her black hair hung limp, and on the back of her white shirt was a smear of fresh blood.

Got her from behind, Vance—Cole whirled, zeroed the gun behind him—*Nothing.* Whirled back.

Faron's mouth was taped, his nose bled like he'd been hit. His eyes were dazed, but blinking back to life—alive.

Cole shuffled toward Faron, his Beretta pointing to the wall that must not be a dead end, must have an outlet where Vance ran. Cole stepped past the blood-smeared security guard.

Faron swung down the pipe toward Cole. *Why is he kicking at me?* Then, in that heartbeat, he realized why Faron's nosebleed was fresh, why the guard's back was smeared with blood. Cole whirled.

The apparition charging Cole came from Hell: a horrific face streaked with blood and stain and hunger, a gun in each slippery hand. Both the killer's guns roared.

A bullet tore Cole's left shoulder; another clipped his hair.

Cole swung his gun backhand across the killer's pistols as they fired again—bullets ricocheted off a pipe.

Close, he's too—Cole pushed a pistol muzzle away from his face, swung his Beretta back—

The killer chopped Cole's wrist with the gun in his left hand. With his right hand, he smashed Sallie's automatic into Cole's face.

Cole stumbled, tried to swing the Beretta around to fire. He slammed into a shin-high pipe, fell on it as the killer's guns sent two slugs ripping through the air where he'd been. Cole crashed to the floor, rolled on his back, the Beretta swinging around—

Kurt Vance's leer emerged from a melting mask of dark stain and blood as he raised his two guns, and both he and Cole knew that the FBI agent was doomed.

Three gunshots roared through the dank, yellow basement.

Kurt Vance pitched forward. One gun flew from his gorestained hand. The other gun fired, a reflexive jerk squeezing the trigger and ricocheting the slug off the back wall. The killer crumpled like a puppet shorn of strings.

Lauren stood in the tunnel, revolver grasped in both hands.

"Dalton!" Tears streamed down her cheek. "I couldn't let him kill you!"

Cole pulled himself to his feet, his shoulder throbbing from Vance's bullet.

"Are you hurt? Oh, God, did he—"

Hand is heavy: Beretta, never dropped my—Cole saw the cop's gun on the floor. Sallie's gun in dead damn dead Kurt Vance's grip. Cole felt a graveyard claw grab his spine. "Lauren . . . Where did you get the gun?"

She stared at the revolver she held. "It was my father's . . . I told you, he was in law enforcement."

Dalton moved toward Lauren. "What does that mean?"

"It doesn't matter! Nothing matters! It's over!"

" 'Law enforcement.' Not what you say when . . . He wasn't a cop."

"He was a prison guard! You can it look it up! What difference does it make! Come here, let me—"

Freeze. Beretta still . . . *Go backwards up the killing chain:* Faron dangling from the pipe to . . . Kurt Vance to . . . Chris Harvie, who knew that psycho assassin to . . . Chris's Number One bad-guy contact, Brian Luster, long time hustler and *ex-con* to . . .

"Why won't you come to me?" she said.

Faron, dangling, mouth taped, tried to talk with his eyes.

"Put the gun on the floor," said Cole.

"Why?"

"You don't need it anymore. You're right; it's over."

She whispered: "What do you want me to do?"

"It's OK. You're safe. It's over."

The light in her face changed; a smile twitched her mouth. "We can walk away now?"

"Yes."

Then her gun arm tensed. "You said you'd never lie to me."

"Give me the gun, Lauren."

But she pointed it at him. "Don't do this! You don't have to do this! There are ways—"

"One way." He held the Beretta, not pointing at her, but . . . "One way. Put the gun on the floor."

"No!" With both hands, she locked the revolver on Cole . . . Training swung his Beretta up. "Stop it!"

"You stop it!" Tears filled her eyes. "You couldn't stop him. You couldn't stop it these few weeks. I couldn't stop it after I . . . after we . . . He wouldn't 'betray destiny.' Internet e-mailed him, but I couldn't turn him off; I knew it when he . . ."

"You brought the gun with you because you knew," said Cole.

"That was the plan." Bitterness fought sorrow and hope in her voice. "The old plan. Would have been so easy, walk Faron to wherever Vance was, just him and me and—"

"*Number Two,*" said Cole. "Vance's second job was to die. You were going to kill him the instant he had killed Faron."

Faron thrashed as he dangled from the pipe.

"It worked with Oswald," said Lauren. "Obvious psycho dead before he talked. Me as the witness and lucky avenging angel. Vance needed a glorious mission to make the world recognize what he was. Him thinking he had two steps to glory kept him from betraying me before—"

"What about Monk?"

She stabbed the gun at the air. "That wasn't supposed to happen! That was another damn thing Faron made happen! Monk . . . I was skimming cash to send to Vance; Monk found me. Sat him down at computer to show him I wasn't . . . I had to! Didn't know the fucking FBI already had ruined everything!"

She sobbed. Her gun shook, but the muzzle stayed locked on Cole. She whispered: "We can work it out! We can be together!"

Her gun pointed at him, his Beretta stayed locked on her.

"We were a lie! You came to my apartment to keep me—"

"Safe," she said. "To keep you from this and safe. If you'd let me then, now, if you let—"

"We are a lie!"

"No, we aren't. You weren't lying to me. What you brought back to life in me wasn't lying to you. Or I wouldn't be here now, or you'd be dead now, and my heart would be, too."

A dark lake on the floor spread around Cole's shoes.

"You know that's true," she whispered.

"Doesn't matter. There's too much to answer for."

"If Vance killed Faron, all the answers are done."

They ignored muffled sounds. Cole stepped back. Lauren followed him step for step, like dancers, like cats circling meat dangling from a snare. Rubbing his face against an arm chained above his head, Faron freed the tape over his mouth.

"Why?" he shouted.

Lauren and Cole jumped—kept their guns zeroed on each other.

Faron said: "Lauren, I gave you everything I could!"

"You took everything I had!" She stepped past the body of the man she had shot. Cole stepped with her, trying to keep Faron out of the center of their circle, out of the line of fire.

Faron said: "I don't know what—"

"That's the big truth!" She shouted at the man dangling from the pipe. Kept her eyes and gun pointed at the man who aimed his gun at her. They circled around Faron, slowly, side-step by sidestep. "You never knew! You never cared about—"

"That's wrong! You know I—"

"All the big ideas, you cared about them, and—"

"You, I gave you all the love I had!"

"Not enough, not near enough. You said it yourself last year. All these years, it was just so easy for you. Think the big thoughts, do the big deeds, let me make it all work!"

"I don't unders—"

"For years I gave you everything! Remember the fire that almost wiped us out? But, like . . . wow! We were insured, and the money bailed out your failures, and you went on to make . . .

"*I* made that fire," she said. "Knew we needed it, knew *you* needed it, and anything you wanted or needed . . . nothing was . . . My father knew he owed me. Knew he had to help me."

Cole said: "He was a guard at the prison where—"

"Brian Luster," whispered Lauren. "I paid him to set the fire, but Luster wanted more than just money. And I paid. I let him . . . he made me . . . all for you, and it was . . . and you didn't care and—"

"You never told me! I wouldn't have let you—"

"You never wanted to know!"

Circle, get close to her, let her focus on Faron, grab . . . Oh, God, Lauren, Lauren!

"You made me," Lauren hissed. "You made me what I . . .

"Then," she yelled, "then you had your damn *epiphanies*! Your damn *awakenings*! And you didn't give a damn about—"

"No!" said Faron. "I wanted you to share—"

"Yeah, well, how was I going to waltz into heaven after you'd turned me out as your whore in Hell?

"Last time . . . I tried one last time," she said. "Got you back in my bed—remember? Did Dalton tell you?"

What? Don't—

"The money the computer showed I took. Oh, yeah, I had a hysterectomy. *After* I had the abortion.

"Two payments, Dalton, only you never checked what they were for! Two payments, two . . . procedures. After I found out that he'd come back to my bed because he felt sorry for me, after he told me how he wouldn't burden any child with being—"

"You never told me!" cried Faron, twisting to find her face. "I never knew you were—"

"I was damned if I was going to give you any more of my flesh!" Her gun trembled. "I could have had that baby! And afterwards, when I went back to . . . and they found the infection I got from the abortion, and then they cut out any chance ever . . . You took it. You took that last chance from me, too.

"Then you told us how you were going to give away the empire I built for you with my flesh and blood and . . . give it away to . . . buy me out with *money*, make me just another rich old woman with *no one* and *nothing I built* left to call my own!"

"You didn't have to kill me," said Faron.

"But I *could*. I couldn't reach you any other way, but *that I could do*. And save at least some of what was mine for me, too."

"Let her go, Cole."

"Faron—"

"He won't do it," she said. "He's just like you. Some big, heartless 'it' is more important to him than a woman who loves him.

"Who he loves," she added softly.

Circling around Faron, Cole said: "Lauren, put the gun—"

"Let her go, Cole! You got your killer and she's paid—"

"You fucking men!" she yelled. "You're both, you're still, you're deciding about *me*! *For* me! No more!"

"Get out of here, Dalton." She shook her head. "Mrs. Dalton Cole and you loved me more than *no babies*. Get out of here."

Her gun flicked to Faron as he dangled between them from the pipe, and she yelled: "I said get out of here!"

"Lauren! Don't! If you love me—"

"This has nothing to do with you!" Her revolver now centered on Faron's chest. "This is me not failing at everything!"

"Come with me!" he cried.

"Where?"

"You'll be alive!"

"I was dead before you, and you'll send me back there anyway."

"I'll have to shoot you!" yelled Cole. "That will rip me apart! If you care about me, you won't make me do that!"

"You can't stop me! You shoot me to stop me, this close, aiming at him, I'll still squeeze off—You can't stop me!"

"But you can leave," she said. "When you come back, it will all be over. Everything. And you'll be safe. Stay, and I might have to shoot you, too. I got three bullets. I only want to use two. Go now, please, go now. Nothing you can do to stop what's coming, and anything else you try ends—"

"*Duck!*"

Cole flinched. Lauren reflexively ducked, too, her revolver barrel jerked up, and she whirled to look behind her—

Nick's .45 boomed. The heavy slug slammed Lauren off her feet. Her revolver spit a bullet into a pipe and freed a geyser of steam.

Cole screamed "No!" as he watched her slow fall in the mist.

61

Monday morning, nine days later, the front page of the *Washington Post* covered a catastrophe in Africa with a picture of a dying child, a summit in Europe to reach an agreement to confer, a White House aide who had met the wrong person at the wrong time in the wrong place and told the wrong lie about it, the new murder record for D.C., a bizarre pop star's latest scandal, Congress's stalemate over vital legislation, and the political sojourns of three Very Important Persons, all white males, who were expressing grave concerns about the current administration's ability to carry out the people's mandate.

The day before, the *Post* ended its coverage of the psychopath who had teamed with a vengeful ex-lover to murder Faron Sears, only to be foiled by a crack team of FBI agents and D.C. police who discovered the killer's trail of interstate felonies while providing assistance to police in Montana. The *Post*'s two-page Sunday analysis explained how celebrities were flames for moths who wanted to live forever.

That Monday, the sun shone, the air was clean, and life ached to burst forth. No TV vans waited in front of Faron's headquarters when Dalton Cole drove up. The stiffness in his healing shoulder bothered him as he parked the BuCar. The old code got Cole through the steel gates. No one answered his buzz at the door, so he tried the code for that lock. The door clicked open.

Cole found no one on the first floor. Phones rang unanswered. On the second floor, a strip of yellow police crime-scene tape hung from the doorjamb of the Operations Room.

A phone rang there, too. Cole found Faron in his third-floor meditation room.

"Where is everybody?" said Cole.

The man sat with his back to Cole. He stood and faced the person who had saved his life.

"Jon left for New Jersey last night. You'll get a letter asking for a contribution to his Senate campaign. Jeff left this morning for Chicago. He'll take over that project, the transition of my companies to employee ownership. I had to make Nguyen responsible for Jeff before he would leave."

"Somebody better keep watch on Mr. Wood," said Cole.

"There'll be no shortage of eyes for that, even with Justice ending its 'review.' "

"Why did you call me?" asked Cole.

"So you'd come here."

"I've been—"

Faron cut off the lie with a shake of his head. "Me too. Have you talked to Nick lately?"

As agents uncuffed Faron from the pipe, after they had pulled Cole away from Lauren's body, his clothes soaked with her blood, Nick had faced his partner, said: "No choice. You know that."

Cole had said nothing.

"One of us had to do it or she'd have shot him first."

Cole had said nothing.

"When she flinched, I squeezed the trigger."

Cole had said nothing.

"You know I was right to do it. Right now, you probably hate me for it. That'll pass fast. What won't pass will be the big question: Would you have pulled the trigger on her?"

Cole had said nothing.

"You're never gonna forget that question," Nick told him as the crime scene crew flashed pictures in that yellow tunnel. "But no matter what you tell yourself, you'll never know. All you can do about that is let it go, because it doesn't matter, you didn't have to make that choice."

Cole had said nothing.

"One thing," Nick said before they led Cole to the ambulance for the bullet in his shoulder: "Never ever tell me thank you."

Monday morning, Cole told Faron: "I finally talked to him yesterday."

"He told me he's going to back to the Cold Case Squad," said Faron. "What about you?"

"They told me I can write my own ticket. As long as your case is closed by me like everyone publicly believes it to be."

"What did you and your bosses never tell me?" asked Faron.

"Doesn't matter. Let it go."

"Does it affect Sallie?"

"No, not at all."

Faron nodded, led Cole out of the empty room. He looked at the rainbowed shaft of light falling on the floor. Closed the door.

"She left me," Faron told Cole as they walked down the hall.

From downstairs came the peal of unanswered telephones.

"For the right reasons. Not for what I did in the past or what happened then, but for who she is. Who she wants to be."

Faron opened a door. Cole realized it was to his bedroom.

Cole said: "Would you have left her?"

"Never," whispered Faron. He smiled. "She told me it was her fate to fight the devils so I could help the angels. No middle earth where we could live together. The girl can leave the church, but some church stays in the woman.

"She wants to work on your next squad." Faron walked to the bed where an old suitcase that looked like a physician's bag waited, its mouth gaping.

"The Bureau will give her whatever it can."

"What about you?" asked Faron.

Cole stayed in the doorway. "Anybody who gets in her way has me to answer to."

"She doesn't need either of us."

"No, she doesn't."

"You and I have unfinished business," said Faron.

"Not that I'm aware of." Sunshine warmed the room.

Faron said: "Lauren."

Cole said nothing.

"What happened between Lauren and me caused horror and pain."

"Do you want me to say that it wasn't your fault?" said Cole. "OK. It wasn't. She chose to do all that."

"No," said Faron. "You're wrong. I was careless."

He snapped the bag shut.

"Lauren made terrible, evil choices," he said, "but I made convenient ones. I loved her as much as I could, but I knew that wasn't enough for her. The moment I knew that, I should have let her go. But staying with her was easy, made my life work. I let her hope for what I knew would never be true. My profit from her dreams turned them into her nightmares."

"You might be a genius," said Cole, "but you're only human."

"I'm not a genius. I just can't help seeing." Faron said: "She did love you. And she was worth loving. And I'm sorry."

Cole nodded.

"The price of life is that you pay." Faron lifted the bag off the bed. Walked over and shook Cole's hand, held it.

"Thank you," said Faron. "You are a true and good man."

Faron wore a denim shirt over a skier's navy-blue long underwear top, faded black jeans pulled down over boots.

"Will you walk me out?" he asked Dalton.

"Where are you going?" said Cole as they went downstairs.

Faron led Cole to the Operations Room, touched the yellow crime-scene tape, left it. Didn't answer the ringing phones. A laptop computer waited in the wardrobe that Sallie had burgled. Faron added it to his load, led Cole down to the main floor.

"You can't just walk out on a political movement you started!"

"The whole point is the Movement," said Faron. "Once I became the point, after an assassin made that clear, I realized that if a person stayed at the center, then everything would center on the person. Then assassins made as much sense as elections; then all we've created would become only what already was."

"You're abandoning everything you convinced other people to believe in?"

"Just the opposite. It's simple. The world that we live in can change only if we change the way we live in the world."

"Oh, gee. We'll miss those brilliant—"

Faron held up the laptop. "I'll be *here* if you look. Only it won't be me, it'll just be the pure expression of—"

"Ideas in the Internet don't feed babies starving in Harlem."

"No. But maybe they can help reshape a million minds that let those babies starve." He led Cole to the reception room. A parcel wrapped in brown paper waited on the table.

"With all your billions of doll—"

"I don't have them anymore." Faron opened the parcel. "Kept enough so I won't starve, but most of it went to employee ownership groups and the Chicago project, foundations and scholarships."

"When?"

"I activated the switch about an hour ago." He nodded toward a ringing phone. "Wall Street must have found out."

Out of the parcel he lifted an old black leather jacket that closed with buttons and reached past his hips and still fit when Faron put it on. "Lucky that back then I bought it big enough to hide guns."

"Where will you go?" asked Dalton.

"Outside." And he smiled.

The steel gate clanged shut behind them when they stepped onto the sidewalk. Like the gate to a prison.

"What do I say to you now?" Cole told the man on the sidewalk.

The smile Faron Sears gave him curved with the earth.

"Say, 'See you.' " Then he walked away.

Cole watched until the man was just a silhouette in sunlight.